Merlyn ...

He smiled slightly, taking full note of my awareness of him. I could not summon a sound to my lips. Even though I had been certain that Merlyn lived, the sight of him standing hale before me stole the words from my mouth.

As always he had.

Merlyn leaned in a dark portal in the wall, one that had not been there a moment past. It yawned like a cavern opening into darkness and I thought I might have summoned him from hell's own gates.

His white linen chemise hung open to reveal his tanned throat and chest, though it was tinged with dirt at the cuff. There was a pallor beneath his tan and shadows beneath his eyes.

And there were other changes. That familiar knowing smile curved his lips as he watched my perusal of him, but his gaze was wary. There was a tightness in his smile, a tension in his stance that was alien to me.

Merlyn's gaze never wavered from mine. He arched a dark brow.

"So, wife of mine, are you disappointed that I live?"

Please turn to the back of this book for a preview of Claire Delacroix's upcoming novel, *The Scoundrel.*

P9-DCC-893

THE
ROGUE

CLAIRE DELACROIX

WARNER BOOKS

An AOL Time Warner Company

WARNER BOOKS EDITION

Cover design by Diane Luger
Cover illustration by Sal Barracca

Warner Books, Inc.
1271 Avenue of the Americas
New York, NY 10020

Visit our Web site at
www.twbookmark.com.

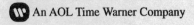 An AOL Time Warner Company

Printed in the United States of America

First Printing: October 2002

10 9 8 7 6 5 4 3 2 1

With thanks to my agent, Dominick Abel,
my friend, Ingrid,
and my husband, Konstantin.
Without their enthusiasm and assistance,
this book would never have made it off my desk.

Thank you all.

December 24, 1371

Christmas Eve
Feast Day of Saint Gregory
of Spoleto, and Saints Thrasilla
and Emiliana

I

The raven came first.

It landed upon the window sill in the kitchen of the silversmith's wife and croaked so loudly at me that I nearly dropped my ladle into the hot wort.

"Wretched bird! Shoo!" I waved my hand at it, but it merely tilted its head to regard me with bright eyes. "Fie! Away with you!"

I knew as well as any the repute of these birds, but had less desire than most souls to be in the company of a creature so associated with superstition.

I had sufficient trouble without being found in the company of drinkers of blood and harbingers of death. The silversmith's wife would be rid of us for once and for all, if anyone in this village whispered that I kept a raven as a familiar. Such tales were all nonsense, of course, but I dared not risk an inopportune rumor.

"Shoo!" I flicked a cloth at the bird, which seemed untroubled and unimpressed by my antics. The creature bobbed its head and seemed to cackle at me, no doubt enjoying my discomfiture.

"Begone!" I picked up an onion, the bird watching me with knowing eyes all the time, then flung it across the kitchen with all my might.

I missed the raven by a good three hand-spans, though the onion splattered against the wall most impressively. The bird screamed and took flight, uninjured and apparently insulted, which suited me well enough.

I sighed and rubbed my brow as I eyed the mess. I not only had to clean the shattered onion but would have to explain to my patroness why I had seen fit to destroy her foodstuffs—without admitting to the presence of the raven, lest her superstitions be fed. How sweet it would be to have no need of Fiona, with her sharp face and sharper tongue!

I had learned long ago, though, that there was nothing to be gained in bemoaning one's circumstance. I stirred the wort again and fought the urge to grumble.

My ale is fine, I dare say, the very finest. But with no kitchen, no pot, no spouse, the law decrees that I cannot be granted a license to brew. My ale has long provided what little coin my family had, so I am compelled to brew. What choice have I but to ally with this wife or another?

Fiona it was, for she would have me as her partner, if by her spouse's command. It would take a more foolish woman than myself to not perceive that though I did most of the work, Fiona kept most of the coin—and one less aware of nuance than I to not note that coin and spousal approval were not sufficient in Fiona's view to suffer a witch in one's kitchen.

We were convenient to the silversmith and his wife, and it was for this, not a matter of principle or Christian duty, that they tolerated us. I have learned not to be surprised that charity is so circumscribed, nor that principles can be so readily forgotten.

Once this massive pot was strained and flavored with my particular combination of herbs, I hoped for brisk sales over the holiday season. The ale would spoil in several days and, as I worked, I worried anew that I had made too much.

I could not risk the loss of any of my investment in ingredients. Competition was fierce in Kinfairlie for ale-making, there being so few other sources of profit. I had a good repute, but the harvest had been mean and all the other brewsters would be making similarly large batches.

I frowned and stirred the wort while it came to the boil.

Making ale is a tedious trade and one requiring much heavy labor. I am not afraid to work, indeed I welcome labor. A heavy day ensures a solid night's sleep, at least, and a reprieve from the multitude of worries that plague me.

This day was the first day of the so-called Twelve Days of Christmas, though I should undoubtedly have to explain to young Tynan again and again why there were fourteen days in total so designated. The prospect made me smile.

The wort began to sputter and splash. It was a feat to move the cauldron from the fire myself, but I would have to do it again. I cursed Fiona, who contrived to be absent whenever her assistance might have been helpful. The pot was large enough and hot enough that even once it was away from the heat, it continued to chortle.

It was when I had wrestled it from the fire and halted to wipe my brow that I heard the hoofbeats. I turned, eyes narrowed, and listened.

Three fleet steeds, their hooves shod with iron. Dread prickled down my spine. Not plough-horses, for they pranced too lightly. Palfreys lightly burdened, perhaps. And a fourth steed. Larger. Faster. I listened, wanting to be certain, my heart thumping with its own certitude.

The fourth beast was a destrier. There could be no doubt.

I closed my eyes, swallowed, and prayed that the beast's rider was not who I feared it might be. There was no reason it should be him. After all, Kinfairlie's meager tithes have been hotly contested since the liege lord and manor were lost. We have become accustomed to various nobles assaulting the town in search of tribute.

Especially before a holy day.

The hoofbeats came closer. When the raven cried, even at a distance, I knew.

The silversmith's house faces the main square of Kinfairlie, where markets are held and criminals are hung, and it was here that the new arrivals came to a halt. I stiffened, but did not go to the door. The steeds' hooves clattered to silence, the destrier neighed and no doubt tossed his head.

"I seek Ysabella of Kinfairlie!" roared a man, his voice achingly familiar.

Merlyn. My heart lunged for my throat.

For years, I had imagined how we might meet again, how I would scorn him with blistering wit, yet now I merely whispered his name beneath my breath like a besotted damsel. In truth, I did not know whether to be frightened or relieved, to be joyous or disappointed. He had come in pursuit of me, after all this time, a boon to my pride if not a good omen for my future.

"Ysabella!" he shouted anew and I wondered if he was drunk.

I glanced over myself and smiled wryly at the embellishment of fermented malt upon my skirts. No doubt the hair had escaped my braid, my face would be hot and nigh as red as my hair. It was a far cry from the reunions I had so oft envisioned, when I was garbed in richness and hauteur, my words as sharp as lances.

My appearance would do very well to show my spouse his importance—or lack of it—to me.

I crossed the kitchen and opened the heavy wood door. Even though I braced myself, my heart stopped. Merlyn was just as imposing as before, his two young squires fighting to control their palfreys. He was garbed in the black and silver he favored, the hues of his house, the hues that made him look more dangerous and dashing than even he was. I looked hastily at his companion. Stalwart Fitz was still with Merlyn, his face only slightly more lined than before.

"Good morning to you, Merlyn," I said, feigning an indifference I hardly felt. "What brings you to Kinfairlie?"

He urged the steed closer, then dismounted, casting the reins aside. His smile was confident, roguish, and enough to set my very flesh to flame. His gaze swept over me, leaving a tingle in its wake and I gripped the door lest I cast myself at him like a harlot. His breath made a cloud against the sky that darkened too early in this season.

"Well met, chère," he murmured, with the intimacy one reserves for lovers.

And I flushed scarlet, heating from nipples to hairline. Worse, I could not summon a sound to my lips.

Merlyn knew it, curse him, and grinned with wicked satisfaction as he closed the distance between us.

I could not draw a breath. I knew the dark truth of Merlyn, and yet, and yet despite all of that, despite my moral certainty that he would burn in hell, I still yearned to touch him again. He infuriated me, yet I had not felt so alive in all the years we had been apart as I did in this one moment, holding his gaze in winter's cool air.

I had assured myself that my attraction to Merlyn had been born of my ignorance, but he approached with all his wretched surety and the loss of my ignorance did not keep his allure at bay. Far from it. If anything, I desired him more ardently than ever.

To think that I had long fancied myself a clever woman.

"I seek *you,* chère," he said, his words husky.

I caught the scent of his flesh and lust unfurled within my gut, memories flooding my thoughts of nights—and days— spent entangled in each other's arms. I squared my shoulders, determined to resist him and failing utterly.

"What else?"

He claimed my hand and bestowed a kiss upon my knuckles, his eyes filled with an answering heat that weakened my knees.

I snatched my hand away, hating that I so quickly fell beneath his spell once more. "And it has taken you five years to remember the way to Kinfairlie village? God in heaven, Merlyn, even the slowest child can walk to Ravensmuir in a day."

I inclined my head curtly, excusing myself, and retreated into the kitchen. I knew full well that he would follow, though I bristled when he did so. I stirred the wort vigorously, showing a belated care that my investment did not burn.

"You might at least leave the door ajar," I snapped. "But then, when have you had a care for my reputation?"

"Always, despite your conviction otherwise." Merlyn's words were more harsh than I expected. I pivoted and his gaze locked with mine as he flicked the portal closed with his fingertips. He did not apologize, he did not so much as blink.

I raised a finger. "You . . ."

He interrupted me with resolve. "I am your legal spouse, and there is no law writ that says a man cannot be alone with his wife."

I turned back to the brew and stirred it with an enthusiasm undeserved. "And you have developed a sudden interest in law?" I asked archly. "How strange. I was certain that your sole commitment to the law was to break it."

Merlyn laughed. I felt him pause behind me and heard him doff his gloves. He cast them on the board and I caught my breath when I glimpsed them from the corner of my eye. Had he chosen scarlet ones apurpose this day? Did he mean to prompt memory in me?

I knew him well enough to understand that nothing was accident with Merlyn Lammergeier.

Even knowing he approached, I still jumped when his warm fingertip landed on my bare nape. His gentleness always caught me unawares. I inhaled sharply, hoping my indication of disapproval would halt him.

It did not, but then, I had expected as much. I stared at the wort as Merlyn's finger traced a beguiling path around the neckline of my ancient dress. I felt the barest whisper of his breath before he kissed me beneath the ear.

I jumped truly then, swatted him and moved to the other side of the cauldron. I looked daggers at him, but he was unrepentant.

"The fire still burns," he murmured, his eyes gleaming. No doubt he reveled in having some power over me.

"Trust me. It is doused beyond reviving." I scrubbed the hot mark of his kiss with one hand as he laughed.

Merlyn blew me a kiss across the cauldron. "I have missed you, chère."

"I can tell by the speed with which you sought me out."

He studied me for a long moment, then slapped his gloves against his palm. "You are vexed that I did not come sooner."

"I expect nothing of you, Merlyn Lammergeier. Indeed, I would appreciate your absence." I indicated the door. "Do you still cede to the request of a lady?"

Merlyn sobered. "Not this time." He fixed a gaze upon me that was so intent that I nearly squirmed. "Why did you leave Ravensmuir?"

"How can you ask me such a thing? Is it not obvious?"

"No."

"Then you should have asked sooner. I have forgotten by now." I stirred and blushed and ignored him as best as I was able.

Which was not particularly well.

When he finally spoke, Merlyn's voice was no more than a whisper. "I was certain that you loved me."

I scoffed, irked anew that he made no sweet pledge himself to persuade me to come back. "You never held my heart, Merlyn, and even if you had, it would have been lost to you the moment that I learned that you had lied to me."

He watched me, as a cat does afore it springs upon its prey. "What lie is that?"

"So, even you cannot keep them straight." I surveyed him with disdain. "You trade in religious relics and we both know it well."

"In the greater service to the Lord, that all his faithful might have access to saintly intercession on their behalf." A smile touched Merlyn's lips. "It is my solemn Christian duty."

"Nonsense! You do it for coin!"

"My expenses must be compensated." He began to circumnavigate the cauldron again, though I moved too, and kept the pot between us. "And who am I to argue with an abbot or a bishop so anxious to gain a foreskin or a lock of hair that the coin fairly spills from his fingers?"

"Who are you to trouble yourself with ensuring that the relic is genuine?"

"Chère," Merlyn chided, "there is not a relic in all of Christendom with a provenance above repute in these days."

"Except perhaps the ones that you and your brother Gawain have wrought. Do they not have impeccable credentials?"

Merlyn's eyes lit with surprise, then something that might have been admiration. His tan crinkled beside his eyes when he smiled. "How do you know of this?"

"I guessed, once Gawain made his confession to me."

Merlyn leaned forward, suddenly intent. "Is this why you left Ravensmuir? Because of my brother's tales?"

I dropped the ladle and propped my hands upon my hips. "I did not leave Ravensmuir, I left *you*, Merlyn. I could not abide with a thief and a forger and a liar."

Merlyn was not in the least bit insulted. "I am not a thief, chère." He had the audacity to smile. "Perhaps you misunderstood, but acquisition has long been Gawain's part in our endeavor."

"I could not abide with a forger and a liar, nonetheless."

His smile flashed briefly and my cursed heart skipped a beat. "Ah, while you could have remained with a mere liar. You should have said as much, for I long ago surrendered the forging to Fitz. He shows a tremendous talent for the details."

I glared at him. "Liar. You told me that your trade was in

textiles. I thought you an honest merchant, but you lied to me."

Merlyn prowled the width of the kitchen, his expression so serious that I knew he meant to mock me. "And this is the root of it? For the sake of a single lie, I could have been happily wedded all these years." He turned and granted me an inquiring look that I knew better than to trust.

I stirred with a vengeance. "I am certain you would have left many comely wenches disappointed."

"Perhaps not." There was laughter in his tone, though whether he enjoyed the idea that I might be jealous, or whether he was amused at the idea of monogamy, I could not say.

Asking him to clarify would only humiliate me further, and the realization made my anger boil as surely as the wort. Truly, if ever there had been a wicked wretch draw breath, he stood before me—yet still I felt my blood quickening to Merlyn's presence. My flesh still sizzled where he had planted that kiss.

"One lie is not the sum of it," I insisted. "You cannot make a jest of this, Merlyn. I could not live with who you are, I could not be a part of your crimes. I dared not become like you, a lawless renegade devoid of morals and ethics."

"So, you live in poverty and destitution instead." He spared a skeptical glance for the kitchen which must appear humble to him, the kitchen which was in fact neither my own nor within my means.

"My coin is honestly earned. You cannot say as much. How often does Gawain steal back what you have sold, that it might be sold again?"

He laughed, for I had surprised him again, and his eyes sparkled as they had on a long-ago afternoon. I held his gaze, my own expression stony. "The art of this trade, Ysabella, lies in not asking too many questions. I do not ask where my brother makes his finds."

"Just as you do not ask how there could be three crowns

of thorns surviving from the crucifixion which featured, as I
recall, solely *one*."

His smile was unrepentant. "Who are we to decide which
is genuine and which is not?"

"So, you sell them all. It is reprehensible. Do you not
think of those people, imagining that they touch a relic of
import when they in truth are caressing a fistful of brambles
from Ravensmuir's moat?"

"We are not so graceless as that." Merlyn looked at me as-
sessingly. "Yes, that *was* five years or so ago," he mused,
clearly thinking of the three crowns. "Was that Gawain's
tale?"

"Much of it. He was in his cups and unaccountably proud
of himself."

"Who else was enjoying his tales?"

"Just we two." I cleared my throat, feeling an odd compulsion to protect Gawain from Merlyn's wrath. "I believe
he thought that I already knew the truth and that we enjoyed
the jest together."

Merlyn's voice hardened as he crossed the chamber.
"Who did you tell of what you knew?"

"No one. Why?"

He seized my arm, compelling me to meet his gaze. "No
one?"

"What ails you, Merlyn?" I fussed, but his intent matter
unsettled me. "Who would I tell?"

"Swear it to me, chère," he insisted. "Swear to me that the
tale never crossed your lips again."

He was serious, more serious than ever I have seen him.
A goose crossed my grave and I shivered. "What has happened, Merlyn?"

"I doubt that you truly wish to know." His gaze was un-
wavering. "Swear it."

I held his gaze for a long moment, startled not only by his
intensity but the fear he awakened in me. "I told no one."

"Not even your sister, Mavella? Or your mother?"

"My mother died shortly after we left Ravensmuir," I said, though I immediately wished that I had not.

Merlyn released my arm and a lump rose in my throat at the compassion in his gaze. "I am sorry, chère. I know that you were close."

I nodded, embarrassed at my tears. I pushed up my sleeves and made to strain the wort, for I could not linger over the task any longer, and I would not have Merlyn believe that his presence changed my routine a whit.

Merlyn moved with astonishing speed to seize my left wrist. He turned it so that light played along the ravaged flesh of my inner arm. I have a scar from wrist to elbow, one that I oft forget now that the wound is healed, but one Merlyn had never seen before.

"What is this? Who did this to you?" To my surprise, his voice shook with rage.

"The wort must be strained from the brew while boiling hot. I have seen worse injuries than mine." I tried to shake off his grip without success. "It is nothing."

Merlyn's eyes narrowed. "Does it hurt?"

"No longer."

He ran a gentle fingertip along the considerable length of puckered flesh and awakened a most unwelcome sensation. "Did you have care for it?"

I scoffed with feigned impatience. "A witch should know to heal herself."

I had his attention now, though I would have preferred otherwise. "What is this? Who has called you a witch?"

"It is nothing of import. Our lives are no longer entwined, Merlyn, and what happens to me is of no import to you. Your steed awaits you, as do your unholy relics and comely wenches. I have labor to do—if you will excuse me."

He watched me grip the pot. "You drained the mash alone once before and it spilled," he guessed.

I straightened to regard him sternly. In truth, I did not trust myself to do this deed beneath his eye. "The silversmith's wife did not come to aid me as she had promised, which is not uncommon as you can see. The brew would have spoiled if left any longer and the cost of the ingredients would have been mine to bear. I had no choice but to act alone, as I intend to do now."

"So, you will inflict another wound upon yourself. How then, will you and your sister survive? You are too proud, chère. You should ask for aid."

"My patroness does not oblige."

"You should have come to me for aid."

"Oh yes, that I could blacken my soul with some trade in disreputable relics." I snapped at him, stung that he who labored in such sin dared to criticize me. "That would solve all my woes."

"I make no jest."

"Nor do I!" I shook a finger at him. "It is a raw wager to be born a woman in this world, to be poor, to be scorned, to be denied the truth. The sins of Eve and the taint of womanhood are mine to bear simply for the crime of being born a woman. I have made my choices and survived as best I could . . ."

"By letting your neighbors believe you to be a witch?" he demanded, then arched a brow. "You could be burned alive for the accusation alone."

"I did not begin the rumor of my otherworldly powers, though it is true that I did nothing to deter the lie," I admitted. "There has been a time or two that I lifted my fingers in that ancient hex sign to perpetuate the tale."

Merlyn leaned against the table. "Would this be a *lie*, chère?"

"If I have permitted a lie to taint my life, it is because my sole alternative was to die."

He clutched his heart. "I bleed for your pain, chère."

That he should mock me was beyond infuriating. "And so you should! If I, protector and provider of my small family should perish, who then would ensure the welfare of my sister and brother? Who would feed them? Who would make ale to sell so that they had at least bread to eat each day? Who would clothe and shelter them? Who would take them in?"

I advanced upon Merlyn and poked him in the chest with one finger. "You? I suspect not. It has suited me to be known as one with arcane powers, only because that has kept a certain kind of wolf from our door."

Merlyn's eyes were glittering and I sensed the anger coiled within him, though I could not guess the reason for it. "You blame me for this."

I knew I tickled the dragon's belly, but I did not care. "And why not? What choices had I?" I flung out my hands. "I was neither maiden nor widow nor wife. I was without the legal comforts of marriage but denied the opportunities that would have been mine otherwise. I could not have my own license to brew, as an unwed woman might. I could not wed again. Worse, I was shunned and less likely to receive charity from our fellow villagers. To be called a witch was the least offensive of choices I did have. I could have become a thief or a beggar, I could have abandoned my family, I could have become a whore."

Merlyn's eyes narrowed. "It was you who chose to leave Ravensmuir, chère." His lips drew taut. "And interestingly, it is you who calls me a liar."

I could have struck him. Instead, I drove my finger into his chest again. He did not so much as flinch. "I do blame you. I blame you utterly for my circumstance. Had you not been the rogue you are, I would have remained by your side for all of our days, Merlyn. A nuptial pledge such as we exchanged is no small thing." I took a shuddering breath. "I abandoned you only because I feared for my soul in being wed to a criminal. I left you because a woman of any merit would have no other choice."

Merlyn folded his arms grimly across his chest. "So, here we stand. Rogue and witch."

"I am no witch!" I replied hotly. "Look at me! What manner of witless fool would not expect a witch to change the contributing factors of her family's misery? Why would a witch not summon riches for herself, or coax the return of a suitor for her sister, or conjure a meal for her starving brother?" I glared at Merlyn, expecting him to refute me, but his eyes narrowed.

"What brother?" he demanded with such ferocity that my breath caught.

"The brother my mother died bringing into this world!" I turned my back upon him, choking on an unwelcome tide of emotion. "Good day, Merlyn."

I stirred my wort, furious that it cooled, furious that Merlyn was responsible, furious that I responded to him as vigorously as ever I did.

He did not leave.

I had not truly expected him to. I refused to acknowledge him, though the kitchen was thick with the tangle of emotions left between us.

"I came to seek your aid, chère," he said quietly.

"You shall not have it. I want no part of your crimes."

"Even if I give you my word to share the truth with you?"

I shook my head impatiently. "Merlyn, you cannot discredit a lie with another lie."

"How is it that Gawain—a man occupied in the same trade as myself—is given more credence by you than I am?" Merlyn's words were tinged with bitterness.

I turned, my voice faltering. "You have never given me your word."

"Because you never had the courage to make your charges to me!"

"I could not believe whatever you said to me now."

Merlyn's eyes flashed. "Even if it was the truth?"

"I doubt that it would be."

He made a sound of frustration and I glanced back to find his expression grim. He closed the distance between us with one step and caught my chin in his hand. His voice was unexpectedly hoarse. "What if I were to reform my ways? What if I were to pledge to you that I would abandon my father's trade?"

My mouth went dry. I wanted to believe him and my lips parted before I recalled that I had been fool enough to be deceived by Merlyn's lies five years ago. "Prove it to me."

"I give you my pledge."

"It is not enough, Merlyn. Not now."

He studied me, seeking some encouragement that I hoped he would not find. Disappointment slowly filled his gaze, the myriad stars that always lurked in his eyes dimmed, and I felt a wretch for having denied him his will.

No doubt as he intended me to do.

"I hope you do not regret this choice, chère," Merlyn whispered, then kissed me with possessive ease.

I nearly melted against him in my surprise. A thousand yearnings awakened by his presence nigh betrayed me, but I recalled suddenly that he meant to bend me to his will.

And a man with nothing to lose and no ethics to steer his course would use any weakness against another. I let him kiss me, and managed just barely to hold myself aloof.

Merlyn's gaze was flinty when he lifted his head, his disappointment nearly tangible. "You should have spoken to me before you left," he insisted, with what might have been hurt in his tone.

He held my gaze for a long moment, and I felt the odd sense that I had failed him. I knew very well that it was the other way around, but beneath his regard, my conviction faltered.

Had I given Merlyn a chance? Had there been an explanation that might have exonerated him? Had I been unfair?

Did he truly mean to change his ways?

Before I dared voice my doubts, Merlyn turned on his heel and walked away. He donned his gloves as he went, leaving the door open behind him. He crossed the square without a backward glance, a telling choice to my thinking. He swung up into his saddle, gathered the reins in his gloved fist and gave his spurs to the destrier. The beast tossed its dark head and galloped away.

I, in my weakness, clung to the edge of the door and watched Merlyn go. A thousand doubts assailed me and I just barely restrained myself from calling after him. In fact, I might have done so, if the village boys had not drawn closer.

They had gathered to stare at the steeds, and now circled closer as the sound of hoofbeats faded.

One bold and gangly boy who imagined himself on the lip of manhood swaggered toward me. "Ysabella," he taunted, then leered. "Ysabella, I have a missive for you from your spouse. He says you have need of a reminder of your nuptial night!" He grabbed his crotch and made a lewd gesture as the other boys hooted my name.

I slammed the portal and leaned back against it, my anger at Merlyn fed once again. How could I forget his cruelty so readily as that? How could I dismiss the crimes he had wrought against me?

"Curse you, Merlyn Lammergeier!" I cried to the empty kitchen. "Curse you for your careless cruelty! And a pox upon my own self for forgetting your wiles."

I returned to my wort in poor temper—though in truth, I was more angry with myself for failing to learn from experience, than with my spouse for persisting in being the rogue I already knew him to be. I wrestled the cauldron back to the fire, knowing that Merlyn would haunt my dreams.

I was not to be disappointed. The man could be relied upon in some matters, at least.

It is market day in Kinfairlie village some five years past, a fine spring day. The sun is glorious, the wind filled with warmth. May Day is nigh upon us and there is frolic in the air, as there so oft is when spring shows her face after an ar-

duous winter. All the village is merry. It is a day filled with possibilities, a day when any dream could ripen unexpectedly. I am but eighteen summers of age and my footstep is still light.

I hear the nobleman before I see him. The horse could belong to no other, its shod hooves and proud gallop revealing its value, size and lineage.

The nobleman has ridden his destrier through the throng and between the stalls as his ilk so oft do. The sound of that massive stallion's hooves carry over the chatter of the market. Conversations fall silent at the familiar sound, the villagers fearing what toll a nobleman will take of us now.

This one has not come for coin.

I feel the nobleman's presence, feel his gaze upon my back, feel my cheeks heat with the awareness that I have been chosen. Dread rises within me. His is a stare so burning that it cannot be ignored. I try desperately to do so, nonetheless.

I am not so young that I do not know what happens to a peasant girl who snares a laird's desire, let alone one who boldly meets his eye.

Indeed, I know my own assets. To be red of hair is not so much of a liability, not if one's hair is long and thick and curly as mine. I am tall and strong, though not without a few curves. I know that I have become desirable, by whatever measure is used by men, but I do not intend to give away what meager advantage I have.

Marriage is my sole chance of better circumstance, but marriage is not what noblemen offer to village wenches who arouse their lust.

He walks the horse not two steps behind me, but says nothing. Though I know my color rises, I do not acknowledge him. People halt to watch, some nudging and smiling, some whispering, some shaking their head with disapproval. As I hasten my errands, and he patiently stalks me, I know the dread of a mouse cornered in the kitchen. Are noblemen not said to adore the hunt above all else? I hope against hope that this lord will choose more willing prey.

Had I known more of Merlyn then, I would have understood the futility of this hope. Merlyn never sways from winning his desire. He is the most patient man ever born, or perhaps the most determined one. He always has a surety that he is right, and that certainty ensures that he never abandons his objectives.

However disreputable they might prove to be.

I spare a glance back and my heart plummets. The nobleman's horse is fine beyond belief, blacker than black, larger than one such as me might imagine a horse could be. It is so high-stepping and proud that it seems another kind of creature entirely than the sole plough-horse in Kinfairlie. I turn and race away, a glimpse of the steed enough to make me flee. Unwilling to lead him to my home, I lead him upon a chase through the alleys of Kinfairlie.

He laughs and clicks his tongue to the horse.

I duck through every street—for there are not many—and every twisted alley that should have been too narrow for his steed. Yet I fail to lose him nonetheless.

Breathless and exasperated, I spin to confront him in the relative security of the marketplace.

That first sight of him nigh steals my breath away, as does his alarming proximity. My heart lodges in my throat as I note the black of his garb, the golden bird with outspread wings that forms the clasp of his cloak. He can be no other than the scion of the Lammergeier family who have rebuilt Ravensmuir keep. Their wicked repute has preceded him and my fears redouble.

He is beside me in a heartbeat. I have to look up, over his knee, to meet his gaze and then, I am lost.

Oh, this is a wickedly handsome man, of that there can be no doubt. Black of hair and broad of shoulder, he would be striking by his features alone. His lips curve in a knowing smile, his carriage is proud and confident. He has been born to wealth, and grown tall and straight beneath its advantages. His smile is crooked, confident.

His eyes temper my fear and awaken my curiosity. They brim with merriment, sparkling as though wrought of stars. He seems amused yet mischievous at the same time. There is a shadow of knowingness deep within those eyes, an awareness of dark secrets, a certainty of not only his own allure but of my reaction to it.

The reaction of any woman to him.

"What do you want of me?" I demand, knowing full well the answer.

The rogue's smile broadens. He leans down from his saddle with a male grace unfamiliar to me, and flicks his gloved fingertip across my cheek. It is a possessive and intimate gesture, one that makes the old women in the market begin to whisper and cluck.

I am struck to stone. His glove is soft, softer than I had believed leather ever could be, and his touch is gentle. The glove is dyed to the most remarkable shade of crimson.

I am tempted to close my eyes and lean against his unexpected caress, tempted to welcome the softness against my cheek, tempted to forget every warning I have ever heard.

I do not succumb.

"I desire what all these men desire of you," *he whispers, his words deliciously low.* "I desire what you promise with the sway of your hips."

"I promise nothing to any man." *I give him a disparaging glance.* "And grant them even less."

"Are you wed then?"

"Nay." *I spin and walk yet again, my fear changing to intrigue with startling ease. I had expected violence of him, a capture and a rape, not an inquiry.*

Not a caress.

Not a flirtation. I almost smile when I hear the horse trot behind me.

"Have you been spoken for?"

"Nay."

"Pledged to the convent?"

"Nay."

"Then, what is your name?"

"It is not for you to know."

His voice brims with laughter. "And what, my lady not-for-you-to-know, would it take for you to grant a smile to a suitor?"

I glance back to scoff. "You are no suitor!"

He feigns such affront that I nearly laugh. Indeed, I enjoy myself overmuch with this handsome rogue.

"But one glance and the lady knows my intentions. What an uncommon prize of a woman!" His eyes gleam down again. "I can only assume that you refer to knowledge in the biblical sense."

I survey him from unruly hair to fine boot toe with apparent disdain. "In your case, I most definitely do."

The villagers laugh.

He catches at his heart and pretends to be injured. "The lady wounds me."

The crowd gathers closer, much entertained, nudging each other as they strain to catch every word.

I prop my basket upon my hip, toss back my braid and scoff. "Understand this, sir rogue. I would grant such knowledge more willingly to a farmer than to one of your ilk."

He is not insulted, as I might have hoped. He laughs aloud, the rich sound tempting me, among others, to join his merriment. "Do you not imagine that a nobleman could pay a finer price?"

"Oh, undoubtedly he could, but I doubt that he would do so." Certain our parlay is done, I walk on.

He clicks his tongue and the beast strolls after me.

A crowd of villagers begins to follow us, clearly enjoying our wordplay. Their interest makes me realize that my conquest has become a spectacle. I do not take kindly to being the butt of a jest. The fact of my neighbors' entertainment steals the pleasure of matching words with this handsome nobleman.

And truly, I know what he wants and I know what he will do once he has it.

"Why would you think as much?" he asks, his low voice making a part of me tingle in a most unwelcome way.

I have never been shy and my next words prove as much. "Village women are so much chattel to noblemen," I declare. "They plough our furrows and plant their seed, then abandon the fruit to others."

My fellow villagers roar with laughter.

The nobleman's lips twitch. "And what man, fair damsel, will win the right to plough your fields? Would you choose him solely for his experience at farming?"

The crowd jostle around us, all certain that we do not truly speak of fields tilled.

"Of course not."

"No?"

"It is my suspicion that all men are born with the knowledge of farming, so there is no merit to be found in considerable experience."

His smile puts a dimple in his chin. My heart skips a beat, though I try to hide any response from that bright gaze.

"What then?" His tone is teasing, though his eyes are solemn. "What then are your terms, my lady not-for-you-to-know?" He dares me, but he does not guess that I will rise to his challenge.

I smile, feeling my pulse quicken at his proximity, even though I know he will not accept my demand. "My virgin fields, of course, shall solely be the right of my legal husband to furrow."

The villagers alternatively gasp and roar, thinking the matter resolved by my audacity. I turn away, certain of that myself.

But the nobleman seizes my elbow and pulls me to a halt. His gaze burns with unexpected avidity. "Then marry me," he says and I cannot summon a word to my lips for shock.

Does he mock me? Certainly, there is a reckless gleam in his eyes.

"But bed you first, I am certain," I scoff. "Or take vows before your priest, who will be revealed to not be a priest with morning's light."

I pull my arm from his grip and turn away. "You make a jest at my expense, sir, and I need not linger to hear more of it. Unlike you and your kind, I have labor enough to fill my waking hours." I march blindly across the market with the unwelcome sense that amusement has been provided at my expense.

"I make no jest." He speaks with such volume and resolve that the marketplace falls silent.

I glance back in surprise.

He stares fixedly at me, the merry glint in his eyes gone and his smile banished. He is the image of a man resolved, if inexplicably so. There is a majesty about him that draws every eye, that compels every voice to silence. We all stare, knowing we have never seen the like of him.

And I understand suddenly that such men are different from those I know. This resolve, this commanding presence, is why men follow other men, even to their deaths.

He holds my gaze for a long moment, then he raises his voice to address all in attendance.

"My name is Merlyn Lammergeier, newly pronounced Laird of Ravensmuir by my father's own dictate. I seek a bride to grace my home."

"Merlyn," I whisper, trying his name upon my tongue though I know I should not.

He turns his horse that he might address all of the rapt crowd, the creature arching its neck as it circles in place with perfect composure. The wind lifts the ends of Merlyn's cloak and the steed's tail. The vivid blue of the sky shows the hues of Merlyn's garb and his eyes to advantage, the sunlight glints on the gold of his cloak clasp and the silver of his steed's harness. They are magnificent, the two of them, as far beyond our daily lives as might be imagined.

"Let it be known by all that I would wed this woman honorably on this very day, that I will do so in the chapel before whosoever of you will witness the match."

I stare at him in shock. Is he mad?

Do I care?

"What about the banns?" cries one bold woman as I grapple with the whimsy of his offer.

"There is no consanguinity between us," Merlyn declares, then winks at me. "Unless you have kin in France."

I shake my head, marveling.

He nods but once, the matter resolved. "And I have no kin here. I am certain that a donation to the chapel can see such trivialities waived. We shall be wed by the priest of the lady's choosing." He turns back to face me and his eyes shine. "If my lady's terms are truly as she declares." He smiles, and as his voice falls low, I have a sudden sense that I wager with the devil himself. "If her deeds are truly as bold as her speech."

The villagers laugh, jostling each other at this unexpected marvel, then turn to watch me. It is the first but not the last time that Merlyn astounds me with his choices.

Nor is it the last time that he makes my heart thunder.

"Are you certain of your choice, Laird Merlyn?" shouts a bold villager. "This one has the sharpest tongue of any damsel in Kinfairlie!"

Merlyn's gaze darkens, his smile turns seductive. "I have a fancy for maidens with sharp tongues." He coaxes the steed closer and offers his hand to me. "But is this lady of bold speech equally bold in deed? Is she bold enough to accept me, the heir of the Lammergeier? Or have I guessed wrongly that she is sufficiently stalwart to face any challenge?"

There it is again, that mischief, that certainty that not only is his family's repute well known but that I will not rise to his dare. Perhaps it is a test of whether I will make a fitting bride for him.

Perhaps it is a warning.

The truth is that I do not care. I know only that Fortune smiles upon me. I know that Merlyn has wealth, I know that he is handsome, I know that he is not a fool. I know that he makes my heart leap. I know that even if he is a rogue, even if he is mad, that as his wife I could still live well enough on his coin. I know that this chance would only be mine if I seize it immediately.

And most importantly of all, I know that I want to surprise him. I am seduced by that dimple and by that dare in his eyes.

He is irresistible, and he desires me. I have no intent of granting him the time to change his thinking.

I hand my basket to the woman beside me, an elderly neighbor of ours. "Take this home to my mother, if you will, Anna, and please bid her hasten to the chapel if she would see me wed to Laird Merlyn of Ravensmuir by Kinfairlie's own priest."

The crowd hoots with glee but I see only Merlyn's brilliant smile. My heart lurches, but I take his hand as if there is nothing uncommon in what I do. I catch my breath at his strength and surety when he grasps me around the waist and pulls me directly into the saddle before him.

And I find the evidence of his desire pressed against my buttocks, my breath deserting me as his lips touch my ear.

"So, you are indeed as audacious a woman as I suspected," he murmurs, his voice making me shiver. He seems untroubled by what has always been perceived as a liability in my character by others. "Your intrepid nature will serve you well at Ravensmuir."

I wonder then if there is more to the tale of him, more to his need for a bride than I might be pleased to learn.

But such concerns grow no roots in my thoughts, not then. He kisses me, possessively, thoroughly, exhilaratingly, coaxing the spark between us to a smoldering blaze. When he lifts

*his head, he smiles knowingly at me, fully aware of the hunger
he has awakened within me.*

*"Well met, bride of mine," he whispers. He flings his cloak
around me and spurs his steed to the chapel, his hand rising in
the shadows to cup the weight of my breast. My flesh tingles
in a startling new way. I know with dreadful certainly that I
have been claimed by a demon, and that with my own
consent.*

*But I do not step away from the flame Merlyn kindles. The
devil has chosen me as his handmaiden, and for the moment,
I do not care.*

December 25

Christmas Day
Nativity of Jesus Christ,
Feast Day of Saint Eugenia
and Saint Anastasia

II

The darkness had only just begun to recede and the coldest air of the morning was slipping beneath the tattered hide tacked over the sole window in our chamber. I lay abed, tasting Merlyn upon my tongue and wishing I did not.

I was thinking that it was time we rose for mass at dawn. Tynan had finally fallen into slumber and I was reluctant to wake him. So, I lingered abed, waiting for the bell of the chapel to toll, savoring the haze of my dream.

I heard the hoofbeats of a fine horse once more.

My drowsiness was immediately banished. I knew from the proud clatter of shod hooves that this was no horse bent beneath the weight of the plow, nor even a mare pulling a wagon. No, this steed pranced, it fairly danced, and the bells upon its harness jingled with the unmistakable sound of silver. It was as if I summoned Merlyn back to my side.

Again.

I rose and wrapped my arms around myself in the darkness, both waiting for a summons at my door and hoping it would not come. A man's footfall made the loose wooden step creak, and I did not so much as breathe. My sister Mavella sat up in alarm, however, our gazes meeting across the room.

We had become accustomed to harassment, accustomed to wicked tales with no basis in fact, accustomed to those who took satisfaction in our tumble from favor to lowly status. We were poor and we were spurned—and the taste of it was yet more bitter, given what had once been mine. To have tasted sweetness only makes its lack more harsh.

Though I knew I had made the right choice in abandoning Merlyn, there were days and nights when I cursed the price. We had become so adept at cheating death that the feat was unremarkable—and my brother knew no other life than this.

I did not jump skyward at the light rap upon our door, though Mavella caught her breath. Unlike my sister, I was certain that it was not the usual trouble at our door this morn.

It had to be Merlyn. He should not have been able to enter the village at this hour, for the gates should have been barred, but when there is little to protect, men are less vigilant in their watch. A far more stupid man than Merlyn could slip past Kinfairlie's sentries without notice.

Even a less wealthy one could manage it.

I peered beneath the hide, and my heart nearly stopped at the sight of the stallion tethered below. The beast tossed its head proudly, making the bells jingle merrily again, its gleaming coat as black as a midnight sea.

As black as its master's heart.

The rap upon the door came again, oddly tentative to be from Merlyn's own hand. I crossed the floor with suspicion, though I did not open the portal. My sister stood, her hands clutched before herself, and watched me with wide eyes.

"Who troubles my household at this hour?" I demanded with the impatience of one roused for no good reason.

"My lady Ysabella?"

My breath caught in recognition of that voice, no less the music snared within it. Fitz!

But why would Merlyn's most trusted manservant arrive at my door alone? I glanced back to the window, but knew no other lesser steed stood with the destrier. And no nobleman, however generous, would grant such a beast to even his most beloved servant. No, that was Merlyn's mount.

I feared the portent of the steed being here without Merlyn.

"It is Rhys Fitzwilliam," the caller continued, though I knew that well enough. "I would speak with you for a moment, my lady, if you please."

I pulled open the door. My dread redoubled when I found Fitz's countenance pale.

Something clearly had gone awry.

What shall I tell you of Rhys Fitzwilliam? He is a man who savors life's pleasures—that the board of the Lammergeier groans with many such pleasures is evidenced by Fitz's girth. He is not corpulent, but neither is he slender. He is, shall we say, a sturdy man. He is of a height with me, though perhaps twice my age. His face is tanned and lined, and his eyes can sparkle with merriment most unexpected.

Not on this morn, however. Fitz looked woebegone, strained as I had never seen him.

Fitz is oft underestimated, for his appearance is that of a gruff but good-natured man, a simple man who cares more for his comfort than much else. A man, perhaps, who has the urge to say more and to do less. But he has a will of steel not unlike Merlyn's, and one perhaps less easily anticipated. Never did I see Fitz shirk from a thankless or unpleasant deed that had to be done.

His thoughts are difficult to read, his impassivity a trick he learned without doubt from his liege lord. I do not know how long Fitz has served Merlyn, perhaps all of Merlyn's life. I wondered once how many secrets of the Lammergeier were known to Fitz and solely Fitz outside the family, how many quiet missions he had undertaken to see their interests served.

That he showed his dismay was no good sign, in my estimation. I gestured that he should enter, struck wordless.

Fitz's very presence was incongruous in our home, for he was garbed as the servant of a wealthy lord. To his credit, he did not so much as glance at his humble surroundings, nor did any trace of judgment touch his features. I offered him a cup of ale and a seat at the wellworn table.

He accepted neither, but stood, hands locked together. I poured the ale despite his refusal, suspecting that he had ridden long and hard, and that he sought to not strain our finances.

"My lord Merlyn is dead, my lady," he blurted, his voice thick.

My hands froze in the act of pouring the ale, then I knew this to be another of Merlyn's jests. My lips tightened and I filled the cup, then set it firmly upon the board.

"Do not be ridiculous, Fitz," I said sternly, feeling my sister's wide-eyed gaze upon me. "It is the sickly and the failing who die, who fade until they cease to breathe or to be. Merlyn's is a defiant and vibrant nature. He will live to eternity just to spite death." I indicated the ale. "Sit and restore yourself, for you must have come far in haste at Merlyn's bidding."

"It is true, my lady." Fitz bowed his head. "He is lost to us. Merlyn is dead."

Mavella looked between the two of us as she crossed herself and whispered a prayer. Tynan slept on, oblivious to the turmoil within me and the pain in Fitz's lined face.

I was certain of myself until I saw the tear easing from Fitz's eye and sliding down his cheek. He held my gaze relentlessly, neither moving nor wiping away the tear.

I turned my back upon him, shaken by the anguish in his eyes. "No, Fitz," I said, my voice trembling slightly. "Not Merlyn. It cannot be."

Fitz's silence was more eloquent than any argument he might have made. I heard the rustle of cloth and turned in time to see him produce the only token that would have persuaded me.

"Sweet Mary," Mavella said and crossed herself anew.

My eyes widened in recognition of the box Fitz placed

carefully upon my table, a box as finely wrought as the table was rough.

There could not be two such boxes in all of Christendom—and the one I knew was Merlyn's pride. Even for that fortnight that Merlyn and I had lived as man and wife, he had never suffered to be parted from that box. It held his every treasure, coins and gems and deeds and secrets, and he would never suffer it to fall into the hands of another.

At least while he drew breath.

Fitz pushed the box toward me with one heavy fingertip.

I recoiled. That Fitz carried this box, no less that he surrendered it to me, was all the evidence a thinking woman needed.

Merlyn was dead.

I rose and went to the window, pulling back the hide to study the steed below. Tears pricked at my eyes and my throat was tight as I fought to make sense of this news.

It was incomprehensible to me that Merlyn no longer reined in his steed just shy of the lip of a cliff, that he no longer spat into the wind. Inconceivable that he was not somewhere beyond my vision, laughing into the wind, his blue eyes flashing with mischief and merriment. Impossible that his heart did not thunder beneath the fingertips of some wench, that his triumphant smile did not flash in some shadow.

"Where is he?" I demanded, glancing back at our guest. "I must see him dead to believe it."

Fitz shook his head. "I had to act with haste, my lady." He sighed heavily. "Such a duty must be accomplished before rumor spreads. No churchyard will have a Lammergeier if they know the truth of his identity."

"Where is he?"

"I took him to a monastery, you need not know the name, and called him a pilgrim I found assaulted upon the road."

In better circumstance, I might have laughed at the irony of such an occupation being associated with Merlyn.

Fitz continued. "I gave him no name and no doubt they thought me a thief whose crime had gone awry."

"I would see him."

"You cannot, my lady. I dare not raise their suspicions further." He looked discomfited. "So anxious was I that my donation was too great. They questioned that a pilgrim would have so much coin, then that I could show such interest in the eternal rest of a stranger." Fitz very nearly squirmed. He was sorely agitated.

"You could have buried him at Ravensmuir," I said softly.

The older man shook his head and spoke with resolve. "I have learned to look away many a time, my lady, but a man must be buried as befits a man. A man must be buried in sacred ground. A man must meet his maker as it is preached he should."

"Even if it takes a lie to do it." I turned away, saddened by how sordid this tale was, saddened that Merlyn had had so little chance to repent.

Then I shook my head. Merlyn had had a lifetime to repent and had not chosen to do so. Even given the chance of confession and absolution, he would have changed nothing at the end, I am certain.

"How did it happen?" I asked, staring blindly at the road below.

"He was assaulted from behind, stabbed and cast into a ditch."

"Were you not with him?"

"He forbade it." Fitz cleared his throat. "I sought him out when he did not return."

"Where did he go?"

Fitz shrugged. "I know only that it was late and I found him. I did all I could, my lady, but it was too late." I heard him sit heavily then, heard the scrape of the cup upon the board as he seized the ale, heard him drink lustily of it.

My fingers tightened upon the hide, an unexpected thirst for vengeance awakening within me. "Who, Fitz?"

"God only knows."

I glanced back at the bitterness in his tone and found his eyes shining with the same desire that I felt. Fitz's expression turned grim and he gave the box another shove in my direction. "It is yours, all yours, from this day forward, my lady. May you bear its burden with grace and good fortune."

"The box?"

"Ravensmuir."

I left the window, so astounded was I by this revelation. "But that cannot be . . ."

"It is. Merlyn insisted upon it." Fitz spoke with vigor, as if he would have no argument from me in this. "The deed to the keep is within the box, if you would care to see it." He fumbled with a key, trapped upon a length of silken cord and my eyes widened.

That cord had graced Merlyn's neck. I had once tangled my fingers within it. Indeed, it might yet be harboring the warmth of my husband's flesh.

Though warmth had abandoned Merlyn.

Grief caught me by the throat and I looked abruptly away, hoping against hope that I might hide my unwelcome response from this astute servant.

I shook my head, then said the first thing that came to my lips. My voice was flat. "I cannot read the deed, Fitz."

"I would read it to you."

"I believe you, Fitz. Leave it be." I looked out the window again, eying that black stallion which seemed now to appear despondent to me.

It had probably witnessed its lord's demise.

I shivered and turned back to the shabby room, needing to ask yet more. I sat opposite the manservant and studied his features. "Why me, Fitz? Why did Merlyn not leave Ravensmuir to his brother Gawain?"

Fitz coughed delicately. "They have been estranged, my lady."

"As have Merlyn and I. We disagreed just yesterday."

Fitz inclined his head. "I believe the rift with Gawain was a greater one."

"That is hard to believe."

"But true nonetheless."

In this moment, I wished that I had not denied Merlyn the day before. I would never know the truth of his scheme and it was my own fault. I sighed and frowned, feeling suddenly tired. "They are all great rifts now, Fitz, for there is no chasm greater than the one betwixt life and the grave."

No one spoke. Distantly, I heard the sounds of the village awakening, of goats bleating as they were milked, of women cursing and chickens clucking, of the chapel bell beginning to toll.

It was Christmas Day, a realization that seemed most incongruous with Fitz's news. How to rejoice when one's heart is leaden?

Fitz set the ale aside and lifted the box in his hands, offering it to me again. The key lay atop it, the silken cord twined like a red snake. "Will you accept Merlyn's legacy, my lady Ysabella?"

I was about to decline, my pride decreeing that I had need of no crumbs from Merlyn's table. Indeed, what difference is there in making coin with sin and accepting the luxury that can be bought by such stained coin? Once I had seen no moral distinction. I thought my knowledge of what was right to be the same today as it had been five years past.

Then my gaze fell upon my brother Tynan, bundled to his eyes upon the thickest pallet we possessed. The deep auburn tangle of his hair was dark against the rough bedding, against the pallor of his brow. My heart ached that he had known so much want in his few days, that I had been able to give him so very little.

I had taken health from him, denied him prosperity and comfort, by the very act of leaving Ravensmuir, even though

I had not known of his pending arrival when I made my choice.

I suddenly realized that I could fix that failing.

I could take Ravensmuir, I could claim it for Tynan. I straightened as the idea took root. I knew that this was the choice I should make.

It was the choice that I would make.

"It could be said that Merlyn owed me much," I said quietly, "and, although this is not the prize I might have sought, it is the one I am offered." I took a deep breath and met Fitz's gaze as I accepted Merlyn's box. "Ravensmuir will do well enough to settle the balance."

A ghost of a smile lit Fitz's face. Perhaps he was relieved that his lord's will was fulfilled so readily—certainly none would expect biddability of me.

My sister watched me, her uncertainty evident. I forced a smile for her. "We shall spend Christmas warm and well-fed for a change. How soon can you be prepared to depart?"

It was bitterly cold by the time we left Kinfairlie village behind us, by the time I had made some excuse to the silversmith Malcolm Gowan and shaken free of his wife Fiona's shrill demands by persuading her to sell the ale herself. The entire transaction would have irked me more, had I not known that better fortunes lay before us.

No matter how destitute Ravensmuir had become, it would offer a finer life than the one we had come to know.

The dark sky brooded, the clouds a leaden blanket too heavy for the sun to push aside. The wind was vicious as it can only be when it rises in the east. There was a storm coming and we walked quickly, that we might reach the shelter of Ravensmuir before the onslaught of rain began.

We were four—Mavella, Tynan, Fitz, and myself. And the

black stallion, of course. Fitz had offered me the mount, but I know little of horses and this one's vigor frightened me.

Indeed, closer inspection only confirmed my earlier thought. There was a wickedness in the glint of the eye of that stallion, a restlessness about the beast. It was as vibrantly alive as Merlyn had been. It fought the bit and defied Fitz frequently, as if unfamiliar with the burden of him.

Merlyn's steed was a beast of a temperament well matched to his own. I refused to think of Merlyn's visit, refused to consider that I might have prevented his demise by making a choice other than the one I had.

The world was better to be rid another criminal, was it not?

To my dismay, in the shadows of my heart, I was not so certain. The world seemed a darker place without the prospect of encountering Merlyn again. I told myself that the weather solely was at root of my dismal mood but did not believe it for a moment.

I reminded myself that I had made the right choice five years past, the sole choice. I knew that Merlyn and I could not have survived each other—just as the hawk and the hare could not have made a good union.

But surely there is no weakness in admitting that I was encouraged by the knowledge that he sailed onward, boldly conquering all that crossed his path. Surely there is no fault in being glad that some soar as freely as the birds when I myself was securely tethered by concerns and responsibilities. I had borne my burdens more easily, knowing that he flew unfettered.

Our short marriage had not been all bitter, nor even all sweet. No, for all my decision to leave, there was tenderness in my memories of my husband. Merlyn was a man, as few men have the audacity to be—more handsome, more virile, more lacking in conscience, and more charming than God should have permitted any single mortal to be.

Yes, if he had not been a criminal and a murderer, I would have been in his bed until the end.

Until this day.

And now I would never lie abed with him again. I was shocked to realize that a faint hope of reconciliation had lurked in a dark corner of my mind, a hope that now died as surely as Merlyn had.

Could any man's sins be sufficient that he deserved such a sordid death as Merlyn had met?

By the late afternoon, the keep rose dark before us, just as the cold onslaught of rain began. Ravensmuir occupies a point of land which juts into the grey of the North Sea. The keep itself rises to an impressive height, presenting a solid stone face to the inland side, the bulk of it aligned roughly north-south. It is built to withstand a considerable assault. The coastline is rocky and treacherous there, wild with the splash of the surf and as untamed as the family that claimed it.

Not a light glowed from a window, not a sprig of greenery graced the gates. All was grey and desolate. The weather made the keep appear even more forbidding than I knew it was and we trudged onward in silence, oddly disheartened by sight of our destination.

There was only the sound of the rain and the crash of the sea as we approached, the thump of the stallion's hooves. Even Tynan's incessant questions of Fitz were silenced.

The gate to Ravensmuir's inner courtyard is a tunnel that burrows through the body of the keep and opens in the courtyard beyond. That tunnel houses not only a gatekeeper's chamber but three wrought-iron portcullises.

I had a moment to wonder whether Fitz had the keys to the gates, for I certainly did not, and another moment to fear that we would spend this night in the cold rain, before I saw that all of the gates stood open. Our arrival must have been noted long before, an unremarkable detail as the last mile of the road is dead straight for precisely that purpose.

A boy and a woman stood just inside the tunnel, waiting, sheltered there from the rain. I knew immediately who they were, though I wished with vigor that I would be proven wrong.

The woman stepped forward, apparently unaware of the rain, and my heart sank. Ada Gowan had changed little— she was but more taut and more severe, and better at pretending to be wrought of stone. She is not that much older than me, perhaps five years, though she looks twenty years older.

Uncharitable of me to say as much, perhaps, but I will recount the truth here, warts and all.

Ada was garbed in black, a most costly hue. I had never considered that Ada was a vain woman, for she is not particularly comely. But on this day, the expense of her choice was so considerable that I wondered. She was dressed in mourning garb, an affectation of those with considerable wealth. Her black wimple was drawn up to the bottom of her chin. The black veil encircled her sour features along with the wimple, and emphasized the lines carved in her face.

I wondered how she had known so soon that Merlyn was dead.

Her brother, Arnulf, was typically expressionless. He is tall and heavily wrought, larger than one would expect for a youth not yet ten summers. Arnulf is not keen of wit, though he is strong and can labor endlessly. Perhaps he has not the intellect to know when he is tired. I suspect his main advantage in Ada's view is that he will do whatsoever she bids him to do, and that without a single query.

Ada eyed us all as if we were rats come to her door, or beggars. I was very aware of the faded blue shade of my best kirtle, though I lifted my chin and stood protectively beside my sister as Ada surveyed our small party.

"You have no need to voice your tidings, Rhys

Fitzwilliam," Ada said, her tone harsh. "We know the truth of it."

"I beg your pardon?" Fitz's surprise told me that he had neither come here first nor sent word of Merlyn's demise.

Ada's eyes glittered. "We know our lord Merlyn is dead." She gestured to the courtyard far behind her. "The ravens left as one when the light of the dawn touched the sea. It is a sign that our lordship's quest has failed."

I shivered at this news, despite myself.

There was an old tale in these parts that any who made their abode upon this point would know the site blessed for them if the ravens took up residence. And if ever the ravens departed, it was a portent that the family would no longer thrive there.

Merlyn's family took this fable most seriously. He had laughed slightly years ago in his recounting of it, but I had seen the solemnity in his eyes. He had fed the ravens in those days, and had named them all. I had accused him of mingling names and birds, for I could see no difference between the three dozen which occupied the courtyard. I had always thought them ominous birds, though their sudden absence was even more forboding.

Ada's tale chilled me, but I was well aware of my brother's wide eyes. I would not have him frightened so easily as that.

"What superstitious nonsense," I said disparagingly. "For all we know, they will return this night."

"Indeed, they might," Fitz agreed.

Ada snorted, then glanced suddenly at my sister. Mavella flinched, as if struck by a blow, and averted her face.

A smirk that might have been triumphant touched Ada's lips, which infuriated me as nothing else could have done. Had she not done damage enough? Ada and I glared at each other, years of antagonism crackling between us.

Then, Ada curled her lip in a snarl. "I suppose you have

come to pick the bones clean, Ysabella. It is your nature, after all, to covet what is not yours to have."

I itched to slap her, as was now my right, but I spoke in my most dignified manner to prove her expectations wrong. "I have come because Merlyn left Ravensmuir to my care. I am Lady of Ravensmuir from this day forward, Ada, by virtue of being Merlyn's widow and heiress."

"No!" The color drained from Ada's face.

"Oh, yes." I smiled, determined to show more grace than she.

"It is so, Ada," Fitz intervened with authority. "The documents are all in order."

Ada's mouth contorted with rage before she managed to choke out a word. It was one I should have expected, but I flinched all the same. "Witch!"

"Ada . . ." Fitz began, but I held up a hand for silence. I would hear Ada's charges against me.

"The omen is come true, then!" she cried, her outrage clear. "Doom has swallowed the Lammergeiers of Ravensmuir, doom that was hatched years past when Merlyn was beguiled into taking you to wife." She spat on the ground before me. "The loss of my lord Merlyn is but the beginning of the end."

Clearly, Ada did not believe that I would punish her audacity. It was refreshing to meet some soul who put so little faith in my rumored powers of sorcery.

But then, if anyone should know that the rumors of my arcane abilities are nonsense, it should be Ada Gowan.

"I appreciate that your grief at the loss of my lord Merlyn may have affected your greeting," I said coldly, letting Ada see that I appreciated no such thing. "But I and my siblings are in need of a hot bath and a hot meal."

Ada's lips drew to a line so tight that they disappeared. "We were not prepared for your arrival."

"But you had made arrangements for Merlyn's return, for he was so recently in residence." I was well aware that my siblings eyed me with surprise. I dredged up my memory of every lesson Merlyn had granted me in noble conduct, and thought I did passably well.

I let my voice drop. "I counsel you to play no games with me, Ada. You will prepare a bath in the bathing chamber, you will ensure that chamber is warmed, you will see that a hot meal is prepared, that wine is poured and that both the great hall and the beds are made ready. And you will do this promptly." I smiled a smile that was more akin to baring my teeth. "Your pledge of obeisance to me can wait until the morning."

Ada's eyes flashed fire. She opened her mouth and closed it again, spots of color burning in her cheeks. "I will not . . ."

"Then you may leave now and seek employ in another household. It will not trouble me." I spoke with indifference when once I would have shouted. "I believe Dunbar might be the closest keep, and surely you could reach it in several days of hard walking." I smiled again. "Of course, I could not grant a steed or a wagon to someone fleeing my service."

She glared at me, her outrage worsened by my composure. I was delighted that I was finally better at her ploy than she. My siblings were silent. Fitz coughed into his hand and, if I had not known better, I might have thought he disguised a chuckle. Ada's brother watched us, his gaze flat.

Finally Ada straightened, then inclined her head stiffly. "As you wish, my lady," she said, as if the words were poison upon her tongue.

With that, she pivoted and marched back through the gates. Her brother hesitated but a moment before he ambled after her, leaving the four of us in the rain.

Another soul might have been daunted, but I was bolstered. The first clash in this latest battle with Ada had fallen in my favor. I fully expected that Ada would flee that night, but I did not care. She could not steal all of Ravensmuir and whatsoever she left would be more than we had had this very morning.

"Do you intend to linger in the rain all the night long?" I demanded gaily. Fortune had smiled upon us and I was determined to make some merriment, the better to forget my misgivings about Merlyn's demise.

I beamed at my silent siblings. "It is Christmas Day, after all, and our circumstances are vastly improved. Surely that is cause for some cheer?" I nodded at Fitz, then strode into the hall of Ravensmuir as if it were my own.

Because, of course, it was.

III

There is something in the wind when foul fortune is pending. Dogs are made uneasy with it. Cats will coil themselves into watchful balls before the fire when they sense it. And I, too, since my burn was inflicted, feel it in the wound.

Indeed, I began to itch with it as soon as we crossed the threshold of Ravensmuir. I was certain that I was watched, that some hungry gaze kept vigil over me. It was an eerie sensation and made the hairs prickle on the back of my neck.

I attributed it, though, to Ada's sour welcome and refused to bend to her malicious will.

The great hall was cold and barren, not so much as a candle lit within its echoing expanse, and it seemed to me to be haunted by Merlyn. He must have stayed here recently, if not several nights past, and the yawning emptiness of the keep seemed to echo with that.

I peered into every corner, expecting to find him laughing at me. I glanced over my shoulder a dozen times, anticipating that he would be lurking in the shadows, a gleam of triumph in his eyes that he had fooled me yet again.

There was nothing but dust in the shadows.

Dust and memories.

Unexpected tears stung my eyes, but I blinked them away. I would not weep for Merlyn Lammergeier. I knew too much of his dark secrets to mourn his passing.

All the same, I was uneasy. Perhaps Merlyn's ghost would have preferred that I mourned him as diligently as Ada. His specter would have to wait an eternity for that.

Indeed, I sought festive cheer with a vengeance, as if I would thwart even this meager expectation of me.

"Look at this old hall," I declared to none in particular. "It has not seen a merry Christmastide in years. Matters shall be different now that we abide here."

"These rushes are withered and filthy beyond belief," Mavella said, poking at them with her toe.

"We could make it clean!" Tynan said with the enthusiasm of one who will do little of the work.

We had need of some task to occupy us. We lit candles and set to work while we were yet dirty, sweeping the old rushes and dust from the hall. I did not expect that Ada would contribute, for she clearly had not tended to the chamber in years. Fitz began a song and Tynan sang with him, the two of them making such a ruin of the tune that Mavella and I were compelled to join them.

"We have need of a Yule log," I said, for the empty fireplace was not only cold but disheartening.

"What is a Yule log?" Tynan asked. I ruffled his hair as he stood beside me.

Mavella and I exchanged a glance of guilt, for the boy knew so little of festivities. Celebration costs coin and for all of the boy's short life, I had spent what coin we had upon food and fuel for the fire. We had considered ourselves fortunate to have tallow for a candle on Christmas Day.

"You are clearly too young to remember the merriment of past Yules," Fitz said heartily, though his eyes revealed that he understood the truth. He smiled at Tynan. "A great hall has need of a great log, to warm the hearts and the hands of all who come to the hall on this festival of festivals."

Tynan tugged at my hand. "Who will come, Ysabella?"

I looked to Fitz, who said nothing, then shrugged. "Traditionally, all of the peasants come to share at the bounty of their lord's table."

Tynan frowned. "What peasants?"

"I do not know whether there are any sworn to Ravensmuir any longer."

Certainly, there was no village and no cultivated fields near Ravensmuir. Originally, Ravensmuir had been the summer abode of the lord of Kinfairlie. In former times—well before my own days!—its sustenance came from further inland, from the fields pledged to Kinfairlie proper. The destruction of Kinfairlie keep had been just before the first onslaught of the plague, the one which had killed nearly half the peasants hereabouts. Perhaps whatever peasants remained had simply taken up the lands left vacant near Kinfairlie village.

The Lammergeier had claimed suzerainty of Ravensmuir, though I did not know what else they had claimed.

Fitz shrugged, which meant that either he did not know or he would not tell. I supposed any villeins pledged to Ravensmuir would come to the portal in search of that free meal.

Tynan frowned. "No lord gave us dinner in Kinfairlie."

"No, because Kinfairlie keep is burned and gone, and Kinfairlie village is pledged to none in these days. You know that tale," I chided. "There is a Lord of Kinfairlie no longer."

Tynan brightened, his recollection prompted, and began to recount the tale he had heard so many times. It was a favored one of his, for he had a boy's taste for violent tales of chivalry. "For the keep of Kinfairlie was attacked by wicked men who wished to seize it."

Mavella continued. "And when the Lord of Kinfairlie refused to surrender to them, they burned his keep while the lord and his family were trapped within its walls."

"Then they burned his second abode at Ravensmuir!" Tynan said. "They thought to frighten the lord into surrender, but he was too brave to be frightened. Then the wind came from the sea and fanned the flames and the fires burned too heartily to be halted."

"That is sufficient . . ." I began.

But Tynan continued in his enthusiasm. "And it is said that the twin fires of the burning of Ravensmuir and Kinfairlie keep challenged the very light of the sun. And none escaped the blaze but Mother."

Mavella nodded. "Mother, who was in service to the Lady of Kinfairlie and had been dispatched down the treacherous sea cliffs to seek aid from Tantallon or Dunbar."

"After Kinfairlie was reduced to ashes, the bad men sowed the fields with salt and left Kinfairlie for all time, their scheme thwarted," Tynan continued, though he had difficulty with the last word.

Mavella nodded. "No one remembered their names, for the plague came fast on their heels and killed half the people who had occupied Kinfairlie manor and all who had seen their faces."

"And the priests declared that it was reparation for the sins of all those who lived upon Kinfairlie's lands, and demanded penance of us all," I concluded.

"Do you remember?" Tynan asked.

I bent and tickled his tummy. "No. I was smaller then than you are now."

"None of us were born yet," Mavella said.

"That *is* smaller than me!" Tynan giggled and squirmed away from my tickling finger, then tilted his head to regard me. "But Ravensmuir is here, not burned. We stand inside it. How can that be?"

"Because Ravensmuir was rebuilt and Kinfairlie was not."

"By who?"

I crouched down beside him. "Ravensmuir was rebuilt by Avery Lammergeier, who sailed across the seas and laid claim to part of the ancient realm of Kinfairlie. After the keep was built, he gave his holding to his eldest son, who was named Merlyn. And when Merlyn died—" I choked unexpectedly here, but cleared my throat and continued beneath Fitz's bright gaze "—he surrendered Ravensmuir to me." I forced a smile. "And now, we shall live here."

Tynan frowned as he considered information that was new to him. "But why?"

"Because Merlyn is—*was*—my husband."

Tynan's brow puckered as he thought about this. "Then why did we live in Kinfairlie village and not here?"

Fitz lifted his brows quizzically, as if he too would be delighted to know the answer. My sister took sudden interest in the stonework.

"Because Merlyn Lammergeier was a bad man," I said with as much care as I could muster. "I did not realize his wickedness when I pledged to wed him, because he omitted to tell me much of the truth and lied to me about the rest. But as soon as I learned of his crimes, I left Ravensmuir. That is why we lived in Kinfairlie village."

This only fed Tynan's curiosity. "What did he do?"

"He was a thief," I said, unwilling to enumerate all of Merlyn's crimes.

"Then he must be in hell," Tynan said with quiet conviction. His eyes brightened suddenly as he studied me. "Are you sad for him, Ysabella?"

I touched Tynan's face with a fingertip, barely recognizing my own voice when I spoke. I could not lie to a child. "Yes, Tynan. Yes, I am."

Fitz looked away.

"We have need of a Yule log," I said again, more firmly and before my brother could concoct another question.

To my relief, this time the suggestion was taken.

The four of us raided Ravensmuir's woodshed and quickly claimed the largest unhewn tree that had been dragged there. Ada and Arnulf watched sullenly as we pronounced it our Yule log, and garnished it with greenery.

We sang its tribute with an old song our mother had taught Mavella and me, one that she said had been sung at Kinfairlie. Fitz also seemed to know it, though it was all new to Tynan. We danced around the log, each trying to persuade the other to be merry, then we hauled it into the hall. Its root filled the great fireplace at one end of the hall and the wood was so dry that it lit immediately, casting a heartening glow over the hall.

"It is so big!" Tynan whispered.

"It must burn through Epiphany," I told him. "Each day we will push it a little further into the hearth."

"And on Epiphany, we shall store the last coal safely in the cellar for good fortune until next Yule," Mavella added. She nodded at me. "I remember Mother's tales of Kinfairlie."

Tynan's lips set as he stared into the flames. "I should like to have heard her tales."

"Then we shall endeavor to recount them all to you," I said as cheerfully as I could manage. The ghost of my mother seemed to hover at my shoulder. Perhaps hers was the presence I felt this night, not Merlyn's.

I certainly should have preferred it that way.

We warmed our hands and congratulated ourselves on our efforts, then reveled in the hot bath that Ada tartly announced. Fitz took himself off to the stables with some mumbled excuse about the horses and squires.

Eventually, Ada brought us a hot venison stew and rough bread, without apology for either the simplicity of the fare or her delay. Probably she knew that it was a far finer meal than we would have shared this night, had Fitz not rapped upon our door.

It was curious to dine in the great hall, for we were but three and the chamber was intended to house hundreds. We clustered together at one end of the high table, Tynan's giggles echoing loudly in the nigh empty chamber.

Even comfort, companionship, hot stew and the welcome flames upon the hearth could not dismiss my unease. Indeed, the falling darkness seemed to feed it. My trepidation was rooted in more than Ada's ominous greeting, more than the fact that my sole memories of this place included Merlyn, more than the echoing emptiness of Ravensmuir's halls, more than the yearning for my mother.

It was guilt.

Could I have prevented Merlyn's death by aiding him?

I felt that specters hid in the shadows, whispering accusations to each other, that untold doings occurred just out of the range of my vision. There was wickedness afoot, for I had no doubt that this hall had witnessed many crimes, and that wickedness breathed upon my very neck. My burn itched with an unholy vigor that I knew was a portent of ill.

Indeed, I could not stop glancing over my shoulder.

I jumped for the hundredth time when one of Tynan's shouts seemed unaccountably loud, then looked up to find concern in my sister's gaze.

"You must be tired," Mavella said, then smiled with fatigue herself. "It has been a day of many changes, after all."

I was exhausted and saw no reason not to blame that for my fey mood.

"Yes, I am," I agreed. "I will retire, then." I opened my arms in an expansive gesture as I stood, then smiled. "May you both sleep well in this new abode."

"We will find some plump pallet and each claim a chamber for our own," Mavella declared and Tynan's eyes widened that such a deed would be possible. For all his days, we had not only shared one meager room, but lived all the events of our life within it.

We embraced, and I took solace in the goodness of my siblings' hearts. I was fiercely glad to have this opportunity, for their sakes.

I had turned from the table to fetch a lantern before I realized a most simple fact. I, as the new lady of Ravensmuir, would sleep in the lord and lady's chamber, in the lord and lady's bed.

In the bed where I and Merlyn had met lustily so many times.

My heart leapt in an awkward fashion, then fluttered like a caged bird. When I might have granted myself a reprieve for this one night, Ada stepped out of the shadows, her gaze bright.

"I shall show you to the solar, my lady," she said with undisguised anticipation. "Only that I might unlock the doors for you, of course. I would not have you forget the way."

"How kind of you, Ada," I said with a sweetness that made my own teeth ache.

I knew that she wished the perverse pleasure of witnessing my first glimpse of that chamber in half a decade. She meant to see my weakness but I would show her none.

I followed her to the far end of the great hall, irked anew, and spared a glance to the windows that framed a glimpse of the sea beyond. A ship was silhouetted there and was evidently anchored, for its masts were bare.

"Are there guests at Ravensmuir?" I asked.

"Beyond yourselves?" Ada asked archly.

"I refer to the ship riding at anchor."

"My lord Merlyn arrived upon that ship." Ada shrugged. "It seems that they too await a laird who will never arrive. I wonder what their fate might now be."

I wondered about their cargo more than their fate, and hoped it would not prove to be my concern. I had no desire to be burdened with the remnants of Merlyn's disgraceful trade. Perhaps that was why he had left the keep to me—perhaps it had been a sly joke, a vengeance achieved by embroiling me in his wicked deeds.

I rubbed my temple with a tired hand. Morning would be soon enough to learn the worst of it.

There was a small antechamber between the hall and the door to the lord's solar. Ada paused there to fumble with the keys. She held the lantern high with one hand, the light casting her figure in silhouette. She finally found the key and fitted it to the lock, then pushed upon the door. The portal to the chamber beyond was as black as a tomb, a faint scent of burnt wick and beeswax wafting to my nostrils.

"My lord labored late his last night here," Ada commented, pleased that she knew more of Merlyn's recent deeds than I.

Did she know he had sought me out?

The lantern light flickered over the broad wood table and simple chairs in this chamber, the dark paneling and heavy trunks. There was another scent in the chamber, a faint but familiar one that was quickly consumed by the stronger smell of burning oil.

It was the musk of man, of a particular man, of horse and sea and wind and the tang of Merlyn's own skin.

It nigh took me to my knees. The scent, as scents so often do, awakened my every yearning. I could taste Merlyn's kiss again and my heart raced at this false evidence that he was near.

Ironically, Ada was oblivious to the very response she wished to witness. She had turned already toward the stairs that wound upward to the solar proper. I braced myself against the sights and memories I would find above and climbed in her shadow. She crossed the solar quickly to light the brazier, then turned to ensure that she could see every nuance of my expression.

I schooled my features before stepping out of the nook

that hid the stairs. Then I let my gaze flick over the familiar
room as if I had never seen it before. I looked at everything
except the bed, which occupies the better part of the room,
knowing I would be hard-pressed to remain impassive when
my gaze first fell upon it.

Tapestries, richly wrought of red and gold, hung on the
walls in that chamber; trunks were set around the perimeter
of the room; candlesticks and braziers were scattered on the
floor and across the tops of trunks. Nothing had changed
since my departure, save the collection of dust in the corners, and I might have been cast into the past, save for one
detail.

A pair of red leather gloves lay discarded on one chest.
They were Merlyn's gloves, the very gloves he had slapped
against his palm the day before. My innards tightened at the
sight of them and I forced my glance to slide over them.

There were a trio of high small windows on the far side of
the chamber, and all were shuttered against the west wind. I
flung them open, one after the other, then looked over the
sleeping countryside beyond. I eyed the stars above and the
waning moon, and took a deep breath of the chilly night air.
Ada clicked her tongue in disapproval.

I turned to face her with a smile. "Merlyn always preferred to smell the wind."

She averted her face for a moment and I wondered anew
how much she mourned his passing.

Let alone how much she knew about it.

A cold shiver slid down my spine and I resolved to lock
the door of the solar and secure myself against all in this
keep, at least until I knew more.

I could no longer ignore the bed. I clutched Merlyn's box
more tightly against my ribs, then turned, well aware of
Ada's gaze upon me.

Even braced for it, the sight nigh stopped my heart.

This was no common bed. It was not even the bed of a
great lord, it was a magnificent and enormous bed befitting

some potentate whose exalted rank I cannot imagine. Perhaps kings sleep in beds so fine as this, but I doubt it. I doubt that there has ever been or ever will be another bed of this ilk.

The bed's corners were marked with heavy pillars, which rose to meet the timbered ceiling. Each was carved with a doughty griffin at the base then swirled upward, as if wrought of heavy rope. At the foot of the bed, a massive bird of prey was carved between the top of the two pillars and the ceiling, with his wings outspread. The tips of those wings stretched beyond the pillars, and his menacing beak was wide open, as if he meant to devour the heart of any fool come to sleep here unbidden.

It was a lammergeier, the predator for which Merlyn's family was named, the same predator whose silhouette was inlaid in the lid of the box I clutched, the same predator whose shape adorned the clasp of Merlyn's cloak.

The lammergeier is a sheep vulture, the largest bird of prey known to mankind. Its origins lie in the mountains of the east, uncharted and poorly known. It was the sacred bird of the Scythians and of the Goths, revered for its strength and the ferocity of its attack.

Merlyn told me these details on my nuptial night when I was startled by this very carving. It was still daunting in the candlelight. He had told me also that this carved bird was nearly the size a lammergeier is said to be—its wingspan one and a half times the height of a man.

They must be formidable and terrifying creatures, though if the likeness is a good one, then there must be a wild beauty and grace in them as well.

Not unlike the men who bear their name.

Beyond that carving, the bed was merely rich, if richness can ever be inconsequential. The mattresses were three and so thick with goose-down that one had the sense of sleeping in the clouds. A single one of them would grant sweet luxury; three seems most decadent. The bed was hung with silken brocade, so deep an indigo as to be black, embroidered in silver thread with that heraldic bird of Merlyn's family. The hangings were backed with cut velvet of the same hue, a rich foreign fabric which I had only seen and touched once.

In this bed.

With Merlyn. His presence was stronger here, as was the lingering scent of him, as if he might step from the very shadows to greet me again. Memory assailed me, and my lips burned with the recollection of his recent kiss.

I closed my eyes, feeling a phantom parody of his touch slide across my flesh, and willed myself not to flush.

"I trust you will not be troubled that I have yet to air the linens," Ada said, her gleeful tone implying that she expected precisely the opposite. "It is but one night since my lord slumbered here."

"He was not here last evening?"

"No. He did not return from his errand." Ada smiled thinly. "I apologize for my lack, but you must be so tired from your journey that you could sleep in a stable."

"Which is undoubtedly what you would prefer." I had not intended to say as much but the words slipped over my lips.

We stared at each other, Ada's hostility suddenly unguarded.

"He should not have granted Ravensmuir to you," she spat. "It was a mistake. It must have been a jest he never intended to see honored. He could not have bequeathed Ravensmuir to you—he would not have done so, had he lived another day!"

She then stepped back, alarmed that she too had uttered words she had not intended to say, and clapped a hand to her mouth.

I could not resist temptation. "My lord Merlyn had a great fondness for blunt speech," I whispered wickedly. "Perhaps it is his specter that forces the truth from our lips."

"Do not say as much!"

I advanced upon a horrified Ada. "Perhaps he left Ravensmuir to me for that very reason, that I might conjure him back from the dead. You know my repute as well as any, Ada."

"You would not!"

"Indeed, are you not the one who called me the Witch of Kinfairlie? Does that mean that you, above all others, most believe it?"

Ada paled slightly and stepped back. Under the eye of that carving, it did indeed seem that all the dark arts were possible.

I pursued her with measured steps. "Perhaps I will use those gifts which you accused me of having. Perhaps I shall summon Merlyn this night and set him to haunting this place. Perhaps I shall dispatch Merlyn's specter to torment you, Ada Gowan, in retaliation for the wickedness you showed my sister."

Ada glanced quickly over the chamber, then met my gaze again. She spoke boldly and scornfully, though she clung to the crucifix strung on a lace around her neck. "And what would you know of my lord Merlyn? You, who fled his bed in a fortnight?"

"In name and in body, I was Merlyn's wife, just as I am his widow, and now his heiress."

"You were his harlot! You will not stay this time either," Ada insisted even as she eased toward the stairs. "You will not last the night in this chamber!"

"Perhaps it is you who will flee in the night, Ada," I said, fully expecting as much.

"You should have been tried and executed for your sorcery!"

The depth of her hatred for me was sobering. I watched her as she glared at me and tried to find reason in her accusations. "To whom do you think Merlyn ought to have bequeathed Ravensmuir?" I asked quietly. "Surely not to you?"

"What I think and what I do not think is not for you to know," she snarled, but I did not miss the flash of her eyes.

Fear? Or had it been greed? I would have to think about her words and their import. Later, after I slept and my thoughts were more clear.

After I made my peace with Merlyn's death.

I spoke crisply, as if untroubled by this chamber. "I should prefer to break my fast early on the morrow, the better that we might review the inventories."

Resentment darkened her eyes. "As you wish, my lady."

Ada would have turned away, but I put out my hand and the gesture made her pause. "I would have the keys, if you please."

"You have no need of them."

"Indeed I do." I strolled after her. "In fact, I feel a certain threat toward my own health on this evening and I would secure my door against it."

"My lord Merlyn never locked his chamber door!"

"My lord Merlyn is dead. I would prefer not to join him in that state this night." I put out my hand again. "Just as I would prefer not to find myself locked into this chamber at first light, the keys tied on your girdle on their way to Dunbar."

Ada's eyes glittered as she studied me. "You are not the Ysabella that once I knew."

"No, I am neither eighteen summers of age nor readily cowed any longer. I have learned much in these past years, Ada." I gave her that cool smile which seemed to trouble her the most. "Give me the keys, and give them to me now."

To my surprise, she chose not to further defy my command. I had thought I might have to wrest the keys from her, but Ada untied the rings of keys from her girdle and sourly surrendered the smallest ring to me. "The keys to your chamber, my lady." The title she uttered with a sneer, but already I grew accustomed to that.

"And the others?"

"I have yet to secure the stores this night, my lady. I would not disturb you by bringing the keys to you later this night."

She lied and we both knew it.

But the truth was that I would need the knowledge of Ada in the days ahead, as much as it galled me to admit as much. And there was something she desired of me, something that had compelled her to make this concession. I would unravel her reason for that later. For the moment, I would compromise in the hope of prevailing at the greater battle.

I smiled. "Then good night, Ada. May you have pleasant dreams."

She looked as if she might have said something else, but instead she turned away. Her footfalls echoed on the stairs, then the door to the chamber below closed audibly.

I lit a candle with the coals in the brazier and followed Ada, sifting through the keys until I found the one that locked the outermost door. I then climbed the stairs again and dropped the latch to bar the door at the top of the stairs, praising the fact that the Lammergeier were so concerned for their own security. There was none within this chamber but me, and there would be no others all the night long.

That took the steel out of my shoulders. I leaned back against the door for a moment and closed my eyes, breathing deeply of Merlyn's presence and glad to finally be alone. Rain began to fall in heavy drops against the stone walls, though the wind had died. The sound was rhythmic and peaceful. I breathed deeply of the night air and felt somehow soothed.

I put Merlyn's box upon the pillow, running a fingertip across the inlay work on the lid. Merlyn's box is wrought of some exotic wood, its surface dark and burled. It is polished to a gleam and it snared the lantern light now, glowing as if dusted with gold. It is twice the length of my hand, the width of one hand from longest fingertip to wrist and almost the same depth. Its lid is inlaid with a white lammergeier, the bird's wings outspread and its hooked beak open.

Five years ago, I had stood in this very chamber with my new husband. Merlyn had caressed the inlay with his thumb, a gesture I now echoed unintentionally, while he told me that the bird was wrought of ivory. I did not know what ivory was, which he found amusing, as he found it even more amusing when I challenged his explanation. Elephants, I had informed him, did not truly exist outside of fireside tales, as every woman of sense knew.

Or so I had been certain then. I stroked the inlay now and smiled. I had learned much from Merlyn in a mere fortnight, the mere fortnight that we had lived as man and wife.

Perhaps I had learned more than I truly wanted to know.

Merlyn's box held everything precious to which he could lay claim—it contained documents and deeds and coins and keys and the occasional jewel. It still did, though my single treasure—of worth to me alone—now nestled in the silk lining with the box's contents, as well. And the key hung upon the worn red silken cord looped around my own neck, not Merlyn's.

My hand rose to that silken cord, my fingers coiled in its softness. A lump rose in my throat as I fancied I could still feel the heat of Merlyn's flesh trapped within the cord. I caught my breath and abruptly turned away from the box, my gaze falling immediately upon those gloves.

Crimson gloves.

I crossed the floor without ever having decided to do so, and yet, I could not stop until I stood before the gloves. They were fanciful and lavish and I smiled at the evidence of Merlyn's taste for opulence. The gloves were lined with white fur, the ermine I knew he favored, and they were barely worn.

They were undeniably Merlyn's.

I sighed his name without intending to do any such thing.

Then, I touched a finger to the fur, catching my breath when its silky softness swallowed my fingertip. I stroked the length of fine leather, then picked up one glove.

It was heavy for all its fine construction, the palm already stained dark from use. The fingers were curled slightly in the shape of Merlyn's hand, curled as his fingers would be around the leather reins of his destrier's bridle. I half expected it to still be warm from his touch. I lifted the glove to my face as if he cupped my chin and closed my eyes, remembering.

Yearning.

There were tears in my eyes when I impulsively slipped my hand into the glove. My fingers were immediately engulfed in softness, lost in the greater size of Merlyn's glove. It was more like a gauntlet upon me, the cuff coming nearly to my elbow. I was assailed by the scent of Merlyn, the memory of his playful manner, the certainty of his death.

Merlyn was dead.

I bent my head over the fine glove and stained its fine leather with tears.

I thought I had only a few tears to shed for Merlyn, but a torrent was loosed once the dam was opened. I cried and could not stop. I wept for my dead husband, in the solitude of his chamber, breathing the last vestige of his scent. I wept that I would never see him again, I wept that all chances were now lost forever.

When my tears finally slowed, still I felt bereft, as lost as a child, and in dire need of solace.

With nary a second thought, I crossed the chamber, shedding my chemise and shoes as I went and leaving them cast upon the floor. I climbed through the heavy curtains as naked as the day I was born, as naked as I had been on my wedding night. When I realized that Merlyn's gloves were still gripped in one of my hands, I nestled them upon the pillow beside the box. It was foolish and I knew it, but I could not put anything of his from my side.

Not on this night, at least.

I kissed each leather fingertip like a benediction, then slid beneath the coverlet. I was embraced by the furs that still covered the mattress, engulfed by the heady musk of him upon the pillows, swallowed by sweet memories.

Merlyn was dead and gone, never to love and laugh again. And I, I mourned him alone as I would never mourn him before others.

Indeed, I wagered with his specter in the shadowed bed that night. I agreed in my weakness that I would allow him one night and one night alone to haunt me.

I should have guessed that Merlyn would make the most of such an offer. My eyes drifted closed, my fingertip stroked the cuff of one glove, my gaze fixed on the distant sparkle of stars. Sleep came quickly and deeply.

As did my dreams.

The solar is silent and cool after the boisterous if tiny celebration in the great hall. I shiver in mingled cold and anticipation, only now fearing what I have done. I have never been in this chamber. I have never been alone with a man.

I have never been alone with this man. In truth, I know very little of him.

But he is my husband by dint of my own pledge. And if his intent is foul, no one celebrating our match in the hall below will even hear me cry out.

I have made my choice and now must pay the price. How unfortunate a moment for my bravery to flee!

I wrap my arms around myself in trepidation. The lantern's glow gilds luxurious appointments far beyond my experience. Gold and brass studded with gems. Ornate wooden furniture polished to a gleam. Glass and silver. Silks embroidered with gold, furs from distant lands. For all its richness,

*this is the chamber of a man, scattered with weapons of war,
boots and books.*

This is the lair of my lord and master.

My spouse moves from my side and I watch his silhouette,
finding him even more enigmatic in shadow. He lights a candle, grants me a slow smile, then lights a dozen more. I gasp
when he lights a dozen after that, and a dozen more, setting
the room ablaze.

"The cost, my lord!" I protest. "The waste!"

He laughs, a rumble deep in his chest and turns to me.
Candles light the wall behind him, shrouding his features. The
light emphasizes his broad shoulders and his height, it glints
blue in his ebony hair. Only his eyes sparkle as he watches
me, and, inexplicably reassured, I shiver from something
other than fear.

"A lucky man has but one wedding night to celebrate," he
whispers, the low pitch of his words making me shiver. "I have
no care for the cost. I would see my beautiful bride."

I swallow, suddenly feeling too young and too common to
hold this man's eye for long. "Yes, my lord."

"No," he murmurs and crosses the room more quickly than
I would have believed possible. He is like a great cat, or a
wolf, some untamed creature stalking his prey, stalking me,
on silent feet.

But unlike most prey, it is not my nature to flee.

My face is suddenly cradled in his hands, his bright gaze is
bent upon me. Confused, I try to shake free of his grip but he
holds fast.

Gently, firmly.

"Not 'my lord'," he chides, laughter in his eyes. Perhaps I
am beguiled. Perhaps that is why my mouth is dry and I cannot move away. "We are wed, Ysabella, and from this moment forth, you will call me by my name."

"If you so desire, my lord."

His smile flashes, dangerous, heart-stopping. "I do so desire. And my name is Merlyn."

I swallow again, catching my breath when his fingertip touches my throat and traces the movement. There is marvel in his eyes when he meets my gaze again. Marvel? I watch and wonder and realize that I have some power in this game.

Yet I am afraid, though I do not know precisely what I fear. I am not naive of what happens between men and women— no village girl can be—but this room, this lair, unsettles me. The unfamiliar privacy unsettles me. The quietude unsettles me.

Mostly, my spouse unsettles me. My impetuous acceptance of Merlyn Lammergeier's proposal seems suddenly to be the most foolish choice that ever I have made. We are too different, our expectations too broadly apart.

But one does not cower before a hungry dog if one means to escape unscathed. He waits and I know what he desires of me.

"Yes, Merlyn," I whisper with a boldness I do not quite feel.

And the reward of his smile startles me utterly.

I smile back at him. The air heats between us and I can see the hunger invade his gaze, hunger mingled with restraint and admiration. He whispers my name, his breath fanning across my flesh like a caress, and I shiver anew.

His fingers slide into my hair and I close my eyes, tipping my head back to rest in his palms. His lips brush across mine, launching a thousand tingles in the wake of his touch. There is an unspoken question in his ardent but tentative touch, one that reassures me tremendously.

The choice is mine. Here is the nuptial gift from my spouse, the one he does not even know he offers, the precious treasure he grants unwittingly.

Because he offers a choice, there is no choice. He has set me alight as surely as the candles in the chamber. A new flame has been touched to my flesh with a single kiss. I am trembling, my heart pounding, my desire awakened, and I know that only he can sate me.

He desires me and I desire him—this is the commonality of our match, this is the rock upon which we will build a marriage.

I echo his gesture, winding my fingers into the thick silk of his dark hair. I lean against him, feel the muscles of his chest, feel his erection against my belly.

I trace the shape of his lips with my fingertip, suddenly glad of the light so that I, too, can see all of my mate. I see my own hand shake slightly when he takes my fingertip gently in his mouth. He grazes the skin with his teeth, our gazes lock. He watches me, he flicks his tongue across the tip of my finger, and I melt into fathomless desire.

"Yes, Merlyn," I whisper. "Oh, yes."

I have but a glimpse of his smile before he claims my lips in a possessive kiss, a kiss that leaves nothing in the night save Merlyn Lammergeier.

December 26

Saint Stephen's Day
Feast Day of Saint Dionysius

IV

I awakened to find my cheeks tight with dried tears and sunlight streaming through the east windows. The air was cold and crisp. Much refreshed, I lay abed and savored the fleeting shards of my dream. I assumed that I had pleasured myself in the night, for I was languid and sated.

But then, I smelled an earthly scent that was not my own, a scent that had not been there the night before. I smelled it despite the locked doors separating me from the keep, despite the greater barriers between myself and the gates of hell.

I smelled *Merlyn.*

Or more precisely, I smelled Merlyn's seed. And it was then that I knew that I was no widow, for Merlyn was not dead.

Which meant that I had been deceived.

Worse, I had been fool enough to fall for a deception perfectly typical of my estranged spouse. My own gullibility enraged me as nothing else could have done. My temper is slow to kindle, but there is no more sure way of igniting it than with mockery.

The faithless rogue had not only deceived me, but he had seduced me while I mourned his demise! He *knew* I should never have permitted him between my thighs while I was awake, so he came to me in darkness, shrouded in dreams.

Wretch! Nothing would have given me greater pleasure that morn than to fatally draw Merlyn's blood myself! I flung myself from the bed and dressed in haste.

By the time I found the harridan Ada in the kitchens, my mood was blacker still. She was clearly startled by my appearance—I assumed because of the earliness of the hour. Then the two squires seated at the board studied me with wide eyes, before looking quickly back to their meal. Arnulf made a long, if surreptitious, survey of me.

I had not troubled with my hair and it hung loose down my back in an unruly tangle. My feet were bare in my shoes, but I had already decided not to waste time returning to the solar for my stockings.

Ada's face pinched with as much disapproval as ever. "My lady?"

"I will have the remainder of the keys, if you please."

She retreated, her expression guarded. "And if I do not please?"

"Last evening we agreed you should surrender the keys this morning."

Ada shrugged. "I have changed my thinking. It would be most inconvenient for me to not have them in my own possession."

"Do you defy me in this?"

She held my gaze in silent challenge. Slowly, disdain crept into her gaze and her lips curved in a sneer. "Yes," she whispered. "I do."

I guessed that Ada was only so bold because she too knew the truth. A fit of madness came upon me then, wrought perhaps of grief and sleeplessness and duress. I was convinced that she meant to aid Merlyn by keeping the keys from me, that the two of them conspired together to mock me for some unfathomable purpose. I was certain that she was privy to his scheme as I was not, that she changed her thinking because Merlyn had bidden her to do so.

And I seethed at the injustice of it all.

"You know the truth of it!" I shouted at her. Ada backed into the wall but I gave her no quarter, for her retreat proved her guilt to me. "You *know* where Merlyn is, you aid him in his jest! You hide him from me and heed his instruction instead of my own!"

"No, I . . ." Her hand fell to her girdle and I heard the tinkle of the keys hanging within the folds of her robe, hidden beneath her sheltering hand.

I seized her black sleeve. "Then, how did you know he was dead? Fitz had not returned and no others come this way."

"The ravens . . ."

"That is only superstitious foolery, Ada. You are more keen of wit than that." But I was not certain of this even as I uttered the words, for her expression turned fearful.

One squire murmured a blessing and crossed himself. I saw now that the two boys had pushed back from the table and Arnulf had huddled against the wood pile. All were staring at me as if I had been struck mad.

I realized belatedly how I must appear and forced myself to take a deep breath. I released Ada's sleeve and she backed away, taking great trouble to rearrange the folds of her garment even as she watched me.

Though I spoke softly, there was still a thread of anger in my tone. "Tell me where he is, Ada."

She huffed. "As he is dead, no doubt my lord Merlyn will be found in a churchyard somewhere."

"I think not."

Ada glared at me. "Ask Rhys Fitzwilliam."

"You tell me."

She brushed down her garment with elaborate care, then granted me a piercing look. "I have no time for your folly this morn, my lady, and indeed, I do not possess the answer you seek."

"Then give me the keys."

"I have need of them."

"Then you shall ask me for them, as required. The keys are mine, Ada, and you know this well. They should be in my possession alone."

"And suddenly our ladyship knows so much of the running of a large keep," she snipped, her sarcasm undisguised.

"Give me the keys."

"No."

Her defiance infuriated me anew, for my patience wore thin. I snatched at the keys, laying claim to the ring. I wrested them from her grip and though Ada fought hard for control of the ring, she shrank away from me when she lost them.

"And if you feel the compulsion to warn Merlyn, then tell him that he will regret my discovery of him."

Ada sniffed. "Perhaps you forget, my lady, that my lord Merlyn is dead."

"I know he is not." I gave them each a hard stare in turn. "As do all of you, I am certain."

I strode from the kitchens without waiting for an answer and set to my task. It was clear that Merlyn did not wish to be found, but I am stubborn and I was angry.

We had matters to discuss, Merlyn and I.

Ravensmuir is not an old keep, though its site has been occupied since ancient times. What I know of it was told to me by my mother, or by Merlyn. There were vicious battles over the once-rich holding of Kinfairlie, as in so much of this region, the last of those battles having ended with Kinfairlie's keep razed to the ground.

The ruins of Kinfairlie keep have been left untouched ever since. The ghosts of the tormented family are said to still haunt the site, rumoured to interfere with any attempts to build there. I do not know whether that is true, but I know from my mother's account that that unfortunate family was burned alive, trapped in the keep that should have been their sanctuary.

Their screams had haunted the serving girl who had failed to bring aid to them in time.

Only Kinfairlie village remains of what had once been a proud holding, though it no longer has a manor to serve. It is a place of poverty and disillusion, the place in which I was raised and to which I returned after leaving Ravensmuir and Merlyn. By accident of war and plague, Kinfairlie village still has no overlord and is frequently preyed upon by warriors in need of funds.

But the villagers remain, hoping that the status of freemen bestowed upon other local towns might one day be bestowed upon them. Even in hardship, none are anxious to swear themselves to the service of one lord or another. Memory runs too long.

Though it is harsh to say, we are peasants all—bred to obey, not to lead. Had there been a persuasive speaker or a man with a firm scheme ever born in Kinfairlie village, perhaps matters would be different. As it is, we simply continued, endured, and waited for we knew not what.

Meanwhile, after the destruction of the Kinfairlie strongholds and the onslaught of the plague, the Lammergeier quietly laid claim to the abandoned ruins of Ravensmuir. Merlyn told me once that the place had suited them, though he did not explain why, not then.

Now I can well imagine that his family desired no witnesses of their nefarious deeds. Merlyn's father, Avery Lammergeier, built this new and formidable keep at Ravensmuir relatively unobserved. The other local lords fought bitterly with each other, with the English, and with the grim reaper himself. By the time they noted Avery's deeds and decided to act, it was too late. The fortress was built and Ravensmuir secured.

Merlyn told me with some pride that the stone had all been brought from France, for Avery wanted the walls to be of the same material as Chartres Cathedral, so near the origins of their family. I do not know whether this is true, or some fanciful tale of Merlyn's making; I could not always tell when he made a jest. I understood that Chartres was inland and I cannot fathom that a family of seafarers would originate in such a place, but then, I know little of Merlyn's origins and less again of foreign lands.

I am an ignorant, illiterate village maid, albeit one whose mother insisted that her daughters speak as finely as the ladies of the court where she once served.

Once Ravensmuir was completed, it could not be taken by force. A stout wall extends from either end of the keep proper to barricade the point completely. On the inland or west side, great ditches are wrought of the land beyond Ravensmuir's gates, their valleys filled with mire and their peaks cultivated with briars. Only one road cuts a path to the gates, and it runs dead straight for several miles. A single horse can be seen from the watchtower long before its arrival.

One might say that the Lammergeier are protective of their privacy—or that they have much to hide.

Behind the wall and extending to the east are two smaller wings, each an echo of the other. The south wing is occupied by the kitchens, with the kitchen hearth at the eastern end of the wing. The household servants sleep on the second floor, and the wing's roof is thatch.

The north wing holds storage, though the bulk of that wing comprises the stables. The second floor here is used by the shepherds and ostlers, when any are resident, for their sleeping quarters. There is a smithy at the eastern end of this wing, where the fire can be easily restrained.

The keep itself is several stories in height. The lowest floor is not lavish and tends to dank darkness. Here are the quarters for the gatekeeper and whatsoever low staff the lord has in the hall proper. The second floor is larger and grander, its ceiling four times the height of a man.

The majority of this floor is occupied by the great hall, which has two rows of small windows facing the sea, rich tapestries hung beneath them. It is a grand chamber, with four fireplaces, all embellished with the emblems of the Lammergeier. With the tapestries illuminated by candle-light, the tables set with fine linen and the fires raging—which is how I first saw it—the room is both impressive and welcoming.

To the north end of the great hall lies the laird's chambers, one room atop the other, where I had just spent the night. Above the great hall and the lord's solar is another low story which runs the length of the building. Separated at the south end and with a private ladder from the gatehouse, is a small watch chamber with windows to the west, south and east. There are also ladders at either end of the great hall to the remainder of this floor, which provides a warren of small chambers for sleeping, all heated by the chimneys rising from the great hall.

The two wings combine with the keep proper to define three sides of the central courtyard, like an embrace wel-coming the sea. There is a well in the midst of the courtyard and a kitchen garden toward the coast. On a point which juts into the sea is the chapel of Ravensmuir, humped like a bee skep. The path toward it is as overgrown as it was when first I came to Ravensmuir.

Ravensmuir is a massive keep, much of it unused in these times, but I went through it room by room, floor by floor, cupboard by cupboard, my blood boiling hotter with every step.

I discovered my sleeping sister, a veritable angel with her golden hair and fine features, in a chamber on the third floor. If ever a child was left by the fey, it is Mavella, too finely wrought to be a mere mortal.

I tiptoed through her room, and found Tynan in the adja-cent chamber. He managed to look unkempt and on the verge of plunging into some mischief even in sleep. There was a healthy bloom of color in his cheeks, which encour-aged me that I had chosen aright in bringing us here. I brushed the unruly lock of hair back from his brow with the tenderness that flooded my heart in his presence. I smiled briefly before I crept from the room, closed the door and continued my hunt.

Merlyn evaded me.

No doubt, he did so deliberately. My fury mounted with every chamber that proved empty, with every cabinet that was unlocked to no avail. I discovered antechambers and nooks I had never guessed existed, every one of them devoid of my spouse. I could feel Merlyn watching me, I could smell him, and I fancied more than once that I could hear the mockery of his laughter.

But I could not find him. Curse the man!

By the time I reached the stables, I was more livid than ever I have been. I knew that Merlyn deliberately chose his ploy to prove himself more clever than me. I searched every stall with murderous vigor. I nudged past the gentle beasts who regarded me with amiable incomprehension, and even dared to peer within the destrier's stable.

A silver wolfhound had greeted me at the portal to the stables then followed me, like a sentinel posted to observe my every move. It watched me explore the last stall, its expression curious.

As if it wondered why I sought Merlyn here. Even the dog knew more than I!

I cried out in frustration, then glared about myself. I had searched every corner of the keep, to no avail. I kicked a bale of hay with vigor and found such satisfaction in the way that it scattered that I repeated the deed.

"Curse you, Merlyn Lammergeier!" I kicked another bale, venting my anger. It flew apart, filling the air with golden dust as the straw scattered across the floor. "A pox upon you!" I shouted and repeated the deed.

The dog thought this a marvelous game. It pounced on the bundles, shaking mouthfuls of the hay and growling. Its manner made me smile, its wagging tail the surest antidote to a foul mood that I can name.

Indeed, I began to enjoy myself as I kicked the bales yet higher. We made a merry mess, the two of us, and I did not care.

"A plague upon you, Merlyn, and all your kind, all your kin, all your friends and confidants!" I shouted without restraint. "A curse upon you and all those you have favored in your wretched life!"

I caught a sudden whiff of the sea, but paid it no mind in this drafty stable so close to the shore. No doubt the wind mustered anew. I kicked another bale toward the dog. The beast jumped and snatched a mouthful out of the air, then raced in triumphant circles about me.

I laughed, then attacked another bale. "Curse you, Merlyn! Curse the lot of you Lammergeier to hell and back!" The dog backed away and barked.

But it did not bark at me. It barked at something—or someone—behind me. My breath caught before I heard a familiar voice.

"How reassuring to know that I shall have your company upon that long journey."

I jumped. I pivoted, my heart lunging for my throat, knowing before I did who I would see.

Merlyn.

He smiled slightly, taking full note of my awareness of him. No doubt he was pleased. I could not summon a sound to my lips. Even though I had been certain that Merlyn lived, the sight of him standing hale before me stole the words from my mouth.

As always he had.

Merlyn leaned in a dark portal in the wall, one that had

not been there a moment past. It yawned wide and black, a cavern opening into darkness, and I whimsically thought I might have summoned him from hell's own gates. Certainly, there was nothing but unfathomable shadows visible behind him.

Upon closer inspection, he looked haggard, my Merlyn, as if he had fought an ordeal since we last met. His white linen chemise hung open to reveal his tanned throat and chest, though it was tinged with dirt at the cuff. His dark chausses bore a tear upon one knee and his fine leather boots were scuffed, which I knew he would not normally tolerate. There was a pallor beneath his tan and shadows lurked beneath his eyes.

And there were other changes, once I took the time to truly look. That familiar knowing smile curved his lips as he watched my perusal of him, but his gaze was wary as seldom it had been in my presence before. There was a tightness in his smile, a tension in his stance that was alien to me.

He could not have looked more mortal if he had tried.

I wondered how well I looked to him, then recalled the enthusiasm of our reunion the night before and flushed like a maiden.

And—curse Merlyn!—he chuckled, giving me a glimpse of the carefree allure he had once carried so easily.

The hound wagged his tail at that sound, evidence that the lord of the manor was no unfamiliar intruder. Merlyn extended his hand and the beast ran to sniffle at his fingers. He scratched the dog's ear, and I was struck as I had been struck so many times by the gentleness he could show when he chose. It made his occasional harshness seem more cruel by contrast.

Merlyn's gaze never wavered from mine and I finally recalled his comment. "I will not accompany you to hell or anywhere else," I said, keeping both my distance and a measure of my resolve.

"We shall see," he said in a low tone that made me shiver.

He arched a dark brow. "So, wife of mine, are you disappointed that I live, or relieved to find me hale?"

He was not hale, any fool could see as much, but I was not so churlish as to comment upon it.

"I am disappointed that you are not already dead, yet relieved that I shall have the opportunity to kill you myself." Some of my usual bravado returned. Merlyn watched me with undisguised amusement. "And I suppose it is a relief to be certain that I did not lose my wits last night."

"Did you not? I thought you quite . . . uninhibited."

I was discomfited, yet our gazes locked in recollection of what we had done. The stable seemed unaccountably warm and my mouth went dry, my entire body filled with unwelcome yearning.

I should leave. I knew this. I should tear myself away from the spell he cast so readily, and mitigate its power with distance. It was dangerous to linger, but I could not bring myself to leave. Not so soon as this.

Merlyn sobered, his gaze slipping over me. "You look well this morn."

I folded my arms across my chest, my tongue turning sharp in my unwillingness to be charmed. "You look dreadful."

"I thank you, chère, for the reminder." That coy smile appeared, for his choice of endearment was an entirely different reminder and not an accidental one, I was certain.

At our nuptial feast, he had called me "chère" and, with the indignation of the young and ignorant, I had charged him with not even knowing my name. To the merriment of our few guests, I had soundly chastised him, not realizing why Merlyn merely listened and smiled. When he told me of my error, I was so humiliated that I wished to die.

I have told you that I do not take kindly to being made the butt of a joke. Even now, the recollection fired my temper.

"Will you never let me forget my ignorance?" I demanded.

Merlyn smiled. "It was charming. Indeed, I treasure the memory of your indignation."

"Liar!"

"I tell no lie. Do you know, chère, how fetching you are when your eyes flash? You seem filled with the fire of life, a maiden wrought of flame." When I did not reply, he shrugged. "What a relief it was to encounter a woman untutored in manipulative games. Your honesty is the trait I recall most affectionately about you."

"Why? Because it contrasts so well with your skill in the telling of falsehoods?"

"Me?" He feigned innocence in a way that had once made me laugh.

"Yes, you! Clearly your repentance does not run deep." I approached him boldly, wagging a finger at him as if he were a badly behaved child. "Lest we forget why I seek you out this morn, I am sorely angered with you."

His eyes gleamed. "Yes, that was most clear last night."

I ignored this unworthy comment. "You sent Fitz to lie to me, Merlyn. You had him lie about your demise to tempt me to this place, for some dark purpose of your own devising."

"To seduce you soundly, I suppose."

"If not more."

"You should have protested more vehemently, chère," he chided with a gentle shake of his head. "A man could easily misconstrue your intent when you behave as you did."

"Meaning what?"

"That I had no plan to seduce you. I came solely to speak to you." Merlyn stretched out a finger and traced the outline of my lips. The gentle caress stopped my heart, so unexpected, so seductive. Again, I knew that I should retreat, but I could not summon the strength or the desire to do so.

Merlyn was alive and, in the secret corners of my heart, I was fool enough to be glad.

"Until you moaned, of course." Merlyn bent closer, touching his lips to my cheek and whispered. It was all I could do not to melt against his touch. A sound of yearning escaped my lips, much to my own mortification. I felt myself flush.

"Yes, like that, chère." His fingertips slid along my jawline, then down my throat. I lifted my chin and strained toward him, greedy for his touch.

"Until you arched against my hand, like this." He murmured hoarsely, then ran his lips across the tender spot beneath my ear. I closed my eyes. His hand slipped to cup my breast and his thumb slid across my nipple.

"Merlyn!" His name fell from my lips, without my intending to utter any such thing.

His gentle laughter fanned across my skin. "Until you whispered my name, exactly thus." His voice roughened. "Yes, exactly thus, chère."

I knew he would kiss me then, I knew that I was powerless to stop him. I opened my eyes and found him watching me from close proximity, as contented as a cat whose prey has been neatly cornered.

I granted him too easy of a victory. Doubts flooded into my thoughts and I pushed him away, making a show of wiping the imprint of his kiss from my flesh. My accusation fell doubly harsh from my lips. "Unless you lied also to Fitz?"

Merlyn's expression would have revealed nothing at all to another, but I knew he was irked with me. He seemed suddenly taller and darker, more forbidding, though he had not moved a hair. His gaze was both brighter and darker, a sign that did not bode well for me.

"If you would hear my confession, then you will have to come with me." He gestured to the gaping maw behind him and offered his hand in invitation.

I took another step back, though I would never have admitted whether I was more repelled by the dark mystery of that space or the enigma of the man who offered the invitation. Certainly I was not anxious to share a confined space with the man who could so easily persuade me to be seduced.

Did I fear Merlyn's plan for my fate, especially that I now knew he lived? Not truly, not in that moment. I suspected that he had need of me, though I could not imagine why, and that his need for my aid would protect me for a while, no matter how dark his ultimate intent. Truth be told, I had greater fears—of my own weaknesses, or at least of revealing them to a man who might well use them against me.

"I should think not," I retorted. "Whatsoever you have to say can be uttered here, as can an apology."

"I should apologize for granting what you so clearly desired?"

"I did not desire you in my bed."

Merlyn almost smiled. "Again, chère, your certainty was somewhat difficult to read in your response."

I straightened. "Then let me be blunt. I have no intent of leaving this stable with you, not for any reason, nor to enter that black hole in your company."

Merlyn's gaze flicked across the stable. "I would confide in you, but it is not safe here."

"In your own abode?" I rolled my eyes, though his pledge intrigued me. Merlyn sharing confidences? That would be worth a risk or two. "With the family of your own designated heiress? You make much of little, Merlyn."

His gaze hardened. "Do I?"

"Indeed. Whereas I have much to lose by following you into darkness. Am I the sole one who knows that you live? Did you lure me back to Ravensmuir to begin matters again betwixt we two?"

"The prospect has a certain allure, you must admit."

"You find allure in whatsoever you find useful," I charged, but he did not deny the accusation.

As if he meant to persuade me, Merlyn left the opening then, and strode toward me. He lifted a hand to my cheek and ran his thumb across my flesh once more. I held his gaze stubbornly, hoping he could not discern the fullness of the response he awakened so easily in me.

His smile broadened, and I knew my hope had been a futile one.

"So many matters remain between us, chère," he murmured.

There is something beguiling about the man's very voice, especially when he drops it low. A woman could be coaxed to do much by the splendor of that voice. It is a temptation to many sins and pleasures.

"So many questions lie unanswered," he continued, "but there is only one I would have from you now. Did you endeavor to see me killed? Did you wish to see me dead?" His gaze searched mine, and no doubt he saw my astonishment.

"Before this morn?" Had I been a hen, my feathers would have ruffled in agitation. "Before this *moment*?"

Merlyn chuckled, apparently reassured and not in the least bit fearful of me. "Before I came to speak to you abed last evening."

"You did not come to *speak* to me."

"I did." I must have looked unpersuaded, for he smiled slightly though his gaze was still filled with doubts. "Did you, chère?" His gaze locked with mine and I could not deny him such a simple answer.

"No, Merlyn."

"Did you tell any that you had seen me?"

I arched a brow. "You rode into Kinfairlie in the full light of day. None needed to ask me whether you were there, for you left witnesses aplenty."

Still he insisted, his gaze boring into mine. "Did you send word to any man of my presence?"

"No, Merlyn. I had labor to do."

"Swear it to me, chère."

I was surprised by his insistence, struck by the uncertainty in his eyes. "I swear it."

I saw his relief, felt the warmth fairly pour from him. He had not truly believed that I was responsible, but he had not been certain.

I was inordinately pleased that he accepted my word. "Why did you come to me at all?"

"I have missed you," he whispered, his gaze dropping to my lips.

"And it took you five years to seek me out?" I tried to scoff, though the words sounded breathlessly. "It is somewhat difficult to perceive any enthusiasm in that."

Merlyn's eyes gleamed. "Did you expect me to retrieve you, like a stray hound?"

I looked up, and this was my mistake. I was snared by the thousands of secrets in his gaze, caught by the bemused smile that curved his lips. Time stopped as we stood there, enraptured with each other, trapped by our own desire. I felt a trembling begin in my belly, a trembling that only Merlyn could awaken and that only he could sate. He slid his fingers into my hair, cupping my face, stroking my cheeks with his thumbs.

His eyes are grey in their midst, Merlyn's are, grey around the pupil and blue around the rims. They darken to the hue of the sky at the first appearance of the stars when he is impassioned, as they darkened in that moment.

I thought he might kiss me, indeed I expected as much, but he stepped abruptly away, releasing me so quickly that I stumbled. He strode to the gaping portal, then glanced back over his shoulder at me, his expression inscrutable.

"There has been too little trust in our match, and too much left unsaid."

"We have no match," I said sharply. "We have not had one these five years, for I could not trust a man who makes his trade in falsehoods."

"Perhaps I have reformed my ways."

"Perhaps the moon is wrought of cheese."

"Trust me now." Merlyn extended his hand to me. "For

the first time and the last. You, chère, hold the key to my survival."

I was disappointed, if you must know, that Merlyn merely found me useful, and more disappointed that he had not touched his lips to mine.

"You are not the first to desire something of me, Merlyn Lammergeier, nor will you be the last. I am disinclined to do what is convenient for you."

Merlyn's gaze remained intense. "But I will wager that I am the first prepared to compensate you for your aid."

"Abed?" My tone was arch.

"If only it were so simple." He smiled wickedly, then sobered. "I have surrendered Ravensmuir to you in anticipation of your aid. Surely it is a price worthy of your favor?"

"And if I do not aid you?"

He grinned then, the reckless rogue who once had made my heart skip. "Then I shall indeed return from hell," he vowed. "If I am not dead, then I shall have no heiress. This holding shall return to my hand again once my existence is witnessed anew."

Fear clutched my heart that Tynan should be denied security again. "I will not permit it!"

Merlyn's smile disappeared and he spoke with resolve. "You shall have no choice. Take the matter to any court in the land, and you will lose. A will is only enacted when a man is dead."

He was right and I knew it. I looked away and his tone turned dangerously thoughtful.

"I half-believed that you would spurn Ravensmuir, for you are a woman of high principle. I feared that all my planning would come to naught. Indeed, chère, your enthusiasm to return to the place you fled so hastily is a great surprise to me."

Merlyn snared me with Ravensmuir, and, though he knew his bait had worked, it was clear that he did not know precisely why. My thoughts churned as I avoided his gaze.

If I told him why I had accepted his legacy, he would guess the greatest secret that I had. And I was not prepared for Merlyn to have yet another weapon in his arsenal.

Aware of his watchful gaze, I shrugged with apparent insouciance. "I have missed the comforts of wealth. Perhaps Ravensmuir suits me as well as your death did."

Merlyn's eyes narrowed.

I smiled pertly at him. "Perhaps you should tell me your tale here."

He offered his hand again. "It is not safe." This he said with such force that I believed him. "Trust me, chère."

I met his gaze and saw the plea he could not articulate. He did need me. I knew then that I would go with him, though I refused to examine why.

Merlyn smiled as I stepped toward him, then caught my hand in his. His grip was strong and I only shivered slightly in trepidation when he pulled me closer. He bade the dog to remain, then reached into the shadows and pulled the wall of the stable back across the makeshift portal. Some latch not apparent to me settled in place with a click.

We stood then in blackness, hand in hand, and I began to doubt the wisdom of my choice. The dog whimpered in the stable beyond, its sniffling echoing loudly in the small space. I could smell stone and salt and water. The crashing of the waves on the shore echoed more loudly than it had in the stables and the air was both damp and chill.

And it was dark.

Darker than hell, blacker than a rogue's heart. My heart began to race and I felt the perspiration of anxiety slip between my breasts. I closed my eyes, but shivered all the same, and Merlyn pulled me closer to his heat.

I knew but a moment's solace before he released my

hand. He put his hand on the back of my waist to urge me forward. "The way is quite level. In a moment or two, your eyes will accustom themselves to the darkness."

That would not ease my fear, but I did not tell him as much. My eyes had adjusted much already, but not enough to reassure me. I could see very little other than the faint image of the path directly before myself. The path turned and twisted, the rock worn smooth by a thousand footfalls. Countless openings gaped on either side of the pathway, offering even more ominous shadows, and the path Merlyn chose was not evident as a greater one.

I quickly lost whatever sense of direction I might have had. If Merlyn intended to confuse me, he did an artful job of it. I could not be certain in which general direction lay the stables, much less retrace our footsteps. I doubted that I could open the wall myself in darkness. I drew slightly closer to my companion, though I would have preferred not to do so, for I was keenly aware of my dependence upon him.

I have never been fond of closed spaces or of darkness. The sense of being surrounded by rock, of being enclosed, makes terror rise within my chest. I could not imagine entering this place alone—or surviving it alone. Even with Merlyn, even knowing that he knew the way out, I was sorely distressed.

For there was no guarantee that he meant to take me out. I realized too late that with Merlyn, there would be a price.

There always was. He had coaxed me into a place of weakness to ensure that I had no choice but to accept whatever terms he offered. The folly of my own choice turned my uneasy gut.

Why did I so readily forget the kind of man I had wed? Why did I trust him over and over again, even knowing that he was not trustworthy? I knew his crimes. I knew that I could not trust my desire for him.

Yet each time he reached for me, I met him halfway. It has

never been my ambition to die foolish, but it seemed on that
day that I was closer to doing so than ever I had been.

Merlyn halted suddenly, and I felt him lean closer to me.
My breathing was shallow. "You are troubled."

I spoke boldly in an attempt to disguise my fears. His
price would be higher if he knew how desperately I wished
to be free of this place. "What woman would not feel
trapped, confined with a man whose motives she does not
know?"

I felt Merlyn study me, perhaps guessing more than I admitted.

"Believe, chère, that in my presence you are safe."

I would have made some comment but he caught me
close. So weak was I, so relieved was I by the touch of another, that I clung to his strength.

Merlyn kissed me with that possessive ease that could
make a woman forget her own name. I gasped in my relief,
then kissed him back, emboldened by the darkness and my
own need.

I tasted his surprise and deepened my kiss, finding it most
gratifying when I put my hand upon his chest and felt the
thunder of his heartbeat. Our kiss turned savage, hungry, demanding and exhilarating.

Indeed, his touch pushed the terror of the darkness aside.
I could have sucked the marrow from his bones, so grateful
was I for the solace he offered. The ardor of my response
shocked him, I knew it, and I savored the fleeting sense that
I had surprised the most unpredictable man I had ever
known.

We parted with reluctance, the ragged sound of our
breathing all too loud. He muttered my name like a curse,
then stepped away. I panicked at the prospect of becoming
lost, fearful now that Merlyn did not offer an anchor in his
touch.

"Merlyn!"

"Your trust is meager, chère," he muttered.

A moment later, I heard him strike a flint and was relieved when he touched the flame to a candle and light fell upon us.

The candlelight made him look yet more diabolical, only one side of his face lit and the other falling into shadow. His hair fell unruly over his brow and when he smiled at me in the intimacy of that light, I thought my heart would burst.

In gratitude for the light, of course. No more than that.

"Better?"

I nodded, then sat upon a rock to hide the fact that my knees threatened to collapse beneath me. The threat of the shadows seemed to confine the glow from the candle, but the light was better than none at all. I wiped the slickness of my palms against my garb and took a steadying breath. I focused upon the light, not upon the shadows filled with a thousand horrors that surrounded us.

Before I could thank him for his kindness, Merlyn spoke. "Who is the boy?" he asked.

I jumped in surprise, then looked away from him. "This is what you would discuss?"

His brows drew together. "Who?"

"He is my brother, Tynan," I chattered. "He was born in Kinfairlie village, after we returned there, which is why you do not know him."

Though he said nothing, I knew Merlyn did not believe me.

"Who else should he be?" I demanded, angered by his judgmental silence. "Who else should my mother have brought into the world? I attended her! I pulled the child from her womb. I laid him upon her belly as she died!"

I stood and turned my back upon him, feeling my tears rise to choke me. It has been years, but still I listen for my mother's footsteps.

Merlyn cleared his throat cautiously. "When did Elizabeth die?"

I nodded without turning and my voice was low with the

grief that haunted me. "Within a year of our departure from here. Childbirth at her age proved too much for her to bear." I took a shuddering breath. "With her last breath, she pushed her son into the world."

I remembered the anguish of losing her all too well. The silence stretched long between us and I feared that I would weep for my mother there, in front of the last person I wished to witness any vulnerability of mine.

"I am sorry," Merlyn said quietly. "You must miss her."

The compassion in his tone unsettled me, for I had not expected understanding, let alone sympathy. "I would not wish to meet a person who did not miss their deceased mother," I retorted more savagely than was necessary.

"What of Tynan?" Merlyn's tone was mild. "Surely he cannot miss the mother he never knew?"

I inhaled sharply. "Did you bring me here to provoke me?"

Silence again, pressing against my ears, challenging the veracity of my tale without a word.

"He looks like a Lammergeier," Merlyn said.

"He looks like a child," I snapped.

"Ysabella . . ."

There was a warning in his use of my name, and I knew better than to vex him further. I tipped my head back to stare at the hewn rock overhead and forced myself to speak evenly. "It is true that I do not know his exact parentage, Merlyn, though it is somewhat graceless of you to compel me to admit it."

"And what is that to mean?"

I shrugged. "Perhaps you found my mother fetching. It is a sordid possibility, though not out of the question."

Merlyn laughed, though there was little mirth in the sound. "Not I. I was . . . otherwise occupied for that fortnight."

I felt him draw close, the warmth of the candle nearer, the heat of Merlyn yet more tangible. My own shadow loomed large on the hewn stone before me, and now was joined by his larger one. I took a shaking breath as his grip landed upon my shoulder, his fingers tight.

"You may recall that my mother was fond of your brother," I added hastily. "She and Gawain spent much time together in those few weeks."

"As you did."

"I spoke to him only once."

Much hung unsaid between us and the silence stretched long.

Then Merlyn spoke. "I suppose it is only my suspicious nature that compels me to note that neither Gawain nor Elizabeth are here to confirm or deny the tale of them."

"Is Gawain dead?"

"No."

"Then you might ask him when next you meet."

"That seems most unlikely to happen." Merlyn gripped my shoulder so tightly that I was startled. "I would prefer to have the truth from you."

"You have the truth from me!"

"No, I do not." His words were low, dangerous. "You lie, Ysabella, you lie to me about the boy."

"I do not!" I flung out my hands. "Is deception so bred in your bones that you cannot imagine that others do not lie to you at every turn? Merlyn, I do *not* lie. That is your affliction, as I recall."

He removed his hand, disgust in his gesture, and turned away. "Forgive me if I offend the Witch of Kinfairlie." He turned back to face me, his eyes snapping with an anger that he held under tight control. "Will you curse me now?"

My fists clenched and unclenched, hating that he so unerringly noted the falsehood that had shaped my recent life. "I would do so if I had the power."

"You are not a witch but you call yourself one."

"I let others call me as much."

"Either way, you support a claim that is not true, yet you

insist to me that you do not lie." Merlyn's tone was scathing. He exhaled with undisguised disgust, his words harsh. "There was a time, Ysabella, when you had a thirst for the truth. There was time when you would settle for nothing less than complete honesty."

"There was a time when I believed and trusted my lord husband. That time is gone, not my love of the truth."

He turned his piercing gaze upon me. "Then why do you lie to me about the boy?"

"I do not."

"You lie," he declared through gritted teeth. His fist clenched.

"I do not!"

"You lie!" Merlyn strode away impatiently, taking the candle with him.

"How dare you assume that I lie, on the basis of no evidence at all?"

He did not grant me a reply.

"And what do you know of the virtues of telling the truth?" I cried, my voice rising with every question. "Have you not made a *life* of spreading falsehoods? Have you not earned a living by the cultivation of lies?"

Merlyn did not pause.

"Did you not lie to your new bride about your trade? Did you not lie about your own death? Did you not deceive me that I might come to Ravensmuir, and lie about the ceding of that title to me?" I shouted after him. "Does the inability to speak honestly not course through your very veins?"

Merlyn paused then and glanced back at me, his expression guarded. "Perhaps it does," he acknowledged quietly, too quietly to be trusted. I took a cautious step back, though it was too late. "Let me then grant to you some advice for those moments when you lie, my lady wife, as you clearly are unfamiliar with the necessary protocol."

I retreated another step, distrusting his ominous tone.

"Do not let your voice rise," Merlyn said softly. "Do not

challenge expectations too greatly. Do not speak overmuch in explanation, for all of these actions will reveal your dishonesty."

I feared then for my future, for he spoke with the quick precision of one who is sorely angered. "Merlyn . . ."

But he continued, his tone harsh. "Choose your lies well, and with understanding of your victim. I, for example, should have been less angered that you had borne me a child unbeknownst to me, or that you had rutted with my brother, than be expected to believe some fantastic tale that the child carries no Lammergeier blood." I gasped, but Merlyn did not pause. "It is in my nature to take poorly to any implication that I am slow of wit."

"Merlyn . . ."

He drew closer, appearing larger, darker, more dangerous and more unpredictable than I could recall. He loomed over me, his eyes blazing. "And finally, when you mean to lie, ensure that your deception will not be immediately discerned. People, as a rule, do not care to be deceived. Matters may proceed poorly for you if your ruse is discovered while you are in a somewhat disadvantaged circumstance." His gaze held mine and I panicked.

"Merlyn!"

He blew out the flame. The cavern plunged into blackness, leaving the image of his determination burned in my mind.

I gasped, then screamed his name, but Merlyn did not reply.

His boots ground on the stone, first from one direction then from the other. I guessed that he used his knowledge of the space to my disadvantage.

When he spoke, his words were bitter. "I sought you out, Ysabella, I sought you out solely because of your love of truth. I had need of an honest ally in whom I can place complete trust. I foolishly believed that person might be you."

I struggled to locate him, but to no avail. I snatched at the air in pursuit of his voice, trying desperately to lay a hand upon him. But Merlyn could move with the silent grace of a cat when he so chose.

"I sought you out to aid me in uncovering the truth. I thought that you alone, you *especially*, held the truth in high regard." I had no care for what he told me. "I thought you noble. I thought you unlike any other woman I had ever met. I thought I could trust you. And what have you immediately done—what, Ysabella?"

"Merlyn, have mercy . . ."

"You *lied*!" he roared with such volume that I feared the stones would tumble all around us. His voice seemed to come from everywhere and nowhere, his shout bouncing off the stone on every side of me.

The darkness, though, was the sum of my concern. It made me yearn to claw my way through the very stone, to dig my way back to the light again if necessary. It made me desperate and rash and more frightened than ever I had been in all my days.

I cried his name in anguish.

"If you no longer hold truth in such esteem as once you did," he hissed, "then there is nothing, *nothing*, that we might say each to the other now."

I knew then that he would leave me there, alone in the darkness.

Forever.

"Merlyn! No!"

Not one sound reached my ears, no matter how I strained. Not one breath, not one whisper, not the rattle of one dislodged pebble.

"If I no longer hold truth in such esteem, it is your own doing!" I cried in desperation. "I have done what I had to do to ensure my survival. Merlyn, have mercy upon me!"

But there was no answer.

Merlyn was gone.

I whirled in place, uncertain which way to turn. I begged, I groveled, I cried out shamelessly for his mercy.

To no avail. By the time my entreaties finally fell silent, I could hear only the thunder of the sea and the pounding of my own terrified heart.

V

In the telling, his choice seems a cruel one. And it is true that Merlyn has been manipulative in his time, as well as demanding. But to his side, it must be credited that he never knew of my terror of the darkness.

While I was resident at Ravensmuir the first time, there was seldom complete darkness in our chamber. He lit candles when we loved, and we loved most of the night most nights. Even the night just past, the solar had been lit with the first young sliver of the waning moon diffused through the clouds. I had opened the shutters upon my arrival for precisely this reason.

Merlyn and I had not lived together long enough that he might know all of my secrets, especially those—like this one—that I protected so carefully. And even if he guessed at it, he could not have understood the fullness of my terror. He is not a fearful man himself and perhaps never understood what it meant to be terrified right to one's bones.

Perhaps I give him more credit than is due. But the fact remains that when I managed to calm myself slightly, I noticed a light flickering in the distance.

Merlyn had left a beacon for me. Relief took me to my knees and I sobbed there for a moment before I could compose myself. Perhaps he was less cruel than I had assumed. Perhaps he yet desired something of me. Perhaps I did not care in my gratitude for his gift of the light.

Though Merlyn was the last person whose company I wished to keep in that moment, the light was lure enough. I was less afraid of Merlyn than I was of the darkness. I stood, brushed off my skirts and pursued him.

It was, without doubt, precisely what he intended me to do.

The lantern's glow grew brighter as I made my way along the passageway. Much to my relief, the twists in the tunnel had concealed some of the light and it was brighter than I had first guessed. The sound of the waves and the smell of sea salt also increased with every step.

I had to ascend to the opening from which the light issued and was slightly out of breath when I finally stood on the threshold of what I discovered to be a room.

Merlyn was in this chamber hewn from the rock, a trio of oil lanterns burning brightly around him. He sat on a crate wrought of wood and had shed his chemise. Fitz was there, to my astonishment, though neither man glanced up at my arrival.

Merlyn winced as the manservant dressed the wound upon the back of his shoulder. It was a deep and ugly gash, and fresh blood was leaking from its corners. It had evidently opened in Merlyn's recent adventures and Fitz clicked his tongue in chastisement as he carefully stitched it closed once more.

Merlyn had worn his chemise the night before when he came to me and I understood why. I had felt cloth beneath my fingers, but not the binding beneath. Here too was the reason for his pallor—though he had not died, Merlyn had certainly had a foretaste of his demise.

That the procedure was painful was evident only by the tightness of Merlyn's expression. He looked more grey and more grim than he had even in the stables and my heart wrenched. I was unsettled by the sight of him being less than formidable and was glad of this respite from his perceptive gaze.

Here was a timely reminder that someone had tried to kill him. By the size of the wound, he or she had come close to succeeding. I reminded myself that what was truly remarkable was that no one had tried to kill a scoundrel like Merlyn sooner.

He had lost weight in recent years, I noted, but I looked again and saw that he was more sleek than gaunt. All sinew and strength, he was, like the dangerous predator for which his family was named.

I looked away, the hunger in my loins most unwelcome. The chamber was filled with crates, no doubt from the ship that bobbed empty at anchor, its hold crammed with the disreputable goods with which this family continued to make their fortune.

Bolstered by my disgust, I announced my presence. "Your death blow, I can only assume?"

Neither man seemed surprised by my comment and I wondered whether I had been as unobserved as I had assumed.

Fitz grunted in reply, then frowned as he stitched the end of the wound closed. "Almost done now, my lord. Hold steady."

Merlyn visibly gritted his teeth, then eyed me warily. "Do I detect glee in your tone, chère?"

One credit that I must grant Merlyn is that his temper, while fearsome, is neither violent nor enduring. He says what he must, often quite loudly, but once the storm has erupted, it quickly passes. I have never seen him strike anything or anyone. He seems to express his fury purely with volume. It was clear that his usual mood was already partially restored.

It is a trait we share. I, too, am slow to boil and loud in my temper, though it is not dangerous to others and fades quickly.

"There are some who would say that you had gained your just reward in this."

His eyes narrowed. "How so?"

"Like rewards like, does it not?" I strolled into the chamber, eying the crates stacked against the walls. "It seems most apt to me that you should be murdered. The sole surprise is that none took a knife to you before this."

"Such venom," he chided, though his brow had darkened. "So, you *were* glad to hear of my death?"

"Why should I not be? I am Lady of Ravensmuir, and honorably widowed as well. I might wed quite well, given the change you have wrought in my circumstance." I cast him a bright smile which only seemed to deepen his scowl. "Indeed, Merlyn, you suit me better dead than alive."

"That was not the sense I had last night," he muttered.

"A man came to me as a dream," I retorted, discomfited that Fitz should be privy to this detail. "How are you to know who I dreamed you were?"

Merlyn impaled me with a glance that made me flush with certainty that I had called him by name in that moment of moments. I turned away from him, and surveyed the contents of this chamber with curiosity that was not entirely feigned.

The room was stacked with boxes and bundles of all sizes. The floor was reasonably level and the sole way in and out of it was through the portal by which I had just entered. Nooks had been created or naturally occurred in the walls, and the lanterns had been nestled within them. Their flames flickered despite that shelter.

It was not an uncomfortable place, though it would have felt somewhat damp without the heat of Merlyn's gaze upon me. I had never been here, never guessed that such a chamber existed, though I had assumed all those years ago that there must be a hidden storeroom somewhere. It would not do for a customer to witness three crowns of thorns. Additionally, a valuable inventory was better hidden from prying eyes.

"What have you this time?" I asked, nudging one crate with my toe.

"It is safer for you to forget that ever you saw this chamber," Merlyn said grimly. "And yet more so to have no inkling of its contents. Have the sense to hold your tongue for the rest of your days, chère, or you may share what might have been my fate."

I was, despite myself, touched by his apparent concern for my survival. Merlyn, though, was emotionless. He donned his chemise with abrupt gestures, leaving the fine cloth to fall loosely around his waist as he surveyed me. I could see the expanse of his bare chest through the gaping neck when he leaned his elbows upon his knees, though I strove to give no hint of my awareness of him.

He is a finely wrought man, Merlyn Lammergeier, but perhaps I have mentioned as much. He moves not unlike a powerful and large cat, elegant yet able to destroy an assailant with his hands alone.

Have ever you seen the lions that kings oft bring from the lands far to the south? I never have, though I have heard tell of them and I have wondered whether Merlyn shares a resemblance with them.

Save, of course, that his hair is so black. Perhaps his brother Gawain would be more like those tawny beasts, for his hair is of a golden hue. Perhaps it is fitting that dangerous Merlyn is as dark as a demon loosed from hell, while charming Gawain seems touched by the favor of the sun. I always thought the light and the dark of their respective coloring gave a hint of their greater character.

Oh yes, it is Gawain who laughs and is merry; Gawain who would charm a woman with pretty speech and promises; Gawain who is as reliable as a chance beam of sunlight. It is Merlyn who is dark and ominous, who whispers secrets and leaves much unsaid, whose presence fills your ears and presses against your flesh.

Perhaps there is an unholy allure between darkness and light, perhaps I with my corona of flaming hair could never have resisted a sultry beast like Merlyn Lammergeier.

I was struck by his vitality in that cavern and then by my own awareness of his masculinity. That cursed tingle awakened in my belly and, flustered, I blurted out the first question that rose to my lips. "How could any man be fool enough to believe you dead?"

Merlyn smiled. "I shall take that as the rare compliment it is, chère."

"The matter was closer than I would have liked," Fitz muttered. His manner was dour, but Merlyn seemed to be recovering his vigor.

"Of what merit is a life lived without risk, Fitz?" he demanded. "What man would desire to live sixty or even seventy years if he did not cheat death with some frequency? There is no difference then betwixt life and death if a man takes no more chances than a corpse."

"So you say." Fitz folded the remaining length of clean linen with quick efficiency. "I should like to try such a life before making any criticism of its failings."

Merlyn eyed me, his words soft. "And what say you, chère? Risk or safety?"

"Perhaps a taste of both. I would welcome the surety of a regular meal after these past years, though I know such attraction would pale in time." I may have shown more resignation than I might have preferred because he sobered as he watched me, his mood dispelled by mine.

He tired from his wound and I tired of his mysteries.

"Is this your decision then?" I asked. "That you shall live again and I shall return to Kinfairlie and we shall continue as we have done? That you shall keep your secrets and savor your risks and I shall yearn for a hot morsel at intervals while I watch my siblings suffer? To what purpose have you summoned me here, Merlyn? To watch me weep when you snatched away your supposed gift?"

"I cannot imagine that ever you would show another the weakness of tears," he said, his tone hard.

I turned away.

"You have lived a hard life since leaving this place," he suggested, perhaps inviting my confidences.

"I have lived as best I could and made what choices I must," I retorted. "It is of no matter."

His dark brow arched. "You are irked with me."

"And why not? You pledge a fortress to me, then vow to reclaim it. You send Fitz to tell me of your death, then reveal that you are alive. You come to me as a dream, then spill your seed as only a man of flesh can do. You surprise me, drag me into darkness, then accuse me of lying and abandon me to my fear." I inhaled shakily. "Worse, I should have known better. I should have expected such trickery from you, but I was fool enough to believe otherwise. Yes, I am irked with you, Merlyn! Who would not be?"

"I told you she would not approve of this course," Fitz murmured.

Merlyn rose to his feet and crossed the chamber to where I stood shaking, then took my hand in his. He kissed the back of my hand with embarrassing thoroughness, his gaze locked with mine. A quiver awakened deep within me, undermining all my sensible reasoning.

"Do not do that." I tried to pull my hand away.

Merlyn not only held fast, he kissed my palm and dispatched a thousand hungry shivers over my skin. He watched me, as if assessing my response, and I have no doubt he discerned the simmer of my unwelcome desire for his touch.

"I am sorry, chère," he said for my ears alone. "It is no excuse, but I was sorely vexed with you, and thus behaved unchivalrously. I did not believe you capable of lying . . ."

"You apologize when it is convenient to your aims," I

charged and Fitz snorted. "Clearly, you have need of my favor now."

"Of course, I have need of you."

I parted my lips to protest his change of the meaning, but Merlyn kissed my palm, his heated gaze holding mine in silent warning. Fitz, of course, could not see his gesture. Merlyn bit my thumb gently, running his teeth languidly over the flesh in a way intended to weaken my knees.

It worked. I could see down the neck of his chemise, could see the thicket of dark hair upon his chest, could see the erection straining his chausses, could smell the heat of his skin.

And I longed for a night abed with him again, one in which I did not imagine that I dreamed. No, I would have an afternoon abed, with sunlight spilling over us, all golden and warm and rich.

My resolve weakened, consumed by my growing desire. He mouthed kisses against my palm—fully, wickedly aware of the power of his touch. "Forgive me, chère."

"You do yet need something of me then," I replied, if not as coolly as I might have preferred.

Fitz gave a bark of laughter. "I told you she would not be easily led." He nodded to me with approval. "It is a clever wench you wed, my lord, and you would not be the first man to rue such a choice."

"I do not rue it." Merlyn straightened and flattened my hand against the heat of his chest, holding it captive against the thunder of his heart. His bright gaze pinned me in place and my mouth went dry. "Indeed, it is my lady's intellect upon which I must now rely."

I studied him. "You do need me."

"I told you that I have repented of my crimes and would live an honest life."

I tried without success to pull my hand from his grip. "It is the nature of those who narrowly escape death to repent.

You will revert to your true nature before your wound is healed."

"No, chère."

"You expect me to take the word of a liar? You tell me what you know I wish to hear in order to win my aid, no more than that."

"You took my brother's word and shaped your life for the worse upon it."

I managed to tug my fingers free and stepped away from him. "That was different."

"Was it?"

"He was right about you."

Merlyn's voice hardened. "But the fact remains that you believed him, while you will not believe me. A man could take offense at such favor."

"Then, take offense. It is of no import to me. You are a rogue and a sinner and I have learned to know better than to believe your lies."

Merlyn inhaled sharply and paced back across the cavern. "I ask you only to discover the name of the man who desired to have me killed. Surely you would do as much for the sake of justice, if not for me."

I watched him, sensing that he told me but half of the tale. "Ada said you departed upon a quest on Christmas Eve."

Merlyn nodded tersely. "I had a message from the Earl of March, requesting my presence. He asked that I come late to Dunbar, that my arrival might not be witnessed by curious eyes, and said that the gatekeeper would expect me."

"And?"

Merlyn shook his head. "I never reached his gates. I was attacked from behind at a curve in the road."

"You were surprised."

He smiled wryly. "There are places in Christendom, chère, where a man is vigilant. This has never been one of them for me, hence the appeal of Ravensmuir. It seems that matters have changed."

"And it seems that the Earl of March is the man you seek."

"Not necessarily. He might not have sent the missive, or even if he did, he might have known nothing of my assailant's plans."

I was intrigued by this puzzle despite myself. "And if I find the name of the man responsible, then what?"

Merlyn's expression hardened into dangerous lines. "Then I shall see to the rest."

"That is not the pursuit of justice!"

"It most certainly is."

"Justice is rendered by the king's justiciar, not wrought in retaliation! Do you intend to murder in return? Do you intend that I should abet your crime? And for what price? Truly, Merlyn, you have not thought beyond your own revenge in this! What if I think murder reprehensible?"

"You do not know all of the tale."

"Forgive me if I assume that you will not share it with me! Perhaps someone sought to kill you in vengeance for what you once did. Perhaps his cause is not unjustified. Perhaps you do not share the whole tale because it shows you in poor light. Perhaps you cannot tell me all of the tale, if you even desired to do so." I propped my hands upon my hips. "Surely, Merlyn, of all people, I can understand the desire to throttle the life from you!"

He settled upon a crate to watch me. "Perhaps I miscalculated the allure of Ravensmuir to you."

"Perhaps you did." I crossed the room to confront him. "Or perhaps you miscalculated your own path."

"And what is that to mean?"

"That you have no ability to compel me to do what you desire me to do." I spoke boldly. "A corpse cannot change the terms of his will."

His gaze brightened fiercely. "I told you that I could return to life."

"And grant the assassin whose identity you do not know

another chance to finish what he has begun. How clever a ploy! Someone desired to kill you, Merlyn. I have no doubt that person will lust to finish the deed. In fact, he now has greater cause to see you dead, for you alone might be able to provide testimony of his attempted crime." I leaned closer to him and dropped my voice. "You dare not risk returning from the grave if you mean to live."

Fitz whistled through his teeth.

Merlyn pushed to his feet and walked across the chamber. I had the sense that I had disappointed him, though when he turned to regard me again, I could not be certain. He stood, no doubt deliberately, beyond the circles of light cast by the lanterns, his features wreathed in shadows.

"I thought you would aid me to seek the truth."

I folded my arms across my chest. "You thought wrongly. High justice is the right of the king and the king alone."

"I will tell you all you need to know."

I arched my brow. "Instead of telling me all that you know? How typically evasive of you, Merlyn. There was a time when I found your many enigmas intriguing. Now I know that you merely hide the wickedness of your intent from those who might not approve."

Merlyn's silence was all the answer he intended to give, but I was not done.

"I want you to understand what you ask of me, Merlyn." I took a deep breath, my words coming low and hot. "I have spent five years tarred by the speculation of what I might have done in my brief association with the Lammergeier. I was innocent, I fled this keep as soon as I knew the dark truth of your deeds, Merlyn, but still, I have suffered for my fleeting association with your family."

Merlyn might have protested but I hastened onward. "Worse, my family has suffered. Would my mother have died if a physician or a healer could have been persuaded to at least come to her side? Would my brother have eaten better if we were not regularly cheated of our due? Would he have grown taller and stronger? Would my sister have found a fitting spouse if she had not been tarnished by our stay at Ravensmuir?"

I shook a finger at him, noting that his features had set to stone but not caring a whit if I injured his pride. "You may have been able to smooth your way with coin, but I had no such advantage. I will not become embroiled in your schemes. I will not make matters worse by becoming guilty, as well. I will not be complicit in your crimes and I will not be an accomplice to murder."

"Even if it means returning to Kinfairlie and poverty?"

I lifted my chin. "Even that."

We stared at each other, adversaries in yet another matter. The fact was that I did not expect the issue to be readily abandoned. I anticipated a long battle of wills, one that would challenge my convictions. I assumed that Merlyn would bend his considerable charm to changing my thinking.

But he did not.

His weariness suddenly showed in his face: he looked older and more gaunt, more tired. It seemed the wound took more from him than he would care to admit. My guilt grew a modicum, fed by new doubts—was I unfair? What if he truly did mean to put his trade aside and repent of his ways? Should I not aid him in that?

Fitz noticed the change in Merlyn's manner as soon as I did, and he stepped closer. "I know you have much to do this day, my lord," he said briskly. "And I must return to the keep. Perhaps I shall see her ladyship back to the hall."

Merlyn's gaze met mine and I saw that he was not deceived by Fitz's excuses before his gaze flicked away. "I have nothing more demanding to do this day than to sleep, and you know it well, Fitz." He spoke dismissively, ignoring me.

"Shall I escort my lady to the keep?" Fitz said.

"If you prefer, Fitz. See that she is blindfolded, though, if you will." Merlyn's gaze burned into mine. "It would not be wise for Ysabella to ever find her way back to this place alone."

His use of my name, instead of his usual endearment, stung as it was doubtless intended to. And so I was warned, not to return to this place in general and not to peruse Merlyn's goods in specific.

Fitz apologized as he blindfolded me. He turned me a few times in place to ensure that I was dizzy, then laid claim to my elbow and led me stumbling from that chamber.

"This matter is not done, Ysabella," Merlyn said quietly. Though I could not guess his proximity, the hair prickled on the back of my neck. I wondered whether Merlyn would come to my bed again to persuade me and could not bear to think of what I might surrender.

A wicked part of me looked forward to his persuasion.

Merlyn said nothing more, not so much as a word of farewell, and I felt oddly bereft of his presence as soon as Fitz marched me out of the small chamber. The air was colder in the caverns beyond and though I feared to trip, Fitz did not allow it.

We walked a long way in silence save for our footsteps and the murmur of the sea. I have no doubt that we doubled over our course and took a circuitous route, as well. We could have walked to Edinburgh and back for all I knew of it. I was footsore and in dire need of sustenance and still we walked ever onward.

It was only when we stood upon a level floor that felt to be wrought of wood, that Fitz halted and spoke to me. I could smell a fire burning and the cooking of a stew of some kind. My belly growled in complaint, indeed it did so loudly that I nearly missed Fitz's murmured words.

"He thought you the only soul in all of Christendom that he could trust besides myself," he said, accusation heavy in his words. "But you had to lie to him."

"I did not lie to him!"

"He believes that you did and it is much the same. You should forgive him and trust him."

"Forgive him? For using me to his own ends? For telling me but a small fragment of the truth, and threatening to reclaim Ravensmuir if I do not do his bidding?" I pulled the blindfold from my eyes. A thin line of light made its way beneath the panel before us and granted some illumination. I glared at Fitz. "I will not forgive him."

"You should aid him."

"I will not condone crime, even for my lord husband."

Fitz shook his head. "You do not know all of the tale."

"And no one intends to share it with me." My tone was sour. "Does he not see the mire of his own thinking? He claims he needs my intellect, then treats me like a foolish child who cannot be trusted to see right and wrong in the details."

"The man has been betrayed and you are nigh a stranger. How can you expect him to trust you?"

"Surely trust undeserved is what he asks of me! Truly, Fitz, I have already been betrayed by Merlyn. It is only sensible that I show caution in taking his errands now."

Fitz studied me carefully and I had the sense that he too was disappointed in me. "Do what you must, lass," he said finally. "But understand that you and I alone know of my lord's survival, and if Merlyn is betrayed this time, he shall know who is responsible."

The implication was clear. Fitz would never betray his lord, thus any such betrayal would be mine.

"If betrayal would lead to his demise, then I have nothing to fear," I retorted, having no intent of being intimidated.

Fitz smiled coolly. "You should still have to contend with me, lass."

His gaze hardened and I knew that I could expect no mercy from this man if he deemed me disloyal.

I flicked my gaze away from him. "May I leave, or am I to be a prisoner forever?"

Fitz lifted a latch and a small door, no larger than that of a cupboard, opened before us. I ducked through the opening, though was not immediately certain where I was. It was not the stables, for the other three walls here were wrought of thatch.

When I glanced back, Fitz had silently closed the opening behind me and I could not discern where it had been. No wonder I had not found it earlier! I leaned on the wood of that wall and felt along it for a moment, but could find no hint of the door. The light was poor, though, and I resolved to return later with a lantern.

I pivoted, and in looking again, realized that I was in one of the storage rooms in the wing that held the kitchens. I made my way around the sacks of flour and ducked beneath the herbs of previous summers still hanging from the rafters. I left the room and made my way down the stairs, entering the kitchen just as Ada entered the opposite door.

She smirked. "Did you find my lord Merlyn in the storage rooms? You were mistaken this morning in thinking you would find him alive. Perhaps it was the wine you found early this morn."

Although it was tempting to prove her wrong, I was not yet prepared to betray Merlyn's presence. I tossed my loose hair, noting how she watched it with suspicion. It was too sweet to torment Ada, after all the torment she had granted me and mine.

"You are right, of course—I found him dead," I replied, giving her but a moment to look smug. "He was not a phantom as I had suspected, but a demon. It seems my lord Merlyn has indeed been dispatched to the underworld, as so many so oft did threaten."

You must admit that my words were not strictly a lie.

Ada paled. "Do not utter such blasphemy!"

I strode toward her boldly. "Indeed, he is a demon of such rank that he has offered a wager to me. Would you like to know of it, Ada?"

She shook her head and her hand rose to her crucifix, though her eyes revealed her curiosity.

"A lifetime of my daily service to his memory was the term," I whispered to her with great delight, "in exchange for an eternity of nightly service from him."

She was shocked, though she savored the salacious detail. "Wicked woman!" she cried.

I laughed, well pleased with myself and shook my tresses again. "Is it true, Ada, that when a witch looses her hair, havoc will reign? I think I shall wear mine unbraided from this day forth."

Ada crossed herself as I left the kitchen and I felt suddenly good for a widow recently bereaved and doubly threatened before breaking her fast. My mood had nothing to do with the fact that Merlyn yet lived, of that you may be certain.

You can imagine that after my journey through the labyrinth, I looked less than my best. I had not begun the day in my finest garb, to be sure, and after my encounter with Merlyn, I felt the need to lift my spirits. I knew I had made the right choice, yet I could not shake my sense that I had failed him.

Merlyn had once seen fit to outfit his bride, and he had made acquisitions with a customary lack of restraint and disregard for expense. I had seldom touched the garments then, but I hoped that the trunk might still be in the solar. Merlyn, after all, had been absent from Ravensmuir. If the trunk had remained tightly closed, then there might not be damage from moths.

The garments were wasted without a woman wearing them, and they had been a gift to me in the first place. I intended to share them with my sister, if Ada had not helped herself to the store in our absence.

I particularly wished to look more regal when next I encountered my troublesome spouse. I had no doubt that I would see him again and a person stands taller when garbed well. With Merlyn, I had need of every advantage I could muster.

He desired me, perhaps as much as I desired him. Perhaps I could use his ploys against him and win advantage in the promise of passion. The prospect lightened my step considerably.

The trunk was still where I recalled it to be. I flung back the lid, impatient with hope, and smiled. But one glimpse of that trunk's contents and I resolved to burn my old blue kirtle, mended so often and worn so long.

I selected an undyed linen chemise first, savoring as I once had the marvelous fine texture of its cloth. It was so much softer against the skin than the woolsy-linsey to which we were accustomed. I had always intended to buy myself one such chemise if we had the wealth to spare. That one luxury would sate me, though none might see it but myself.

But there were more luxuries than that to be regarded— indeed, the trunk was filled to bursting. I do not know how long I spent examining each piece and admiring its unique details.

Eventually I decided upon a gown of deepest green, the wool woven so fine that it slipped through the fingers like silk. The fabric alone was richer than anything I had known, but there were untold lengths of cloth in the fullness of the skirt. It hung in gathers, pooling around my feet, intended to do so as a mark that the wearer had no need to toil through muck or to labor at all. The sleeves buttoned from elbow to wrist with tiny ivory buttons that were fiercely difficult to fasten oneself.

I managed. The sleeves were cut long so that they gathered most attractively around the lower arm. The bodice fitted snugly to my sides, showing my figure to advantage, and for once I did not regret giving my meal to Tynan on so many occasions.

I donned a brocade surcoat which was shorter than the gown—it was fitted, with open sides and ermine trim, and ended at the curve of my hips. The brocade was thick with gold embroidery.

I recalled that Merlyn had once told me that this ensemble made my eyes look more green. "Bewitching" he had called me when I wore this kirtle to the hall. I thought to change it, then resolved that if he were bewitched again, he might well adjust his terms.

It seemed unlikely, but I would not change.

The knitted lace stockings were still there, as were the gold-hued garters that Merlyn had once unfastened with his teeth. I felt myself blushing in recollection as I donned them. Some searching revealed the green leather "poulaine" shoes with their pointed toes. They were packed so carefully in the bottom of the trunk, stuffed with rags to hold their shape, that I knew I could not have packed them away. I would never have thought of such a trick.

Who had packed my garments? Who had folded them away with such care? Who had fingered them in my absence?

I pushed such fruitless speculation from my mind and combed out my hair, coiling it simply at the sides and tying it with a green ribbon before letting it hang loose down my back. I had no jewelry but still felt as lavishly garbed as a queen.

I turned at the shuffle of footsteps upon the stairs and smiled when my sister appeared.

Her eyes widened at the sight of me, then she bowed low,

pretending I was some haughty noblewoman. "I beg your pardon, fine lady, I came to seek my sister and have interrupted you instead."

I laughed and caught at her hand. "Ah, but I shall bestow lavish garb upon you as if you were mine own sister," I teased.

Mavella plucked at the sleeve of my gown. "I remember this."

"All of that garb is yet here." I threw back the lid of the trunk but Mavella sobered, her gaze flicking over its contents.

She sighed as she bent and stroked the fine damask of one surcoat. "Ah, Merlyn," she whispered, her voice thick. "He had an eye as to what would favor a woman."

"You should choose something for yourself."

"You would squander his gifts?"

"I would share."

Mavella studied me for a moment before she spoke. "You have a sharp tongue, Ysabella, but your heart has always been tender. When you spoke harshly yesterday, I thought you mourned Merlyn in your way. But on this day, you are merry—there is a sparkle in your eye and color in your cheek."

Caught, by my own blood.

I averted my face and tried to disguise my mood. "It is Christmas, a time of merriment, and we shall have a hearty meal this night for the first time in years. I but celebrate what good fortune has come to us."

Mavella was unconvinced. "Is your grief so shallow as that?"

I gestured to the trunk, not wanting to betray Merlyn's secret. "Choose a garment, any garment, and let us gather greenery for the hall."

My sister did not move nor did she look away. "I thought you loved Merlyn."

"No!" I spoke with a heat that only made her expression

turn more thoughtful. "Merlyn was a scoundrel. I was well rid of him then and better rid of him now."

"Is that so?"

"You know that it is, Mavella!"

Mavella shook her head. "I know no such thing. You left the man you loved for the sake of principle. You were right, if lonely, impoverished and unchallenged."

"I do not regret my choice . . ."

My sister interrupted me. "There was a fire about you, Ysabella, when you were in Merlyn's presence, a spark that abandoned you when you abandoned him. You have been brittle these years in your unhappiness."

"You do not know that I have been unhappy."

Mavella smiled sadly. "We have both been unhappy. In my case, the choice was inflicted upon me, while you made your own choice. Either way, we chose not to begin again, not to heal, not to forgive, not to forget." She considered me. "I had forgotten how brightly your eyes could sparkle and how a flush could become you better than any powder."

"Mavella, I tell you that I feel no need to mourn Merlyn."

"I do not care for the reason, Ysabella. I was but surprised that his death did not cut you more deeply." I felt myself flush but she looked back to the trunk, her hand sliding across a silken robe. "It is nearly the beginning of a new year and I would make a wager with you."

"What kind of wager?"

"Merlyn has granted us the gift of a new beginning. Let us seize it, let us greet the coming year with open hearts. Let us forget and forgive, let us put the past where it belongs."

Mavella spoke with a ferocity uncommon for her and indeed, she began to tremble as she clenched her fist before herself. "Let us *live*, Ysabella. Let us be happy. I have had enough misery to last me all of my days and nights. Let us rejoice that we are yet alive, for Death can come suddenly for any of us."

"Amen to that." I embraced her, then tightened my grip when I felt her shaking like a leaf.

"I saw Alasdair," she whispered unevenly into my shoulder. Her grip tightened on my gown. "Before we left Kinfairlie."

I pulled back to regard her. "You said nothing of this."

"I could not speak of it." Mavella shook her head without looking up.

"Was he alone?"

Mavella shook her head once. My heart ached for her. Alasdair had been her love and the light of her life, until he spurned her and left Kinfairlie. I knew that my sister still yearned for her lost love.

"Did he see you? Did he speak to you?"

"No and no again." She took a shaking breath. "He carried a child, a young child, and they laughed together. The rumors were true—he wed another. And he is happy, as I am not." Her words faltered and I hugged her fiercely, my own tears gathering at the unfairness of her circumstance.

Then she spoke with force. "There is a lesson here. Alasdair has lived all these years, Ysabella, while I have waited. He has put the past behind him, where it rightly belongs, while I have wallowed in it." She lifted her chin. "I shall do this no more. Wager with me that we shall live this year ahead."

"I take your wager, Mavella." Even as I said the words, I thought of Merlyn's pledge that life was worth little without a taste of risk.

I was startled to find myself agreeing with him.

We embraced tightly and wiped a few tears, then Mavella heaved a sigh. "God bless Merlyn for this opportunity. God bless him for waking me from my slumber. I do not care what he did in his life, Ysabella, but in dying he made a good choice." She smiled at me. "He righted his debt to you and he granted us a rare opportunity. Surely that will be counted in his favor when he faces his judgment. God bless Merlyn Lammergeier."

She looked up expectantly when I did not immediately echo her blessing. But I could not form the words. I stared at her mutely, unable to bless Merlyn, unwilling to admit that he yet drew breath.

"Indeed." I managed to nod once and Mavella's gaze softened.

She touched my cheek with a gentle fingertip. "You do mourn him. I knew you had lost your heart to him, scoundrel or no."

I had to turn away. I immediately spied a sapphire gown in the trunk, one wrought of some shimmering fabric from the East. It was woven with silver, embroidered with silver upon its hems, and adorned with dozens of tiny silver buttons. It was an altogether splendid garment, as well as a perfect distraction.

"This would be perfect for you," I declared and pulled the gown from the trunk.

My sister gasped. "Nay, Ysabella, I could not!" But her eyes shone as they had not in years and she reached out to touch the cloth with a tentative hand.

She was half smitten with it already.

"It is too small for me through the waist and hips. You must take it or it will be wasted."

It was not that hard to persuade her to don the garment.

"Oh, but it is too long."

"It pools upon the floor most attractively."

"This is impractical, Ysabella," she insisted, though she could not tear her gaze from it. "It will be stained before a single day is through."

"How so? You are a lady of leisure, Mavella, and such garb is most suitable for you in these days. We could turn up the hem later, if you so desire."

My sister spun, luxuriating in the quality of the cloth as she decided. I knew she would accept it. It favored her wonderfully, the brightness of the hue taking years from her countenance. She even preened a little, then turned to me with a radiant smile the like of which I had not seen in six years. I had forgotten how beautiful she is.

The sight brought a lump to my throat.

"I thank you, Ysabella." She bowed low like a fine lady, then fingered the cloth with awe. "This is the finest gift that ever I have had."

"And this," I said, touching her smiling lips with my fingertip, "is the finest gift that ever I have had."

She laughed, thinking I made a jest, but it was true. My sister's smile and her newfound hope for the future was the best Yuletide gift that ever I could have received.

I realized with some dismay that I did owe Merlyn a debt of gratitude, for this moment was of his making. What had once been a clear matter of principle already became as slippery as a fresh eel.

That was perhaps Merlyn's intent.

But was Mavella's smile sufficient to persuade me to agree to Merlyn's terms?

I had no doubt that Merlyn would seek me out. He had need of me, this I knew, and he never abandoned an argument he was losing. I guessed that he would appear suddenly, seeking to have surprise upon his side when he set to changing my thinking.

I was prepared for him. Not only did I hesitate before opening any portal that night, not only did I peer in every shadowed corner even as we decked the halls, but I sat awake in the solar until long into the night, expectant.

But Merlyn did not come. Beneath the shadow of the carved lammergeier, hours passed with no hint that he yet breathed. I wondered and I worried. Was he absent because he could not come, or because he had chosen not to come?

How serious was his wound?

What manner of fool was I to fret for his welfare?

In the darkness, my doubts festered. Was it possible that Merlyn truly intended to change? And why had I so readily trusted Gawain's word, as I was unprepared to trust Merlyn's? Had I merely been younger and more gullible then?

I could admit to myself in my dark solitude that I had been afraid to ask Merlyn for his version of events, afraid in those days to grant him any chance to sway me to his side. Was that why I held fast against his new assertions?

I punched my pillows and tossed restlessly in the chilly solar.

What did I truly know of Merlyn? He had wealth. He had charm. Though I called him cruel, he had never raised a hand against me. He could become angered as he had in the labyrinth, but I knew the sting of realizing that a trusted soul had lied. And he had not truly abandoned me, even in his anger—he had left the light to summon me. His cruelty was less than even I might expect.

I rose and noted how far the crescent moon had moved, how close it came to dawn. And still, Merlyn did not come to me.

I was disappointed.

Perhaps he did not need me as much as I believed he did. Perhaps I only wished he would seek me out again. In the darkness I could admit to myself that I was curious as to who had assaulted him.

And why.

I had fewer qualms about Merlyn's lust for vengeance than I would have liked him to know. Did I dare draw close to the untrustworthy flame that was Merlyn yet again? I knew there would be pleasure abed, but my choice could endanger others. If Merlyn deceived me and there was some foul price to be paid, it could be exacted of my innocent siblings.

My thoughts circled fruitlessly, seeking a solution that I did not have sufficient information to find. Eventually, I fell into a fitful sleep.

It is night in Ravensmuir and I lie abed, alone for the first time since my arrival here ten days past. My husband does not come. I have not seen him since midday and the passing hours feed my doubts.

Has he left me?

Has he taken a mistress? Indeed, there could be a mistress resident in this massive place and I would never guess at her presence.

Is he displeased with his common bride?

He comes finally on the cusp of the dawn, clearly irked that I am yet awake. He is distracted as I have never seen him, though he summons his charm to apologize prettily. His smile, though, does not reach his eyes. His gaze slides away from me, a shadow claims his features, and I know that he lies when he concocts a tale of where he has been.

It is the first lie between us.

It stains the air.

It leaves an odor like a rank perfume. It feeds questions and doubts in my mind. It makes me hold back from him when we make love. The wedge is driven between us and I cannot help but resent him for choosing to invite it, for deciding to lie.

For nothing will ever be the same.

I dream, on that night and again on this one, of a priceless treasure slipping through my numbed fingers. The gem flashes, momentarily in my grip, then turns slippery. I am powerless to snatch it tightly, unable to halt its tumble into a fathomless abyss.

As it disappears from sight, swallowed by darkness, the sun disappears without warning from the midday sky. Two pin-

points of light burn painfully bright on the horizon and I reach for them in hope.

The yawning maw of blackness devours both lights. I tremble in terror. A shadow has swallowed the world, a shadow so complete that I cannot see my own hand before my face.

Then, just when I can endure it no longer, somewhere in the distant darkness, a scream begins. Its volume rises, it grates like nails on a stone, it fills my ears to bursting.

It is a child, I know this, a child in anguish and in need of solace. I scramble in the darkness, hoping to aid somehow, knowing that I cannot arrive in time. The scream grows to terrifying volume, its pain and plaintiveness making me fear that the child is lost forever.

December 27

Saint John the Evangelist's Day

VI

I sat up with a gasp. My heart was racing.

But no child screamed for aid. The solar was filled with nothing more threatening than the glow of the moon and the stirrings of the wind. I could smell the promise of yet more rain and hear the waves of the sea. I reassured myself that I was safe and took a deep breath.

Then choked upon it when I saw something glitter and spin on the far side of the chamber.

The silhouette of a man was barely discernible as he held his hand high, that glittering trinket evidently strung on a cord. It glimmered again as it spun and I realized what it was.

The key to Merlyn's box.

The key that hung upon the red silken cord around my neck. My hand rose to my chest, fearing what I would find, and closed upon nothing at all.

"Merlyn," I whispered, my heart racing with hope that I guessed aright.

His smile glinted in the shadows; his voice was low and dark. "The beauty awakens, not requiring my kiss to tempt her back from dreams. I confess myself disappointed, chère."

"It is the kiss of a prince that awakens the damsel in the tale, not that of a blackguard," I retorted, pulling the furs up over my bare breasts.

Merlyn chuckled, then unfolded himself from his seat. He came and perched upon the side of the bed. "Whereas the blackguard comes only to ravish the damsel?"

"Indeed." I put out my hand with imperial poise. "You appear to have something that is mine."

Merlyn rolled the cord between his finger and thumb, setting the key to spinning again. "You should wear it always, chère. If you carelessly lay aside your treasures, any rogue could claim them in the night."

That I sat in the company of a rogue holding my prize only emphasized his point. I was not convinced that he spoke only of the key, but was not in any mood to accept an implied compliment.

I reached for the key, but Merlyn held it out of my grasp.

"It is evident that locking and barring the door is not sufficient to keep rogues at bay," I snapped.

He smiled, then lifted the cord in both hands, obviously intending that I should dip my head through its circle. Of course, then I should have to lean closer to him, and he would have a glimpse down my cleavage. He knew I slept nude and he was man enough to want a glimpse.

Scoundrel. His gaze met mine in silent challenge and I set my lips as I took his dare. Indeed, I let the furs dip low in my grasp, so they only barely covered my nipples. I bent my head and leaned forward, smiling at the slight sound of his inhalation. He released the cord with startling speed, so I jumped when the cold key fell against my flesh. The key slipped between my breasts and Merlyn watched its downward progress.

I flicked back my hair and smiled at his obvious interest. "Did you come to persuade me to agreement, then?"

"You made mention of a wager to Ada," he whispered, his eyes dark. My breath caught as he eased closer. His hands landed on the bed, on either side of my hips, imprisoning me within his embrace. I leaned back, trapped against the carved headboard even as Merlyn loomed over me.

"Now, what were those terms?" He pursed his lips, as if struggling to remember, though I had no doubt my words were in the forefront of his thoughts.

He looked as devilish as I once remembered him being, and the sight was not the only reason my heart raced.

"Your aid by day in exchange for my favors abed at night, I believe it was. Is that not right, chère?"

"Merlyn, no."

He arched a dark brow. "And why not? It was your own suggestion and one most amenable to me." His lips quirked and his warm gaze slipped over me. "Do you fear that you could not be persuaded? I cannot imagine that you would be so reticent." He smiled. "And I cannot imagine that I would find the burden of persuading you so onerous as that."

I closed my eyes as his kiss feathered across my brow. I feared precisely the opposite—that Merlyn's fiery touch would persuade me to abandon the last vestige of my sense. I heard myself sigh as his lips touched my temple.

Merlyn's heat melted my resistance, his touch gave me far less than I desired, his gentle kisses dissolved my determination to fight him. He knew that force would make rejection easy, so he teased and tempted, he seduced. His lips touched my brow, my temple, my ear, the corner of my mouth. I felt myself hungering for his touch, burning for the pleasure that I knew he could grant, aching for the fire we two could light between us.

I turned my face abruptly away, though the feat took an unholy effort. "I cannot aid you without more knowledge, Merlyn," I said and barely recognized the husky words as my own. "You ask too much of me."

"Then, you will assist me?"

I turned and met his gaze steadily. "I cannot make such a choice, not without the details. And surely, Merlyn, a person is more likely to cleave to an agreement made willingly than one which has been beguiled from their lips."

He smiled, then leaned his weight upon his elbow. "Do I beguile you, chère?"

The last thing the man needed was a boost to his confidence. I gathered the furs high, not wanting to give him the satisfaction of my seeking a chemise, then granted him my most bored glance. "Of course not. Say what you must and be done with it."

But Merlyn neither moved nor spoke. He studied me for so long that my flesh prickled with awareness of him. His gaze slid over my face, my hair, my bare shoulder, my tight pose, then returned to my face again.

"You have changed," he said softly, as if surprised.

"I have not changed save that I am older. As we all are." I knew, of course, that I had changed, but I did not intend to explain my choices to Merlyn.

"No, it is more than that." The shadows made him look mysterious and alluring. He leaned closer, stretching his legs out on the mattress beside me, and studied me with care.

"And I say you are wrong." I yawned elaborately, hoping to disguise my awareness that my husband was again in my bed and that I warmed to his very presence. It was all too easy to recall the wondrous things we had done to each other here. "How fascinating, Merlyn. We have found another matter upon which we can disagree."

He touched my shoulder with a warm fingertip that stopped my heart, then slid his touch down the length of my arm. I struggled to hide my shiver. "You are more inclined to speak your thoughts than you were even then," he said with quiet certitude. "You are harsher than once you were, more judgmental, more severe. You are more tough than the maiden I knew."

His perceptiveness alarmed me and sharpened my tongue. "Had you ever tended chickens, Merlyn, you would know that the tender do not survive and that the oldest hens oft have the toughest meat."

My bold words were effectively undermined when he slipped his hand beneath the furs and cupped the weight of my breast in his hand. His eyes sparkled when I caught my breath.

Merlyn slid his thumb across my nipple, encouraging it to bead, and I know he delighted in how readily I responded. "Surely you do not call yourself an old hen, chère? This flesh seems most soft."

I fixed him with a challenging stare. "Tell me more or leave."

Merlyn's hand slipped away, and I was not entirely glad to lose his touch. He got to his feet, and I feared that he would leave.

Then he glanced back to me, his expression almost contrite. "You are suspicious, as well. Is this my legacy to you?"

I lifted my chin, hating that I could soften toward him so readily. "Perhaps so, Merlyn. You certainly taught me that matters are not always as they appear, nor even as a man might insist they are."

Merlyn's voice hardened. "Give me one example of a deed I have done to earn your bitterness. Not one recounted by Gawain or any other, but one that you yourself witnessed."

I knew a perfect example well enough. "That is an easy task, Merlyn. Your reply to my request for an annulment will suffice."

"How so?" He was wary, despite his query, as if he guessed himself guilty. "You sent a missive and I replied. Where is the crime in that?"

"You knew that I would not be able to read your reply!" This was an old wound and the recounting of it heated my words. "You *knew* I would have to have it read for me, and that the only place to have that done is in the market! You knew that the entire village would hear the contents of your missive."

If I longed for a rebuttal, an explanation that would prove him innocent, I was not to have it.

Merlyn's features set to stone. "Indeed I did."

I gasped. "You shamed me apurpose!"

"I ensured that the relationship between us was made clear, for the benefit of all parties."

"Benefit?" Outrage rose hot in my throat. "If you believe that what you wrote was for my benefit, then you are more a fool than I ever imagined, Merlyn Lammergeier."

"And what is that to mean?" he demanded. "You asked for an annulment, and I explained why it was not possible."

"You made me look a fool!"

"I did no such thing."

"I beg your pardon, my lord Merlyn, but I remember the matter somewhat differently."

"Do tell." Merlyn watched me, his gaze snapping.

It is somewhat difficult to make a regal argument reclined nude in one's bed, but I did my best. "You regretted to inform me that a marriage could only be annulled for three reasons."

"Indeed."

"The first—" I held up my thumb "—if the bride was unwilling. As I had accepted you of my own volition, you knew this was not so."

"And so I still do."

"The second—" I held up my index finger "—if the bride and groom are related within unacceptable degrees of consanguinity, which you also knew to not be so."

Merlyn nodded, his expression grim and unrepentant.

I faltered, but then I saw the gleam in his eyes and knew that he knew what had infuriated me so.

But still, he made me tell him.

Cur!

Angered anew, I held up my next finger. "The third—if the match has not been consummated."

"Ah, yes," Merlyn murmured. "Do you find fault with my understanding of ecclesiastical law?"

I had the definite sense that he laughed at me, though his expression remained sober.

"No, not that. I find fault with your assurance that you recalled the consummation of our wedding night with greatest pleasure . . ."

"As I still do."

"And you offered that if my recollection was lacking, you would be delighted to return to Kinfairlie and refresh my memory."

Merlyn grinned. "It is true. But my recounting of the truth annoyed you?"

"You knew I could not read your missive myself!" I shouted, furious that he still did not see the issue. "You knew that I would have to take it to the scribe in the market and you knew that he would read it aloud."

Merlyn paused, watching me carefully.

I shook a finger at him. "It was an entire month before I dared show my face in the village market. To this day, boys will follow me, snickering while they insist that they have a missive for me from my spouse, then grabbing at themselves in case their meaning is not clear."

Merlyn frowned. "Chère, I meant no disrespect . . ."

"But you granted it to me all the same! Do you know nothing of village life? Do you know nothing of how vicious people can be? I was already mocked, as you might have guessed, for having been spurned by the Laird of Ravensmuir."

He straightened. "I did not spurn you."

"I let them believe what they wished to believe and that was the conclusion they made. I was not about to confess the wicked deeds of my spouse."

"You protected me . . ."

"I did not choose to confide in the gossips of Kinfairlie!" I declared, interrupting him before he could think overmuch along such lines. "We had long been accused of holding ourselves above others, and that was a chance for malice to reign."

"Your mother certainly never comported herself as a peasant."

"She was no peasant! She was a noblewoman's hand-maid, orphaned and sent to serve in the household of a for-mer ally of her father. And she insisted that we speak properly, as she had been taught to do, rather than mutter and growl like those common born."

"Which fed resentment, no doubt." Merlyn's eyes glit-tered. "Your return to Kinfairlie provided all the fuel neces-sary for malice."

"Oh yes. Clearly, we were not so fine as we believed. Clearly, you regretted your hasty courtship. Clearly, you re-gretted an unfortunate choice of bride. The gossips were proven right a hundredfold. But Merlyn, with your missive, you made the matter ten times worse!"

I closed my eyes, snared in that horrible afternoon, seeing again the dozens of leering faces savoring my discomfiture. "I remember the heat of my shame, I remember how my face burned, I remember how they mocked me even as I stood there. I dare not let myself be cornered alone even to this day, lest they choose to deliver their missive and out-number me so that I cannot halt them." I swallowed. "You know that there is no law in Kinfairlie, Merlyn, for there is no laird. Do you know what it is to taste terror when you hear footsteps behind you?"

"You could have left the village."

"To go where?" My tears rose hot again, as they had on that long-ago day, but I could not halt. "Have you ever tasted despair, Merlyn? I was not well, my mother was very ill, we had no coin to speak of, no income, no patron, and yet a child would be born in our household within the year. We were trapped in Kinfairlie, as surely as if the gates were barred against us, and you stole what few op-tions we had."

"Surely not!"

"I could not marry again, to see us secure, for I was still wedded. I could not gain a license to brew as a single woman, and could not have one as a married woman for there was no spouse to guarantee my pledge. You neither claimed me nor released me. You left me trapped in poverty, Merlyn, powerless by your choice."

He spared me a simmering glance. "You could have returned here."

"To the man who lied to me? To the man who mocked me? I think not!"

Merlyn's expression turned conciliatory. "Ysabella . . ."

"Those words meant *nothing* to you, Merlyn, yet everything to me. I hated you that day with every fiber of my being."

He stared at me, something in my tone having given him pause. We eyed each other for a long moment and I did not temper the fury I still felt.

The truth was that I had hated Merlyn that day as one can only hate what one has loved.

Once vented, my anger was spent. The wind left my sails and I felt smaller than I had just moments past. It is a curious thing about bitterness and anger—they fester solely in the dark shadows of our hearts and, once exposed to even fitful moonlight, disperse like wraiths. I folded my arms about myself, feeling more naked without the burden of my resentment. In hindsight, I was ashamed that I had confessed so much so readily.

"I am sorry, chère. I never thought . . ." Merlyn's voice faltered uncharacteristically.

I peeked through my lashes to find him looking most troubled. He shoved a hand through his hair and swore. He crossed the chamber and caught my hand in his, giving me no chance to snatch it away.

He appealed to me, his eyes telling me much that his hoarse words did not. "It is true that I knew that you could not read, and that I anticipated that you would have the missive read in the marketplace."

He paused for a long moment while I wrestled with my disappointment that he was guilty again of the charges I made against him.

"I thought matters would be simpler for you if people knew that your spouse was not disinterested in your fate." He took a deep breath, and he lifted my chin with a fingertip as if he would will me to believe him. "I thought my name might protect you, chère, or the fear of my name, even if you would not allow me to do so. My sole intent was to put the terror of the Lammergeier into those who might otherwise have tormented you." He smiled at me and I knew he would make a light jest. "Clearly, I underestimated our wicked repute."

I was within a hair of believing him. I wanted to be persuaded that he had tried to protect me. I wanted to forgive him, but the anguish of that day was still too sharp within me.

I turned away, pulling my hand from his grip. "How curious then, if you were so concerned for my welfare, that you never once sought me out."

Merlyn met my gaze, his eyes a stormy blue. "I did, just days past, and you did not welcome me."

I had no argument for that.

"You fled my home without explanation. You asked for an annulment. A man could readily conclude from those choices that his attentions were unwelcome."

I froze at the hurt underlying his words.

Had I wounded Merlyn by leaving him? The possibility was stunning. I faced him anew and found it telling that he averted his gaze from mine.

Or was this yet another facet of his game to win my aid?

"You do not fool me, Merlyn," I said with low heat. "You speak loftily of trust between us, but the sole thing you desire is my trust of you, granted preferably without restraint, without your making the effort of behaving in a trustworthy manner. Indeed, I believe the true mark of the Lammergeier is a refusal to trust any person not of their own brood."

I thought he would argue with me, but he simply glanced down at me, his gaze steady. "I am not accustomed to sharing my secrets, chère," he confessed and I saw a hesitancy in him which I had never witnessed before. "I have not your talent for speaking with clarity and passion of matters that have long been hidden." Merlyn frowned. "And I am spared of your conviction that my choices have been the best ones."

There was sincerity in his manner. Though I was uncertain whether to trust it, I touched his sleeve. "I cannot aid you, Merlyn, not unless you share with me what details you know."

He parted his lips, then sealed them again, frustration creasing his brow. His silence told me that Merlyn knew little of trust.

A mere week ago, I would have laughed if any soul had insisted that I had anything of merit to share with Merlyn.

But I knew how to trust, and Merlyn did not. I knew how to protect what was mine by virtue of love's bonds, what I protected for the sake of love alone. Merlyn protected what was his by sovereignty, by purchase and by trade, because it was his legal right and duty to do so.

His uneasiness, his doubt and his silence told me much. The tide turned for me then, for I knew that if he did mean to change his ways, the course would not be an easy one for him.

I decided to encourage him.

I reached up and framed his face in my hands, a gesture that startled him into meeting my gaze. "Trust cannot be wagered or bought, Merlyn." I reached up and pushed the hair from his brow, my fingers tangling in the thick waves of it. "I am not so harsh a listener as you fear."

He smiled at me, his expression wry. "You think not? You demand solely the truth, chère, no more than utter honesty. And you have the audacity to insist that it is not a heavy burden."

"It is not," I whispered. "Not when the burden is shared." I stretched up and brushed my lips across his.

Merlyn caught his breath and became very still.

"You can tell me of it, Merlyn, and I shall listen, and once you have begun, it will not be so difficult as you fear." I stared into his eyes, willing him to believe me this time, then I kissed him in silent demand.

I had never before initiated a kiss with him, or indeed with any man, and I was clumsy in approaching him. But Merlyn did not seem to find fault.

Indeed, I heard him moan softly, then he caught me close. He let me lead, but responded with an enthusiasm that could not have been feigned. Our kiss blazed with that familiar heat and I wound my fingers into his hair, arching against him like a wanton. I kissed him with a hunger I had never yet shared and he responded in kind.

Then he pulled away, looking more disheveled and uncertain than ever I have seen him. He smiled down at me, resolve dawning in his eyes. "You shall have your desire in this, chère," he whispered, "though you may well regret it."

Merlyn paced the solar like a caged beast, his footsteps relentless. He was not comfortable with his choice and I knew it well, so I let him linger over the beginning. He was so restless that I knew he intended to do as he had pledged.

I was fascinated, shocked, and thrilled. I had never expected that Merlyn might surrender one of his secrets to me.

He must have greater need of my aid than I had imagined.

I waited, content to let him take his time. The chamber brightened as the sun rose, the sky turned to a burnished silver then was tinged with blue, a ray of sunlight touched the wall of the solar.

Finally, Merlyn spoke. "The root of this matter lies in both my father's trade in relics and events long past." He sighed and perched on the side of the mattress. "When I was a child, I thought my father was a powerful sorcerer, for he seemed to conjure rare marvels at the most opportune times."

I snorted. I could not help myself.

Merlyn spared me a glance. "Imagine how magical it appeared to a child, especially one inclined to think his father marvelous. We would visit an acquaintance and, at some point, usually after a fine meal, our host would tell of his endowment of a local church or monastery, then would express a desire for a fine relic to give the crowning glory to his gift.

"It would have to be a prestigious relic, of course, one fitting of the lord's stature. One that would bring pilgrims to the chapel, one that would ensure that his endowment would have financial security for all time, one that would ensure his gift, and his grace, was eternal."

"Of course."

"Our host might rhapsodize about the perfect relic for this place. Typically, he had already reflected long about the matter and sought only an audience to hear of his dream."

I hugged my knees, sitting forward, intrigued by Merlyn's tale and the music of his voice. "And your father listened."

"He was always a most gracious guest." We smiled at each other for a heartstopping moment, then Merlyn frowned. "And I listened as well." He shook his head and fell silent again.

I prompted him without a thought. "What kind of relics would these hosts desire?"

Merlyn shrugged. "Perhaps a fingerbone of a saint who had been born locally before rising to great repute; perhaps a lock of hair of a great saint with a tenuous link to the foundation itself. Perhaps the skull of an apostle rumored to have visited the locale in his travels." His lips twisted. "The majesty of the desired relic tended to reflect the host's view of his importance."

"And the fatness of his purse."

Merlyn nodded, his gaze slipping over the tapestries and rich appointments of the chamber. I supposed they had been acquired by his father, with coin gained by this traffic, and looked about myself with newly assessing eyes. Indeed, this entire keep must have been built with the earnings from such sources. I had not previously thought about the roots running so very deep.

"Our host would then look to my father, who was known to travel extensively, hoping for news that such a relic could be had."

"And he would produce it from his trunk?"

"Never so vulgar as that, chère!" Merlyn clicked his tongue in mock disapproval. "No, my father would sigh and shake his head. He would confess that he had heard nothing of such a precious token, for surely one would hear tell of an invaluable relic being translated or acquired."

"He delayed to make the prize seem more rare."

He spared me an incisive glance. "You are skeptical, chère."

"I have seen much of men in my days."

Merlyn held my gaze, his own expression inscrutable as the silence stretched long between us. I did not tear my gaze away. "Yes," he mused. "I expect you have."

He cleared his throat, frowned, and continued. "They would then discuss other known relics of this particular saint and the location of those relics, expressing admiration and awe of each in accordance with the miracles attributed to it. Finally, my father would assure our host that he would listen keenly for any news in his travels that might be of interest."

Merlyn pursed his lips. "It was the most curious thing, for inevitably, usually within a year or so, he not only heard a rumor of such a relic, but he managed to acquire it, at not inconsiderable expense, as a favor to his great friend."

I laughed without humor.

"Yes, it is so obvious now what he did." Merlyn shrugged. "The friend, of course, would be so overjoyed that he would not only compensate my father for his cost of acquisition but add a stipend for my father's loyalty and trouble. The entire matter would be conducted very quietly, to protect the purchaser from vandals."

"But in reality to ensure that your father remained above suspicion."

"Indeed. So, the relics simply appeared, 'found' in the lord's family treasury, 'lost and retrieved' from dear cousin George's crusade or some such tale."

"But where did the relics come from? Did your father counterfeit them?"

"No, at least not initially. My father worked every snippet of information loose from his host in their initial conversation, as the host invariably had done much of the research of what was available and where it was located."

"Then he stole it?"

"Again, I do not think this was his original strategy, though it definitely was part of the trade later. I suspect he began innocently enough. My family had long traded in textiles, and had a particular speciality in silks." He met my gaze, his own bright and compelling. "I told you no lie in this. My father traveled often to the East, at least thrice a year, and had a considerable trade in such fine cloths. And we have all been known for finding the occasional interesting trinket.

"I have no doubt that he truly did oft purchase a thumb bone or femur in Damascus or in Tripoli—perhaps he believed they were genuine, perhaps he was told a tall tale, perhaps he knew them to be false but guessed they would please an acquaintance."

"But why take the trouble?"

Merlyn shrugged. "Who can know? He may have begun this as a means of securing alliances useful to his main trade and even supplementing it. Relics do not take much room to ship and they please noblemen. The nobility, after all, are the primary purchasers of silken cloth."

Merlyn's brows drew together. "But I can surmise that at some point, my father must have looked at the sorry array of fingernail clippings for which he had just paid an exorbitant fee and concluded that he could do better."

"And fetch a better price," I muttered.

"As one might expect from a man in his trade, my father was much concerned with the appearance of things. My first task in this endeavor was creating new boxes for the relics before they were taken to the noblemen desirous of them. He said a gift should be presented in the splendor it deserved. I showed an early talent with woodworking, so he apprenticed me at nine to a craftsman he knew, a Christian man in Cairo who wrought exquisite boxes of fine woods and inlaid their lids."

I looked immediately at the fine box which held Merlyn's deeds and seals. "Did you make this box?"

"No. I never mastered the art of inlay—I doubt that my father ever intended for me to learn a trade so well as that."

"Then why . . ."

"It behooves a trader to be able to recognize the caliber of workmanship," Merlyn said stiffly, his fingers sliding once again over the box as his voice softened. "Joseph wrought this for me, as a parting gift when I left his household." He fell silent for a moment. "They were good people, and good to me."

I understood that they had passed away and said nothing to shorten his moment of mourning.

Merlyn continued. "But I could make a plain box well enough, and if the wood is sufficiently fine, the grain is all the ornament it needs. My father purchased exotic woods in his travels and brought them home to me. I made boxes for the relics he acquired and my mother lined the boxes artfully in silk." Merlyn shook his head. "I remember my pride the first time we had completed such a box. My father took it, nodded approval, then dropped it onto the stone floor."

I gasped but Merlyn's tone was hard. "It was no accident. He then stained the silk lining with ash from the fireplace. He scarred the outside of the box, he buried it in the garden for a month, then confessed himself pleased with the results. He said that it was important to the client to believe that all of what he purchased was ancient."

"The silk would have rotted in a lifetime or less," I felt obliged to observe.

Merlyn's eyes twinkled. "While in contact with a holy relic? Tsk tsk, chère, I thought your faith more resolute than that."

"My faith is resolute. It is the quality of the relics in which you trade that I question."

"Ah, but the clients seldom did." Merlyn sobered. "It is true, chère, that people will believe what they most wish to believe. In every deception, there are two willing parties— the one who deceives and the one who permits himself to be deceived."

Did he allude to our relationship? I dared not guess.

"Surely you do not suggest that your father's clients deserved to be tricked?"

Merlyn shook his head. "No. I suggest only that if they had kept their wits about them—if they had questioned the survival of the silk, for example—then they likely would not have been deceived."

I could see the merit of this argument, but it did not absolve Merlyn and his family in their trade, at least not for me. My expression must have showed as much, for Merlyn abandoned the point. "My father's willful aging of the box troubled me, for it seemed a deception even though he insisted it was an innocent one. For a long time, I thought, or perhaps I hoped, that the false aging of the box was the worst of it."

"Then you discovered differently."

Merlyn frowned. "I was twelve or thirteen years of age and was traveling with my father more frequently to learn the family trade. It was why I had been compelled to leave Joseph and his family—my father had need of my assistance. There was too much labor for one man and he meant to initiate me that I could assume responsibility for some portion of the trade. It was not long before I began to question the extraordinary correlation between the noblemen's desires and my father's sudden discoveries. I dared to say nothing at first, of course."

"Of course? Why?"

"Matters were troubled in our family and tensions rode high." Merlyn sighed. "My parents had always argued, but there was new heat to their antagonism and they argued less furtively than once they had. It has been said, chère, that not all desires can be sated with coin. Our visible wealth had grown considerably since I was a child—we lived in a finer house and with extraordinarily fine goods. My mother had five servants in the house where once she had had one, but lines of misery etched deeper in her brow with every year."

"Surely this troubled your father?"

"By that time, he was oblivious to little beyond the trade that had long eclipsed his traffic in cloth. He was becoming more bold, his discoveries beginning to defy belief."

"Surely some soul questioned him?"

"I did." Merlyn swallowed. "I finally challenged him one

day, skeptical that none had yet found the jawbone of John the Baptist when that apostle's skull was claimed to be held in two different places."

"What did he tell you? Did he lie?"

"Worse." Merlyn's hand gathered into a fist. "He took me into his confidence."

I watched him and wondered how a boy bore the burden of knowing his father a criminal, also knowing it would be disloyal to betray his father's confidence. That Avery had made Merlyn part of his scheme said little in that man's favor, in my opinion.

I wondered what kind of man would urge his son to join him in such a trade.

I wondered how any son would perceive that he had a choice.

"What did you say?"

Merlyn impaled me with a glance. "What do you think?"

His voice was hoarse, his eyes a bright unearthly blue. He was aloof, elusive, unknowable. He held my gaze, his own defiant.

Merlyn was still, his every fiber waiting for my reply. I understood that my assessment of him would determine whatsoever else he told me.

If anything.

But I could not lie to him, not even to hear the entire tale.

"I would like to think that you did not," I said, holding his gaze unswervingly. "I would like to believe that you continued to be troubled by this trade, and even that you rejected it. I would like to think that Gawain lied to me. But, as you noted, the years have made me skeptical." I gestured to the room around me and shook my head. "It is clear that your father found favor with you, for he made you his heir. Still you have coin to spare, still you have crates stacked in the labyrinth. You must prosper at this unholy traffic."

He did not so much as move. "Would you like to think I

did not do so because you find the trade offensive? Or because you believe my heart could not be so black as my father's?"

"I do not know. You can be so cruel and yet so kind, Merlyn. I cannot fathom which is the true measure of you."

"But what does your heart tell you?" he insisted, as if he had spied the doubt within me and would ferret it out, forcing it to the light.

"That every wickedness I know of you is by repute and mine own interpretation." My voice caught in recognition of the truth I had unwittingly uttered, then I continued hoarsely. "And that every goodness I know of you is from my own experience of your deeds."

And my husband smiled, his expression like a ray of sunshine in the blackest night. He spoke with quiet urgency. "Perhaps there is something of me that you do not know, something that would make the two halves seem one."

"Then tell me of it, Merlyn."

He took a deep breath. His arms were folded across his chest, his gaze fixed on some distant late star visible through the high open window. "I did not readily embrace my father's trade, chère. We argued, and I left both my father and my family home. I walked away from the taint upon his coin."

My heart took flight with hope, hope that Merlyn was the man I had once believed him to be. "What did you do?"

"I had learned enough of the trade in cloth to know what was good and what price was fair. I began in trading cloth in Venice, then painstakingly built up enough coin to invest in a trading venture to the East. I fared well enough, though times were hard more than once. My coin was honestly earned, though, and that made the struggle worthwhile."

I was jubilant that the tale he had recounted to me years ago as to his own trade was not entirely untrue. "That is not without merit."

"And it was not easy to be alone in the world, without kith or kin," he said sourly. "It is lonely, chère."

I touched his hand and his fingers closed over mine.

"I was certain that I would never see my family again after our parting. But to my astonishment, my father strode one day into my shop. He said that he wished to repair the rift between us. He invited me to journey to Ravensmuir with him, that we might become close once more."

"Did you believe him?"

Merlyn frowned, at a momentary loss for words. "He had aged greatly and I was shocked by the sight of him, no less by the news that my mother had passed away. I was torn, tempted to deny him. But there is a duty of a son to a father and I believed that too much had been left unsaid between us. I thought that I might reform him. I thought that at least we might come to an understanding."

"You have been a most optimistic man in your time," I teased but Merlyn did not smile.

I rose from the bed, wrapped a length of linen about myself and sat at his side, wanting only to encourage him. Though he did not look at me, he seized my hand and held it against his chest. I could feel his heartbeat, the most reassuring thunder that ever there was.

"I was surprised to learn once we arrived here that my father intended to grant Ravensmuir to my own hand, as a gesture of goodwill between the two of us. I was incredulous when he drew up the deed, but I saw it signed and witnessed and I saw it become my own. I always loved this keep and I was glad to hold it myself."

His gaze flicked to mine, a glimmer deep within his eyes. "And so, with sufficient wealth to end my solitude, I sought a bride with whom to share my good fortune, a woman who would be undaunted by an odd family, a woman who loved life as well as I."

My mouth went dry. "Me."

"I knew the moment that my eye lit upon you, chère."

Merlyn smiled at my evident surprise and his grip tightened on my hand. "It was only days later that I learned that my father wanted my aid in a new scheme of his. He insisted that a genuine relic had come into his possession, a relic of such value and history that it would fetch an uncommon price."

I frowned. "But I never met your father. He was not here."

"Yes, he was, chère. He remained in the caverns, for he wished none to witness his presence."

I might have questioned this, but instead I watched Merlyn closely . . . and I remembered. I remembered the time he stayed away from our chambers for most of the night, I remembered the tale he recounted of having had a bad dream regarding his steed and how he had felt the urge to check on the beast.

I remembered how he had evaded my gaze, how I had known that he lied. I remembered the shadow that crept into his eyes as its partner slid across my heart.

"He came the night you claimed you had the foul dream."

Merlyn nodded. "The night that I told you I was in the stables, I was truly in the labyrinth, arguing with my sire."

My mouth went dry. I remembered how Merlyn had disappeared for an entire day not long afterward, how Gawain had found me alone and disconsolate, how that gilded brother had whispered infection in my ears.

Now I wondered how much of it had been true.

"And that last day? Where were you, Merlyn? What happened?"

Merlyn shook his head and continued with his tale. "My father's difficulty was that he had offered this prize to no less than three noblemen, all of whom wanted it, all of whom he had promised it to at different times. Evidently, they had learned of each other and were each pressing him for delivery. He was excited as I had never seen him, agitated and uneasy. He insisted that one had tried to kill him to wrest the relic from his grip."

"Why did he not just deliver it to one of them?"

"He was determined to gain the best price and deliver upon his own terms. My father had a rare ability to sense when a client will pay more and he insisted that at least one of these men would double his price given a few more days. No doubt that is why they knew of each other, at least by repute—he probably ensured as much." Merlyn's disgust was clear.

"But who were they?"

"He never surrendered their names. I have assumed them to be of the ilk of his customary clients—kings, powerful abbots and barons of the realm."

I sensed a link between past and present, and was anxious to learn more. "Tell me more of the relic."

He frowned anew. "I never laid eyes upon it, nor knew what it was. I thought this yet another of my father's tall tales. I was impatient with what I saw as his manipulation of me and resented being torn from my legitimate trade for this game."

"You did not think the relic was genuine?"

"I was not even convinced that it existed. He never showed it to me and he never named it. And I did not believe that another man was trying to kill my father. I thought this a thin tale to win my sympathy and my aid. Oh, we argued mightily, my father and I."

"You never told me."

Merlyn shook his head. "I could scarcely tell you part of the tale, chère. And what would you have thought of the Lammergeier if I had told you all of my father's deeds? I had already told you that I did not participate in my father's trade, and now he drew me down into the mire." He looked at me. "What would you have thought if I had told you that I meant to join him in his trade?"

"But why would you do such a thing?"

"He offered to surrender the relic at the root of it all to me if I aided him."

"And if you did not?"

Merlyn met my gaze. "Then he would rescind the grant of Ravensmuir to me. It had not yet been witnessed by the king, a matter that I did not realize could be so readily used against me."

My heart stilled. "Without a holding, you would have no right to wed."

Merlyn reached up and tucked a tendril of hair behind my ear. "But you, chère, had already met me abed. And I had pledged to be wedded to you in truth, not realizing my father's reason for so quickly encouraging me to seek a bride. I feared to prove your every suspicion of noblemen true and feared it more than I feared my father's intent."

"You were offered a bargain with the devil himself."

"I said as much to him. But, in the end, in weakness for my own blood, I agreed to his scheme." Merlyn grimaced. "Like father, like son."

"Not truly," I insisted hopefully, having had some glimpse that Merlyn was not wrought the same as his father.

My husband lifted my fingers to his lips and brushed his own against my knuckles, though still did not look down. I could not understand why he was suddenly so grim, so cool.

"You were gone two days at the end," I whispered, long-ago heartbreak still echoing in my words. "I did not know what had happened to you."

Merlyn cast aside my hand and paced across the room, putting distance between us and turning his back to me. "What happened that day was that my father died and I became heir to his trade. What happened that day is that I gained possession of Ravensmuir, the right to wed and a fat purse."

He turned, his gaze burning as his voice dropped. "What happened that day was that my bride chose my brother's poisonous tale over any truth that I might have told her.

What happened that day was that my new bride fled, rather than speak to me directly about her suspicions."

His anger irked me as little else could have done. This was not my fault! "Suspicions which proved true!" I cried.

"But are not without explanation."

"Then share those explanations with me."

"Pledge to aid me first." We glared at each other, each persuaded of our own position.

"You have not told me enough, Merlyn."

"I have told you more than I have ever told another," he said impatiently. "And it has gained me nothing. This is a waste of time and trouble. Do I have your pledge of assistance or not?"

I folded my arms across my chest. "No. I dare not enter an agreement without knowing the fullness of the tale. Who tried to kill you? What do you know of that? Where is the relic? There are too many questions remaining, Merlyn, for me to agree to this on trust."

He eyed me with disappointment and disapproval. "You fear to risk your own hide."

"I fear to risk my siblings' hides."

Merlyn closed the distance between us, his expression intent. "But do you not understand, Ysabella? You already risk them. Someone has tried to kill me, to win the relic my father promised but did not deliver, the relic he believes that I now hold." I stared at him, only now understanding the import of his tale. "And that someone may well now target you, assuming that you have inherited the prize along with Ravensmuir."

My heart skipped but I did not look away. "Then I have but two choices: complete ignorance of your schemes, or complete knowledge of what has gone before. There can be no half measures, Merlyn, not when lives are at stake."

"I dare tell you no more without your pledge. Grant it to me."

"No, Merlyn."

"What if I challenge you to take this chance?"

I shook my head with resolve. "It would be a fool's wager, one that I might not live long enough to regret."

His lips tightened then, and he crossed the room, moving so quickly that I did not discern how he opened the panel in the wall. He paused on the threshold and looked back. "This is your final choice?"

I nodded, not nearly as convinced as I would have him believe.

"Then may you sleep well upon its repercussions."

Before I could ask what he meant, Merlyn was gone, the panel sliding securely back into place behind him.

VII

By the time I descended to the hall to break my fast, I was thoroughly annoyed with my demanding spouse. Half the tale had left me with more questions than answers.

Even knowing what I did, even fearing what I did not know, still I was tempted to grant Merlyn what he requested of me. I was overly touched that he had entrusted even one of his tightly held secrets to me, for the telling had not come easily to him.

It was evident that a lack of sleep had addled my wits.

When I came to the great hall, Ada was not there, nor even my siblings. There was a stranger, idly nudging at the Yule log, loitering in my hall. I hesitated, wondering at this.

He was not just any man. I saw even before he turned at the sound of my foot upon the stone that he had been shaped by wealth and privilege. He was a knight, garbed for war in his gleaming armament and mail.

His tabard was thick with embroidery, his cloak was wrought of heavy red cloth worth a king's ransom in these parts. He was fair, his hair of coppery gold, and I thought for a moment that he might be an older Gawain come to make acquaintance again.

But this man was taller, broader, more solidly wrought. Gawain also did not dress for battle like this, though his garb was no less rich. This man's heraldic device was one I did not know—his insignia that of a prancing golden stag on a black field.

When the guest turned, I saw that he was older than Gawain as well. Merlyn was some ten years older than I, his brother slightly younger than him. This man had seen at least twenty summers more than I. Winter touched his temples though he still was handsome. His ready smile and appreciative gaze hinted at great virility.

Was he known in this place? Was he a comrade of Merlyn's? I could think of no other reason why he had been admitted to the great hall without my approval—or even my awareness!—and left unattended. To be sure, I know little of such protocol, but one does not build a keep to defend oneself and then let any soul who so chooses wander through the gates.

"My lady Ysabella, I assume," he said, then bowed low at my slight nod. That he knew my name only confirmed my suspicion that he knew Merlyn. His voice was both mellow and rich, not displeasing in the least. He took my hand and bestowed a polite kiss upon its back, his touch lingering in a way that said much of what he thought of the sight of me.

I found his open appreciation bold and untimely, but was most aware of my inexperience of noble courts and manners. And truly, it was a treat to be in the company of a man whose thoughts were easily read.

"You have me at a disadvantage," I said, knowing that color stained my cheeks. "For I have not the luxury of knowing your name."

"Sir Calum Scott of Dunkilber," he said, taking no offense to my relief. "I must say that you are a most pleasant surprise, Lady Ysabella."

"Me?"

"I had expected that you might be a dowager who scowled fiercely at my uninvited presence."

"Even in this festive season?"

"Even then!"

We laughed lightly together as those in social circumstance do, though I wondered how he could not have guessed my age if he were a friend of Merlyn's. Men did not wed women decades older than them—at least men desiring children did not, and Merlyn, judging by his lust abed, had desired an heir.

Or six. I blushed again, my thoughts filled with unexpectedly earthy memories. Calum noted my pinkened cheeks, though his satisfied smile indicated that he thought his own presence responsible.

"And why then are you here, if you were not invited and expected to be spurned as a result?" I asked lightly.

"I came to share my condolences, of course. It is only proper, after all, and one cannot be daunted from duty by what another might say or do." Calum smiled and tucked my hand into his elbow. He led me around the room and we paused as one before each tapestry as if more interested in the work than we were.

"How intriguing that you thought me aged."

"Was Merlyn not aged?"

I laughed. "Hardly that. Did you not know him?"

"We had not the opportunity to meet. I have held Dunkilber for only three years and though I have called here before, the lord has been abroad." He winked at me. "Had I guessed his lady was so fetching, I would have called more diligently."

Ah, so Calum knew nothing of our estranged marriage, perhaps having assumed that I had sometimes traveled with Merlyn. He must be comparatively new to this region. That made matters simpler.

I had a suspicion that Calum was a man much enamored of women's charms, and truth be told, his attention was as a balm to me. It had been long since a man flirted with me, at least a man whose motives were so readily displayed as this one's. Merlyn's squires hovered discretely at the doors, having appeared from some hiding place too late to have halted Calum's arrival. A trio of other boys arrived, wearing

Calum's colors. He nodded in acknowledgment of them and I guessed that they had been ensuring the welfare of his steed.

"I like a woman who is unafraid to share her thoughts," Calum said with great approval. "And I like it well, my lady Ysabella, that we are neighbors now."

"Are we?"

"Surely you know that Dunkilber manor is four miles from here?"

"No, I did not." I had heard once or twice of Dunkilber, though I could not recall in what context. I did not know its location precisely.

I granted him a coy smile, determined to know his motives. I had no doubt that he would tell me. Calum appeared to be the kind of man who held no secrets, whose expression betrayed any attempt to lie and whose heart belied any intent to do so. "Do you come to pledge fealty to me then?" I teased.

He laughed and gallantly pressed a kiss to my knuckles. His lips were dry and firm, his embrace not unpleasant. "Would that I could, fair lady, but my fealty is pledged already to the Earl of March at Dunbar keep." His eyes twinkled merrily as he eyed me over my own hand. "Though there are, admittedly, other kinds of allegiance betwixt men and women."

He meant to flirt and I knew it well. This was a delightful change from those who damned me and spurned me and tried to bend me to their nefarious wills. "Do you mean to court me, sir?" I asked, enjoying myself.

"The mere crook of your finger, lady fair, and I should be so encouraged."

"But I know nothing of you, save that you come to my portal garbed for war. Is it perhaps a different conquest that you seek than that of my heart?"

Calum laughed again, untroubled by my query. "Ah, one hears rumors aplenty when a lord meets an untimely demise.

I knew not what to expect upon my arrival here. Indeed, the earl himself feared that brigands might have seized this place and demanded of me, as the closest of his vassals, to ensure that such a tragedy had not occurred." He bowed slightly. "I come at my lord's bidding, garbed for any eventuality. As I mentioned, my lady, you are a most welcome surprise."

I wondered then whether the earl had a desire for Ravensmuir. His lands lay to the south of those of old Kinfairlie and he had been the earl for many years. He most certainly would have been earl when Merlyn's father had been seeking a buyer for his mysterious relic.

I resolved to send the earl a message, by way of this affable knight. I smiled but spoke with resolve. "Ravensmuir was bequeathed to me by my spouse and the deed so inscribed is safely within my care. My lord Merlyn and I had a legal match and an enduring one—let no man contest the truth of it."

"I can well imagine that a man would be happy with such a comely bride." Calum's eyes gleamed, though he spoke with care. "But be warned, my lady, these parts are not devoid of men who seize what they desire to be their own. Your keep lies between those of two powerful men, and the balance betwixt the two has changed with Scotland's change of king."

"Indeed?"

"Indeed. William, Earl of Douglas, whose holding lies north of here at Tantallon, has risen to favor with the newly crowned King Robert II, while George, Earl of March, who abides at Dunbar keep to the south, has lost his regal ally in the death of King David II. You are caught betwixt the pan and the fire, my lady, and solely Ravensmuir's lack of tithes will keep these great men at bay."

He glanced around the hall with an assessing eye. "Though Ravensmuir does not seem to lack for wealth despite its dearth of tilled fields and diligent peasants. Beware, my lady fair, for there will be those seeking both this holding and the source of its revenue."

I interpreted that as a warning against his lord's intentions. "I thank you for your counsel."

Calum's voice softened further and his expression turned somber. "But if you find yourself beset, if you have need to defend this keep against the desires of others, know that you may call upon me."

"Even against your liege lord, the earl?"

Calum smiled. "Surely Beauty, my lady most fair, and Justice are the greatest liege lords of all?"

And he kissed me, most audaciously, upon my very lips. I was surprised, but he was very quick and I had no chance to retreat. His embrace was not abhorrent, though it could not compare to Merlyn's own.

I did not pull away—when I might have done so, it occurred to me that I might have need of alliance. I took his warning to heart and kissed him back as boldly as he kissed me.

A warrior and his attendant skills might serve me well, after all, when my spouse could not be summoned from Hades on demand. And a kiss, however boldly initiated, was a small token to encourage a military man's support.

Is boldness not a most desirable trait in a knight?

We spent the morning together, Calum and I, and he offered a most enchanting diversion. It was clear that he hungered for feminine companionship and he made more than one hint that he sought a bride. It seemed that wealth and security had come relatively late to his hand—I did not enquire as to the reasons for that, as matters had been most unsettled locally in recent decades and it was surely no reflection upon him—and he chafed now to take a wife.

I was somewhat irked, you might be certain, that my sister did not deign to appear. Here was a man anxious for a wife and an allegiance to Ravensmuir, but Mavella slept opportunity away!

Ada admitted at midday that Fitz had taken Tynan and Mavella upon a tour of the keep and bailey. This news not only set any worries I might have had at ease, but gave me the chance to tell Calum of them.

Calum was charming, and he might prove to be useful. Here was a man unburdened with secrets and mysteries, a man who was exactly as he appeared to be. Simple men have their allure, especially when contrasted with creatures like Merlyn. He told me of his adventures while we shared a simple midday meal, and to my relief, he did not comment upon the meager offerings at my table.

In fact, he offered me counsel in the finding of assistance, clucking his tongue all the while over the mismanagement practiced by the Lammergeier family. He seemed to assume that I had lived abroad while my husband ran this holding without a woman's helpful touch. It was interesting to be regarded as an exotic, fragile creature from across the seas, especially for me, who had always been assumed to be sturdy, common, and resilient.

To my delight, Mavella joined us at the gates when Calum was taking his leave. She was radiant in the sapphire kirtle and Calum's eyes lit at the sight of her.

It would be an ideal solution for the two to wed—Calum would have his bride, Mavella would have a pleasant spouse, and we all would have a warrior and his army to defend our gates in the short term. It would be perfect.

Calum rode away after much fulsome praise of the two of us and many blushes upon Mavella's part. He himself made many a lingering backward glance. His squires had gathered outside the gates to await him, and now rode in his wake, kicking up dust as they galloped down Ravensmuir's road.

"Where is Tynan?" I asked, as we waved farewell.

Mavella sighed. "He wished to see the horses again but I had need of a respite."

"From his endless questions?"

"From the sight of Fitz bleeding the horses." Mavella grimaced. "Did you know that it was a tradition upon Saint Stephen's Day to do as much, for their health in the year ahead?"

"No. But Saint Stephen's Day was yesterday."

Mavella sighed. "Fitz said that today would serve well enough, as none had done it yesterday."

"It cannot be harmful. That brute stallion seems vigorous enough."

Mavella rolled her eyes. "He did not take kindly to the procedure, I can assure you. To witness more of that labor was not for me."

"I am certain that Tynan is enthralled."

We shared a smile.

"Indeed he is. Did ever you know that he could run so fast? And he asks so many questions of Fitz that the poor man barely has time to reply!"

I laughed, delighted that both of my siblings were so lively again. "Perhaps he will sleep early this night."

"Ah, you dream, sister mine." Mavella flicked her skirts. "Look, I have marked the hem in our visit to the stables. Just as I assured you, the gown is too long." She wrinkled her nose, then her expression turned mischievous. "Though I do not wish to remove this glorious gown for even the time required to clean and hem it."

I snapped my fingers. "Then you shall have another."

"Oh, my lady is most indulgent." Mavella gave a bow so elaborate that she lost her balance and nearly tripped over her luxurious hem. I had to seize her arm to keep her from falling, no small feat once we two began to laugh.

"Calum is charming, is he not?" I asked.

Mavella sobered immediately. "He is old, Ysabella."

"Oh, do not be so coy! His eye landed upon you. You could do worse than to wed a knight with a manor to his name."

Mavella's voice softened. "I do not care what a man holds. I care solely whether I hold his heart."

"Then, win Calum's."

She stared after him and shook her head. "I am not convinced that men of war have tender hearts, let alone that they could surrender the advantage of them to another." She looked suddenly so saddened that I knew she recalled her lost Alasdair.

I gave her a hug, hoping to encourage her to trust another man with her affections. "If any woman could soften the heart of a knight, it would be you. Now, you know there are a dozen gowns in that trunk. Come choose two or three."

"I shall let you choose. I shall ask Ada for a needle and thread that we might shorten this hem. Already I have shown that I am not wrought for leisure!" We laughed together. Mavella headed for the kitchen with purpose and I strode to the solar.

My footsteps echoed as I hastened through the hall—which seemed more achingly empty since Calum's departure—but the Yule log crackled and cast a heartening light. I decided this hall had need of guests and music to be at its best, and began to wonder how I might ensure that such a solution came about.

A wedding, of course, would be a hearty beginning.

I anticipated a leisurely afternoon of chatting with Mavella, ensuring that she would be garbed to perfection when next she met Calum of Dunkilber. I climbed to the solar and stopped short at the summit of the stairs, my smile fading.

Merlyn stood within the chamber, arms folded across his chest, his irked gaze fixed upon me.

Merlyn's eyes were dark, a stormy hue that hinted at troubled seas ahead for me. He arched a brow when our gazes met, though he said naught. He clearly had been waiting for me and my heart lunged for my throat.

The room was falling dark already, only one lantern lit to dispel the wintery shadows. The light gilded Merlyn's features but I could not guess his thoughts with any exactitude.

He was annoyed, I thought because of our parting this morning. Why it should have angered him so vigorously only now was beyond my comprehension—but then, so was much of Merlyn.

He wore a black tunic marked in silver with his family insignia, black chausses and tall black boots. An indigo cloak that fell to his ankles was held upon one shoulder with that fine golden clasp, wrought in the shape of the family bird, and the silver fur lining shimmered slightly when he moved.

Merlyn's garb was somber compared to that of the knight who had just departed—he looked wrought of shadow and as inclined to fade to nothing as a shadow could be. I could not, in this moment, imagine how or why I had thought his vigor diminished in the caverns the day before.

He was indomitable once again.

His voice was low when he spoke. "Have you changed your thinking? Do you intend to aid me?"

I shook my head, shaken to silence by my sudden fear that he meant to leave.

And yes, by my unexpected desire for him. He noted the change in my garb, for his gaze swept over me, but I was disappointed that I could read no responding heat in his eyes. I hoped, for a foolish moment, that he intended to sweep me into the bed and persuade me to his view.

But Merlyn donned his gloves, his lips drawn to a taut line. "I suspected as much. Know that I have seen fit to persuade you to share my view, chère."

His manner frightened me. "And what is that to mean?"

Without further explanation, he strode across the room and lifted one hand to the wall. The wood panel there slid back at his touch, revealing a gaping entry on the far side of the bed.

"This keep is a veritable warren," I muttered, "riddled with holes from top to bottom."

"My family oft have need of discreet arrivals and departures."

"I can well imagine that vermin must oft escape the witnesses of their deeds."

"While you are entirely innocent, chère?" His was not truly a question, though his tone was surprisingly harsh. "I think not."

"And what is that to mean?"

"You seem to have wasted no time in finding a suitor for your hand, and indeed, you expend little time in the courtship. Clearly you make haste to end your days as a widow." Merlyn spat the words and I saw now the reason for his annoyance. "Perhaps it is timely for me to depart, so that you can share this bed without fear of interruption."

I propped my hands upon my hips, unwilling to give him any hint of my intent. "While you have been chaste all these years? What of all those merry wenches who would have been disappointed if I had still been in your bed?"

"I gave them nothing," he said fiercely.

"Save a child or two?" I was guessing, hoping for a morsel of news about his doings, though I dared not examine why. I certainly was not jealous of any woman who caught Merlyn's eye!

Just as he could not be jealous of Calum. No, he simply preferred to control my every decision and I knew that he had not invited our guest.

His eyes flashed now as he gestured at me. "Do you intend to wed and bestow Ravensmuir's seal upon another before I can prove that I live?"

"And what if I did?" I demanded, annoyed that his sole care was for Ravensmuir. "I shall take a thousand lovers and grant them each a stone of this hall, if only to vex you!"

Merlyn advanced upon me, shaking a heavy finger. "You will not!"

"Suddenly you have a care for me, but only because another man shows his desire, only because Ravensmuir is at stake." I tossed back my hair and glared at him, for he stood directly before me now. That familiar heat rose between us. My blood was a-boil, as it had not been all of this day in Calum's company. "You have a curious way of persuading a woman to take your cause, Merlyn."

"And what way would you prefer?" he purred.

He eased closer and I could smell the heat of him. My heart was racing and I tingled from head to toe, every increment of my flesh screaming for his touch. Oh, we had loved once after we had argued over some petty nonsense and I will never forget the majestic fury of that mating.

I could think of nothing else in that moment, nothing but Merlyn's burning kisses and his heat within me, nothing but the way we had rolled and bit and tormented each other to greater heights. Indeed, I was blushing, my cheeks were burning, my nipples taut and my fists clenched. It seemed to me that he too recalled that fiery coupling, for his eyes were darker than dark, as if he burned with a secret desire.

Then he suddenly looked away. "I have no time for this," he muttered and stepped toward the shadowed portal.

Oh! I would not be a mere inconvenience!

"Hiding your thoughts from me, cher?" I whispered audaciously.

Merlyn froze on the lip of the chasm and looked back at me, his expression grim. "You accuse me of lying to you about my trade, so you would wed another man in haste, knowing less of him than you knew of me. You learn little from your errors, Ysabella."

I noticed that again he ceased to call me his chère. Indeed, he bit out my name as if it burned his tongue.

"Who spoke of marriage? The man came to meet his neighbor."

"And offered a kiss upon the mouth, so early as this? A kiss that was not merely accepted but returned with enthusiasm?" Merlyn clucked his tongue chidingly. "It is either marriage or relations abed without a priest's blessing that you offer your neighbor."

"You watched!" I gasped, then lunged after him.

Merlyn caught my chin in his hand, his eyes glittering. "You may be certain that I am watching you. When my own fate relies so heavily upon your choices I can do little else. And when you make such poor choices as to trust a man of the ilk of Calum Scott, then you have need of a watchful eye upon you."

"You insult the man's character solely out of jealousy!"

"I warn you, chère."

"Not to favor any man but you. Aye, I understand that well enough, Merlyn Lammergeier, and still I will do whatsoever I desire." I pushed his patience and I knew it well, but mine was nigh expired. "You are dead, husband mine, and a widow must assure her future among the living."

Merlyn's eyes narrowed but not quickly enough that I didn't note the familiar spark in their depths. His thumb moved persuasively across my jawline, a new note coloring the mingled heat of our breath. His next words rumbled low in his chest.

"Tell me," he whispered, his voice dark, "how does his kiss compare with mine?"

I said nothing, but held his regard defiantly, hoping with all my heart and soul.

And it was but a moment before I had my desire, before Merlyn claimed my lips with all the possessive ardor I had hoped he would. He drove the taste of Calum from me and deluged my senses with himself, solely himself. There was no comparison and he knew it well—he had witnessed Calum's tepid embrace, after all.

When he eventually lifted his head, we both were disheveled and short of breath. He pressed his gloved thumb against my lips before I could comment and his words were rough. "Do not lie to me that his kiss burned brighter than mine. I *know* this truth."

I took a ragged breath and pulled away. "You will not persuade me to do your will, not with mere kisses."

Merlyn smiled a smile that fed my distrust. "Which is why I have taken the liberty of granting you some encouragement."

Too late I was suspicious, too late I recalled his earlier warning. "What manner of encouragement?"

"Have you seen the boy this afternoon?" Merlyn asked with false innocence, then snapped his fingers as if in recollection. "No, of course, you were *entertaining* a guest."

I snatched at his sleeve in fear. "What have you done with Tynan, Merlyn? Tell me!"

Merlyn smiled his most wicked smile. "I have invited him upon an adventure and he, intrepid boy that he is, has accepted."

I was stunned.

He watched me avidly, noting every detail of my response.

"You have stolen him." I met his gaze, incredulous. "What will you do to him if I fail to follow your bidding?"

Merlyn turned away. "It matters little what I would do,"

he said with surprising heat. "It matters only what you *believe* I might do."

I knew then a terror greater than any I have ever tasted. "I beg of you, Merlyn, do not involve the boy in your schemes. I will do anything . . ."

"Now, you would make a wager." He shook his head, appearing much saddened by my choices. "It is clear that I found the correct means of encouraging you, when simple trust would not suffice."

"How could I trust you, after all I know of you?"

"You know nothing of me," he growled, then flung me away from him in annoyance. He strode down the stairs half hidden by shadows, even the echo of his boots fading in no time at all. I leaned out into the hidden stairwell, smelling dampness and darkness and goodness knows what, my heart hammering.

"Merlyn!" I shouted.

The fading echo of his boots on stone was my only reply.

Whether by accident or design, Merlyn had left the portal agape. In any other circumstance, I would not have pursued him into the blackness. But Tynan's life was at stake. My own fears of the dark were as nothing compared to my need to protect my brother.

Worse, time was of the essence. I seized the lantern and lifted it high, my heart fluttering in terror at what I must do. I gritted my teeth, swallowed my rising bile, and stepped into the darkness in pursuit.

I had descended but six steps when a gust of wind buffeted me. It smelled strongly of salt and sea, but I was more concerned that it gutted the lantern flame.

I was plunged into menacing shadows.

I cried out and stumbled up the stairs in retreat, racing toward the light emanating from the solar. But I touched the rim of the opening en route and inadvertently hit a lever of some kind. The portal slid back into place with a swish. Despite my scrabbling fingers and my terror, it clicked resolutely into place.

The darkness closed around me like a shroud. My heart nigh stopped. I felt around the perimeter of the door with wild hands, but found only smooth wood and stone. This added to my frenzy and my fear. I hammered upon the door and shouted, careless that I might reveal Merlyn's secrets in my own desire to be rescued.

But none answered. And who would even hear me? The solar was separated from the hall, Mavella was with Ada in the kitchens and too far away to hear my cries. The squires were undoubtedly in the kitchens or with the steeds. Fitz was complicit with Merlyn and Tynan was gone.

I was trapped.

I smelled my own perspiration, as before, and felt the chill of it on my flesh. I shook like a leaf in the autumn wind and my breath came in uneven gulps. I settled against the door and whimpered like a child despite my efforts to control myself.

It was blacker than black, my prospects no less dark. I was trapped in the labyrinth of tunnels of Ravensmuir, with only one hope of escape: my unpredictable and wicked spouse.

"Merlyn!" I screamed, but there was no reply.

Of course not. For all I knew, he had planned this situation to weaken my resistance to his scheme. He had done as much the day before.

There was nothing for it. I would have to seek him out.

Trembling in terror, I felt my way down the hidden stone staircase, knowing full well that I would never find my way free alone. I had to find Merlyn.

Worse, I had to rely upon Merlyn's chivalry, without the conviction that he had any.

I do not know how long I was trapped alone in those caverns. I know only that it felt like an eternity. I could smell my own sweat and taste my own terror. I scraped my hands upon the stone and stumbled more than once upon the hem of my lavish kirtle.

I often felt the sudden space of other openings yawning to one side of me or the other as I descended and I tried to choose my course with some hope of retracing it. I inclined always downward, for I guessed that was the direction of Merlyn's escape. It grew damper and colder with every step that I took and I began to fear that I had chosen wrongly.

I shouted for Merlyn at intervals. There was no response. I pursued him despite my fear and my growing conviction that I descended closer to hell and further from safety with every step.

I fell when I did not guess a staircase yawned before me. I screamed as I tumbled down half a dozen steps. The twisting nature of those tunnels saved me, for I landed against a wall with a thud and this was what halted my fall. I leaned back against the cold stone, shaken and shaking. Emptiness loomed to my right.

I had scraped my knee sufficiently to tear my stocking and draw blood. The wound was warm and wet on my fingers when I felt for damage, the viscous heat of it sickening me.

I rose on trembling legs and continued my course. Once I descended that twisting and irregular staircase, the walls opened wide with an abruptness that startled me. I reached out but my hands grasped at emptiness in every direction. I knew I stood in a cavern, one which threw my own calls back at me mockingly.

Was I beneath Ravensmuir? Under the courtyard? Or had

I descended to some grotto near the ocean? I could not say and could not retrace my steps.

I might be lost here forever.

Or until I starved.

Or worse. What other creatures shared this space with me? Did some demon watch me with sharper vision than my own?

Terror assailed me there, in that cavern occupied by creatures that I could not see. I fancied that spiders crawled upon my flesh, that snakes coiled about my feet, that the rock above me would fall in a sudden crash and entomb me alive.

I fled in the direction I thought I had come, but collided with a solid stone wall that seemed endless to both left and right. This loosed a frenzy in me and one wilder than what I had endured thus far. No doubt I had simply turned the wrong way and was but a few feet from my objective, but fear paralyzed my thinking.

I pounded upon the stone until my fists bled, nigh insensible in my terror. I scratched at it with my nails. I kicked at it, certain a door was hidden behind it, I tried to climb up it. I whimpered and I cried and I shrieked, not caring how witless I appeared for there were none there to see. Something soft brushed my fingertips, perhaps a spider or its web, and I shrieked like a madwoman, so certain was I that Death in some horrible guise had found me.

And then I heard it. A footfall resonating on stone. I thought that the first was a figment of my imagination.

The second made me wish that it was. I was immediately convinced that some creature consigned to darkness stalked me.

The third persuaded me that my fate was sealed. I knew that I would be tormented and no doubt devoured by this nameless beast, but still I tried to escape.

I gasped in relief when I found an opening in the rock face. I lunged through it, not caring where the path led. I raced along the uneven corridor, tripping and stumbling, weeping in fear and scattering small stones noisily as I fled.

To no avail. The creature pursued me with relentless determination, its footsteps echoing behind me with terrifying regularity. It did not stumble, it did not waver. It followed me as surely as a hungry dog follows a sack of bones.

The corridor terminated so abruptly that I ran directly into the wall at its end. I bit my lip in so doing and tasted my own blood, but my hands were working feverishly across the surface. The footsteps echoed more loudly behind me with every passing moment.

No one would build a corridor that led nowhere. I could not have found a dead end, especially as this ending would lead to my own demise.

But I did not find a portal before the demon's breath sounded close behind me. I spun and braced my back against the wall, searching the shadows for some hint of my assailant. I could faintly discern the outline of an enormous creature that walked upon its hinds. Wings spread behind it and its eyes glinted.

I understood in a flash. The Lammergeier kept one of their namesake birds entombed beneath the keep! This was the dark secret of Ravensmuir. This explained the departure of the ravens—they had known the predator would be loosed and had fled for their own survival.

The beast lifted claws toward me and the last of my sensibility snapped. I screamed, covering my face with my hands as I cowered against the stone.

"Do not hurt me, I beg of you, I will do anything . . ." My protest became so much nonsense as the beast seized me with those harsh claws. I whimpered and struggled, even trying to bite its grip.

"Chère," Merlyn whispered as he gave my shoulders a shake. "What have I ever done to make you fear me so?"

I choked. I froze. It took me a long moment to comprehend that it was Merlyn who held me, not some foul creature.

"Chère?" He shook me again, concern more evident in his tone.

"Merlyn!" I am ashamed to recount that I clutched my spouse. Indeed, I almost fainted against his chest. He closed his arms tightly around me and sheltered me against his warmth. I could make no sense of his presence in my troubled state, even though I had ventured this far solely to find him.

"You called me," he whispered, and stroked my hair as one reassures a child awakened by a nightmare. "Did you not think I would heed you?"

"No. Why should you begin now?" I shuddered and burrowed my face against his chest.

Merlyn chuckled, his humor silenced when his hand slid up my throat. He meant to cup my chin, I knew this gesture of his well, but he hesitated when the wild flutter of my pulse was beneath his hand.

"You are truly terrified," he said, marvel in his voice. "I always thought that you feared nothing at all."

"Only darkness," I admitted in my weakened state, knowing even then that I would regret it. "Only caves."

I shuddered once more and his embrace tightened protectively. I felt his response to my presence then and it reassured me greatly that Merlyn found me alluring even in my terror.

"Yet you risk your deepest fear to save the boy from me." There was consideration in his tone, consideration I should have known not to trust. "You think poorly of me indeed."

I chose not to review his crimes in this moment, for I had

need of his aid. "He can be no pawn between us, Merlyn. Leave the boy alone, I beg of you. Do your worst to me, but do not involve Tynan."

I felt his gaze upon me and it was long before he spoke. "Do you wish to return to the solar?" he asked, disregarding my plea.

"Tynan?"

Merlyn traced my cheek with his fingertip and no doubt noticed how I trembled. "You care greatly for his welfare, perhaps more than one would expect."

"Perhaps in your family but not in mine. He is my blood! Tynan is the last vestige we have of my mother and to be bereft of them both would be too high a price." My words were anxious, hasty. "I could not bear to lose him."

Merlyn's tone turned chiding. "I do not intend for you to lose him, chère."

I had no chance to ask what he meant. He claimed my hand then and strode back the way we had come, his pace sure. He knew every crook of that corridor, every place where I might stumble. Though he set a brisk pace, he warned me of each hazard and caught my elbow when I fell too far behind him. He guided me with a confidence I could only envy.

All this Merlyn did with no lantern—either he knew the labyrinth as well as his own hand, or he could see in the dark, like so many birds of prey. I realized now that what I had mistaken for wings was his cloak, for it flared behind him as he walked.

I breathed more easily when we began to climb the stairs, ascending as we did toward light and what I fancied to be salvation. Merlyn was fast behind me, ensuring that I could not stumble backward, yet quick to tell me of every twist and turn. One hand he kept upon my waist and there was not much distance between us, another fact which greatly reassured me.

Though reassurance and gratitude were not the only

things I felt. With each step we took toward the solar and every breath that smelled less of sea and more of keep, my desire for Merlyn also increased. I liked the weight of his hand upon my back, I liked his surety, I liked his protectiveness. I liked that he took me back to the light and I liked the heat awakened in me by his presence. I wanted to reward him abed for proving to be more chivalrous than my expectation. I wanted to reward myself for surviving—I wanted to feel utterly alive.

I could not fight my instinctive response, nor did I dare to trust it. At least, not until Merlyn returned Tynan to me.

Merlyn, mercifully oblivious to my musings, paused before a smooth wall. Sadly I could not see what precisely he did. The panel slid back with a click as it had before, and the solar was before us again. I stepped over the threshold with undisguised relief.

Merlyn lingered in the shadows, watching me carefully. "Your terror is not feigned."

I was indignant. "How can you suggest such a thing?"

"I certainly cannot believe it, not given the sight of you."

I looked down and nearly wept at the damage I had done to the fine gown. It was not only soiled beyond repair, but it had torn when I had tripped. I lifted the hem and found both stocking and knee crusted with blood, then raised a hand to my throbbing lip and found blood there too.

I met Merlyn's gaze incredulously.

He smiled with a warmth unexpected. "Such small wounds will all heal readily enough, chère, and the gown is of no import. It can be replaced. I am glad that I found you before you did greater damage to yourself." He might have turned away, but I pursued him, snatching his sleeve.

"Merlyn! What of Tynan?"

"I am reassured—" he paused to study me and I dared to hope "—that the means I chose to ensure your assistance was the most effective one. Indeed, it appears to be a better guarantee of your aid than I had imagined."

My heart stopped in horror. "No! You must release him!"

"Must I?"

I took an unsteady breath and held fast to his sleeve, knowing I would have only one chance to persuade him, hearing my words tumble over each other in my haste to be heard. "Merlyn, you made a confession to me this day; now I shall make one to you. I shall tell you of my deepest fear."

"Darkness?"

"No. Even that is nothing compared to the terror that has tormented me these past years. These years in Kinfairlie, my greatest fear was that Tynan, so clever, so handsome, so well wrought, would be destroyed by our circumstance. I dreaded every day and every night that he might die young, I dreaded every winter that he might not survive until spring, and yes, I feared that it would be my fault. I feared that by one choice I made in ignorance of his pending arrival, I would condemn him."

My tears began to fall, but still I dared not halt my confession. "He had no father. He had no mother. I could not donate him to a monastic order as an oblate to save his life, because I had insufficient coin with which to secure his place. You know as well as I that such favors must be bought.

"And so I did what little I could. I gave him the lion's share of the meat, and I brewed ale until the bones nigh broke through the flesh of my fingers. When I took this burn from the mash, I went directly back to the kettle without a pause. I made whatever wagers I had to make to see something on our board each day and a roof over our heads each night. I found every measure of strength that I needed in the sweet innocence of his face."

I took a shuddering breath, well aware of Merlyn's attentive silence. "And yes, I lied for Tynan. Every lie that ever I have told has been for the sake of Tynan, whatever you believe to the contrary, and I would tell each and every one of them again without hesitation. I would tell them twice! I would give my soul for Tynan, and that without regret."

I could not look up at Merlyn. "Even as his presence has given me hope and joy, Merlyn, I have feared for him. It is true that this burden made me more harsh, as you mentioned, for it is not easy to watch those you love suffer and pay the price for your choice."

My tears rose to choke me but I continued doggedly. "It is not easy to know that the chance you had to trade your soul for their comfort is gone. It is not easy to know that it is too late to repair the damage you have wrought yourself."

I stepped away from him and stood straight. "My first instinct was to decline the legacy you left to me, but I accepted Ravensmuir for the sake of Tynan. I accepted it that he might have a future, that he might have a chance. Tynan would not have grown up as he had, if you had not deceived me as you had. It seemed fitting to me, when Fitz brought the news, that your death would redress the balance."

We stared at each other across the chamber and my voice dropped to a hoarse whisper. "Do not take Tynan, Merlyn. Do not sacrifice the life that I have labored to save." I felt my throat work. "Do not be so cruel as this."

A shadow crossed Merlyn's features and I was certain that I had swayed him to my side. "Your love is fierce, chère," he said softly, a suspicious shimmer in his eyes. He shook his head, as if marveling at me, and his next words were hoarse. "What child could not grow straight beneath the shelter of such a love? What child could not be blessed simply from knowing such devotion in his life?"

I clutched at Merlyn's strong fingers, needing to know the truth. "Then tell me that you will not take him."

Merlyn lifted my hand to his lips and kissed my palm. He moved slowly, as if burdened by a tremendous sorrow. I assumed this was because he knew his thinking to have been wrong, because he regretted his choice.

But his words, when finally he spoke, tore my very heart in two. "It is out of your hands, chère. You had best make your peace with that."

I was stunned.

As I stared at him in silent shock, a voice carried from the stairs to the chamber below. "Ysabella?"

Merlyn lifted a finger to his lips. In a heartbeat, he was gone and the panel was closed, as if he had never been before me, as if he was no more substantial than a nightmare.

I pivoted in time to see my sister's fair hair appear in the stairwell, her head bent as she gave full attention to her footing.

"Those steps are narrow enough to be a menace," she began with a smile, then sobered when she saw me. "What has happened to you?"

"Me?" I was tempted, sorely tempted, to break my vow to Merlyn and tell Mavella all I knew. But he had crippled me with only part of his own tale and I had heard enough this day to know that matters could be entirely different than I believed. I did not know what havoc I might wreak with such a confession.

I could not guess what price Tynan might be compelled to pay if I broke my pledge to Merlyn.

Mavella tsk-tsk'd, oblivious to the chaos of my thoughts. "Your lip is cut and your knee is bleeding."

"I fell," I lied. "Upon those very stairs." I feigned dizziness, feeling somewhat weak in the knees in truth. "I must have hit my head."

Mavella rushed to my side, taking my hand in hers, her eyes widening. "But you are filthy, as well!"

"I suppose Ada has not cleaned the corners of late."

She seized my elbow as if I were an invalid. "Come, sit on the bed. Let me tend to you . . ."

And so my sister was easily distracted from the evidence that did not entirely mesh with my hastily concocted tale. I was sickened, not only by my failure to retrieve Tynan but the fact that I told my sister a new lie.

It was Merlyn Lammergeier who made a liar of me, as always it had been, Merlyn whose deeds trapped me in a web of falsehoods that grew ever tighter around me.

We were in the hall, much later, before Mavella noticed Tynan's absence. The boy never missed a meal, even at home, and Ravensmuir's board tempted him to something akin to gluttony.

"Rhys Fitzwilliam has taken him with him on a journey to a neighboring keep," Ada informed my sister sourly. I had only a moment to wonder whether the tale was her own concoction or the one told to her before my sister touched my arm.

"But how? But why?" Mavella's grip tightened when I dropped my gaze, damning myself by my inability to hold her eye. "You knew of this!"

Yet again Merlyn's choices made a liar of me. I could not tell the truth without potentially endangering Tynan.

I shrugged, sickened by my part in this. "Tynan wished to learn to ride." It was the best explanation I could concoct so quickly as that.

My sister was incredulous. "But alone, with Fitz, a man we have not seen in years? How do we know that he will heed Fitz's instructions—and that Fitz knows much of boys? And riding? Ysabella, he could be sorely injured." She seized my hand, her gaze searching mine. "We have never been parted since Tynan's birth. What compelled you to this choice?"

I had to look away. "Your tale of bleeding the horses

made me realize it was time he lingered with men, instead of solely in the company of women." I spoke as calmly as I could manage. "He is becoming a man himself, Mavella, and must know of things we cannot teach him."

She folded her hands together tightly at that, her expression prim. She did not approve, I knew this, just as I knew that the greater part of her disapproval was caused by what she saw as my failure to include her in my decision.

But she did not know that it had not been *my* decision.

As I picked at my meal, I wished with all my heart and soul that I truly was a witch. That way, I might raise my hand in the old hex and know that I would have restitution from my husband's sorry hide.

I ate little that night and slept less. The food was as sawdust in my mouth. There was no chatter between Mavella and myself, though she turned the occasional weighty glance of accusation upon me.

I was heartsick, and my sense of ill only increased once I returned to my chamber alone. My confidence eroded badly when Merlyn did not appear, for it was evidence that he had left Ravensmuir in truth, and thus I fretted the night away. Where had they gone?

What would Merlyn do to Tynan?

I had my answer in the early hours of the morning, as unwelcome as it was. My restlessness had brought me to the great hall. I looked across the sea beyond the courtyard, seeking answers in the dance of the moonlight upon the waves.

The sea sparkled, silvered by the caress of the moon's light, and rolled as the tide retreated. My gaze rested repeatedly upon the dark silhouette of the ship anchored offshore, the ship that Ada claimed had brought Merlyn to Ravensmuir. I had an inkling of an idea then, but there was no time for a plan to form in my addled thoughts.

The sails began to unfurl. I did not believe my eyes. I blinked and stared, but I made no mistake. It was as if a shadowy crew stole the ship by the night, but I knew that Merlyn would never permit such a deed.

As I watched, transfixed and powerless, the sails billowed and swelled. Slowly, silently, as if snared in a dream, the ship began to sail to the east. I watched the ship depart upon the tide, powerless to halt its course.

With startling clarity, I understood. Merlyn had ensured that I could neither retrieve Tynan nor argue further with him. My husband had stolen my brother and sailed away.

I cried out as I clutched the sill. I knew then that I might never see Tynan again. The sea, after all, is a perilous mistress, one that could seize an unexpected toll even if Merlyn had chosen to let the boy live. And I had no faith that my husband would make such a choice.

I had failed Tynan utterly, failed to protect him, failed to ensure his safety, failed to keep him fast by my side. I had failed in the only responsibility of consequence that I had ever been granted.

Worse, there was nothing I could do to repair the matter. It was my darkest fear brought to life.

A cold resolve settled within me as the ship faded out of sight. I took a deep breath and straightened with newfound purpose. There was one thing I could do. I would solve the riddle Merlyn had set before me.

I was not consoled that my decision was precisely as Merlyn had intended it to be. I could have hated him anew, but instead, Merlyn's tale of his father came unbidden to me. Indeed, my spouse had learned early that the only way to ensure that someone did your bidding was to leave that person no other alternatives.

It was bittersweet to see that I could have shown Merlyn

otherwise and averted the hardship Tynan would be forced to bear.

It was bitter to realize that I had been my spouse's sole chance of reform only as Merlyn left my side, perhaps forever.

December 28

The Feast of Holy Innocents
"Childermas Day"

VIII

There must be a rule, writ somewhere, that once one makes an enemy of another soul, one will eventually require that very person's aid in some critical undertaking. As the sun turned morning's skies to brilliant blue, I realized that the key in solving Merlyn's riddle might be held by Ada Gowan.

I would have to solicit her assistance.

I grit my teeth and donned my old blue kirtle, hoping that Ada might be more inclined to confide in me if I dressed as if I had just come from the village. It was a slender hope, as we had never been confidantes, but my wearing the elegant garb of my new station was fairly certain to raise her ire.

I could not guess how Merlyn would know when I completed the task he set before me, but he was not a man who left loose ends. Perhaps Fitz lurked in the shadows with some means of sending word to his master. Perhaps Merlyn meant to return after some specified time. It mattered little—I would complete this task in haste to ensure that Tynan was returned as quickly as possible.

I combed and braided my hair, then made my way to the kitchens. If I did not hasten, it was because I was undecided how best to approach the matter.

Ada charted my course.

She straightened, her eyes flicking fire, then turned her back upon me. "If you have come for your pledge of fealty, then it will have to wait until the bread is baking and the meat is upon the spit," she said by way of greeting. "Or the

fine nobles of this abode will find the board bare at midday,
my lady." The title she spat, though I expected little else.

I seated myself beside the table smoothed by years of use
and arranged my skirts as if untroubled. "I can wait for your
attentiveness, though I have come for another matter altogether."

She spared me a suspicious glance, though it was clear
that her curiosity was awakened. "And what might that be?"

I smiled serenely. "I should not wish to disturb you from
your tasks, Ada. Tell me, is there any aid I might offer to
you?"

She was in the midst of cutting fat from a hind of venison
but fairly slammed the knife onto the board at my offer. "Oh,
I see how your plan unfolds, you need have no fear of that!
You sweetly offer aid, then will find fault with me for not
managing this household myself. You will not send me from
the gates, but will humiliate me first, laying too many burdens upon my shoulders then blaming me for my own inability to complete them all. I see the workings of your
mind, Ysabella, and you do not fool me."

She snatched up the knife and waved it under my nose,
her malice washing over me in waves. "But I shall thwart
you, this you shall see. I shall fulfill every one of my responsibilities and you will have no cause for complaint, no
charge to make against my services. You will not have the
best of me!"

It was on my lips to ask why she cared to prove herself instead of simply leaving, but I realized that Ada might have
as much need of me as I had need of her.

Perhaps she had no other place to go. Certainly if she had
directed her venom at others as she had with my small family, the hills might be rife with her enemies.

I chose not to pursue that matter, just as I did not comment upon the sudden appearance of a full hind. No doubt
she intended this meat for Merlyn's return—and now, it
would only spoil if not cooked. I guessed that she granted

me the leavings, and only prepared such a roast because she had no choice.

"Surely Merlyn would have allowed you to have a village lass or two to aid you?"

"I have no need of prying eyes and loose tongues around my kitchen, of that you may be certain."

Her brother shouldered his way through the door to the bailey, burdened with firewood. Ada hastened to his side to direct him. At her command, Arnulf set to stacking the wood beside the hearth, his gaze straying repeatedly to me. I ignored him, though it was uncomfortably silent until he completed his task and left. I plucked a dried fig from the bowl there and made much of eating the luxurious treat.

Ada's lip curled as she watched me. "Savor your pleasures while you can, Ysabella."

"What is that to mean?"

"You are no more a noblewoman than I, indeed even less so. This will not endure."

"I am not the first to elevate my circumstance by marriage, and the fact remains that Ravensmuir's seal and deed both rest in my care."

Too late I recalled that I had left Merlyn's box in the solar, though I had locked the door behind myself and I wore the cord with the key. As Ada's eyes gleamed, I wondered how many keys to that chamber there might be.

Perhaps Merlyn's warning had not been a vain one.

Ada grimly stirred up the coals and hefted the meat onto the spit, then placed the spit over the fire. She turned the spit, watching as the flames seared the outside of the roast. The meat sputtered and sizzled, the fat hissed as it fell.

I forced myself to be conciliatory. "You can have aid in the kitchens, Ada, if you desire it."

"And you will enjoy that you can accuse me of becoming old and feeble and incompetent."

"I will enjoy that those beneath my hand are not overly burdened."

"Perhaps I like the burden," she retorted. "Perhaps it is not so much more work to have you and your sister here than my lord Merlyn and his manservant." She spared me another knowing glance. "Perhaps you will not remain here any longer than they ever did."

I bent my attention upon the figs though I was intrigued by her inference. If I showed too much interest, Ada would confide nothing simply to vex me. "I thought Merlyn had not been here in five years."

Ada laughed, and it was a harsh sound. "You think he cannot have been here, because he did not seek you out! He was here, though it will not do your pride any favor to know of it."

"I could hardly be insulted if he came but once and for so short duration that he could not make his way to Kinfairlie village." My heart was pounding as I said this so very idly.

Ada turned, eyes flashing. "He came more than once!" she cried, triumphant. "And each time, he remained for a fortnight, if not more. That was more than ample time to get himself to Kinfairlie village, if he had so desired."

She leaned over me and I felt the heat of her breath. "You had best face the truth of it, Ysabella—if you had not left Merlyn, he would have discarded you. He knew that you were not a worthy bride for a man of his rank and wealth. No doubt your departure saved him an unpleasant task."

I managed to look disappointed, if perplexed.

Her voice dropped to a hiss. "Is it not true, Ysabella, that he left you cold in your nuptial bed all those years ago? Is it not true that he tired of you even in that fortnight? One might ask who had abandoned who."

I met her gaze steadily, refusing to rise to her bait and doubly glad Merlyn had confided the tale of his father to me. I spoke with a sweetness I did not feel. "But Ada, if he had no regard for me, then why did he leave Ravensmuir to my hand?"

"Clearly, it was a mistake."

"Do you call Fitz a liar?"

"Perhaps my lord Merlyn did not mean to die." She turned back to the meat and said nothing more. I could fairly hear her thinking—without doubt, she knew more than what she had already revealed.

I rose, feigning interest in the kitchen's contents. I touched this and that, sniffed the bread appreciatively, picked up one utensil after another. She watched me covertly, her expression oddly reminiscent of that of her brother, and feigned fascination with the hind. Her back was straight and stiff, her disapproval of my presence more than clear.

What had Merlyn done here on his visits? Why had he come?

My pride stumbled over the fact that Merlyn had been as close as this to Kinfairlie, repeatedly, and he had not sought me out until now. These tidings fed my annoyance with Merlyn and his secrets.

That annoyance did not, however, aid me in discovering all of what Ada knew. I prepared to grant Ada a hearty prod.

"You are right in one matter," I said, my tone mild. "For no man intends to die before his dotage, nor indeed do most choose the day. But beyond that, I think that you are wrong. Merlyn would see nothing writ which he did not mean and in fact, he came to see me on the day before he died . . ."

"He did not!"

"He most certainly did. Ask any soul in Kinfairlie."

She turned to the meat, her determined expression revealing her intent to do just that.

I continued merrily upon my course of lies. "He tried to persuade me to return here, to live as his wife once again. I cannot imagine why he delayed in making such an argument, but it is clear that our marriage was of great import to him . . ."

"He never wished to have you return!" Ada cried. "He

was glad to be rid of you! He was glad to have matters resolved so easily."

I shook my head, leaving silence for her to fill.

Ada fumed. "He was tricked, plain and simple, he was tricked into making his will thus, tricked by that cursed Rhys Fitzwilliam who always showed an unholy favor for you. My lord Merlyn was tricked as he lay dying and had not the strength to know what he did."

"We embraced warmly when he came to me again. His will merely reflects his intent." I sat down and wiped an invisible tear. "How sad that he was beset by bandits just when he rode to join me abed. How sad that we came so close to living happily together once again."

Ada abandoned the meat in her fury and strode toward me. "You *lie!* He did not come to you that night!"

I widened my eyes, all innocence. "Where did he go?"

"He had a missive to deliver, and it was not to you."

"To who?"

She opened her mouth, then closed it again, her expression turning sly. "You are trying to trick me. You would have me reveal that I know too much of my lord's affairs, so that you might accuse me of indiscretion."

I shook my head. "No, Ada. I would know who killed Merlyn."

She retreated a step. "Why?"

"That justice might be served."

Ada rolled her eyes. "That you might charge me with slandering my betters. I will not aid you in this endeavor."

Her betters? Did she know about the summons from the earl?

I waited, without success. Ada eyed the meat, clicking her tongue when she saw that her inattention had allowed one side to burn. She cursed softly and cut the burned bit away, letting it fall into the fire. She did a credible job of pretending that I was no longer there.

"I would see Merlyn's murderer brought to justice, Ada. I would see Merlyn avenged."

"It will never be done."

"Why? Is the man responsible of too lofty a station?"

She smiled at me over her shoulder, but her gaze was knowing. "How am I to know? There were no witnesses of this crime, from what I am told."

Her coy manner infuriated me as nothing else could have done. "You served Merlyn for years and his father before that! How can you care so little that his murderer walks free?" I jumped to my feet. "Or are you a part of this, Ada? Have you seen compense from whosoever stalks the Lammergeier? Have you gained from Merlyn's death?"

"How dare you charge me with gain, when you have claimed this very keep!" She spun to face me, her eyes burning with a fury that made me step back. "And for what? You rolled to your back for a fortnight, while I, I have labored for seven years for mere suzerainty over Ravensmuir's kitchens—and even that, you may steal from me!"

She advanced upon me, shaking a finger as I stood, astonished. "Understand this, my fine lady. My debt to the Lammergeier has been rendered in full. It is their debt to me that is yet outstanding. I owe them nothing, nothing at all, and I owe you even less."

I was confused. "But what do they owe you?"

Ada smiled as she composed herself anew. "You might know the answer afore you die, Ysabella of Kinfairlie."

"What is that to mean? You speak in riddles."

"My lord Merlyn is dead because his quest failed." Ada's eyes gleamed. "Because the quest failed, some thwarted soul will come to collect his or her due, just as that same soul came a few nights past to collect that due from my lord Merlyn. But you, you will not be able to surrender what is desired of you—and I shall tell you nothing that might grant you any such chance." Her tone turned mocking. "I shall dance when you share my lord Merlyn's fate. Upon that, my lady, you may rely." She whistled as she tended her meat.

It took me a few moments to summon words to my lips. "You have always hated us, Ada."

She snorted. "What fondness could I have for a family of harlots such as yours?"

"We are not—"

"You most certainly are harlots and every soul in the village of Kinfairlie knew it. Did your mother not earn her keep upon her back?"

I stood, my arms folded across my chest, knowing that a furious outburst would gain me nothing. All the same, Ada insulted my own mother. "My mother used her wits and her gifts to see us fed."

Ada chortled. "That is one way of telling the tale. Oh, it was known where a boy might go to learn amorous arts before his wedding night."

"You lie!"

"You are your mother's daughter, of that there can be no mistake." Ada scoffed at me. "And such a fine prize you have won for surrendering your charms, no less than Ravensmuir itself. Your slatternly mother would be proud."

I lost my temper with her at that. "Which is the deeper wound, Ada?" I demanded. "Which was the wound that fed your hatred? Alasdair or Ravensmuir?"

Ada slapped me at that. My head snapped to one side with the vigor of her strike. The air crackled in the kitchen, but I did not care. What had so long been hidden was finally driven into the open and I was glad of it.

"Alasdair was mine!" she cried. "But your whorish sister stole him from me!"

"Alasdair never looked twice at you," I insisted, for this was the ugly truth of it. "But one glimpse of Mavella and he was hers forever."

"Sorcery!" Ada hissed.

"Love!"

She struck me again, then kicked my legs out from beneath me. She was stronger than I had anticipated, but I snatched at her and hauled her to the floor with me. She was wiry despite her smaller stature and angry enough for two. We rolled across the flagstones, pulling hair, slapping cheeks, jabbing elbows into ribs, until she shoved me hard against the wall. The breath went out of me for a moment, and Ada shoved to her feet, panting as she stared down at me, her garb in disarray.

"There is no such thing as love, Ysabella. There is only advantage well-played and fortune well-secured." She spat into the rushes spread on the floor. "You, spawn of a whore and a man with no name, should understand as much." Ada pushed up her sleeves and walked back to the fireplace.

I rose to my feet and adjusted my kirtle. "Only witchery could have made Alasdair spurn Mavella as he did."

She turned to look at me, surprised by my words. "No, you have the wrong end of the stick. It was sorcery that drew his ardent eye from me. He spurned your sister because he was shaken free of her wicked spell."

"If that were so, Ada, then why did Alasdair never wed you?"

She granted me such a poisonous glance that I thought she would strike me again. "Perhaps I no longer wanted him."

"Because a life of servitude tempted you so?" I shook my head as she bristled. "I think not."

We eyed each other with undisguised animosity.

I knew I would have no more confessions from her on this day and my blood simmered so that I did not care. I left the kitchen, wanting only to be away from her presence. I was upset, snared in dark memories and angered anew by what had passed before. I needed to feel the wind from the sea upon my face, clear my thoughts, and name Merlyn's assailant.

You are surprised by such hostility? I cannot imagine why—you would not if you knew all of the tale. Ada had coldly contrived for my sister to lose her love and had no remorse for her deeds, even less for the pain she had caused. Whatever Ada held against me was nothing compared to that initial crime.

Even in the bracing air of the morning, I could see Mavella's stricken face once again. I saw again the light leaving her eyes as her beloved Alasdair deliberately turned his back upon her before all of Kinfairlie. She had never been the same—and it was Ada's fault. The past clung to me like cobwebs, keeping me from the riddle I had to solve for Tynan's sake.

I turned away from the sound of chopping wood, not being anxious to meet Arnulf, and strode toward the sparkling sea. The sky was clear on this day, the wind cold.

The empty horizon disheartened me in that moment. It seemed that I could not succeed in this endeavor, not with so few answers and so many questions. Who sent the summons to Merlyn? It might have been the earl and it might not have been. There were probably fifty noblemen within a day's ride of Ravensmuir who might have afforded Avery's relics, most of whom were secure enough to have held their title five years before.

I recalled Ada's veiled reference, though she too yielded little solid. She might have meant a spiritual better, a monk or hermit or nun or bishop, or a nobleman. I heaved a sigh, knowing there was a vast nunnery at North Berwick and two or three monasteries close at hand. Who knew how many other solitaries and priests dotted the countryside?

And even if I began to speak to all of them, I would not know what to ask them. My determination faltered before such obstacles, and my gaze fell upon the crumbling chapel, isolated upon the tiny jutting point.

Perhaps it was time I sought greater assistance—or at least renewed strength—in my seemingly impossible task. Perhaps it was time that those at Ravensmuir attempted to solicit divine favor.

Indeed, our fortunes could not be worse.

I set out at a brisk pace for the chapel. I did not progress far, however, for my course was obstructed by the thicket of gorse and blackberry that had not been challenged or broken in years. I was not surprised at this measure of the Lammergeier family's faith, no less that of Ada and Arnulf.

On another day, I might have turned back, but I was restless, burdened by the impotence of my situation and in dire need of some useful labor to perform. I had no desire to meet my sister in such a mood, for I might tell her more than I should.

I returned to the keep and fetched a scythe, then set to clearing a path. I am strong, but it was heavy work.

The thorns tore at my hands and my clothing, my old kirtle became more disreputable in appearance with every step. The sun shone hot upon my back as it climbed higher in the sky and strands of my hair escaped my braid, then stuck in the sweat upon my brow.

I savored the ache in my muscles, though. It was good to engage in such simple labor as this, hard work which gave visible results. My goal was not the slippery mire of Merlyn's secrets and mysteries, but the measurable clearing of this gorse. Birds called to each other in the distance, I could hear the crash of the sea just beyond the chapel, the fall of Arnulf's axe fell with regularity far behind me. I could have been far from Ravensmuir, I could have been alone.

I could have been without worries, without scars. My life could have been simple.

Once my rhythm was found, I could have continued forever, though eventually I reached the end of the thicket. I straightened, stretched my back and looked back over what I had done.

A wide straight path now was hacked through the growth. I had aimed to make it at least two strides in width and had sheared it close to the earth, so that the brambles could not reclaim it so quickly as that. In some places it was wider, in others less so, depending upon the power of my swing and the stoutness of the plants that had stood in my way.

I put down the scythe and wiped my hands upon my skirts. The chapel was larger than I had ever thought it to be. It was a rectangular structure, wrought of stone, with only high tiny windows. They had no glass in them, which hinted at the age of the structure, and the tower at the east end was squat and square. The stones were adorned with moss on their north side.

Some kind of low-growing plant flourished around the chapel, so the chapel appeared to stand in a green clearing. Perhaps the point had once been completely covered in this pleasing growth, for I could see evidence of it beneath the closest brambles.

The sea splashed high here and as I made a circuit of the chapel, the spray landed upon my heated flesh. The wind was cooler and I lifted my braid off my neck to feel its welcome caress. The sea sparkled and danced as far as the horizon, to which I looked again for some hint of Merlyn's ship.

Of course, there was none.

I walked around the chapel again, confirming that there was no other path from the keep. Outside of the rampant brambles, there was only the scrabble of rock and coast.

I made to step upon a stone, to test the chances of making one's way around the gorse, and it immediately loosed itself, then three of its neighbors. I stepped back, watching as the stones tumbled and crashed down the steep coast, then splashed into the ocean. That way would not be passable, for the risk of falling was too high for a person of sense.

I felt that sense of being watched again, and spared a glance to Ravensmuir, golden and benign in the sunlight. Did anyone observe me from a high window there? Certainly, there was no one within sight.

I shook off my trepidation and returned to the narrow pair of chapel doors. Together they made a pointed arch, though they fit poorly together and there was only a vestige of ochre paint left upon them.

The hinges groaned as I opened the door. I peered into the shadows within, blinking after the brilliance of the light upon the sea. Several spears of sunlight fell through the dilapidated roof and dust motes danced within them. It seemed an abandoned place, an impression only heightened when a dozen pigeons stirred at the sound of me and flew through a hole in the wooden roof.

It was not an unpleasant place, despite its disrepair. There were diamond-shaped windows in the tower, one at the summit of each wall, and the sunlight poured through them in bright shafts. There was still a large trestle table, which had obviously been the altar, and a fine wooden sculpture of Christ upon the cross dominated the wall beyond. I crossed myself and took a deep breath as I proceeded further.

There were tombstones in the floor, great slabs of stone carved with images of knights and ladies and text, probably their names and deeds. The good dozen souls had clearly been people of wealth to have such tombs as this.

The chapel smelled of wet stone and the floor was marked with the droppings of the pigeons which roosted above. The air was musty, which only added to the impression that it had long been ignored.

Which was why my heart nearly leapt from my chest when someone coughed gently behind me. I spun to find a familiar man leaning against the stone framing the door.

"You are harsh, chère."
Merlyn.

I flung back my hair, well aware that he caught me at my worst, and glared at him. "To hold your crimes against you? It is you, Merlyn, who so readily admit your own guilt."

He smiled slightly, then clicked his tongue. "I meant with regards to Ada." He shook his head. "You are uncommonly cruel, each to the other."

I was not in the mood to suffer criticism from him. "So, you find me harsh with dear, innocent Ada. She is not so innocent as all of that, Merlyn."

"But is she as guilty as you would imply? There is much talk of wickedness, chère, and little evidence of it."

That he should accuse me of acting unjustly was too much to bear. Still riled, I pointed to the bench. "Sit and you will have your evidence." To my surprise, Merlyn did so and waited.

I began crisply. "Let me tell you something of Ada Gowan. Though she has been here at Ravensmuir since before my first arrival, she was born in Kinfairlie village. She was raised there, though in finer circumstance than we lived. Ada shows a face to you here that is unknown to me."

I sat on another bench, keeping my distance from my watchful spouse, smoothed my skirts and frowned. I was surprised at how important it was to me suddenly that Merlyn should understand, that he should not think poorly of me.

"She has three brothers, she being the eldest of the family and the silversmith Malcolm Gowan being of an age with me. One brother there is between those two. His name is Michael and, as he was always a clever boy, his father marked him for the church.

"Malcolm, of course, learned the trade of his father's silversmithy. And then there is Arnulf, born late and simple. Ada's mother was lost in the delivery and if ever there was a lamb in need of its ewe, Arnulf was it. Ada was left the brunt of the task of mothering her simple brother."

"You feel sympathy for her in that."

"In that, yes. I could feel more if she had not ensured that none could nurse much compassion for her. Her lot was not all bad, for her father made a good trade with Edinburgh and North Berwick in finery. Certainly there were none in Kinfairlie who could afford his wares, but the traveling added a glamor to their status. They lacked for little and it could be said quite fairly that the family believed themselves of somewhat better ilk than all the rest of us.

"Ada's father adored his sole daughter. Perhaps she reminded him of his wife, I cannot say, but she was granted every frippery and every favor which she desired, for all the good it did her appearance."

"Chère . . ."

"It is perhaps ungracious of me to speak the truth so baldly. You can gild a lily and make it finer than it was, but a gilded stick is yet a stick. And Ada suffered from the sin of pride—her father's adornments did not become her for they were not worn with grace. She walked with her chin high in the market, our Ada, apparently believing herself a princess among the rabble. She gave no alms to beggars, she spoke to none, she grimaced when any of us dared to come near to her."

I pleated my skirt between my fingers. "And so it was that she reached some twenty summers of age, without spouse or betrothed, for she was too haughty to even speak to any man she deemed beneath her. This was the beginning of the real trouble betwixt Ada and myself."

"How so?"

"It was the miller's son, Alasdair, at root."

A light dawned in Merlyn's eyes. "A miller's son would

have been the sole man with financial prospects for the future, at least in Kinfairlie village." Typically, he saw directly to the heart of the matter and I respected his intellect at least.

"Of course. Even in a poor village, the miller always has his due. All must have their grain ground, all must pay the miller for his services or go without. Ada either discerned this or her mother guided her eye, for she marked the miller's son as the man she would wed. No doubt she thought the match would be a fitting one: they were of an age and each came from one of the two favored families in the town."

"And the miller's son?"

"Alasdair was an amiable young man, honest and hard-working, good-natured, a man unlikely to abuse his ale or his wife. Any father in Kinfairlie would have been glad to have Alasdair's eye land upon his daughter."

"But?"

"But his eye landed upon Mavella."

Merlyn smiled. "She is charming and sweet, as well as lovely."

I was unable to suppress an answering smile of my own. Our gazes met, our admiration of my sister clear, and a tentative link was forged between the two of us once again.

I hastily averted my gaze, distrusting the way the chapel suddenly seemed warmer. I dared not trust this man!

"Alasdair was smitten with Mavella, and she was smitten with him. All the village sighed at their courtship. Mavella came home with flowers in her hair and winsome light in her eyes. The miller's son smiled and whistled all the time." My smile faded. "There was one, though, who did not smile."

"Ada Gowan."

I nodded. "I knew of her disappointment, of course, all in the village did, but I was perhaps not the only one to underestimate the extent of her malice."

Merlyn slipped on to the bench beside me and captured my hand. "What did she do?"

I found his touch reassuring, for my memories were troubling. His thigh touched mine, his heat driving some of the chill of the stone away. I welcomed the scent of him, though I would have protested any such admission. In my weakness, I did not pull my fingers away. "How is Tynan?"

"Well."

I met his gaze and could find no hint that he lied to me.

Merlyn smiled. "Fitz is most competent with the custody of young boys. He did not fare so badly with me." Then he sobered, seeing my worry. "He will let himself be killed before he allows harm to befall his ward. I did not trust Tynan's care lightly to him, chère."

I looked away and swallowed, reassured but not certain I should be. "Rumors began in the village shortly after the miller's son made his intent clear. Rumors there were that my mother and her daughters were sorceresses, that the miller's son had fallen prey to a foul spell. There were demands that we should be tried by the courts for witchery. I with my red hair was immediately suspect, though why it is that the ignorant assume that all witches would be so clearly marked makes no sense to me."

Merlyn bit back a smile. "Nor to me."

"But there was more than rumor. Foul tokens were left in places that we frequented, small dead creatures with symbols carved or burnt into their flesh, trussed with red thread, purportedly of my making." I shuddered in recollection and Merlyn squeezed my fingers. "Those poor creatures!"

I caught my breath when he only waited. "Though at first the tales were greeted with skepticism, there are always some who will listen to any foolery. Over time, the consensus grew. Whispers began about my mother's uncommon beauty and youthfulness, the sparkle she left in men's eyes and the ease with which she attracted them. Of course, there was no witchery in that—she simply made no demands and offered the men pleasure in exchange."

"Elizabeth had a rare ability to savor life's pleasures."

I slanted a glance his way, liking the lack of censure in his tone. "She was no whore."

"Of course not." Merlyn shook his head in recollection. "But neither did she do as one expected of her. She was a ray of sunlight, chère, and even in our brief acquaintance, I saw that she could confound and charm many a man." He smiled at me. "Hers was a rare and generous soul, and you share her spirit."

I looked across the chapel, my heart warmed that Merlyn did not hold my mother's nature against her. Then I chided myself for softening toward him at all.

Confused by my mingled response, I continued doggedly with the tale. "Whispers there were that the miller's son had been targeted by our sorcery and that the grain would be enchanted if Mavella wed into his family. A manner of madness ensued, the claims becoming more wild with every day. All men would abandon their wives if Mavella could but run her hands through the grain. All women would be left destitute by the men whom they had wedded. All men would be enslaved by us three."

"It is hard to believe that people would credit such nonsense."

I nodded. "But over time, they did. No doubt the small tokens left in the belongings of those said to dislike us played a part in that." My voice caught. "And eventually, as surely as the sun rises each day, the ardor of the miller's son cooled. I should have anticipated as much, but I had thought his heart true."

"Perhaps his father insisted upon the change of his course," Merlyn suggested quietly. "He would be less likely to risk folk taking their grain elsewhere to be milled."

"Perhaps Ada speaks aright, that there is no love, only advantage well-secured."

Merlyn's fingers tightened painfully over mine and he spoke with sudden ferocity. "Never believe as much, chère."

I glanced up at this unexpected insistence.

He smiled then, a slow smile that heated my loins. He raised one hand and touched my lips, tracing their outline with his fingertip. His gaze simmered and I could not catch my breath. "You are surprised," he murmured.

Our gazes locked and my flesh tingled. In that moment, despite all I knew, I wanted to be Merlyn's love. I wanted his heat within me and his hands upon my flesh. I wanted to unveil all of his secrets and share with him all of my own.

But that was foolery.

I spoke crisply. "It seems an unlikely sentiment to fall from your lips."

"That you would say as much is a disappointment, chère."

I did not trust this intimacy—no, it was my response to it that I feared most—and tried to ease away. Merlyn let me go, though still he held fast to my hand and kept his gaze locked with mine. "Did I not tell you that I meant to reform my ways, that I had pledged to surrender my father's trade?"

I shrugged, hoping despite my casual manner. "Perhaps you sought only to win my favor."

"Perhaps I do." He frowned and looked at my hand, watching his thumb stroke across its back. "I have missed you, chère. Though you did not voice your concerns, in my heart, I knew why you had left. You are a woman of integrity and honesty." He glanced up, his eyes dark. "Indeed, I never told you of my father's proposition for that very reason. I knew that you would not approve and I feared that you would spurn me for thinking a balance could be achieved."

I stared at him, transfixed.

Merlyn swallowed, a most unlikely hint of discomfiture. "I understand that the sole way to make our marriage whole again is to abandon my trade. I returned to Ravensmuir with the intent of putting this trade aside, of abandoning it and courting you anew."

I could scarce believe my ears. "Why, Merlyn?"

His gaze bored into mine. "Because I love you, chère."

IX

It was a confession I had never expected to hear from any man. That it fell from Merlyn's lips was even more astonishing. I stared at him, but he smiled slowly, nigh daring me to believe him.

Love?

I pulled my hand from Merlyn's and stood, needing distance between us. I paced across the chapel, then turned to face him, my arms folded across my chest. He seemed so sincere.

But then, was that ability not key to his trade?

"You never said as much before."

"I had to lose you to appreciate the prize that had slipped through my fingers," he said. "You had to leave me that I could know you possessed my heart."

My heart fluttered. I wanted to believe him. Part of me was prepared to surrender fully and immediately. But I could not help recalling that his success in his father's trade was rooted in his own persuasiveness. I could not help recalling that he had stolen Tynan to encourage my compliance.

"Forgive me if I do not believe you. My agreement would make matters too convenient for you."

"I did not ask for your agreement, not yet," Merlyn said softly. "I ask only that you listen and do not bar your heart against me."

We stared at each other across the width of the chapel, a thousand desires in the air, a thousand doubts yet filling the chasm between us. My heart thumped painfully against my ribs and my mouth was dry.

Could I believe him?

"I dare not trust the man who kidnapped my brother."

"Perhaps I had another reason to see him away from Ravensmuir," Merlyn said with resolve. "I have told you many a time that I protect what is mine own."

I turned my back upon him at that and pondered what he had said. From what did he protect Tynan? Could it be true? I was surprised at how much I wished it to be so.

"Tell me the rest of the story, chère," he urged quietly, though he did not approach me.

I took a deep breath, relieved to concentrate upon the tale. "One day, my sister went to the market to meet Alasdair as always they did. She was thirteen, smitten with her first love and her last. I remember how she cried out with joy when she spied Alasdair. I remember how she ran across the market to his side. It was as if she flew." My words faltered at the recollection. "I remember how his shoulders stiffened, how I felt that first sense that something was amiss."

"Surely he did not reject her publicly?" There was a welcome outrage in Merlyn's tone.

"He did exactly that. I shall never forget the stony expression he wore when he turned to acknowledge her. He told her, curtly, to leave him be from that day forward, then he turned his back upon her as if she did not merit his attention further."

Merlyn caught my shoulders in his hands. I jumped slightly, not having heard him approach, but did not turn.

"She was shattered, Merlyn. She had never been dealt such a cruel blow in all her life. The wound of her heart was there for all to see. She has never been the same, not until this very week when she resolved to live again."

"But what had Ada to do with it?"

"She is responsible for Alasdair's change."

"How can you know?"

I looked to my shoes. Here was a part of the tale that did not show me to advantage. "I could not look upon my sister's grief for long that day. I glanced over the watchful crowd, even as I hugged Mavella tightly, and I saw Ada. She wore the smile of one well satisfied with what she had wrought. She was gleeful that my sister was in pain. I sent my sister home, then I followed Ada stealthily. I had a sense that she knew more than she told. I was right."

Merlyn watched me.

"She hurried away from the market, singing beneath her breath, no doubt wanting to be in her kitchen when the miller's son came calling for a bride. She was so certain of herself that she never anticipated me, never anticipated that she would be caught."

"But caught she was."

"I guessed her destination and entered her kitchen before she did. It did not take me long to find six more dead mice, their eyes poked out, their tiny bodies abused with her feigned witchery. There was a spool of red thread with which she had trussed so many. She was surprised when she arrived there and I presented what I had found, when I made my charge."

My fists clenched. "And then she laughed, convinced that she had done so good a job that none would believe any accusation I made against her. She was of a wealthy family, after all, and we were no one of merit at all. I was young and angry and fearful that she was right. I slapped her, as she struck me this very day, and we fought like she-cats. There was no one else at home, no one else to hear. I blackened her eye before I left her there weeping."

"Weeping?"

"Of course. She could not show her face in the market until that bruise healed, lest she have to explain its origins. And with the bruise, she presented no vision to tempt a reluctant suitor's heart."

"Did you plan as much?"

I shook my head. "I merely struck out at her. Providence did the rest. Ada had to wait at home for Alasdair."

"And he did not come."

"He wed in haste, but he did not wed Ada. He married the buxom daughter of one of the townsmen, a dark-haired and hearty woman as unlike Mavella as a woman could be." I stared over Merlyn's shoulder at the wall. "She died within the year in the birthing of his son, and the infant died as well."

"How tragic."

"It was a tragedy made more so by Ada's whispering. She said that we had hexed the new bride in retaliation for her taking Mavella's place."

I met my spouse's gaze, uncommonly anxious to persuade him of the truth. "But we are not witches, Merlyn. Indeed, if there is a witch in all of this, it is Ada. She dispenses malice into the world with gusto and it seems that there is some truth in the assertion that whatever one sends out returns threefold. She has had poor luck in her ambitions, poorer luck than it would seem a favored and wealthy daughter could have."

"Are you superstitious, chère?"

I shook my head. "I endeavor to do the best for the welfare and protection of those around me, that others might reciprocate in kind. Ada is the sole exception, and it is because she seeks to grant injury to those I hold in my heart."

"Again, that fierce love is revealed." He stroked my cheek with his fingertip, awakening an array of tingles in my treacherous flesh.

I spoke hastily, thinking to finish the tale and escape. "The miller's son left Kinfairlie after his wife's demise, traveling south to some relations. There were rumors that he wed again. I had heard that he had returned of late, though Mavella alone has seen him. She saw him with a young boy, presumably his son, and he took no heed of her."

"And Ada?"

"She did not linger long in Kinfairlie before she came here to tend to your father's hearth. Her mother died around that time and she had the burden of Arnulf to bear. Her brother's wife Fiona is shrewd with a coin, and perhaps did not appreciate two more mouths to feed. I do not know. Nor do I know precisely why Ada's brother was anxious to give us charity upon our return to Kinfairlie."

"But you guess that he felt remorse for his sister's deeds?"

I nodded and bowed my head.

"What of Ada's doting father?"

"He died about five years before Mavella's failed courtship. After his death, of course, Ada's mother wed again. I did not know her stepfather well, he was from away and not a man inclined to be friendly. He disappeared after his wife died, and I assume he returned to his own blood."

I sighed. "Ada's father, though, was a kindly man, generous with his wealth and apparently blind to the foibles of his children. Or perhaps they grew unchecked in his absence. Perhaps Ada had long benefited from his wisdom and restraint, and knew not how to behave without his counsel. The fact remains that I knew her father well and mourned his death deeply."

"How did you know him so well?"

I looked away, knowing this detail could be misconstrued. "Matters were apparently dour in the Gowan household and it was well known that Robert Gowan and his wife were estranged." I paused. "Robert Gowan came to our abode often and lingered long there. He oft said that my mother made him laugh."

Merlyn smiled in reminiscence. "It was a gift of hers."

"I think he enjoyed the respite from the demands of his own household, and the frequent laughter of our own. He was good company, was Ada's father, and he granted much paternal advice to Mavella and myself."

Merlyn waited, his grip still fast upon my hand.

"He died in my mother's bed," I confessed quietly. "My mother always said that he smiled like an angel at the end, though Malcolm scowled like a demon when he came to collect his father's corpse."

"Perhaps that is the root of the animosity between you and Ada," Merlyn suggested softly.

I considered the possibility, then shrugged. "Perhaps you are right. Not only was her adored father less saintly than she had believed, but Ada discovered the truth of it along with all the rest of the village. There were those who thought this a reckoning long overdue, a humiliation to people who imagined themselves better."

Merlyn seemed to be fighting a smile. "It is hard to conceive of Elizabeth thinking of matters that way."

Our gazes met and we smiled in fond recollection of her earthy merriment. "Oh no, she found it most fitting that Robert died between her thighs. It was where she insisted he was happiest, and my mother long believed that a person dies best engaged in a deed he or she loves."

"God bless her stalwart soul." Merlyn brushed a kiss across my knuckles, awakening untold fires beneath my flesh. His words came very soft and low. "How did Elizabeth die, chère?"

My smile faded and my tears rose again. "Wretchedly. Pustules and boils upon her body, a fire beneath her flesh and madness in her mind."

"And a new babe just out of her womb," he reminded me, his words gentle yet insistent.

"Of course, yes," I agreed hastily and nodded with unnecessary vigor. "That as well."

"You were with her."

"I held her hand. I told her that we had returned to Ravensmuir while she slept and that every finery was at her fingertips. She never understood my departure from this place."

"Nor did I."

"She liked you."

Merlyn laughed, well pleased. "I liked Elizabeth as well, but solely as the mother of my wife."

I ignored his manner. "She took our departure most poorly and when we returned to Kinfairlie, her health began to fail. So I lied at the end, I told her of the fine wines and tidbits arrayed upon the table, awaiting her attention. I told her of sumptuous cloth draping the bed and luxurious furs piled against her chin. She was nigh oblivious, she did not know that I lied."

Merlyn slipped his arm around my shoulders, and kissed my temple. "But your wondrous tales gave her solace, I am sure. Elizabeth was a woman much comforted by finery."

"It was a lie, Merlyn," I said bitterly, shrugging off his embrace. "Yet another lie in a long retinue of lies, another falsehood in the stream of falsehoods that have fallen from my lips since first leaving this place."

I strode away from him, my arms wrapped about myself. Despair assailed me as it seldom did and I knew myself for the failure that I had become. "For years I have blamed you for making a liar of me, but the sorry truth is that I have made the choice to let each falsehood pass my lips. I am disgusted with the person I have become." I turned to study him. "You have chosen the wrong assistant in your quest for truth, Merlyn. You are wrong in thinking me a person of integrity. I cannot aid you."

The words hung between us for a long time, only the rustling of the birds overhead filling the air. Then Merlyn shook his head slowly. "No, chère." He strolled after me like a great cat, his gaze pinning me in place when I might have turned away. "I made no error."

I would have protested, but his thumb landed heavily

upon my lips, silencing me as effectively as the admiration in his eyes.

"Your loyalty is beyond question, once you grant it, and your desire for justice is far greater than that of any I have known. You willingly jeopardize yourself and sacrifice your own desires for the good of those you love."

I shook free of his touch. "Then bring Tynan back to me." As soon as I voiced my demand, I knew that it irked Merlyn.

"Do you not already have my guarantee? Is my pledge insufficient for you?"

"How can you ask as much?" I spun away from him and put the width of the chapel between us. "The sea is a capricious mistress, Merlyn. Even you cannot control all the matters that might go awry."

"No, I cannot," he admitted, but he looked uncommonly pleased.

"And of course, there is your own unknown scheme for the boy," I amended hastily.

Merlyn closed the distance between us with one step, then raised a finger to ease an errant tendril of hair behind my ear. His finger slid over the curve of my ear in a caress that left me dizzy.

"My own wickedness," he whispered against my temple and I closed my eyes. "Which you forgot, if only for a moment."

What he considered a triumph, I could only see as a failure. I ducked around him and crossed the chapel once more. "I thought you gone from Ravensmuir, and good riddance."

His smile flashed. "Ah, but we have a wager, chère, by your own dictate. Having encouraged you to aid me, it would be churlish to not reward your daily efforts with my nocturnal ones."

I cursed myself when a heated flush rose over my cheeks. Merlyn chuckled, doing nothing to ease my discomfiture. He pursued me and I ignored him. I closed my eyes at the

caress of his breath against my nape, the slide of his fingertip down my throat. "Of what did you dream last night,
chère?"

"I did not sleep."

His fingers slid into the hair and I fought valiantly against
his allure. "Nor did I," he murmured. I felt his lips upon my
ear, his breath upon my temple, and I clenched my fists
against the vigor of my desire.

"Guilt clearly kept you awake," I said, belying the weakness of my knees with a strident tone.

Merlyn chuckled. His other hand rose to cup my breast
and I glanced down, appalled to find that my labor had left
the wool damp and my nipples clearly discernible.

I gasped and tried to pull away but he held me captive in
the circle of his embrace.

"You love with vigor and tenacity, chère, and expect nothing in return," Merlyn whispered. I glanced up and found his
eyes filled with that unsettling admiration.

"I am the stronger one. It falls to me to protect my
younger siblings. It is only right and proper."

Merlyn bent and kissed me with such tender vigor that my
toes curled. "You grant more than others expect or even perhaps than they deserve."

"No, I—"

"Hush." His gaze searched mine, his expression intent as
he hovered close. His voice dropped low. "If ever a man
could prove himself worthy of your trust, would you love
him with the same ferocious ardor?"

I knew that Merlyn spoke of no random man, but himself.
I felt the dawning love I had once felt for him awaken once
more, then reminded myself that Merlyn had lied to me.

This was no man to whom a thinking woman surrendered
her heart.

I feared, though, that mine was halfway gone. He had
confided some of his history to me, a rare gift, but I yearned
for more of his tales.

I lifted my chin and swallowed. "I have yet to meet a man worthy of my regard. I do not know how I would love such a man if I did."

Merlyn smiled, as if contented with an answer that should have been unsatisfactory. "It is consoling to know that even though you have yet to find me fitting, your suitor from Dunkilber has fared no better."

I was disgusted with myself for not quelling his expectations when it could have been so readily done. I spun and he let me go. I surveyed the floor with its many carved slabs, pretending that I was not as keenly aware of him as I was. "Does your rabbit warren of tunnels open into this chapel as well?"

"No." He shrugged as I looked back. "There are openings all along the face of the cliff. More than one meets a path; one winds to the lip of this very cliff."

"So, a man caught in the labyrinth is not truly snared at all? This entire holding is within his reach?"

"Not all of it. The tunnels do not reach far inland, so the keep is as far as the furthest."

"How did your family find the time and the labor to carve out such a network of passages?"

"It was here, chère. Most were formed by nature, others had been added and reshaped by smugglers over the years."

"This labyrinth is why Ravensmuir so suited your sire," I guessed and he nodded.

Merlyn looked about himself and abruptly frowned. He crossed the floor quickly, then bent behind the table at the altar. When he stood up, he held a piece of crockery, turning it in his hands. "Did you come to retrieve this?"

It was an earthenware plate. The crockery was fine, the image upon it most familiar. The plate was dun in color with a line of cobalt blue around the rim, a bird with outstretched wings painted in the same blue in its center.

A lammergeier.

"Not I." I traced the bird's outline with a fingertip and met Merlyn's gaze. "Is it from the keep?"

"Yes." He frowned and said no more.

"None could have come the way I came without leaving a path."

"I thought that only Fitz and I knew the labyrinth." There was a rind of cheese and a crust of bread upon the plate, neither nibbled by vermin and neither so stale that they could have lain here more than a fortnight.

Here was a matter upon which we could not suspect the other, and I doubted I was the only one who seized upon this puzzle with relief. I turned and studied the chapel once again, seeking hints of occupancy.

Upon closer scrutiny, the stones in the floor were not laid as flatly or as evenly as one might have expected. There was dirt alongside the one beside me. I bent and Merlyn guessed my intent. He managed to lift one corner of this comparatively small flagstone, revealing that the soil beneath it had been disturbed.

"Someone dug beneath the floor." I looked at Merlyn. "Someone sought the religious relic your father had never delivered."

"Not unreasonably, they sought it in a house of God."

"You?"

He shook his head.

We circled the chapel in opposing directions, pointing out the fresh scrapes upon the larger stones to each other. There were telltale remnants of earth when one looked with especial care, and numerous places where mortar had been removed. One particularly scraped stone in the back corner attracted my eye and I tipped it with considerable effort before Merlyn reached my side.

There were tools hidden beneath it. A small shovel, a bucket, a trowel and a knife. We did not touch them, and Merlyn returned the stone as it had been.

"Someone recently took refuge here, to seek the prize."

"He might still be near," Merlyn said grimly.

My gaze fell upon the plate once more. "And he had the audacity to steal from Ravensmuir's kitchens."

"Or had the endorsement of one within its walls."

That truth made the hair prickle on the back of my neck.

"You should know, chère, that I came this time at my brother's urging."

I was shocked that he confessed as much to me, then that another Lammergeier hid from my view. "Gawain is here?"

His eyes narrowed. "He was here, for he sent me word from here, though I arrived to find him gone."

"And Ada?"

"Said she has not seen him in a year."

"She lies."

"Possibly."

We looked at the plate as one. "Does he know the labyrinth?"

Merlyn shrugged. "Not to my knowledge, but why should he not?"

"Did your father show it to you?"

"No. I knew it was there, for he spoke of it, and I found several entries when I was younger. I only learned its extent after his demise."

"When you came repeatedly," I said bitterly. "Yet did not seek me out."

Merlyn said nothing to that. Indeed, he turned his back upon me and strode back to the plate.

I could not keep injury from my tone. "Is it true what Ada said? Did you return here often?"

His shoulders stiffened but he did not turn and he did not speak for a long moment. Again I had the sense that my departure had stung more deeply that Merlyn would care to admit.

Or that he, yet again, preferred to keep his thoughts veiled.

"Perhaps you came to visit another," I suggested, making

no effort to keep my tone from turning waspish. "Perhaps you have an affection for Ada. She, after all, seems to think that Ravensmuir should have fallen to the hands of another, perhaps even herself."

"Ada?" Merlyn turned, his expression astonished. "What claim might she believe herself to have?"

"Perhaps she shared your bed in my absence."

Merlyn's lips quirked, and he began to laugh. He flicked my chin with his fingertip, merriment crinkling his eyes. "Is this then why you would ensure that I am exhausted?"

I flicked my hand at him, annoyed that he teased me. "She believes herself to have some claim."

"Seven years of labor is no strong claim to a keep's seal," Merlyn retorted, then tipped my chin upward. "Perhaps she has come to think of this place as her own, but there is no reason for it to be to my knowledge."

"Were you here often?"

He nodded. "Several times. The relic with which my father wagered must be secreted here somewhere." His gaze was troubled, and I thought I discerned something that he could not voice.

"Unless Gawain found it."

Merlyn put the plate back on the floor of the chapel, his expression pensive as he crouched beside it. "Gawain is the finest thief that ever I have known."

"And you have known so many as that?"

Merlyn disregarded my comment. "He leaves no evidence of his presence. He leaves no hint that he was the one there, nor even a sign that the sanctuary has been invaded. He would never have left so careless a sign as this plate."

"Unless he was interrupted."

Merlyn bowed his head. "If not worse." I understood his implication. Whosoever sought the relic was prepared to kill to get it.

Had Gawain found it, then been killed for it? Was that why he was gone when Merlyn arrived?

But then, why had Merlyn been assaulted, as well?

I shivered. The chapel was filled with shadows and whisperlike rustles of the birds. There were nests in the supports for the wooden roof of the chapel, the gleam of beady eyes revealing the birds.

Merlyn pushed to his feet, suddenly impatient. "You have been here too long, chère. Even the most diligent cannot pray so long as this. Curious souls will wonder."

"And one might seek me out."

He scooped up the plate, pausing before me. There was hopefulness in his eyes that made him look younger, uncertain. "If a man sought your favor, chère, would you heed his efforts?"

"If a man confessed all he knew, I could do nothing but listen," I replied. A ghost of a smile touched Merlyn's lips, then he kissed the tip of my nose and was gone.

X

Merlyn's was a farewell fittingly given to a child and it irked me as little else he might have done. On principle alone, I did not follow him to the door, nor did I watch him go. Instead, I paced back to the altar and prayed for some aid in this matter.

The wind blew in a gust and wood rattled against wood.

I tipped my head back and looked for the source of the sound. A wooden rosary had been hung over one arm of the crucifix hung behind the altar. Those beads swung in the wind and slapped against the crucifix's center beam.

I had not noticed the rosary before, but there was a patina of dust upon each bead. And the wooden beads were dark, of the same hue as the carved wood itself, as well as hanging in the deep shadows beneath the window.

Indeed, there was nothing remarkable about it or its presence. I exhaled and glanced over my shoulder, feeling suddenly very alone. I wondered fleetingly who had left the beads here, perhaps a pilgrim or a priest, perhaps some long forgotten penitent.

I turned to depart, then spared one last glance for the swinging beads. My gaze sharpened and I nigh gasped aloud.

Tucked onto the support for the crucifix, hidden from casual glimpse by the carving of the dying Christ himself, was a bundle of cloth tied with heavy twine.

Perhaps I have a measure of the Sight, for I knew with unswerving certainty what it was. Here was the relic of Merlyn's father, here was Avery's prize.

Or *there* it was, so highly placed that I could not reach it without Merlyn's aid. And Merlyn, of course, was not only gone without a trace but impossible to summon to my aid.

After a great deal of fretting and stretching, I reluctantly concluded that there was little I could do. And truly, the bundle, if it was the relic, had been secreted safely there for many years. Even someone who had sought it within the chapel had not discovered its hiding place.

Merlyn would be pleased and the prospect of that pleased me. Impatient to see him again, but knowing he had spoken rightly, I schooled myself to pretend I knew nothing of the prize. I retrieved the scythe and strode whistling back toward the keep. I strolled into the kitchen, making a show of wiping my dirty brow.

"That was heavy labor," I declared to none in particular.

Ada's lips tightened. "None asked you to do it."

So, she had noted where I had gone. "But none would have done it for me. And in the absence of the ravens, I thought the occupants of this keep had need of some divine favor."

Ada snorted. Her brother watched me, his task of turning the spit forgotten. I wondered whether he guessed the truth of Merlyn, through some peculiar sense that such people often have. I turned from his oddly knowing gaze.

"I have need of a bath before the midday meal, Ada," I said in a most conciliatory tone, grateful that I could seize upon my labor as an excuse. "Could you provide me with a bucket or two of water?"

"Since I have nothing else to do?" she demanded, looking pointedly at the meal she was preparing.

"I could not come filthy to such a fine board as you clearly intend to lay."

Her face pinched, then she turned away. "I should expect not, as you have a guest again this day."

"I do?"

"Calum of Dunkilber has seen fit to seek you out again. He is in the stables with his steeds and squires."

Annoyance rose within me, though not just with Ada's deeds. My tone was sharp. "Ada, you should not admit any soul to the hall and stables who so much as appears at the gate."

"Oh?" Her brows arched high. "I had thought him an *intimate* friend of yours, my lady. Had I but known he was an enemy to be barred from entry, I should have done so."

"He is not an enemy," I explained with a patience I was far from feeling. "But it is not proper to admit visitors without the approval of the noblewoman who holds the keep and that, in case you have forgotten, is me."

She surveyed me, her expression telling. "While it is proper for a noblewoman to tend her own grounds?"

I shook my head, knowing this argument could not be won. "Bring me two buckets of water with all haste, Ada. And admit none from this day forward without my express permission."

"Arnulf will bring it," she said tersely as I made to leave.

I paused, wondering what scheme she hatched with this choice, then spoke with a resolve that could not be mistaken. "Then he shall leave it outside the solar door and knock to let me know that it has arrived. I will have no man within my chambers."

Ada, curse her, laughed.

I reached the solar before I wondered whether she meant only to irk me or whether she knew more of Merlyn's survival than even he had guessed.

My bath was tepid and rushed. I struggled with the laces on a fine gown and hastened to the hall, arriving breathless to find my sister laughing at some jest of Calum's. Ada was carrying a steaming platter to the board, her brother bore the roast meat behind her, and the smell of the food filled the hall. Merlyn's two squires stood by the board, prepared to serve the meat.

The Yule log filled the hall with welcome heat and a merry crackle, while the green adornment we had labored to hang looked festive. Both Ada and Arnulf were so concentrated on their tasks that they looked almost amiable.

The table was set with linen and crockery. Though it was a disproportionately small table for the size of the chamber, it looked welcoming. Braziers burned on either side, Ada evidently having decided that a visiting nobleman was worth the expenditure as the newly resident noblewoman was not. Sunlight filtered through the glass windows and drew golden patterns upon the floor. Calum's squires clustered together and slightly to one side; a young girl stood near them but alone.

Mavella looked fetching and she laughed merrily. That she had dressed with care for Calum implied much. Certainly, she was pretty with her cheeks flushed and her eyes sparkling.

Had it not been for Tynan's absence and the troubling circumstances surrounding that, this scene might have lightened my heart. Mavella and Calum both turned to smile at me and I forced myself to smile in turn.

"Greetings, Lady Ysabella!" Calum cried with a heartiness of manner that I was coming to associate with him. "How do you fare in this place thus far?"

"Quite well since yesterday," I said. I offered my hand and he bowed low to kiss its back. "What an unexpected pleasure to see you twice in so many days." Though I found his attentiveness slightly extreme, his was a pleasant presence.

He certainly was garbed both richly and with flamboyant flair. He gestured broadly to the hall. "And what progress you have already made in bringing change to this desolate hall." He winked, including Mavella in his camaraderie. "My suggestions cannot have been all bad."

I did not tell him that this presentation of the meal was Ada's doing, and that for the benefit of his second appearance here. Had he not arrived, we might have had to fetch the meat from the kitchens ourselves. "Of course they were not. Come and join us at the board."

Calum beckoned to his entourage. "Then perhaps you will not take offense at my providing another suggestion, even a more forward one."

He gestured to the girl and I guessed his intention before he voiced it.

"This is Berthe, the daughter of my seneschal and his wife." Berthe bobbed her head and dropped her gaze when she came to a halt before me. She then smiled, clearly seeking a sign that she was welcome. She was a pretty girl, plump-cheeked with sparkling brown eyes, her tangle of dark curls tamed into a braid with only moderate success.

Calum continued, all a-bluster with his own generosity. "You have no maid in this place and with two fine ladies such as yourselves, a chamber maid would be most useful to you. As there are no ladies in my manor, Berthe's skills with feminine fripperies have no opportunity to be used."

"Then where did she learn such skills?" Mavella asked. Intriguingly, Berthe's smile disappeared and the girl began to look agitated.

Calum reddened. "There is no shame in admitting that Berthe and her family were at Dunkilber when I took possession of the holding . . ."

"You served the lady previously in residence?" I asked the girl, assuming that the former residents had died. It is not uncommon for an estate to revert to an overlord, who might grant it to a loyal knight like Calum. I assumed he had earned his land with years of diligent service to the earl.

But Berthe's eyes flashed. "She was murdered," she said tightly, and fixed Calum with an accusing look. "In the siege of Dunkilber."

Calum's smile turned chilly as he held the girl's gaze. "Such is the nature of warfare and the reason why responsible men dispatch their womenfolk elsewhere when they decline terms of surrender."

I was momentarily taken back by Calum's icy tone.

But then, men claimed property by force all the time and I knew I should not put too much weight upon this fact. Calum's expression unsettled me, despite my own argument for it, and Mavella stepped away.

The girl shut her mouth mutinously and looked across the hall. Calum shrugged and rolled his eyes as if the girl's manner was worthy only of a jest, but he was irked. There might be another reason for Calum seeking a new home for Berthe. Perhaps it was not entirely comfortable having her at Dunkilber if she could not hide her animosity toward its new lord.

"If Berthe would like to remain here at Ravensmuir, we should be delighted to have her," I said and the girl bestowed a smile of gratitude upon me. "I am certain that you can find a great deal of labor to do in this keep. We are woefully without servants."

"Yes, my lady. I should welcome the opportunity, my lady."

I smiled for Calum. "And I must thank you for your thoughtfulness, though I know not how it can be repaid."

Calum smiled. "A kiss, my lady fair, would suffice."

I offered him my hand and knew I did not imagine that he hesitated. No doubt he had expected a more intimate kiss than the one I let him place upon my knuckles. His gaze flicked to both my watchful sister and the wide-eyed maid, then he smiled and bent low over my fingertips.

His tongue slid boldly betwixt my fingers. When I caught my breath at his audacity, his eyes shone with mischief and he winked.

I straightened and forced a smile. "Perhaps we should eat, before Ada's fine meal becomes cold. Tell me, Calum, do you know where I might find a seneschal of my own?"

I suspected that Berthe's parents might be similarly disenchanted with their new overlord, though Calum proved to be less inclined to be rid of them. We discussed the matter as we took our seats and one of the squires began to cut the meat from the bone for all of us.

It was when the boy artfully laid out a piece of meat before me that I glanced down. The plate set before me, and graced with venison, was identical to the plate I had found in the chapel. A similar bird with outstretched wings filled the middle of the plate.

I looked quickly to one side and the other and saw that only three such plates had been laid upon the board for the nobles, while the servants having been granted trenchers cut of bread instead.

From that point, I had difficulty concentrating upon the conversation at hand.

⇛

I stopped in the kitchens after Calum's departure, purportedly to introduce Berthe to Ada but hoping to discover what she knew of the plates. Ada stood stiffly as I said my piece, and her wary gaze flicked between Berthe and myself.

"I have rules in my kitchen," she said to Berthe. "And you will abide by them if you do not wish a beating. You will do what you are told to do, immediately and without question; you will not have any discussions with my brother; you will eat and drink what you are given to eat and drink and not filch from the platters going to the hall; and you will never touch the plates."

Berthe's gaze danced over the kitchen shelves as she tried to make sense of this last dictate. "There were plates on the board . . ."

"Yes, there were and there were three of them. You will not touch them today and indeed you will never touch them."

"But . . ."

"But nothing you can say will change the truth. It is careless handling that costs a lord his treasures, of that you can be certain." Ada became annoyed. "Here is the evidence of it: twenty-four plates there were originally, purchased on commission by Avery, the first Lammergeier Laird of Ravensmuir and the father of our recently lost lord Merlyn. He ordered them made in Italy as a gift for his bride, then shipped them here upon his own ships. Twenty-four there were and now there are but half of them remaining—*half!*— the others lost through the careless handling of serving girls."

I refrained from commenting that the broken twelve must have been lost while the kitchen was beneath Ada's jurisdiction.

"They are in the pantry, placed high on a shelf, secured against clumsy fingers and still such care is not enough. Just recently, we have lost another, for there were thirteen when last I used them and only twelve were there on this morning."

"You have broken another?" I asked, unable to resist.

Ada's eyes snapped, guessing the wrong reason for my interest. "Thirteen is a wicked number, the realm of witchery. Nothing good comes of thirteen. There are but two possible explanations for the disappearance of that plate. The first is that some fool had seen fit to take it and probably broken it."

"But who?"

"Rhys Fitzwilliam is one to help himself to what is not his

to take," Ada fumed. "And if ever he is fool enough to cross this threshold again, I shall demand to know whether he broke one of those plates then did not confess to it."

"But the second possibility?"

Ada glared at me. "Some sorcery summoned the plate from beneath my very eye, tempted by the wickedness of the number thirteen."

"That seems unlikely," I said calmly, for Berthe looked alarmed. "In my experience, the most sensible and most mundane explanation is usually the truth. Perhaps you or Arnulf broke it."

"I did not! And Arnulf touches nothing in this kitchen, as he has been bidden!"

"Are you certain they are adequately secured? Perhaps one fell?"

Ada threw open the door of a storage room and gestured to a high shelf. "Look there, my lady! Nine plates stacked high and beyond the reach of most. There they are and there they will remain with their clean brethren until I see fit to remove them."

Berthe's brows drew together in confusion, and she bit her lip. "But there are ten plates here," she said, looking to Ada. "You see?" She carefully counted them aloud.

Ada pushed past her and counted the plates herself. She whirled and returned to the kitchen, inhaling fit to pinch her nostrils shut. Three plates sat upon the kitchen table, their surface stained with gravy. Ten plates, plus the three, brought the total to thirteen once again.

Wicked thirteen.

I had to fight to keep my lips from twitching, because I had a very good idea how that missing plate had joined the others. Yes, there was a wooden wall in that storage room, as well as several in the kitchen itself, walls not unlike those that slid back in other parts of the keep to grant access to the labyrinth.

Every one of us had been in the hall when the meat was

served. I could not help but think that a certain man courted my approval.

The prospect coaxed my smile.

"How very strange, Ada. Wicked thirteen haunts you again."

Ada huffed and glared. "There is evil afoot at Ravensmuir, of that there can be no doubt." She turned upon Berthe. "I expect both care and accountability of those serving in this hall. Do you understand me?"

Berthe nodded and bobbed her head. "Yes, indeed. I have never broken any crockery or vessel, madam. And I know nothing of sorcery, nothing at all."

"Then see that you do not begin either here." Ada's words turned acidic. "Is there any other matter that concerns you, my lady, or do you linger for the delights of our companionship?"

"No, Ada. That is all. Could you find sufficient labor for Berthe? I shall not have need of her aid until the evening."

Berthe lifted her chin. "I but await your instruction, Ada." There was a spark in her eyes that told me she was determined to prove Ada's expectations wrong.

I left them together and strolled back toward the solar. I should give some gift to Calum in return beyond my knuckles to kiss. Perhaps I would visit him at Dunkilber.

Perhaps I would send Mavella to visit him. I spun lovely futures for my sister and I even, to my own surprise, hummed a tune beneath my breath.

My humming halted on the threshold of the solar, so certain was I that Merlyn was within and that he would demand a reward for his jest with the plate. I shivered in anticipation. I eased open the door and slipped over the threshold, wanting to grant a surprise to him for a change.

No one was there. I crept soundlessly up the stairs to the solar itself, alert to the slightest creak of the wooden floors.

Nothing.

Nothing but the increasingly familiar and eerie sense that I was being watched. I halted at the top of the stairs and stood there for a long moment. My gaze lifted to the vicious expression of the carved bird over the bed, my pulse hammered in my ears. I could hear the sounds of activity in the great hall, if distantly, and the even fainter rhythm of the sea crashing upon the shore.

The chamber seemed to breathe, though I could not detect anything amiss at all. My burn itched in a most irksome way. The sun had moved onward, past the angle where it shone directly through the windows. The room seemed secretive, dark.

But all appeared as I had left it. I crossed the room and tapped upon the panel that Merlyn had opened, then tried to budge it without success.

How typical of Merlyn to be absent when his presence was desired!

Disappointed and disgruntled, I shed my girdle and kirtle, and laid aside my stockings and shoes. I unbraided my hair and shook it out, then stretched leisurely across the bed. There were aches settling into my muscles from the morning's exertions and I closed my eyes for just a moment's respite.

I must have slept. I awakened to a darkened chamber, my belly growling. I dressed and descended to the hall. Although I was late for the evening meal, Mavella did not comment upon it.

Ours was hardly a court burdened with formalities.

I retired early. Perhaps because I had slept earlier, perhaps because I still thought Merlyn would come, I was restless. I barred the door, and fell upon Merlyn's box, for I had yet to thoroughly study its contents.

I lay on my belly across the mattress, lanterns perched all around the great bed, and turned the key in the lock. The contents were as magical and marvelous as I had expected them to be.

Here must be the deed that Fitz had spoken of. Writ on thick golden parchment, affixed with ribbons and red wax seals, it could be nothing other than the deed to Ravensmuir. And here was a seal, presumably for Ravensmuir, a keep with a bird perched upon it carved into its face.

There were three or four other deeds, none so splendid as the Ravensmuir's deed nor so tattered as my own hidden contribution. I set them aside, their contents a mystery until some trusted soul could read them to me.

There were perhaps fifty coins scattered in the bottom, a fairly meager treasury but one of interest. The coins were all different, some gold and some silver. I knew silver pennies of this type, though most that passed through my hands had been cheated of silver by nips around the rim. These were intact, perfect circles, and so barely worn that the faces pressed into the metal could yet be discerned.

I laid them out on the indigo coverlet in rows, holding a lantern close to study each in turn. The writing was different on them, some more cursive and some more angular, all equally mysterious. The rulers all looked noble and somber. The coins were all cool in my hand, a balm to the flesh.

It is perhaps a legacy of poverty that I find the caress of coin in my palm reassuring.

There was a small velvet sack there, as well, and I caught my breath when I scattered the contents across the bed. Gems they were, rounded and gleaming; ruby and sapphire and emerald; glistening pearls of silver and black; amethyst and amber; opal and onyx.

A king's ransom was spread before me, sufficient gems

for a diadem in a sack I could hide within my hand. I played with them, making patterns upon the dark velvet, watching the light toy in their depths, counting them. Eventually, I gathered them all back into the sack once more and knotted it tightly.

I reached into the box for the one item that was my own. The letter folded to softness with its secret contents had been my sole addition to this box of treasures. I had tucked it within on the morning that Fitz entrusted this box to me, for it was the only thing in our home that I had needed to bring.

It was the true treasure for me within this box, for it was the last remaining clue to my mother's many secrets. She had died with a hundred things in her heart, not the least of which was the name of the father—or fathers—of Mavella and myself.

To be born a bastard, to not know the name of one's own father, is a circumstance to which a woman may become accustomed but one which she will always hope to see changed. I desired nothing from my father—no coin, no name, no legacy—I wished only to know who he was. I wanted to look into the faces of kin and see similarities, I wanted the one detail of my own existence that had been denied to me.

I knew that I would likely never know it—my mother, after all, had been disinclined to share my father's name, for whatever reason. Her death might well have meant that no one alive knew who my father had been. Perhaps she had never told the man. Perhaps she did not even know herself.

Perhaps it was folly to hope that this letter held the secret I most wanted to know.

Perhaps it was a blessing that I could not read its contents and be disappointed by whatever truth it told.

I unfolded the letter carefully and spread it across the bed, running a fingertip across it with a reverence undiminished. The letter was filled with dense black script from edge to edge, on both front and back, the ink worn from the creases folded and unfolded countless times.

I had never even known of its existence until I plucked it from my mother's chemise when dressing her for burial, and had been frustrated at intervals since by my inability to decipher its contents. That she had treasured it was sufficient for me.

My experience with Merlyn's missive had left me too hesitant to pay to have a missive read aloud in the market. I had never even told Mavella of it. It seemed cruel to wave before her what might be evidence of the one matter we most wished to know, yet to not be able to unveil its secrets. I would much rather present my sister with an answer than a clue.

I bent and inhaled deeply, savoring the last vestige of my mother's scent trapped in the paper. Already the cedar scent of Merlyn's box consumed the last of it. I closed my eyes and could almost feel her presence beside me, the weight of her hand upon my shoulder, the love in her eyes as she smiled, the laughter that understroked her every word.

My mother who defied convention and did not care.

My mother whose merry nature lightened any burden.

My mother who would have done anything for us, anything save tell us our fathers' names.

Ravensmuir was silent as I packed the treasures carefully away. No sound carried from beyond the solar but the relentless litany of the waves cascading upon the shore. I sat awake long into the night, half-convinced that Merlyn still would come to me.

He did not. I fell asleep just before the dawn, disappointed yet again by my spouse's mysterious absence.

I am on the small porch of Kinfairlie's chapel, the spring sunlight spilling around my feet. It is my nuptial day. The villagers are gathered near, my mother smiles radiantly beside me, the man who will be my lord and husband holds

*fast to my hand. Someone has cast a wreath of cowslips
over my head and it slips askew, the yellow blossoms
bouncing in the periphery of my vision. I guess that I am
shaking, given the trembling of the flowers, but Merlyn is
as steady as a rock.*

*The priest is displeased. We have made our vows despite
the lack of banns and his seething disapproval. Coin has only
somewhat appeased him. Now, he has asked for the ring.*

We do not have one.

"Surely it is of little import," *Merlyn says.*

"Surely it is an ill portent," *the fat priest mutters.*

*I look up and Merlyn smiles, his eyes twinkling, his tan
crinkling. He looks undaunted by portents.* "Such is the price
of impulsiveness," *he whispers for my ears alone and I fight a
smile that the priest will deem irreverent.*

"I cannot pronounce you wedded," *the priest complains. I
have the sense that he finds pleasure in denying the Laird of
Ravensmuir his will on such a detail.* "I will not pronounce
you wedded."

"Then you shall have a ring." *Merlyn pulls a silver ring
from the smallest finger of his left hand. He winks as he
pushes the considerable piece of jewelry over my knuckle,
onto the middle finger of my left hand. It is still loose on my
largest finger and we share a smile.*

*I have never seen such a ring. Three stars and three words
are carved into its surface. It is a heavy ring—it nearly fills
my knuckle—and its surface is polished to a gleam from years
of being worn on Merlyn's hand.*

"A family piece," *my mother says with satisfaction.* "It is
good luck to have tradition on your finger."

"My own mother wore it," *Merlyn agrees, his gaze searching mine.* "It is all I have of hers."

*I look down at the ring, my heart in my throat, under-
standing that this man I barely know has surrendered to me
something precious to him, and am touched by his trust.*

"I pronounce . . ."

"Not yet." Merlyn bends his head to mine as the priest flutters impatiently. Merlyn ignores the priest as he touches each name engraved upon the ring in slow succession. "Three names with a star between each," he whispers. "A star like the star of Bethlehem."

"Three kings," I guess and Merlyn smiles.

"Here is the name of Melchior."

My fingertip trails behind his, touching each name after he has touched it. I cannot read the words, but I see the difference between the marks and resolve to memorize which is which.

"The smallest of stature," I say, for I know the tale of these kings as well as any other. "The King of Nubia, he who brought gold to the savior's birthplace."

"And here is the name of Balthazar."

"The King of Chaldea, he who brought incense."

"And here is the name of Jasper."

"The tallest of all of them, a towering black Ethiope and King of Tarshish. He who brought myrrh." I gaze at my wealthy spouse in awe. "Surely this is not a relic wrought by these kings?"

"It is not more than a token made to invoke their protection." Merlyn sobers, then presses his lips to my brow. His voice drops very low, so low that even I have to strain to hear it. "For those moments—may they never come—when you have need of my protection and I cannot aid you."

I hold his gaze, fearful of the portent of his words. The priest raises his hand to bless our match and pronounce us wedded, but I see only the warning in Merlyn's eyes.

The chapel fades suddenly into the moor with the startling ability of dreams. Dark clouds obstruct the sun as they did not on that long-ago day. The moon is in the sky and it is night and I am abruptly alone on the moor, alone without so much as a cloak.

Merlyn is gone.

My mother is gone. The villagers are gone. Even the priest has disappeared.

The ring, though, is heavy on my finger. I turn in confusion, seeking some hint of where I am and why. Hoofbeats echo and I am frightened, fearful as to who comes and what message he brings. Clouds scuttle across the moon, enfolding it in a dark embrace. Ravens shriek into the rising wind and far, far in the distance, a child cries out in terror.

It is Tynan and I know it, know that only I can save him. I run toward the sound of his cry, though I can see nothing, no hint of where he might be. I fear that an omen comes to me, a vision of Tynan's death, a demand that I save him with my deeds.

For it is I and my deeds that are responsible for his peril.

I toss in my sleep, knotting the linens about myself, anxious to waken and act. The nightmare snares me, holds me fast, tightens my chest and wraps about me as securely as a spider's web. I hear myself whimper and moan, but am powerless to stop. The child cries again, the sound further away, and I know that I will be too late.

And then, unexpectedly, a hand lands upon my brow. The touch is warm and soothing. Gentle fingers stroke my face, brushing the terror away so easily that it might not have been real. A man's whisper calms me, eases my trepidation.

I know whose fingers these are. I know the smell and the weight of this caress, I know the strength of it. I know the barren left knuckle as well as my own burdened one.

My husband's fingers slide over me in an endless caress, awakening another fire beneath my flesh and one less easily sated. I feel the heat of my lover join me, his muscled length stretched beside me from shoulder to toe. I feel the touch of a reassuring kiss upon my shoulder, I feel his hand slide over my breast.

And I turn to him, knowing how best to be rid of a nightmare.

In some corner of my thoughts, I fear that I lie alone in the *great Lammergeier bed on a chilly winter night. I keep my eyes closed tightly, evading the truth. In darkness and solitude, I can confess my yearning for my spouse, a yearning to which I dare not give voice outside of dreams.*

In the blackness of the night, I moan my husband's name.

December 29

Feast Day of Saint Marcellus,
Saint Evroul
and Saint Thomas à Becket

XI

A scream startled me to wakefulness.

My eyes flew open as the raven on the high window ledge shrieked again. I saw the shadow of its outspread wings against the opalescent light of the morning, then it croaked and bobbed its head.

Silver flashed, tumbling from its beak into the chamber.

Something tinkled upon the floor. The bird craned its neck, seeking the lost prize in the shadows of the solar below.

I leapt from the bed, half believing the massive bird would invite itself into the room. The small item glinted in the pale light as it rolled, shone as it came to rest. The bird crooked its head inquisitively, its eyes bright. It cried out again and flapped its wings, but I snatched up the prize, then stared at it in astonishment.

It was a ring.

But not just any ring. No, no other ring could curdle my blood as this one did. It was the ring that Merlyn had taken from his hand in Kinfairlie church and slipped onto my own finger.

The ring that I had left in the midst of this very bed five long years before—a silver circle left on indigo that could not have been missed, a potent symbol of my rejection of all facets of our marriage—that ring lay once again in the palm of my hand.

My fingers closed instinctively over it. I looked up at the raven. Where had the bird found the ring?

It held my regard for an eerie moment, then cried out as it took flight. Its silhouette faded quickly into the pale sky, any answers disappearing with it.

Had Merlyn donned the ring again? I closed my eyes and willed myself to remember, but I had not seen it upon his hand of late. Had it fallen from his grip at some point? Had he given it to another woman who rejected him and it?

Or had he flung the ring from this window in disgust all those days and nights ago? The bird might well have plucked it from the moor simply because it shone, as birds are wont to do.

I turned it around, looking at the familiar names etched upon it. How strange the timing, how odd that the bird would find the ring only after I returned to Ravensmuir. How odd that I had dreamed of it just the night before.

It might have been a missive.

Merlyn's voice resonated suddenly in my thoughts: *"For those moments—may they never come—when you have need of my protection and I cannot aid you."*

And again.

"You, chère, of all people, should know that I protect what is mine own."

The hairs on my nape prickled.

My mother had oft said that ravens were uncommon birds, that they had not only the intellect of a bright child, but an ability to pierce the veil that concealed the future from our gaze.

Why would Merlyn not be able to aid me? And from what—or whom—did I need protection?

I shivered. I did not care then for whatever worldly truth might be behind this event—I was convinced that the raven brought a warning from Merlyn to me. He was gone, and I might face danger.

I meant to heed it.

I heard hoofbeats again, racing hoofbeats that came from no realm of dreams. I listened, discerned the sounds of two running steeds, neither destriers nor ponies. They came closer.

I climbed atop a trunk to look and spied two riders fast approaching, their palfreys fairly devouring the road in their haste. It was barely dawn and they must have ridden during the night from wherever they had come, a marvel in and of itself. Only fools or desperate men rode at night, when bandits were abroad.

They seemed to be racing each other on the long straight road to Ravensmuir's gates, and the hot breath of the horses made clouds in the morning chill. As they drew nearer, I saw that their colors were different.

I pulled back, hiding in the shadows though I knew that none would note me here. I needed no scrying glass to guess their identities. They were boys, I could see as much, and their competition and differing colors told me the rest.

I guessed that my powerful neighbors, both the Earl of March and the Earl of Douglas, sent word of their pending arrival. Their messengers raced to recount their lord's plans first in my hall.

Had Calum not warned me that Ravensmuir's wealth made it a coveted prize? I wondered to which man Ravensmuir had been pledged. Did the earls come to secure my pledge of fealty? Did they intend to wrest Ravensmuir from my grip if I did not do their bidding?

And how would I see both men sated with one keep to pledge?

I drummed my fingertips upon the sill. I would need cunning, for I had neither military forces nor the ability to glean whatever secrets lay in Ravensmuir's deed.

Unless they sought the prized relic and not Ravensmuir at all.

My heart lodged in my throat. I dressed hastily but with care, then gave my ring a rub to ensure that any saintly aid was solicited early. I had no doubt that I would need it.

I paused on the threshold of the hall to consider my

course. I was without courtiers, without servants, without allies, but I was not entirely without defenses. I had my wits, I had the contents of Merlyn's box, I had the ring upon my finger.

And several hundred armed men were undoubtedly on their way to my door. My spirit quailed.

A ring was well and good, but I would have a protector with sharper teeth at my side. I fetched some scraps of meat from the kitchen and went to the stables to befriend Merlyn's hound.

Let the heralds wait for the Lady of Ravensmuir.

The dog greeted me at the door of the stables, its tail wagging so hard that it could hardly walk. The meat disappeared in short order and my fingers were licked with great delight. I was delighted myself to be remembered with such favor.

It had been long since any had been so glad to see me as this wolfhound upon this day. I made a fuss over it, which it seemed to welcome, then pushed the wiry silver hair back from its eyes. There was cleverness in its gaze, along with canine devotion, and I hoped it would see fit to protect me, should the need arise. The creature seemed to smile at me, its eyes shining and its tail whipping back and forth. It was lean for all its size, too lean as I could feel its ribs.

No wonder it had welcomed both me and the meat.

It left my side suddenly and cocked a leg, keeping one eye upon me lest I escape while it both relieved itself and made its gender clear. I whistled and stepped into the stables with it fast at my heels, for I meant to seek Merlyn's portal to the labyrinth.

I froze just over the threshold, for I was not alone. A boy's dark head bobbed at the far end of the stalls. The hound darted past me and I followed, emboldened by its lack of concern. I recognized Arnulf's voice when he greeted the dog with some incomprehensible sound. The dog barked at him in delight, then ran back to me, nudging me onward.

Arnulf watched my progress with suspicion in his gaze. It was his task that snared my attention more effectively than his presence. He was brushing down the great black destrier, which had clearly been running. The steed was still in a lather and its coat glistened from its exertions.

I remembered all too well the thunder of hoofbeats that had invaded my dreams and now identified the source of the sound. I feared again that Merlyn's steed was present while he was not. Had he been assaulted again—this time, fatally?

I took a wide path around the stall, aware that Arnulf watched me as warily as I watched him. He grunted and worked steadily, even when I paused beside him.

The dog sat upon my foot and leaned its entire body against me. If I took one sidelong step, the creature would have collapsed in a heap, but the contact was not unwelcome.

"Who ran the horse, Arnulf?" I asked quietly, doubting that Ada's brother had the skill or the audacity to ride his lord's prized stallion.

Arnulf shook his head and frowned. He grunted and brushed the sleek steed, as if I were not there. He moved more quickly though, his agitation evident.

The stallion tossed its head, whinnied and flared its nostrils. It was evidently prepared to run yet more, so it could not have traveled far. The dog, oblivious to my concerns, rubbed the back of its head against my leg, begging for a scratch.

For all the cozy domesticity of my surroundings, my wound itched with vigor. I felt unseen eyes again watching my every move, though I told myself it was only because Merlyn had first surprised me in this very place.

All the same, my words fell from my lips in haste. "Have you seen my lord Merlyn this day, Arnulf?"

Arnulf shook his head as if he would force the sound of my voice from his ears. He scowled fiercely and moved around the stallion, putting the steed's bulk between us. The horse stamped with impatience and fought the bit.

I dreaded that Merlyn lay in a ditch once again, this time without Fitz to retrieve him, with none to guess where he had gone.

But I would have no information from this boy. I folded my arms across my chest and frowned, speaking as much to myself as to Ada's brother. "Truly, none could choose a safer confidant than you, Arnulf."

He regarded me balefully over the stallion's rump, then ducked his head out of sight. I exhaled and tapped my toe with an impatience of my own. What could I do?

I strode to the wall that had opened at Merlyn's command and ran my hands over its surface. I could find no way to open it, of course, a fact that did little to ease my agitation.

Had Merlyn surrendered so many secrets to me, because he feared that he embarked upon a mission of no return?

Why had he not simply told me as much?

Why *did* Merlyn persist in such cursed secrecy? It was infuriating that he kept his secrets so secure, leaving none to chance to betray him, but also ensuring that none could aid him. Was he truly witless enough to think himself invincible?

I could have throttled the man from frustration and concern for his wretched hide. I pounded upon the wood, finding where it echoed hollowly and beating there as loudly as I could. "Merlyn!" I shouted. "I demand admittance! Merlyn!"

Arnulf wailed in protest, but I ignored him. The hound snuffled the ground directly at the base of this place, then snorted and stepped back.

I looked down, saw the blood and knew the worst.

I bent and rubbed the fresh blood between my fingers. It

was wet, but not warm and there was more of it than I would have preferred. Merlyn was here, but injured.

And alone.

A frenzy seized me then and I flung myself at the barrier between us. I pounded and I kicked and I screamed. "Merlyn! You must let me aid you! Merlyn, you cannot crawl into a hole to die like a hound!"

Arnulf cried out. The dog barked, its eyes bright.

When Merlyn did not reply, I feared that he could not do so.

My voice sharpened in fear. "Merlyn! Open this portal and open it immediately!" I beat upon the door with increasing frustration when it did not open and none replied, my voice rising higher. "Merlyn! Merlyn!"

Arnulf bellowed. I heard him running toward me. I rapped again and would have shouted, but the boy grabbed me with startling strength and flung me against the wall. The breath was stolen from my chest and I saw stars before my eyes.

Arnulf's fingers locked around my wrist, and he forcibly halted my knocking. When I rallied to fight him, he pulled me bodily away from the wall and cast me across the stable. I fell against the nearest stall, then glanced up with fear. He balanced himself upon the balls of his feet, his hands clenching and unclenching, his gaze fixed upon me.

I forced myself to my feet, bracing myself for another assault. I moved slowly and deliberately, so as not to provoke him though I had no faith the tactic would work.

We stared at each other, breathing raggedly, for a long moment. Then Arnulf was snatching up the stained straw, gathering what was marked with blood and clutching it to his chest. He worked back and forth, muttering to himself in consternation, collecting all evidence of Merlyn's passing. It seemed sufficient to him that I was away from the hidden portal.

I realized my own stupidity and his cleverness. Arnulf did

not wish me to betray his lord's presence. He had seen Merlyn, of course, watched Merlyn retreat safely into hiding, but I risked all by shouting of Merlyn's presence.

He had stopped me in the only way he could. I watched him remove the evidence of Merlyn's presence and knew that no man could expect greater loyalty from another.

Arnulf completed his collection, then fell to his knees before me, shaking his head repeatedly as he held the straw tightly. He knew he had done wrong by touching me, though I could not fault his impulse.

He stretched out one hand, begging me incoherently not to condemn him, and I saw that there were tears in his eyes. He made a mournful sound over and over again, a sound that might have been an entreaty.

The hound sat and watched us both.

"I will not hurt you, Arnulf," I whispered. He rocked, flicking fearful glances at me. He shook his head mournfully and tightened his grip upon the straw.

I lifted one hand over his shoulder, reaching for the wall once more to test my interpretation. He wailed, then snatched at my wrist and forced my hand back toward myself. As soon as I pulled my hand back, he released me. He folded his arms across his chest, clutching the straw, and rocked more agitatedly, flinching when my gaze fell upon him.

He feared I would strike him for touching me.

Yet he feared even more that I would betray Merlyn by revealing the secret labyrinth.

"Merlyn is fortunate to have such a loyal soul in his abode as you, Arnulf," I said. He looked up at me, as if unable to credit my words. How much did he understand? I smiled at him and he caught his breath, looking away as a dull flush rose on his neck. "Is Merlyn good to you?"

Arnulf glanced tellingly to the stallion then back to me.

"Does he let you ride the beast?"

A shine came into Arnulf's eyes. Perhaps Merlyn took

him into the saddle with him, perhaps he let the boy mount the steed. Whatever the details, it was clear that Arnulf loved the horse and that Merlyn was kind to the boy.

I crouched near him and took his hand.

"I thank you for your warning," I said softly as he watched me. "I understand your concern. I should not try to open the portal, not with strangers at our gates, and I will not do so. You were right to give me such counsel." I rose to my feet and offered him my hand. "Come, we shall burn the straw so that none see it."

He was more than compliant in this, leading me with all the enthusiasm of a pup to the cold smithy at the end of the stables. He piled the straw in the blackened space used for the fire, touched the flint still hanging upon the wall with hesitant fingertips, then turned hopefully to me.

He understood more than I had realized, and he must have been forbidden to deal with fire. Or perhaps he once had burned himself. At any rate, he would not touch the flint.

I struck a flame and touched it to the dry straw. Arnulf hovered beside me, watching and pointing worriedly to snippets of straw that escaped the hungry flames. I pushed them back into the fire with the armorer's tongs, until the fire extinguished itself for lack of fuel and Arnulf was satisfied.

He grunted and dashed past me, back to the stables and his unfinished labor. I followed more cautiously, still aware of the weight of his gaze. I trusted him, just as the dog trusted him, just as the stallion trusted him, just as Merlyn trusted him. I suspected that Arnulf had not been spared many kind words in his day.

Ada was his guardian, after all.

The stallion nickered when Arnulf stepped back into the stall and Arnulf made some guttural reply. He began to brush the beast once again, his gaze flicking once or twice to me as if he was yet uncertain of my intent.

Already it was less evident that the stallion had recently

run. There was no longer any blood upon the straw and I
kicked the other straw to hide any path defined by its lack.
The hound thought this a repeat of our previous game, and
leapt and barked, shaking mouthfuls of straw and pouncing
on errant bits.

I was worried about Merlyn. How could I aid him without an entry to the labyrinth? Would he expect to meet me at
the chapel? In the solar?

Had the blood come from Merlyn at all?

Or was this a ploy to feign disappearance yet again?

How I wished Arnulf could tell me more! I watched him,
discontent. The stallion, perfectly content, nibbled at the
boy's hair. Arnulf made a bellow of protest and tried to
duck away. The steed flicked its tail and persisted, its antics making Arnulf grin. Then he glanced at me and made
a gruff sound to the horse, even as he flushed to the roots
of his hair.

"My lady?" I saw Berthe's silhouette in the portal before
she saw me. I stepped forward and hailed her with a wave.
"My lady, there are two heralds in the hall awaiting an audience with you."

"Thank you." I whistled and the dog trotted by my side.
"I will come to the hall now."

Berthe looked horrified. "Oh no, my lady, we must dress
your hair properly. They are the heralds from the earls and
you must appear fitting . . ."

"Of course." I glanced back, oblivious to Berthe's chatter,
and saw Arnulf's head duck behind the stallion. At least I
had no fear that he would—or could—tell anyone else what
he had witnessed.

It was cold comfort, for I could not guess what he knew
of Merlyn's doings, but it would have to do.

⚜

The heralds, as I had suspected, brought word of the pending arrival of their lords on the next morning. I set Ada and Berthe to work sweeping the hall, dispatched the boys to eat in the kitchen, and retired to my chamber. I hoped desperately to find Merlyn there, awaiting my aid.

I gasped aloud when I found another man lounging in the chamber beneath the solar, his boots upon a trunk. His hair was still of golden hue, his features as handsomely wrought as ever.

I distrusted his presence now, as I should have distrusted it five years before.

"Good morning to you, Gawain," I said with a smooth smile. "What brings you to Ravensmuir?"

Gawain's bold gaze swept over me and he gave a low whistle. He smiled cockily, so much more suave and slippery of manner than Merlyn that I was astounded that I had ever given any credence to anything he had said.

"I have come to challenge your inheritance, of course."

I slammed the door behind myself, unwilling that any others should hear his lies. "On what grounds?"

Gawain pursed his lips. "Ravensmuir should have been mine, of course."

"You are not the eldest son."

"But I was the favored one and I was the one who labored at my father's side while Merlyn sought his own fortune." Gawain pushed to his feet to pace, showing the same lithe grace as his brother. "And my father made a promise to me, as well."

"So you say."

"It is true that our father had no time to commit his pledge to me to vellum." Gawain pivoted suddenly to face me and I dreaded what he would say. "But only because Merlyn ensured as much."

I did not believe it for a moment. Words fell gilded from this one's tongue and appeared to do so effortlessly, as if they carried no weight of conviction with them.

Whereas Merlyn's words came slowly, burdened with import and history, burdened with truth.

I knew who I believed, who I trusted. I folded my arms across my chest. "You may once have deceived me with your honeyed lies, but no more, Gawain."

"Believe what you desire of Merlyn." Gawain shrugged, abandoning his argument too easily. "But know this of your neighboring earls, Ysabella. They will be anxious to see you wedded, to ensure the security of this holding so close to their own."

"And what has this to do with you?"

Gawain smiled. "If I challenge your suzerainty before the company on the morrow, who do you think will be believed?" There was no time to respond to his threat before he continued. "Perhaps you and I could come to a mutually acceptable arrangement, one that will also solve the dilemma of Ravensmuir having no laird."

"What manner of arrangement?"

"We could wed, of course." His shrewd gaze locked with mine. "Then you would have the joy of living at Ravensmuir and I would have the satisfaction of holding sway over all its properties. It could be said that we would both possess what we desire."

"I will not wed you!"

"You may have no choice." Gawain smiled at me, supremely confident.

My greater fear was that he spoke aright, that the earls would indeed find his solution appealing. On the other hand, I dared not tell any of them that Merlyn lived lest I make matters worse.

But why did Gawain come to me first? I straightened, for I have cowed before an empty threat before. Perhaps the earls would not approve of him as laird any more than I did. "Merlyn spoke aright in one matter, Gawain."

"How so?"

"He said you were the most cunning and audacious thief

he had ever known. This is the boldest ploy to steal an inheritance that ever I have witnessed."

Gawain's features tightened, then a slyness dawned in his expression. "What if I have something else with which to wager?"

"Unless you mean to confess to your lies, or say your farewells, there is nothing you might say that I would care to hear." I swept past him, my skirts swishing regally across the floor.

He waited until I was at the foot of the stairs to the solar, then spoke quietly. "Not even that Merlyn lies wounded and in need of your aid?"

I spun to face him.

Gawain's expression revealed nothing. "If you have no interest in my tidings, that suits me well enough. I, too, much prefer my brother dead."

I hastened back to Gawain's side, hating the satisfaction that lit his gaze. "Was it you who assaulted him?"

He laughed. "I am not a killer, Ysabella, but a thief. I might neglect to fetch aid for a man mortally wounded if his death would suit me well, but I would not plunge the blade into his flesh myself."

I studied him, uncertain whether to trust him or not. "Tell me where Merlyn is."

Gawain wagged his finger at me. "Not so quickly as that! Let us make a small wager first."

"I will *not* wed you."

"You might show some care in not insulting me," he chided. "Especially as I hold the key to so much." He came closer, leaned against the wall like a man of leisure directly before me, and spoke softly. "Let us be honest, Ysabella."

"I thought that talent beyond you."

He grinned. "A first attempt, then. It cannot hurt."

"What do you want?"

"Let me be blunt. I do not want to wed you, and I suspect

that you do not want to wed me. I do not really want to possess Ravensmuir . . ."

"Then why . . ."

Gawain's voice hardened. "What I truly desire is the relic my father promised to me."

"If Avery did not give it to you, he must have changed his thinking."

"He had no chance to change his mind," Gawain retorted, uncharacteristically angry now. "Merlyn knew our father's favor turned to me and he killed him before he lost all he sought to gain. Merlyn wanted Ravensmuir, he always wanted Ravensmuir, but then he wanted everything else, as well. He knew our father was going to grant the relic to me, and he prevented that gift in the most effective way possible."

I stepped away, not liking the vindictive tone.

"You cannot shy from this truth, Ysabella," Gawain said, pursuing me. "Merlyn murdered our father."

XII

"No!" I cried, not certain what to believe.

"Oh yes. My father wished to feign his death. He made the mistake of soliciting Merlyn's aid." Gawain's expression turned grim. "But only Merlyn returned from their adventure. Only Merlyn strode into this hall."

"Perhaps Avery did feign his death."

Gawain glared at me. "Then how did his corpse come to wash upon Ravensmuir's shore three days later, his pockets filled with stones?"

I looked away, struggling with this revelation about my spouse. I fiercely wanted Merlyn to be innocent of this. "Where is he?"

"He made the mistake of asking me for aid," Gawain snarled. "After all he had stolen from me. My brother lied in his assessment of me, for he is the more cunning thief of the two of us. That relic should have been mine five years past!"

I felt sickened by not only these tidings, but Gawain's bitterness. "What do you want of me?"

Gawain smiled. "The relic."

"Merlyn might have sold it."

"No. He has sold nothing of merit these past years." Gawain rolled his eyes. "Genuine articles, if you can believe the whimsy of that. His fortunes must have been failing."

"I thought you worked together."

"After he killed our father? After he stole my legacy? After he refused to traffic in any relic which he knew had been stolen?" Gawain scoffed. "No longer are we partners!

He may have denied me my due all this time, but I will have the relic now."

"Merlyn might have moved it."

"No. He has returned here and sought it as diligently as me." Gawain caught my shoulder suddenly, granting me no chance to escape his grip. "I know it was in the chapel. My father told me as much, though he never told me where. I came back to search a month ago and turned every stone in that chapel. It was not there because Merlyn moved it."

"You cannot know . . ."

"I think he found it, and that is why I sent word to him to meet me here, that we might make a wager. Sadly, Merlyn is now in no condition to share tales."

My innards clenched. "Take me to him!"

But Gawain did not move. "I think you know where the relic is, Ysabella. Surrender the relic to me and I will tell you precisely where Merlyn lies bleeding." He arched a brow. "You had best hasten your choice. The blood was flowing quickly when I left him."

"Wretch!"

Gawain smiled. "Have we a wager?"

He gave me a choice that was no choice, and I hated that he knew it. "I have found something, but I am not certain what it is."

"Then let us hasten to it and be certain."

"Tell me where Merlyn is."

Gawain smiled coolly. "Of course. *After* you surrender my relic."

We glared at each other. Gawain knew that he could out-wait me.

I hated him then, hated that he knew so well how to win his desire of me, hated that he would steal what I believed should rightfully be Merlyn's own.

And hated still more that there was nothing I could do about it.

"Once you have your prize, you will leave Ravensmuir forever," I insisted, my teeth gritted.

"If it is what I seek, you will never see me again."

"Now that is a wager worth taking."

We made haste across the grass to the chapel, assuming that all in the keep were too busy to note our sudden need to pray. The pigeons fluttered when I pulled open the door, though it was darker within than the last time I had been here.

"Look there." I pointed to the bundle behind the crucifix and Gawain's gaze brightened.

"Have you opened it?"

"I cannot reach it."

He laced his hands together to give me a boost, but I hesitated before I stepping into his grip. "And Merlyn?"

"Fetch it first." Gawain smiled. "Face the truth, Ysabella. I can take this token now, with or without your aid, and you will only have your due of me if I am pleased with your assistance."

I growled something unflattering as I stepped onto his hands, then steadied myself with one hand on the wall. I reached up and tugged the bundle free. It was about the size of a loaf of bread, round and not heavy. It was wrapped in rough cloth and bound securely with twine.

It was heavy with dust. I sneezed and almost sent us both sprawling. Gawain seized the bundle, his expression triumphant.

"Is it what you seek?"

He looked like a child anxious to open an unexpected gift. "Who can say?" He examined the quantity of dust, the state of the knots and the aging of the twine. "This has not been touched in a long time. More than a year."

"We do not have years to linger over this task. Open it!"

Gawain took his knife from his belt and carefully cut the twine that surrounded the package. He laid the bundle upon the trestle table that was the altar, for a finger of sunlight touched there, and carefully unwrapped the outer layer of cloth. He frowned at the wax barrier within. He gave the package a thorough examination which created a most undesirable delay to my thinking.

"Make haste!"

"Nothing good comes of haste," he chided.

"What of Merlyn?"

"He is more resilient than you know." Gawain studied the package anew, and I was surprised by his thoughtful expression. Satisfied by some criteria I could not name, he carefully cut through the wax. There were two more layers of cloth, as if someone sought to ensure that the contents were protected.

I leaned closer with each layer that he removed, my curiosity growing. It could be a jeweled reliquary, I surmised, or the hilt of a great blade with a fearsome relic trapped within it. I had heard once of a spherical crystal, actually wrought of two crystals shaped as half-globes, then set together with a fragment of the true cross between them.

I was so expectant that I cried out in dismay when Gawain finally peeled back the last layer of cloth. He held an utterly unremarkable piece of wood.

"Wood? It is *wood*?" My incredulity quickly turned to annoyance. "What manner of madman would take such care to wrap a piece of wood? Why would anyone hide such a thing in the first place?" I propped my hands upon my hips and huffed. "What a waste of time and anticipation!"

Then I fell silent in terror that Gawain would not keep our wager, that Merlyn would languish untended.

But Gawain did not look disappointed. He turned the wood in his hands, lifting it into the ray of sunlight. His expression was inscrutable, which should have warned me that I was missing a detail of import.

"And it was hidden behind the crucifix." Gawain made a sound beneath his breath that might have been a laugh. He smiled, then ran his finger across some letters carved deeply into the wood upon one side, no doubt to draw my attention to it. He gave me such a wicked look that I knew the inscription was critical.

" 'And Pontius Pilate wrote a title, and put it on the cross. And the writing was JESUS OF NAZARETH THE KING OF THE JEWS. This title then read many of the Jews: for the place where Jesus was crucified was nigh to the city: and it was written in Hebrew, and Greek, and Latin.' "

I stared at him, recognizing the passage all too well. "That is from the Bible, from the account of Christ's crucifixion."

"Yes." Gawain examined the letters again. "The gospel of Saint John. Chapter nineteen, verse nineteen, I believe."

I watched him, my mouth working in silence for a long moment. "You cannot mean what I think you mean!" I sputtered that he would try to tell me such an outrageous lie. "This is not the True Cross!"

"No," he agreed altogether too easily. "If anything, it is what is known as the *Titulus Croce*. The sign that was hung over the crucified Jesus to explain his crime."

"Jesus of Nazareth, the King of the Jews," I whispered.

"*Iesus Nazarenus Rex Iudaeorum*, in the Latin, abbreviated to INRI." Gawain traced this last upon the table with a fingertip, leaving marks in the dust gathered there. I recognized the letters from the inscription over the crucifix in Kinfairlie's parish church.

"That is not what is writ upon the wood."

"*Nazarenus*," he said, writing again in the dust. "Of Nazareth."

"It is still not the same."

"But the Romans wrote it like this: *NAZARENVS*. And if

we include the beginning of the next word, which is *rex*, or king: *NAZARENVSRE*."

I stared at the wood. That was indeed what was carved there, at least in one line.

"And this line?"

"The Greek. Sadly, I do not read Greek as well. The third line is probably Hebrew, which I do not read at all."

God in heaven, what if it was genuine? What if the desire to possess such a prize was at the root of all this wickedness?

I was rationally unable to accept this, though I looked at the wood with newfound awe. "No, it cannot be. It makes no sense. Such a relic would be precious, it would be secured in some place, probably in Rome itself, and guarded vigilantly."

"The tale is that it was for a long time."

"But then?"

"Lost. I believe the last time it was shown was in the twelfth century or so." Gawain winked at me and made to re-wrap the bundle. "Merlyn would have known. He was always better with such details."

I seized his arm. "What do you mean, he would have known?"

"This will do very well for your part of the wager, Ysabella." Gawain knotted the twine with care so that the prize would be protected. He inclined his head in a mocking bow, tucking the bundle beneath his arm as he did so. "Every good fortune to you in this life, Ysabella. Per our agreement, I fear that our paths shall never cross again."

"What about Merlyn?"

"Merlyn?" Gawain granted me a cocky smile. "Oh, he is dead, have you not heard?"

I was outraged by the implication of his words. "You said he lay wounded, you promised, you . . ."

"Oh, I lied, Ysabella." Gawain shrugged, unrepentant, then clicked his tongue. "You should know better than to believe every bit of nonsense told to you, especially by the likes of me."

I was aghast. "You cannot simply leave!"

But he was doing precisely that, striding through the chapel with remarkable speed. I chased him, bursting through the chapel doors as he leapt over the lip of the rocks.

"But wait! Wait!" I scrambled after him and he paused, though he was poised to flee. "The plate! There was a plate in the chapel. Did you leave it there?"

Gawain laughed aloud. "It is not my task to collect and clean the crockery."

"Then you did use it?"

"I am not so churlish as to decline a meal Ada cooked for me."

I took a step after him, my thoughts whirling. "But how did she bring it to you? This gorse was not cut back then."

Gawain shook his head, amused at my confusion. "Foolish Ysabella!" He laughed merrily. "Are you the only one who does not know about the labyrinth?"

Then he was gone with all the infuriating ease that Merlyn oft showed. I lunged after him, but to no avail. He was faster than me, and evidently knew the winding course that made its way down the face of the cliff. By the time I spied the shadowed mouth of the labyrinth, there was no sign of Gawain or the *Titulus*.

I halted and my shoulders sagged. I would never find him in that dark hole. Reluctantly, feeling seven kinds of fool that I fell for his ploy, I climbed back to the chapel, said a prayer, then returned to Ravensmuir's hall.

Too late I realized that I had been tricked out of the one gift with which I might have sated a greedy earl.

I stepped into the kitchens and Berthe came bustling to

my side. "My lady, I have sought you high and low! A caller wishes to see you," she said, her eyes telling me more of her reservations than her words.

Merlyn! Finally, he sought me out! Anticipation hastened my steps to the front gates. We ducked through the portal into the bracing chill of the air. Not twenty steps away, a man glanced over his shoulder. He stood in the building's shadow, his anxiety revealing that his was no leisurely perusal. My gaze strayed beyond him to a mare harnessed to a cart.

The visitor was dressed simply, not richly. His chausses were dark, his boots muddied and worn with use. His cloak was full and dark, his red-blond hair curled long over his collar. He turned a felt hat in his hands with restless gestures, though his fingers halted at the sight of me. He stared at me, his eyes narrowed.

"Ysabella?" he whispered, incredulous, even as I gasped in recognition.

"Alasdair!"

We gaped at each other, each failing to comprehend how the other came to be in this place. He was older, as was I, and somewhat thicker around the middle. There were a few strands of silver in his hair, but he looked well enough.

His ring finger, I noted immediately, was barren.

But then, not all men wore such clear evidence of a nuptial pledge. I remembered that Mavella said she had seen Alasdair with a young boy and steeled my heart against him.

After a long moment of silence, we strode toward each other and both spoke at once.

"Surely you cannot be the Lady of Ravensmuir . . ."

"What brings you to our portal . . ."

We paused and laughed uneasily, shaking our heads. I waved dismissively to Berthe, whose eyes were filled with undisguised curiosity. "We are old friends well-met. Thank you, Berthe. Return to your labor, if you please."

She bowed, took one last lingering look, then disappeared into the keep with evident regret.

"Ysabella!" Alasdair exclaimed, his gaze slipping over me. "I cannot believe it is you."

I shrugged. "It is indeed, and I am Lady of Ravensmuir." I resisted the urge to comment upon matches well-made.

Alasdair fingered his chin and sobered. "Though your presence here makes more sense of what has happened."

"What do you mean?"

He regarded me keenly. "How fares Mavella? Has she wed? Is she well?" His gaze slipped over the high walls. "Is she here?" His face fell. "Or has some lofty lord claimed her for his bride?"

I took a step back, choosing not to answer his questions as yet. "Tell me why you have come to Ravensmuir, Alasdair."

He smiled in a way that made him look boyish. "You will think me mad."

"Perhaps not."

He shrugged in his turn and cast a glance down the road as he sobered. "Perhaps you know that my father died last winter."

"I had heard. I am sorry."

"I thank you. I returned to Kinfairlie to administer the mill, which is my inheritance."

I saw no reason to delay. "With a child."

Alasdair met my gaze steadily. "With my cousin's son." He smiled as my eyes widened. "As I have no child of my own and his five brothers will ensure he has little inheritance, I deemed it fitting to take this boy as my apprentice and heir."

It was a gracious gesture and one I would have expected of the Alasdair I had known, at least before he had shredded my sister's heart. "You did not wed again," I guessed.

Alasdair shook his head firmly. "I could not." He frowned, choosing his words with care. "Mavella has haunted me all of my days and nights. I know that I showed cowardice in bending to my father's demand." His lips tightened. "And I know that I never loved the bride I took with the fervor she deserved, for the memory of Mavella always stood between us. I erred, but many others paid the price for my mistake. I could not wed a second time and make the matter worse once more." He glanced at me. "I have long known this, although last night, I was reminded of my folly."

"How so?"

"You will laugh."

"I pledge not to."

Still he struggled to find the words. "Last night, a demon rose from hell to visit me. You may believe that I am mad, but I did not think myself to be dreaming. I was and am certain that I was awake, that this demon stood before me in the very flesh."

"A demon?"

Alasdair shook his head. "It sounds mad, I know. He was garbed in black, he was tall and terrifying. His face was pale, his eyes glittered, his steed was larger than any that I have ever seen and it fairly breathed fire." He took a shaking breath. "Never have I seen a soul so fearsome. He called to me from my own stoop and when I barred the door against him, he spurred the beast onward."

I watched Alasdair's throat work in agitation. "The steed kicked down the door. The demon entered my abode. He halted the beast by my very pallet. He leaned down, eyes gleaming. He seized my chemise in his cruel grip. He shook me like a sack of bones and he told me he had come to avenge my crime."

Alasdair shivered, then swallowed. "He told me that I had wronged a woman in my time, that I had cast aside a love granted to me by God's own grace, that I had heeded malicious gossip when my heart should have been true. He told me that I had proven love a lie, and that if I did not repent, he would see my soul in torment for all time."

Alasdair hung his head. "I thought immediately of Mavella, for I knew that I wounded her and feared even then that it was for no good cause."

He shook his head. "I know it sounds like madness. I know that no thinking person could credit my tale, but . . ."

"I believe you."

Alasdair spared me a hopeful glance. "You do?"

I had an inkling who this demon had been and thus I smiled. "Yes. I do not think that you are mad."

"Good. Good." He shuffled his feet and turned his hat at this unexpected endorsement. "Well, good!"

"And what happened?"

"I shivered and I begged for mercy and the demon spake again. He told me that my crime could be made right. He said that if an honest love yet burned in my heart, then he had no desire of my soul. He wanted only those whose hearts were as black and cold as a week-old ember. He told me this was my last chance to make amends."

"But how?"

"He bade me ride to Ravensmuir with all haste, he commanded me to arrive here before the sun set again lest he be compelled to take his gruesome penance." He shivered. "He said he would return for me this night, and drag me into his demon hole, there to torment me for all eternity—unless I rode for Ravensmuir this very day."

Alasdair met my gaze. "I did not understand how my arrival here might grant me a chance to apologize to Mavella, but I came. Indeed I dared not do otherwise! Now, it seems more clear. I beg of you, Ysabella, if you know Mavella's whereabouts, then tell me of them. I must see her and I must see her before the sun sinks again."

"Lest the demon return again?"

Alasdair shook his head. "I fear him, of course. But he told me only what I knew, what I had already been summoning the courage to do. I should have sought Mavella out immediately upon my return to Kinfairlie, but I feared she had wed another and I feared to see her as happy with another as I was miserable alone. I know that I deserve no less. I should never have spurned her, but then, perhaps she deserved a more loyal ardor than I could offer."

I studied the long stretch of the road, touched deeply by Merlyn's intervention to secure my sister's happiness.

"I do not care if Mavella is wed, so long as she is happy. I do not care if she spits in my eye, if only I can see her again. It is time that I told her truly what is in my heart. It is time that I grant her the apology she deserves." Alasdair seized my hand, evidently concluding from my delay that I would refuse him. "Tell me, Ysabella, I beg of you, whatever you have thought of me before."

There was no doubting his sincerity.

Nor what Merlyn had done to win my favor. I touched Alasdair's shoulder. "She is here. I shall fetch her." His eyes lit and I knew I should offer him hospitality. "Would you like a place by the fire and a cup of ale? There is food aplenty in the kitchen and the hall."

Alasdair shook his head. "I will stay with my horse."

"I shall send you a cup."

"I have no need of even your reputed brew, Ysabella." He smiled, looking as anxious as a much younger man. "And I would prefer not to plead my case beneath its potent influence."

I hastened back to the portal, intent upon uniting two souls who had been parted overlong, then paused, unable to resist. "You might see a familiar face in this kitchen. Ada Gowan labors here."

"Ada Gowan?" Alasdair frowned as he sought to place the name.

"The silversmith's daughter."

"Oh!" He grimaced. "I shall wait here, if it pleases you."

It most certainly did.

I found Mavella in the hall. A word in her ear and she was on her feet, mystified and showering me with questions even as she followed me. I ignored her queries, then pushed her silently through the portcullis.

"But what madness is this? Do you cast me from your hearth?" she demanded, smiling at my mysterious manner. I grasped her shoulders and kissed her cheek, then spun her to face Alasdair.

She knew him immediately, even at this distance. I heard her breath catch and when he turned to stare at her, she clutched my hand where it still rested on her shoulder. Her voice trembled. "What jest is this, Ysabella?"

"No jest. Alasdair comes to apologize. The boy is his cousin's child, his chosen heir because he has no wife and child of his own."

"Oh!" Mavella's face suffused with color. Alasdair turned his hat restlessly in his hands once more, his gaze fixed upon her. I was glad that she was dressed as finely as she was, glad that he would be humbled and awed by the sight of her.

Because I knew that she would forgive him without a moment's hesitation.

"What should I do?"

"Live, Mavella," I reminded her. I squeezed her fingertips tightly. "You should seize the moment and live, as you yourself pledged that you would."

Her grip tightened on my fingers briefly and she lifted her chin. She kissed my cheek and I saw that there was a sparkle in her eyes and a smile upon her lips. Then she lifted her skirts and strode towards Alasdair, as regal and as fair as a queen of the fey.

I leaned back into the shadows, hugging myself with delight, laughing aloud that she managed only half the distance before she picked up her skirts and began to run. Alasdair shouted with joy and opened his arms to her, swinging her high in his embrace as they laughed together.

They kissed and touched each other's faces and whispered before they walked away, hands entwined as they shared words long overdue. Their heads bent close, gilded in the sunlight, confidants as they had so oft been before. I turned away, tears glazing my vision and my throat tight.

Ah, Merlyn. How could I resist a man who made my battles his own to win? My heart swelled fit to burst. I knew where his steed had been, I knew the demon who tormented Alasdair. I loved him for it, loved him with all my heart and soul, loved him with all the ferocity he had asked of me.

But in the solitude of my chamber that night, when Merlyn still did not show his visage, Gawain's lie grew monstrous with possibility. I thought of the blood in the stables and I feared that Gawain had unwittingly found a root of truth for his falsehood. My wound itched with vigor and even the hound was haunted by dreams.

I take a deep breath of cold, salt-tinged air, and feel the warmth of the dying sunlight upon my face. I see the brilliant blue of a summer sky streaked with the orange and gold of the setting sun. I stand on the lip of the sea and curl my toes around the rocks of the coast. I stand straight and tall, filled with vigor.

I smile, reassured, for I not only know this dream, but the buoyant optimism which it awakens in me. Though I cannot summon it apurpose, it comes when all seems darkest.

It is a gift, from I know not where. I welcome it.

I tip my head back and lift my arms, laughing when the wind lifts my toes from the earth.

I am liberated. I am freed. I am invincible.

And I am flying. I wheel like a gull, as naked as the day I was born. I turn back inland and sweep over the ruins of Kinfairlie manor, then soar to cast my shadow across the forbidding face of Ravensmuir. I laugh, leap and tumble through the air, swoop down to play with the waves crashing against the cliffs.

Then, as always I do in this dream, I dip and turn, fly out over the sea to seek Merlyn, drawn to him like a moth to the flame. The sky is darker in the east, a blue so deep where the heavens meet the sea that the horizon cannot be readily discerned. There are stars out in the east, a thousand stars lighting the sky, diamonds cast on velvet.

I spy the silhouette of the ship almost immediately, its sails full of the wind. He is close, my Merlyn, closer than usual, a measure perhaps of how large he looms in my thoughts this night.

His ship races toward me, the prow slicing through the sea and casting the foam aside. My heart leaps painfully when I see him, his gaze trained upon the sky, his feet braced against the deck, his white chemise fluttering in the wind. He seeks me, as if he has summoned me though I know that is not so.

No, I have chosen to seek him.

Perhaps he always is waiting for me, waiting for me to dream of him, waiting for me to come to him. I cry out as I swoop low, sounding not unlike a gull, and I see the flash of Merlyn's smile. Matters are simple in my dream—there is nothing left unsaid between us, nothing one needs from the other, nothing but joy in our meeting again. Matters are so simple that I nearly weep with gratitude—nothing has ever been simple between us two.

It is as if my husband is another man. There is joy in his smile and a thousand stars shining in his eyes. He is not burdened, this Merlyn—he is hearty and open and his embrace is resolute. His kiss tastes of salt and sea and Merlyn himself, his tongue demands, his hands caress.

I wrap myself around him, twine my fingers into his hair,

meet him touch for touch. I want no less than his all, return his kiss with the ardor of a wanton, demand no less than every pleasure he can give, and am prepared to grant him all of myself.

Because I love him.

I awakened shivering in Ravensmuir's solar, the linens knotted about myself as night and starlight spilled through the windows. I awakened alone. There was no scent on the pillows, no hand on my waist, no warm indent in the bed beside me. The hound whimpered softly, snared in some dream, but I was snared more surely in the tangles of this life.

And I was afraid as I have never been afraid. I feared that Merlyn only laughed unburdened, as in my dream, because he drew breath no longer. I feared that Merlyn came to me in dreams to say farewell because he could not do so in life.

That prospect left me terrified of future days, for I would face them alone. A ring and a hound seemed poor substitutes for my Merlyn.

For I realized the truth of my love for him too late.

December 30

*Feast Day of Saint Sabinus and
His Companion Martyrs,
of Saint Anysia and of Saint Maximus*

XIII

It was Malcolm Gowan who came first to Ravensmuir's gates.

Berthe brought word to me as I bathed, and I bade her invite him into the hall. I did not doubt that he came to confirm the truth of my newfound wealth, and perhaps to ingratiate himself.

Malcolm did better than I expected at that. He bowed low over my hand, pausing to admire my ring. "An heirloom?" he asked, studying it with the keen eye of one who knows good work.

"My husband's mother wore it."

"It is a remarkable piece." He held fast to my hand, apparently unwilling to release my hand lest he be forced to end his perusal.

I pulled my fingers away. "Your sister is in the kitchen, if you come to bid her good tidings for the year ahead."

"I will do so, but first I will render my due." He lifted a small sack and smiled at my confusion. "The proceedings from the sale of your ale," he said, and pushed the sack into my hand. A dozen silver pennies spilled into my palm when I opened it, more than my share of this batch.

Perhaps it was compense of a balance previously withheld.

I met his shrewd gaze. "It seems that the profits are high from one batch of ale."

Malcolm colored. "It befits a man to even his accounts before the dawn of the year. I apologize if such renderings have not been timely in the past."

I saw no reason to argue the matter with him. We both knew what was at root—it was no longer fruitful to take advantage of me. I stepped away from him, saddened by this view of human nature. "You are welcome to break your fast in the hall or the kitchen."

"If you have need of the services of a silversmith . . ."

"I am neither buying nor selling in this time," I said, granting him a steely glance. "As befits a widow."

"But in future . . ."

I smiled coolly. "I know how to find your abode, and know well the reputation of your family."

He flushed then, the back of his neck as fiery as his face. He dropped his gaze, my implication understood by both of us. I stared at the coins, so long overdue and only rendered because my favor could now be advantageous to the Gowan silversmiths.

I hoped he would not plead for trade from me again.

As the morning sun reached over Ravensmuir's towers and touched the moor to the west, I stood at our gates, Mavella on my right hand and the dog seated at my left. We could hear the earls approach, hear the rumble of numerous steeds and the heavy tread of men of war, and I was agitated.

They said they came in peace, but I was skeptical. As they rode into sight, I sought to look unimpressed, as if displays of finery were a bore to one so worldly and wealthy as me, but it was not readily done.

Indeed, the pageantry nigh stole my breath away.

The Earl of Douglas' heralds arrived first, their trumpets sounding at intervals. The boys were garbed in the earl's colors, the coats of their palfreys were brushed to gleaming chestnut. Behind them came the standard bearer, holding the earl's banner high before himself, his mare prancing proudly. And the wealth was startling! The rings on one squire's hand would have seen we three siblings sustained with meat and every manner of fine victual for a year in Kinfairlie village.

Next came the knights themselves, riding their enormous destriers in pairs down the road. Their greaves and helmets flashed in the sun, their visors up and their shields slung upon their saddles. There must have been a dozen of them in all, men with grim countenances who bloodied their hands to earn their way. A few of them were likely mercenaries, for their garb was less regal and their emblems unfamiliar.

"God in heaven," Mavella muttered through her teeth. "There must be a thousand in this party." The knights arrayed themselves in a half circle, the standard bearer and heralds before them, a gap in their ranks for their lord.

"Perhaps two hundred, that is all."

She snorted as if the difference mattered little, which was true enough. "What do they want, Ysabella?"

"I would guess Ravensmuir." I watched them warily.

"Is this not the standard of the Earl of Douglas?"

I nodded. "Sir William, keeper of Tantallon, lord of Liddesdale."

My sister's lips tightened in disapproval. "His notoriety is as considerable as his age."

I nodded. Even we had heard the old tale of William's return from knightly adventures abroad to find his uncle, godfather, and namesake—Sir William Douglas, the Knight of Liddesdale, a legendary wicked knight—the sole obstacle to the claiming of his inheritance.

It had been in 1358 that nephew had assaulted uncle in the Forest of Ettrick. Only this younger William had ever left those woods alive. The charter of Liddesdale had become his own, by grant of a now-deceased king. William had built his stronghold just north of Ravensmuir to show his power, not only over his holding but beyond it.

Mavella had never heeded the details of noble doings. I

shared our mother's fascination with their bickering. For me, their squabbles showed them as common as us villagers. When our mother passed, I continued to ferret out details of our so-called betters. I shared a morsel of recent news with my sister now.

"There was gossip in Kinfairlie market that he challenged the claim of Robert the Steward to Scotland's crown this very year."

"How so?" Mavella asked, though I saw that her thoughts were with Alasdair, now back in Kinfairlie's mill.

Probably he whistled as merrily as Mavella's eyes shone.

At least one matter resolved itself aright.

"William was made royal justiciar of all territories south of the Firth by the new king, after William withdrew his protest of Robert's ascent to the throne. There are those who called it a wager to win his support. There are others who suggest he challenged King Robert purely to gain such a prize. He had little influence with the old king and had fallen far out of favor."

Mavella turned to face me, her expression perplexed. "I thought Sir Robert Erskine was the royal justiciar. He was favored by the king, and was said to hold Stirling's revenues as well."

"Favored by the king who died, Mavella. Even royal favor has no influence from beyond the grave, and royal grants do not oft outlive those who make the endowment."

Mavella pursed her lips. "So, this one has the weight of the king's hand behind him. Tread carefully, sister mine."

I nodded, for there was nothing to be said to that. Sir William was a powerful man and one who had used force to achieve his ends before. And we were far from the king's court. I had no illusions that any king was more concerned with justice than influence and wealth.

I had best think quickly if I meant to secure the advantage of Ravensmuir as Tynan's legacy. I rolled Merlyn's ring around my finger, feeling woefully unprepared for this confrontation.

The earl himself rode alone, with sufficient space before and behind him that his identity could not be mistaken. He had doffed his helmet and the white of his hair shone in the morning light. When he passed through the gap left for his arrival, the knights closed ranks behind him. A bevy of squires and servants took up the rear of his party, and they spread behind the knights until the circle was at least three deep.

I had no idea what foodstuffs were piled in the storage rooms of Ravensmuir, but I dearly hoped that they were plentiful. This was a man I was not anxious to offend with meager hospitality.

William rode directly to me, the reins gathered in his gloved grip. He was a handsome man even for his age, his eyes a cold and calculating blue, his expression uncompromising. Though he halted his steed, he did not dismount to greet me.

I understood the implied slight, but lifted my chin in disapproval and met his gaze steadily.

"My lady Ysabella." He inclined his head. "It is a pleasure to finally make your acquaintance." There was a hint of accusation in his tone, but I did not rise to it.

"Indeed, sir." I replied with just as much formality. "How *kind* of you to make the journey to my abode."

He looked at me again, assessing my tone, no doubt wondering whether my emphasis had been deliberate. Then he spoke with greater care. "It is only fitting that I offer my condolences to the widow of the Laird of Ravensmuir."

He did not address me by my title.

I inclined my head in turn. "And those condolences are gratefully received by the Lady of Ravensmuir."

Did I dare believe that he came in peace? Or would he seize Ravensmuir willfully from my grip once his men had infested my hall? Did I have a choice as to whether to admit him? William's face betrayed nothing of his thoughts. But the other earl had to be fast upon this earl's heels.

Perhaps I could play these competitive men against each other.

William cleared his throat. "I was shocked to hear the news of Merlyn's demise, of course. It is a sorry day that a nobleman cannot ride abroad in certainty of his own safety."

"It is indeed."

His gaze fixed upon me. "Did your lord Merlyn ride alone?"

It was a curious detail to request. "I do not find it tasteful to discuss such sordid details in my bereavement." I let my voice rise, as if I were upset. "Of what matter is it? My lord husband is just as dead, whether he rode alone or with another!"

William dismounted, and bowed low before me. "I apologize most sincerely, my lady. It is the nature of a man of war to forget the fragility of women. I wondered only how Merlyn was found, how he was retrieved, when he was buried." Again his gaze sought some answer in mine and I found myself bristling.

What troubled him was that he had not seen Merlyn's corpse. Perhaps he did not believe Merlyn dead. Perhaps he called me a liar.

Perhaps I did not care for his inference, either way.

"How charitable of you to fret for my husband's immortal soul," I said in a tone that implied otherwise. "But you need not fear, Sir William. Merlyn is safely interred and his passing was blessed, though I prefer to not discuss such grim details." I held his gaze as I lied, recalling all that

Merlyn had told me of the ways of ensuring a lie was believed.

I could not guess whether William believed me or not.

"My regrets, my lady." He bowed again and offered the merest smile. "Know that I would have attended the funeral mass, had I been aware of when and where it was held. Merlyn was an exceptional man."

"My apologies in turn, Sir William." I softened ever so slightly. "I was not sufficiently familiar with my husband's acquaintances in this land to ensure that all were summoned. I took refuge in the comfort of family."

He smiled then, a chilly smile that did little to ease his harsh features. "Still you do not know who was responsible for this vile deed?"

"No, I do not. Do you?"

He inhaled sharply at my audacity. "Would you believe me, my lady Ysabella, if I swore that I would find Merlyn's killer?"

There was no accusation in his tone, no chastisement for whatever suspicion I felt toward him or any other. He had assessed my situation and appreciated that it was not a good one.

"I dare not trust any man until my husband's assailant is brought to justice, sir."

He smiled more broadly. "No one can fault another for showing caution in the wake of danger."

I was uncertain what to make of his change in manner.

A fleeting frown touched his brow when I said nothing and his tone altered once again, becoming cautious. "You spoke of family. Did you and Merlyn have children?"

"Sadly, no. My younger brother will be heir to Ravensmuir."

"How young?"

"He has seen four summers."

The older man was clearly discontent with this news. "A dangerous age for children."

"What is that to mean?"

William met my gaze steadily. "That a young heir oft does not survive to gain his legacy. Childhood is fraught with *accidents*."

My blood chilled. I was suddenly very glad that Tynan was not present to meet these flint-hearted men.

"Is Merlyn's brother, Gawain, in residence at Ravensmuir?"

"No longer," I declared and took Mavella's hand. "My sister lingers to console me in my grief."

"How gracious." William bowed over her hand. He reached to scratch the dog's ears but the hound snarled at him.

I shrugged, thinking what meat I continued to give the beast was well invested. "I apologize but the hound is somewhat protective." I rubbed the creature's chin and it licked my fingers, its gaze never straying from William.

"I suggest you let no other soul feed it, my lady, for the loyalty of a hound fed by one's own hand is the only loyalty that is never in doubt."

"Did you come to warn me, Sir William?"

His expression turned secretive and he looked back at his men. "Among other matters."

Before I could ask what he meant, the clarion call of another herald sounded over the moor. We looked down the road as one, and the Earl of March's party came into sight, just as richly adorned as this party but somewhat less numerous.

"George Dunbar, the Earl of March," muttered William.

"Yes, he sent word of his pending arrival."

"Did he?" William donned his gloves once more.

"Ravensmuir's stable is at your disposal, sir, though I must apologize for the lack of ostler and squires at Ravensmuir. We have kept a minimal household here, given our infrequent visits. I hope there is sufficient fodder for so many steeds."

William nodded brusquely. "I am certain that all shall be suitable."

I was less certain, but continued all the same. "I should appreciate some allowance made for the party of the Earl of March in the stables. I would not have my hospitality slighted, though I leave such details to be arranged between men."

"As is most proper." William lifted a hand to his party, granting me a grin so wicked that I was surprised. "Though I tell you, my lady, that March can sate himself with my leavings. It is a lesson I delight in teaching him these days."

When he might have turned away, I called after him. "A moment, Sir William. My husband's assailant is still at large. You will understand my reluctance to have armed men in my hall when there is a threat against my family and my house."

I watched him struggle with this, for he knew what I would ask. He understood my reasoning, yet it went against his grain to cede it to me.

"I would have your blade surrendered to my hand, Sir William, while you linger at my keep. And I would have your pledge that each of your men will leave their weapons of war outside my hall."

"You know that this is most uncommon."

I held his gaze stubbornly. "You know that my circumstances are most uncommon, and this situation constrains my hospitality."

"It is beneath the dignity of a knight to be asked such a thing."

"I agree that this is a matter better suited to men. Perhaps you and the Earl of March might provide a check each upon the other, to ensure that my will is served in my hall and my family's safety is secured. I ask this of you, relying upon your reputation as a knight and a man of honor."

William's gaze flitted over the ramparts and gates, assessing my keep's defenses, then he studied me, seeking some weakness.

Resignation crossed his brow and I was relieved. Whether he would protect me from himself, from the Earl of March, or simply deceive me into trusting him, I could not say.

William bowed his head, unbuckled his scabbard and offered the sheathed blade to me. "I cede to you, Lady Ysabella, for I too would see Merlyn Lammergeier's murder avenged."

I took the blade and gripped the scabbard tightly. "Then, I bid you welcome, Sir William. Welcome to Ravensmuir."

He bowed, then beckoned his party onward. The knights parted to let six wagons that had been arrayed behind the knights pass through their ranks. The wagons were loaded to the point of sagging, I had assumed with bedding and weaponry. As they passed through Ravensmuir's gates under William's direction, however, I saw that they were loaded with food and wine.

"God bless him," Mavella murmured gratefully.

But I was not so quick to invoke such favor for a man whose motives I could not clearly discern. Indeed, I wondered what would be the price of William's understanding.

I greeted my next guest, George Dunbar, with his lofty condolences and his comparatively humble retinue. Our new king had chosen—or been compelled to choose—Sir William over him, and it seemed that Sir George did not take the change of stature well. It had been rumored that George's sister Agnes was to be King David's new bride—but the roof of Edinburgh keep had fallen in upon David and his men before the nuptial vows could be exchanged.

Before Sir George could secure the advantage he expected to become his own, King Robert had a wife and no need of Agnes, thus the alliance was thwarted.

George was glum, as one might expect, and sighed heavily though without surprise at the news that William had arrived first at Ravensmuir. I had set a precedent he could not deny by claiming William's blade—George recognized it on sight and, no doubt not wanting to be outdone, was quick to offer his own blade as well.

Calum was among Sir George's attending knights, and I recalled that he had said his fealty was pledged to Dunbar. He spared me but a slight smile, intent as he was upon easing closer to his liege lord.

Intriguingly, it appeared that Sir George evaded Calum, though only a watchful soul would have noted as much and perhaps my fanciful eye found evidence of something that was not there.

Once we were seated in the hall, I noticed how seldom knights spoke to Calum. It seemed he had few intimates. I recalled Merlyn's claim that he was unworthy of trust.

But then, relations between men were complicated by matters of alliance and advantage. Perhaps others had had their eye upon Dunkilber and resented that Calum had been granted not only the manor but the glory of besieging it to make his claim. The truth was not of great import, so I put the matter from my thoughts.

There were myriad details, after all, to occupy my attention. Mercifully, there was a great deal of fine wine stored in Ravensmuir's cellars. There were stores that I had not known I possessed yet were most welcome in this moment. Long contented with ale—though surely not of the caliber of mine—the men fell upon the opened casks with delight.

Praise be to God that there were many more casks.

We ate late, well past midday, for there was much to be arranged and settled before the men could come to the board, and indeed, much haste in the kitchen to even see the board laid. I feared the men would be stone drunk before they had a morsel in their bellies, and that madness would ensue, but the kitchen door opened just as the din rose too loud.

The men were ravenously hungry and they ate heartily, sparing attention for little beyond their trenchers and cups. The hall was filled to bursting for once, and I was glad of both the merry blaze in the fireplace and the space we had to offer.

I sat between two old men, George Dunbar and William Douglas. George was less lean than William, less like a hawk and more like a dumpling. His manner was somewhat morose, as I have said. They were not great friends or even allies, for what few words were exchanged between them were terse. Sir George's son John sat upon his left, Mavella sat upon William's right.

I could not eat, even with their blades in my possession. They must have come to wrestle over Ravensmuir and I had to somehow secure my own inheritance. The food was as dust in my mouth.

"I suppose we have both come for the same reason," George said as he pushed back from the remains of his meal.

"I suspect that we have," William agreed. He flicked a glance to me. "You do understand, my lady, that Ravensmuir's succession from Merlyn must be assured and witnessed by your closest neighbors."

"I know no such thing. Is it not the king who must be privy to such matters?"

"As royal justiciar, I am effectively the king in these parts," William said icily.

"As a baron of the realm, I provide an insurance upon the authority of the crown's representative in such matters," George added with a stony glance to William.

"But I fail to see why Ravensmuir is of such interest." I dabbed my lips delicately with my napkin. "There is no wealth in the manor itself. There are no fields, no villeins, no tithes."

"Its location alone is too key to suffer it to fall into the hands of an enemy," William said. George nodded and they both looked expectantly to me. "To whom do you intend to swear fealty?"

"I must confess that I do not know the tradition of Ravensmuir." Tradition, we all knew, was the root of the practice of law outside matters of high justice. "My husband never discussed such matters with me."

"As is proper," William agreed. "It is not a woman's place to engage in such arrangements."

George cleared his throat. "I beg to differ. My own mother defended Dunbar in my father's absence."

"*'Came I early, came I late, there was Agnes at the gate'*," William said flatly, recounting some verse I did not know. "Your mother's deeds are well known, George, though your family tends to forget that she would have had no need to defend Dunbar if your father had not treacherously given it to the English king in the first place."

George colored. "The fact remains that a woman's valor should not be overlooked."

"Nor should her inheritance." William smiled, his expression revealing a fine array of teeth. "Shall we view the proof of your inheritance of Ravensmuir, my lady?"

If there was anything amiss legally, I knew that they would be just as competitive in lodging a complaint against my suzerainty.

If not simply seize the keep as their own.

"Of course." I laid Merlyn's box upon the board and retrieved the key hung about my neck. The hall fell silent as I produced the deed to Ravensmuir, its scarlet ribbons and seals hinting at its pedigree.

I learned long ago that there was little to be gained—beyond mockery—in admitting my inability to read. In this company, I could only assume the response would be worse, for these men might take advantage of my uncertainty of my claim, no less my inability to cite proof of what was my own.

I pretended thus to be utterly familiar with the contents of the deed. I passed the beribboned document to Sir George, he who admired the strengths of women, and smiled.

"I entreat you, Sir George, to read this deed aloud, lest there be doubt among the company that I have embellished the text to my own benefit."

The men harumphed approval and Sir George began to read. The deed, like most of its kind, detailed the property of Ravensmuir, its boundaries and buildings, and the rights of its suzerain to hold courts for peasants abiding upon its land and to defend the holding from assailants, then enumerated the taxes and tithes that might be collected.

And that was where the resemblance ended.

Sir George frowned at the document, the first hint that all was not as he expected. "I thought Ravensmuir was pledged to you and thence to the king," he said to William.

William leaned over me to read the text himself. "I thought it sworn to you and thence to the king."

Both men whistled beneath their breath as they read. Mavella met my gaze with concern. Though I fretted silently, I kept my expression placid, as if I knew the document's contents well. "I trust all meets with your satisfaction?"

"No, it does not." William sat back and drained his cup of wine, then thumped the cup on the board.

George cleared his throat and frowned at the document again. "Though it appears that there is little that can be done."

"The guarantee is in King David's own hand. I know his script well," William noted, touching his finger to one of the signatures at the bottom.

George grimaced agreement. I nigh screamed in frustration that it took men so long to ask the most obvious question.

"Well, what does it say?" George's son John demanded finally.

George read it aloud.

"In deepest gratitude for the services rendered by Avery Lammergeier, Ravensmuir is granted without restraint and without duties or payments due to any overlord, including the King of Scotland himself, and is granted to that same Avery and whatsoever heirs he and his heirs should so designate from this day forward. Avery, styled Laird of Ravensmuir by this edict, and his every heir who follows him, owes no fealty, owes no tithe, and owes no allegiance to any beyond the King of Scotland himself. Pronounced this April the fifth, in the year of our lord 1350 by David II, King of Scotland and witnessed by John Randolph, Earl of Moray, Maurice Moray, Earl of Strathearn, Robert Erskine . . ."

"Without entail?" John interrupted in amazement. "What did Avery do to hold Ravensmuir so freely?"

Or what gift had he brought? I had a sudden inkling as to the identity of one of Avery's patrons. King David was known to endow monasteries and churches for his own salvation and his own honor.

But King David had been dead the better part of a year. It could not be he, or even one bent on winning his favor, who had assaulted Merlyn.

"This is most uncommon," George muttered in discontent, though I knew it was not that unusual.

In the wake of the plague and the decimation of the general populace, the uniformity of deeds and titles had been broken. The lords, quite simply, had less with which to wager. North Berwick had been endowed with new town rights by the king for similar reasons.

Both men's brows furrowed, for they had clearly hoped for an easy grasp of this holding. They fired sidelong glances at me. I squared my shoulders, guessing that they would try to browbeat me into surrendering the right that Avery had secured.

They would not have a concession readily from me.

"We cannot suffer to have a keep of such import so poorly manned," George insisted. "It is a weakness in the defense of the king's own territories, especially when there are rumblings in the south of trouble to come."

I tapped the document with a fingertip, wagering that Fitz had told me the truth. "Am I not decreed to be my husband's legal heir?"

George scowled at the deed. "Yes, there are two addenda, both witnessed as expected, one designating Merlyn Lammergeier, Avery's eldest son, as his heir, and a later one— presumably in Merlyn's own hand—naming his wife Ysabella as his heir."

"Unless it was added after Merlyn's demise," William said carefully. "For he died not only in his prime but most unexpectedly."

I understood his import immediately. "You think that I amended this document?" The prospect was laughable, though I dared not admit my own failing lest it be used against me.

"And who else?"

"Who witnessed the addendum?"

"One Rhys Fitzwilliam." William scanned the assembly. "The manservant of Merlyn, clearly, but is he here to stand witness that this is his mark?"

Fitz, of course, was not present.

"The point of his mark is that he witnessed the deed. A man does not need to witness his own signature," I insisted.

"He does if his hand and his mark are unfamiliar," George retorted. "The matter is suspicious, my lady, and the prize not inconsiderable."

"But this is madness!" I cried. This was no time to be coy. George inhaled sharply. Both men looked away and

Mavella paled at my audacity. I braced myself to fight, but I had no chance to voice my objections.

"On the contrary, it is the first thing of sense I have heard in years!" Ada roared from the back of the hall. All turned to regard her. "Ysabella is but an illiterate alewife from Kinfairlie, not of noble lineage at all, and not fit to be Lady of Ravensmuir!"

The two earls regarded me with alarm but I smiled. "I thank you, Ada, for exonerating me from the charge of having amended Ravensmuir's deed."

Ada colored but did not retreat. "She is a common alewife," she said bitterly. "Daughter of a whore and a man whose name none know."

"Do you challenge her inheritance?" William asked.

"I do. I am more deserving than she," she insisted, though many in the company were amused by her assertion.

"Upon what claim?" George asked.

Malcolm stood but Ada brushed past him, her eyes glittering. Many of the men nudged each other, pointing at her apron and no doubt commenting upon the aspirations of serving women. I felt pity for Ada then, but only for a moment.

She raised her fist, her eyes blazing with anger. "I have the greater claim—Avery Lammergeier swore to make me his legal wife, but he died afore the deed could be done."

The company laughed and Malcolm looked pained for his sister.

"I bore his son!" she shouted, silencing them all with her words. "He pledged to wed me and welcomed me to his bed, and I bore him a son." Arnulf hovered in the portal behind her, cowering slightly when Ada pointed to him. "I called him my brother to evade the shame, but he is a Lammergeier by blood and Ravensmuir should pass to him by right."

Whispers erupted in the hall and my heart sank to my toes. Before I could fully comprehend that Ada and I coveted similarly horrific secrets, she spun and jabbed her finger through the air at me. "I know that this one has stolen everything that ever I desired, and snatched it from my very grip."

She walked toward me, her lip curled. "It was not enough that my father died in shame, it was not enough that all of Kinfairlie mocked us for his weakness. It was not enough that Mavella charmed away the man I deserved to wed. It was not enough for you that every vestige of respect that ever I had, you had seen torn from my name and drawn through the mire. No, it was not enough, Ysabella."

Ada halted before the high table. "You had to seduce Merlyn, as well. You had to use your witching charms upon him and beguile him to wed you in haste. You had to snatch Ravensmuir from my grasp and consign me to the kitchen forever." She smiled coldly. "But justice shall be rendered, Ysabella, and all that you have stolen from me will be returned to me tenfold. I will be Lady of Ravensmuir, as is my rightful due, and you, you will scrub in the kitchens at my bidding." She looked between the two earls. "Gawain makes no claim, which means that Arnulf is the only blood heir to Avery's legacy. Ravensmuir is his right and his due."

"No, Ada!" Malcolm shouted from the back of the hall. "Two ills do not make all come aright."

Ada drew herself taller, like a dark bird, and hissed. "What do you know of the matter?"

"I know that Arnulf is not Avery's son."

"I know who came from my womb. I know what Avery pledged to me."

"And I know what our stepfather did to our home." Malcolm shook his head, then came toward us. The men listened avidly for this was better entertainment than any bard's tale.

"There is no punishment for a man who rapes his wife, nor for one who beats the children he did not beget but is condemned to raise."

"Malcolm, you lie!"

"I tell the truth, Ada. It is time for the truth."

"I tell the truth!"

Malcolm's expression was grim as he shook his head. "This is the truth. My stepfather raped my mother, time and again, and when he got a child upon her, his eye turned to my sister. My mother realized then that his heart was black and she feared to bring another child into her household. She feared that if she bore a girl, that daughter might be abused young."

"No, Malcolm, do not shame us with this nonsense," Ada insisted. "We can have Ravensmuir. We can have our rightful due."

"It is not your due. You have no claim to Ravensmuir." Malcolm turned a cold gaze upon his sister. "My mother went to a woman in the woods, to beg a potion that would make her lose the child. She was coming ripe and the woman argued with her. The risk was great, so close to the babe's time that the mother would die from such a potion and not the babe. My mother did not care, for she was desperate."

He gritted his teeth and turned away from Ada's pleas. "I came home to find her bleeding, my stepfather gone, Ada nigh insensible from his abuse. My mother died that day in our kitchen, but the babe lived. Arnulf came early, though I cannot say whether it was the potion or my stepfather's deeds that made him simple as he is."

I was appalled at what had happened behind the closed doors of the Gowan abode, shocked and dismayed that Ada and her mother had endured it.

Malcolm turned and spoke softly to his sister, who had begun to weep. "Tell them, Ada, tell them the rest."

"You have ruined everything!" she spat at him. "Mine was a perfect tale, one that no one could disprove."

"Except for me." Malcolm slipped his arm around her shoulders, though she shook off his touch. "Enough lies, Ada. We all reap whatsoever we sow and no one else is to blame." He smiled. "Not even Ysabella, Lady of Ravensmuir."

"Avery did promise to marry me."

William leaned forward. "But is Arnulf his son?"

Ada shook her head, her tears spilling. Again, compassion stirred in me, but she lifted a finger of accusation. "I thought his son might make the matter right and fulfill his father's pledge, but no, not with this one loose. Ysabella cast her spells and cooked her potions and chanted her curses, and she snared Merlyn Lammergeier for her own. Surely, you do not intend to let a witch, who should be burned for her crimes, rule Ravensmuir?"

This time her charge fell upon ears prepared to listen.

The assembly began to chatter. The earls exchanged a glance and my own blood ran cold. Witchery is a charge more easily made than disproven and I knew it well.

"Have you evidence to support your accusation?" William leaned forward, much too interested for my taste.

Ada sneered. "Why else would a wealthy handsome laird wed the illiterate spawn of a harlot?"

William smiled. "Men have been known to wed for many a reason."

"You have not heard the last of this!" Ada shouted. "I will see it proven that Ysabella is a witch and ensure that she wins the fate she deserves!"

"Ada, leave the matter be." Malcolm tried to take her arm. "You have wrought enough damage."

Ada struck at him in fury. "I have? And what have you done of the matter? What did you do to see Mother avenged? What did you do to ensure that wretched man had his due? Nothing! No, Malcolm, you were too busy rutting with your new wife to trouble yourself with your family! You let him flee as surely as if you lent him a steed!

"I did not!"

"And what aid did you give us, Malcolm? What did you do once you saw what you saw? You walked away, did you not? You walked out the door and left me amidst that ruin, went back to your poisonous Fiona. You had no time . . ."

"That is enough!" Malcolm shouted.

Ada drew back to hurl more venom at him, but he slapped her face. The blow echoed through the hall, and was followed by silence.

Malcolm stepped forward, contrite. "I am sorry, Ada, I . . ."

But Ada buried her face in her hands and began to weep. Her sobs shook her shoulders and she seemed smaller in her defeat. She appeared so crumpled as to never have been a threat at all.

"Come home with me, Ada," Malcolm urged. "Fiona will welcome you."

"She will not!"

"She will, for I shall insist upon it." He slipped an arm around her shoulders. "You speak aright that I have ignored my blood too long. Come home with me."

Ada let herself be led away, though her weeping did not cease. I could not blame her truly, and felt sympathy for her. I knew how it was to rely upon Fiona Gowan for charity and would not wish that on any other soul, regardless of her crimes.

"We have no evidence of witchery," William grumbled, disappointed.

George smiled, as if there had been no interruption. "Which brings us neatly to the matter of seeing the lady wed to a suitable man." He cleared his throat. "My son, John, for example, is without a spouse."

I spared the man in question a glance and he gave me his most winning smile. I bit my tongue, wanting to know all of my options before discarding them publicly.

"And my man Ethan has need of a bride." William indicated a man of about forty summers who stood at his lord's gesture to bow.

I began to panic, foreseeing that I would be wed again before nightfall. "My lord is not dead a week. Surely it is only fitting that I be allowed time to grieve?"

"All know you were estranged," George insisted. "You can have no need of prolonged mourning."

"A betrothal would be sufficient." William granted me a cool glance. "Provided, of course, that you permitted your betrothed to occupy and defend the keep immediately."

"And occupy my bed without the benefit of vows exchanged?"

Neither earl appeared to have an issue with this detail.

I pushed to my feet and flung down my napkin, hoping to win my way with bravado. "You are all mad! You have no authority here and no right to force me to wed any man. If I wed again, I shall do so at my own choice, in my own time, and after a suitable courtship."

"We dare not wait . . ." George began.

"Find me a runner!" I shouted. "I wish to send a petition to the king that I be defended against the avarice of my neighbors."

"You have no right," George began heatedly, but got no further before a ruckus erupted in the rear of the hall.

The men there turned toward the great portal and as wonder swept the company, cantering hoofbeats could be heard. They were closer than the tunnel to the gates, within the very keep itself! I got to my feet, outraged at the audacity of some bandit.

"This is beyond belief!" I roared. "You come as my guests

and desecrate my hall! I am outraged by such disrespect! The king's justice has taken a rare flavor beneath your hand, Sir William."

"But I know nothing of this . . ."

A great black destrier burst into the hall, silencing us all. It threw back its head and reared, giving a great whinny as its shod hooves pawed the air. The men scrambled out of its path, tipping tables and spilling wine in their haste. Its mane was wild, its tail unfurled like a banner, but it was perfectly beneath its rider's command.

When the beast began to canter toward the dais, stepping high and arching its neck, I heard the murmur of silver bells in its harness. The horse tossed its head and flared its nostrils, stamping impatiently on the floor with its great hooves. Its coat glistened and its sides heaved and I knew it had been running hard.

Then I saw that its rider was shrouded in a great dark cloak, a cloak lined with silver fur. Only the glint of his roguish smile was visible in the shadows within the hood.

My heart leapt, stopped, then raced like a wild thing. Ada cried out in shock. I stood straighter and began to laugh.

I knew the rider's name as well as she.

XIV

The two earls pressing their wills upon me fell silent in trepidation. So they should, by my thinking. A reckoning was come before them.

Merlyn rode the prancing destrier between the tables, and whispers rippled through the company in his wake. He halted before the high table and flung back his hood as the steed snorted and stamped.

My heart leapt at the risk he took, but it was William who uttered my husband's name. Both earls crossed themselves and both looked pale, as if a ghost stood before them.

Merlyn dismounted, then strode forward to take my hand, touching his lips to my fingertips. "I apologize, chère, for my unavoidable delay. I cannot help but note that you have defended yourself and your rights quite splendidly."

I nodded, unable to make a sound. I was both delighted that he was hale and terrified that he would not remain so for long.

"You lied about your demise!" William finally mustered his outrage.

"That it not become fact, yes." Merlyn gave my fingers a minute squeeze, then looked from one earl to the other. "I knew that you would come quickly to Ravensmuir, and I knew that you would compel my lady to wed one of your men before she could request the protection of the crown." His deep voice carried easily over the rapt assembly. "So, I have seen fit to summon the crown myself."

"No!" George protested.

"You had no right to usurp my responsibilities," William argued.

"I had every right," Merlyn said crisply. He gripped my fingers tightly. "A rape will suffice as a consummation, and we all know the truth of that. Would my lady have escaped your ambitions this night, whatever protest she might have made?"

George and William looked away. I noted that Calum appeared to be very angry, though whether his fury was directed at Merlyn or his liege lord, I could not say. He had not, after all, been recommended as a suitor for my hand.

Merlyn continued. "You harbor a murderer in your ranks, or a man who was prepared to commit a murder, and until he is named, it is unclear who is friend and who is foe of Ravensmuir. You would force my lady to wed another, though she is not widowed in truth, and you would undermine the rights granted to Ravensmuir by the king." He smiled at me. "My lady shows good sense in ensuring that you do not sit fully armed within my hall."

Dissent broke out in the company then, each earl defending his actions and more than one man demanding details of my spouse. But Merlyn lifted his hand for silence. "I found the king resident at Haddington. Listen! Your liege lord approaches!"

The distant note of a clarion carried clearly to the hall, as did the sound of many hoofbeats.

The king and his justice arrived at Ravensmuir—and not a moment too soon.

When the king was installed at the high table and his appetite sated, the great hall took the appearance of a court. Merlyn told of the assault upon him. The earls protested my common status and position as heiress, demanding that Ravensmuir's deed be amended.

I realized that they still expected Merlyn to be killed.

"You believe the murderer to be among us?" the king asked.

Merlyn nodded.

"But this is outrageous!" George sputtered. "You cannot make an accusation of murder among men of honor!"

Merlyn granted George a cold glance. "And where is the honor in summoning a man to his death?"

"I beg your pardon?"

"I was on the road, coming to Dunbar at your request and at your designated hour, when I was attacked."

George paled. "But I never sent for you."

"You did. You wished to discuss a relic which you believed to be in my possession."

George shook his head adamantly. "I did not even know you were at Ravensmuir again. Although I always welcome your companionship, Merlyn, I did not summon you."

"How curious that your man insisted that you did." Merlyn turned and glanced over the company. Calum, I noted, set his lips and boldly returned Merlyn's gaze.

"I was summoned to Dunbar to do my lord's bidding," Calum said, "and told to grant to you the message that I did."

"By whom?" George demanded.

Calum pointed to George's son. "By my lord's son John."

John bounced to his feet and pounded his fist upon the board. "That is a lie!"

"It seems the air is thick with lies of late," I said.

"No less your own," William observed tartly.

Merlyn pivoted and clucked his tongue at the two earls. "You should know better, Sir William, than to believe a man is dead without seeing his corpse."

William's lips tightened. "I demanded as much."

"And you, Sir George, should know better than to try to

usurp the rights inherent with Ravensmuir. Ysabella is my heiress, as writ." Merlyn held my gaze. "You all should be so fortunate as to take a bride as stalwart and lusty as mine."

Several men toasted to this happy turn of events, thinking matters resolved. Calum alone looked grim in the assembly. I surmised that both earls were far more happy to have Merlyn alive than the prospect of finding a man to wed me who pleased them both.

The king mused, giving more credence to the earls' complaints than I had hoped. "Merlyn, you cannot fail to see their view," he said. "The borders are restless and a keep held by a woman could be lost readily. Your bride is common-born, and would thus be unfamiliar with what must be done—should she be widowed in truth."

"She is not witless," Merlyn said, but when the king shook his head, my spouse's brow furrowed. "And if the keep is armed, the fields tilled, what then?"

The king's brows rose. "It has not been done in decades, and you, you have never been here oft enough to oversee such a feat."

"I would make Ravensmuir my abode."

"What of your trade?"

"I have left it. My brother is the only Lammergeier to travel abroad in these days. I have a wife and a home to defend."

The king slanted a glance to me, his quick survey revealing his doubts of Merlyn's choice. "Avery must have had considerable treasures to his name," he murmured. My heart sank that the one gift that would have certainly gained his endorsement was gone, disappearing into the distance with Gawain.

By my own fault.

But Merlyn smiled. "Indeed, my father's treasures are still here, in this keep and beneath my hand. As I have left the trade, I shall have to make gifts of them."

The king pursed his lips, no doubt considering the price

of his favor. I was concerned that Merlyn made so bold a hint of his rich possessions, for many men in the company cast glances about themselves with new interest.

Avery's repute must have traveled wide.

"It is time for a new beginning at Ravensmuir, one in which all truths be aired. Let us have another truth before you make your choice." Merlyn rested his hand upon the board before me. "Give me your mother's letter, chère."

I was shocked by his request. I clutched his box to my chest, not dreading the letter's contents so much as having my secrets revealed before all of these men. I dropped my voice to a whisper, haunted by the reading of my spouse's letter in Kinfairlie's market. "Merlyn, not before the entire company."

He met my gaze, his own dark and compelling. "Yes, chère. Here and now. It is time to put questions to rest." He brushed his fingertips across my own and murmured. "Trust me in this."

I was aware of nothing but his gaze. I stared into his eyes, saw his conviction, and knew that the contents of my mother's missive were no mystery to Merlyn. He had read it. He *knew*. He had fetched Alasdair for Mavella, he had seen Tynan safely from the grasp of these earls who spoke of young heirs and "accidents," he had fetched the king to defend our due. He had declared himself alive before an entire company lest I be compelled to wed another.

For all of that, and something nameless besides, I trusted Merlyn.

My heart in my mouth, I unlocked the box and surrendered the softened letter to my spouse. Merlyn smiled fleetingly at me, knowing full well the import of what I did and why. The earls watched with undisguised curiosity.

"How did you come by this?" Merlyn asked me. "Just so all gathered here know the truth of it."

I took a shaking breath. "I found it stitched into my mother's chemise when I prepared her body for burial." I gripped the table in my anxiety. "I had never seen it before and still I do not know what tidings it contains."

"I do, chère. I do." Merlyn spoke with such quiet assurance that I recalled suddenly the sight of him in my chamber, shrouded in shadows, spinning the key upon its silken cord.

He turned to address the rapt company. "It is a letter, from a devoted mother to her daughter, a letter that mother knew her child could not read. As Ada observed, Ysabella cannot read or write, for she has never had the fortune to be taught. She could not have amended the deed to Ravensmuir, she could not have composed this missive."

"It is true," Mavella added.

I gripped my hands together, aching to know what was writ yet fearing to be disappointed. William unexpectedly touched my shoulder in encouragement.

Merlyn unfolded the letter and began to read, not a whisper echoing in the hall to interrupt him.

"My dearest daughter Ysabella,

Herein lies the truth of who I am and how you came to be of this world. This is the tale not only of a long-past night but of a lie I perpetuated for the safety of my eldest child. I have long told people that I served at Kinfairlie keep, I have long insisted that I remember nothing of the burning of that manor, yet neither of these things are true. I dare not make my confession to a priest. I fear to jeopardize my daughter's health, I fear to trust any soul who might betray me.

And those days at Kinfairlie taught me that betrayal can come from any corner.

You know that I am called Elizabeth of Kinfairlie,

but this is not truly my name. I did not serve at Kin-
fairlie, despite my having said as much many times. I
lived there, it is true, but my real name is Marie Elise.
I am the third daughter of the last Laird and Lady of
Kinfairlie. I am the only person from that keep who
survived its destruction."

"She survived!" William said with wonder. I realized that
he must have known, or known of, my mother when she was
young at Kinfairlie.

The company gasped and leaned forward, enraptured. I
closed my eyes, hearing the words as if they were uttered in
my mother's own dear voice, and felt my tears gather.

"None knew me in those days. Few had met me, not
many more had ever seen me. I was a mere thirteen
years of age when Kinfairlie was assaulted, young and
sheltered. My father feared that men might lust for his
daughters and kept us safe within the walls of his
abode. My father feared lawlessness, but still it came to
his own gates and rapped loudly for admission.

We thought that some soul would aid us when the
wolves howled at the door. We thought on each succes-
sive day of the seige that a relieving army would march
over the dark moors and fall upon our enemies. But the
moors were vast and still, the road empty, day after day
after day. And the barrage against our gates seldom
halted. After several weeks, I saw in my father's eyes
that he no longer believed aid would come.

With the bravery and folly of a child, I decided it was
not because my father had few allies, not because my
father seldom came to the aid of another, not because
his request had been denied. I knew with childlike con-
viction that it was only because my wondrous father's
many friends did not know of Kinfairlie's distress.

I appointed myself to redress the error.

There are many ways in and out of an old keep, and children are the ones who know them all. I knew a way through the cellars to the outcropping on the moor. From thence I knew I could walk to Dunbar. My sisters and I had seen it, perched upon the coast in the distance, though I did not know then how far the distance would prove to be. I knew little of the world though I learned much on the morning I chose to seek aid.

By some dark coincidence, it was the same day that the attackers chose to press their assault. No doubt they hoped to encourage my father's surrender, but my father would surrender to no marauding villains. Burning buckets of pitch were lobbed over the walls with first light that morning. Panic ensued when the roof of the stables caught fire and I knew that I had to leave immediately.

I doubt that any missed me. My mother had dressed us all in simple garb, that we might not be known from the servants if the gates were taken. I ducked into the cellar, down the hole that my sisters and I knew, and ran with the certainty that I was my family's sole chance.

In truth, they had no chance. By the time I reached the cavern's end, I could hear the screams behind me and the crackle of flames. I crept out the opening and climbed high to look upon the disaster of my home.

And this was my mistake. Mercenaries surrounded the walls of my home, even as it succumbed to flames, though I was blind to their presence. They could not approach for the heat, while I could not move for the sight before me.

Kinfairlie had become an inferno. The screams of every soul I knew and loved filled the air. I wept in shock and dismay. I recollect that the sun hid its face from the destruction far below, and that the world turned dark. In the darkness that endured for a thou-

sand heartbeats, I could see the fires lick at Ravens-muir in the distance.

I must have stood there, too shocked to move, for a man turned slowly, as if becoming aware of my presence. He was young and garbed as a knight, large, his face blackened with soot. He was angry, his eyes lit with another fire when he shouted at me.

I ran. I ran as fast as I could, but it was not fast enough. He was far larger than me, far more accustomed to running and fighting. He grabbed me and threw me to the ground. He searched me for jewelry and struck me when he found none. When I rolled away from him, hoping to flee, he grasped my hips with painful vigor. I screamed but he knotted my hair around his fist, he held me down.

He raped me thrice.

Then he cast me aside, like so much offal. He left me bruised and bleeding and violated. I struck him when he looked back at the keep, struck him in the head with a stone. He laughed at my effort to avenge myself and came after me again.

I struck him once more, furious at what he had done, terrified that he would do it again. The stone cracked against his skull, his blood flowed from a gash in his temple and he fell to his knees.

It was all the respite I needed. I ran. I leapt over scree and rock and scrambled down the coast. I sobbed as I fled, I dashed the tears from my eyes. I ran faster when I heard him shout after me. I ran for Dunbar, but it proved to be so far that I was out of breath before it drew appreciably closer.

It was then I doubted my own scheme. Who would believe my tale? I had no evidence of my station, no mark that I was my father's child. I had nothing and I was a woman. I knew my assailant's insignia but not his name—what if another wore his colors? Even if I *saw that knight again, even if I pointed a finger at him in utter certainty, I feared that none would believe me.*

Not if he was powerful. I knew of no knights who were not powerful. So, I hunkered down amidst the stones, listening for pursuit that did not come—for he had had what he desired of me—watching and weeping as Kinfairlie burned to the ground.

It took three days.

When the rubble ceased to smoke, I crept out of my hiding spot. The men were gone, my father's lands bare, the crops shriveling. I learned later that the field had been covered with salt, a rich man's curse and one that would take years to be so diminished that crops would grow again. I walked through the ashes of the keep where I had played and I concocted my tale.

Then I walked to Kinfairlie village and recounted the story you have heard. It is not true, Ysabella. It was created on impulse for my own defense. I feared the knight would come again and have a worse due of me if I accused him.

It was perhaps a cowardly choice, but it was done.

Within weeks, I knew that I dared not change my tale. A child grew within me, a child whose presence could confirm my accusation, a child that wicked knight would never suffer to live. I was young myself, but I knew that you were to be my family, that you would fill the yawning hole in my life left by loved ones stolen away too soon.

I never saw the knight again. I do not know if I would know him if I did. But here is the greatest injustice wrought by my selfish lie—that you, my daughter, believe yourself to be common-born. You are no peasant, no bastard spawn of a serving wench. You are the granddaughter of the last Laird and Lady of Kinfairlie, the get of their daughter Marie Elise and a nameless

knight. Your lineage is noble, Ysabella, and none can
steal the legacy of your blood from you."

I felt shock settle into the men on either side of me. I
sensed that William in particular was vexed and he stared
out over the company with narrowed eyes. George fiddled
and fluttered, showing his agitation in another way.

I stared at Merlyn. He was my anchor in a world gone
awry.

"I apologize that I did not tell this to you myself, for
the tale would have been sweeter falling from my lips.
I considered it once, when you and Merlyn wed, for I
thought it fitting that Ravensmuir, once part of my father's holdings, would be your abode. I thought then
that your lineage was evident to the shrewd eye of Merlyn Lammergeier, I thought that he had spied the pearl
hidden in the mire. And I was proud of how you carried
yourself, how you spoke, how readily you assumed the
mantle of your responsibilities. I knew a moment's
pride that I had not fared so badly as that.

But I evaded the telling, and then it seemed my words
would be as salt in the wound—ah yes, daughter mine,
I know you ache for Merlyn. I know you question your
choice. I know that you never will forget him. And it is
true that in my heart, I fear your condemnation for a
lifetime of lies. We have always been close, Ysabella,
and I have no desire to push you from my side, not in
these, my final months.

I regret now that I never taught you to read and to
write, for then you might have read my letter yourself.
It does seem fitting that in the end I prove to be the one
most vexed by this lack wrought of my own choices.

I can have only faith now, Ysabella, faith that you
will find this missive in the event of my demise, faith
that your curiosity will drive you to learn its contents,

*faith that one who is trustworthy will recount its con-
tents to you. I have only faith, but faith is all I have had
since Kinfairlie burned and it has been enough.*

*God bless you, Ysabella. Know that conception in
anger does not preclude birth in love. And bless me, for
I have sinned in lying to you who most deserved the
truth.*

*This is my last confession, though it has not the
blessing of a priest. Pray for me, Ysabella, for my intention was solely to protect you.*

*Yours in Christ,
Marie Elise of Kinfairlie"*

Merlyn folded the letter with care, then handed it back to
me. Our fingers brushed in the transaction and I could not
hold his compassionate gaze. The hall was silent, no man
having a word to say. I folded and put the letter carefully
back into Merlyn's box, my hands shaking.

I locked the box, focusing hard to complete the simple
task, then handed it and its key to my spouse. There was
nothing within it that was mine any longer. This is the gift
of illiteracy—I forget nothing that ever I have heard. I did
not need the letter any longer. I would remember my
mother's words forever, as they would reside in my own
heart.

It was Merlyn who would need evidence that his wife
was nobly born, Merlyn who lived and needed his deeds
returned. My eyes were blind with tears as I stood, and I
trembled at the resonance of my mother's words from beyond
the grave.

"I beg your leave," I said, my voice so hoarse and thick
that I scarce recognized it. "I would excuse myself."

I turned when none spoke and stepped away from the
table. My sister uttered my name, as did my spouse, but I
plunged blindly onward, wanting only to be free of this

company. My unsteady legs carried me only to the end of the dais, then I fainted dead away.

I awakened in the great bed in the solar. Mavella sat beside me upon the mattress, her fingers cool upon my brow as she stroked the hair back from my face. Her smile was the first sight that greeted me. My laces had been loosed and my shoes removed, my braids unfurled. I could hear the murmur of men's voices in the chamber below and would have sat up, but Mavella restrained me with a touch.

"You should rest," she chided.

"I should know what they discuss. No doubt our future is being decided while I lay abed."

Mavella shook her head. "My future is already decided, and I suspect that yours is, as well, now that it is clear that Merlyn yet lives."

I settled back against the pillows in dissatisfaction, guessing that she would not easily let me leave.

"You knew," she said quietly.

I met her gaze and, unable to lie again, nodded. "He came to me, the first night that we were here. That was when I learned the truth of it."

"And that was why you were so gladdened. I am sorry, Ysabella, that I accused you of having a cold heart."

"I dared not tell anyone. I pledged as much to him."

"Of course you did! Oh, Ysabella, I am so happy for you."

We embraced and I sat up, my feet swinging high above the floor, our hands clasped. "Did you guess Mother's secret?"

Mavella shook her head.

"Nor did I," I admitted. "Though in hindsight, I can see why she insisted so oft upon careful speech."

"Why she loved fine goods and victuals."

"Why she had no trade or desire to wed a common man."

"Why she held herself above the others in Kinfairlie village." Mavella heaved a sigh. "They noticed that, even if they did not guess the cause. It is no wonder that she was both admired and resented."

"Her letter tells nothing of your father," I said softly.

Mavella shook her head. "She told me years ago about him. I assumed then that she did the same with you. I knew our fathers were not the same man."

"Then who?"

"Do you remember Rodney?" She smiled as she said his name.

"How could I forget him? He was as a kindly uncle to us. He came so often and brought such wondrous gifts upon the holy days. My earliest memories are of Mother and Rodney sharing a cup of wine, laughing at the board."

"And rutting afterwards." Mavella laughed when I regarded her with shock. "You were not the only one to hear the deed, sister mine. And evidently, it began long before either of us noticed." She smiled with mischief.

"So, he was your father."

Mavella nodded. "Mother said he would not abandon his ailing daughter, for he knew his duty to her and did not wish to burden our household with her illnesses. But all the same, the daughter barely knew him and was scarce aware of whether he was home or away. Mother said a man needs his heart lightened to bear the burden of his life. She was unapologetic."

"She loved him."

Mavella nodded. "And he loved her, I suspect. But they met too late, long after Rodney was snared with responsibilities, long after they might have made a match themselves."

"They missed their chance, but seized what happiness they could," I said quietly. "There is a lesson for us there."

"One we were fool enough to ignore until it was almost too late."

"Almost." I pleated the coverlet between my fingers, my thoughts filled with recollections of Rodney's merry laughter, my mother's smile, the happy if simple times we had had together. "I remember thinking that I would die of grief at his funeral."

"I remember thinking that Mother would die of grief," Mavella said. "Do you remember how his family tried to shame us?"

I nodded, seeing her again. "She marched down the church to place a flower upon his coffin, just to defy them. I remember her telling them that she loved him more than all of them together, that she loved him for more than the weight of his purse which was the sole reason most of them had come."

"And they ensured she saw none of it."

We shook our heads with both exasperation and affection.

"God in heaven," Mavella said. "She never could hold her tongue."

"Now I know why she could so easily hold her head high."

"Yes, she had been raised to it."

We whispered together, comforted by our recollections, then fell silent when Merlyn appeared at the top of the stairs.

"I would have your counsel, chère," he said, his tone bereft of any emotion. I could not have guessed whether he held any tender feelings for me in that moment, for he spoke as a man wrought of stone. His manner discomfited me—I was accustomed to anger or passion from Merlyn, never indifference. Since my heart was filled to bursting, the contrast disconcerted me.

"How so?" I asked and stood.

"The king would have the succession of Ravensmuir decided on this day."

My hands clenched. "They all fear that you will yet be killed."

"It is prudent to plan for such an eventuality." Merlyn's

wicked smile flashed so unexpectedly that my breath was stolen. "I know myself to be mortal, as evidently do they."

"It is writ that Ysabella is your heir," Mavella reminded him.

Merlyn inclined his head. "And you have heard their fears for this scheme. Ravensmuir's location is convenient and its strongholds secure. Even with their pledges of protection, much could go awry."

"Any who claimed Ravensmuir could assault either Dunbar or Tantallon with ease," I said, seeing the import of his words.

Merlyn spread his hands. "And there are no knights pledged to this hall, no mercenaries in Ravensmuir's employ, at least not as yet. It is not unreasonable to conclude that the keep would be difficult to defend."

"Especially by a woman," I concluded, not troubling to hide my bitterness.

Merlyn nodded. "This is their concern."

Mavella rose to her feet, indignation putting color in her cheeks. "They would force you to acknowledge Gawain instead. He has no mercenaries or knights either! And I, for one, would wager my all upon Ysabella afore risking a penny upon Gawain!"

Merlyn smiled again, his gaze landing warmly upon me. "As would I, but I would like to see these men dispatched from my hall."

"You fear treachery in their presence?"

"I fear a stalemate in their presence." Merlyn frowned. "The trap is baited, chère, but the mouse will not venture forth while the hall is full of hungry cats."

My blood chilled as I recalled his claim that a life without risk was not worth the living. "Do you wish truly to die?"

"I wish to have the matter resolved, chère. One must have proof to demand high justice. I would force my assailant to try to repeat his crime, though this time, I am prepared for him."

"Merlyn . . ."

He held my gaze as he sobered. "I have guessed his name, chère."

"But you cannot prove his deeds."

"Not yet."

I understood that Merlyn would say no more until he had the proof to back his accusation.

I took a deep breath, seeing some honor in his choice of secrets but not liking it a whit. "Leave Ravensmuir to Tynan," I said, a plea in my tone for I knew I could not command him to do such a thing. "It was my intent to hold it solely as his regent, that he might have an inheritance of his own."

"Why?" Merlyn's eyes brightened.

I looked at my hands. "We have already discussed our doubts about his parentage," I said carefully. "Perhaps he is a Lammergeier. This way, he can train for the lairdship and all will know his destiny."

Silence stretched taut between Merlyn and I.

"But if some killer hunts the Lammergeier, this will put Tynan at risk," Mavella said fearfully.

"Then praise God that he is away from here," I said with resolve. "Is this why you seized him?"

Mavella caught her breath, but Merlyn nodded slowly.

"I knew they would come," he acknowledged, indicating the men below with a quick move of his head. "Indeed, they could do nothing else. And I feared, it is true, that all the Lammergeier were to be hunted. This matter must be resolved, if we are to live in peace again."

I took a deep breath. "Then it is good that Tynan is abroad. Being openly acknowledged as heir under the protection of the king may serve to protect him."

"You have no other reason for choosing him, chère?" Merlyn prompted, his words soft and compelling. I came close to surrendering my secret to him, but my sister's presence and my own temerity halted me.

I lifted my chin and met Merlyn's regard. "None beyond the fact that he is my brother and my responsibility. I, too, am mortal, Merlyn, and I fear for my Tynan's well-being in my absence. Ravensmuir could secure his future."

Merlyn regarded me for a long moment before he nodded. He smiled as he turned to Mavella. "A man has come to beg the right to wed you, Mavella. He even insists that he has no need for a dowry, so fathomless is his love."

"Alasdair!" my sister cried, her face lighting like a beacon.

Merlyn smiled and this time his pleasure lit his eyes. He was fond of my sister, I saw, and as well pleased as I with what he had wrought. "You favor his suit?"

"Of course!"

"Then, I will offer my congratulations to him, and suggest that he may have the priest in Kinfairlie call the banns." Merlyn frowned at the floor. "I would prefer that you leave with him this day, Mavella. Though it may cause some scandal, you will be safer in Kinfairlie than here. Perhaps Malcolm Gowan and his wife will provide you with fitting accommodations until your nuptials."

Mavella glanced to me, uncertainty lighting her eyes. "If you insist . . ."

"And I would have you take your sister with you . . ."

"No, Merlyn! No!" I leapt to my feet and crossed the chamber. "I will not leave you here alone. We are wed, partners for better or for worse, and . . ."

His thumb landed quickly on my mouth, silencing my protest, and his eyes sparkled. "And how did I guess that you would say as much, wife of mine?" He kissed me quickly on the brow, obviously enjoying how I sputtered that he had guessed my response.

He then pulled his inlaid box from beneath his arm and presented it to me. Our fingers brushed as I took it from him once again. "Keep this for me, chère. The hall on this night will be no place for treasures."

He bent and brushed his fingertips across my lips, then whispered an astonishing command in my ear. Then he smiled and retreated down the stairs.

I could not let him go so easily as that! I seized his shoulder before he disappeared.

"You risk too much in revealing yourself, Merlyn," I said for his ears alone.

"Do you fear for me, chère?" He whispered as did I.

I nodded once, my throat tight. "Your wound is not fully healed. There was blood in the stables."

He shrugged, though there was no such insouciance in the heat of his gaze. "I may have ridden too hard to Kinfairlie, in my haste to win my lady's desire."

"So you then rode to Haddington as well."

He grinned, unrepentant. "We shall see all of this behind us soon, chère."

"If you survive it."

"I have always had an unholy luck."

"As befits a demon?"

We smiled at each other, then our laughter faded and a hunger lit Merlyn's gaze. There was no time to say all that needed saying or to confess every sweet burden of my heart. I bent to kiss his brow as he had so often kissed mine. I found myself trembling, and fearful that I could so obviously be in need of another.

"Be careful, Merlyn. I could not bear to be without you now."

He did not answer me, not in words, but then, I could not blame him for not granting me a guarantee that might not be true. He lifted my hand from his shoulder, then slid his thumb across the silver ring upon my finger.

Before I could speak, he captured my fingers in his grip and kissed the ring. "There is nothing to fear on this night, chère, not when the hall is full of men all watching each other." Merlyn kissed my palm, folded my hand over the heat of his embrace. "It will be when they depart that the peril begins."

And I knew he spoke the truth.

After several moments, I heard the men leave for the hall, the echoing silence of their absence leaving me bereft. The sounds of merrymaking persuaded me to not lend chase. The men were drinking, celebrating, emptying Ravensmuir's cellar of stores, and the hall was no place for women.

Mavella sat on the great bed and chattered happily of what Alasdair had told her. I carefully unlocked Merlyn's box and removed the small sack of jewels. Mavella's words faltered as curiosity had the better of her. I took her hand in mine and she gasped aloud as I spilled the sack's contents into her palm.

"Ysabella! What is this?"

"Your dowry," I smiled at her. "As befits the daughter of Marie Elise of Kinfairlie."

Her mouth dropped open. "No, Ysabella, you cannot do this . . ."

"Merlyn insisted as much and I think his counsel good. This is your guarantee for your children and yourself."

"But . . ."

"Consider it a nuptial gift."

"But . . ."

"Every field has a bad harvest once in a while. Even millstones fall silent in some years. Take it, Mavella, take it with the hope that you be healthy and hale and never have need of it for all the days of your life."

She fell upon me, her tight embrace nigh driving the breath from my very lungs. We began to laugh as we had in childhood, our merriment mingled with tears.

"God smiles upon us in this place," she said, marveling.

"I never dreamed of knowing such good fortune as has found us here at Ravensmuir."

We gathered up the gems and poured them back into the sack. I knew it was not good fortune but the choices of my husband that saw my sister's happiness and prosperity assured. "There is one gift yet owed to you. You have need of a dress for your nuptials, and we shall choose one from that trunk."

"Ysabella, I can take no more from you."

"You will take some raiment, and this will be the gift that all know that I have given you. And we will shorten the hem together tonight, stitching good wishes into every measure." I shook the sack of gems before her eyes. "And when we are done, this sack will be empty, your riches pooled around your feet, and none in this hall or in these lands will be the wiser."

"Oh." Mavella fingered the sack once more. "Are they stolen?"

"No," I said, hoping it was true. "We simply do not wish for you to be taxed by these avaricious earls."

We set to work then, choosing finally a dress of red samite trimmed with ermine, as regal a garment as ever I had seen. Mavella was loath to claim it but I insisted that I could not wear such a hue, due to the shade of my own hair.

She loved the garment—I know this, for she acquiesced with only the slightest argument. We summoned Berthe to aid in the fitting of the gown and the adjustment of the hem—so that all would hear what we did—then I sent the girl to bed.

Mavella and I sat and sewed long into the night, the lanterns flickering as she told me far more than I wished to know of the marvels of Alasdair. I only half-listened, my thoughts whirling.

Though I was happy for my sister, I feared mightily for what the coming days might bring to Ravensmuir's doors.

Mavella eventually fell asleep in the great bed, but I could not be still. And Merlyn did not come, even after the hall fell into the silence of drunken stupor.

I could not sleep for fear of Merlyn's welfare, which troubled me as much as his absence. I had never been so dependent upon another, never relied upon another soul, though many relied upon me. The change in my circumstance made me deeply uneasy, especially as Merlyn seemed determined to court his own demise.

December 31

*Feast Day of Saint Sylvester,
Saint Columba,
Saint Melania the Younger.
Hogmanay*

XV

The sun rose, a blood-red disk wreathed in wraithlike clouds. The very sight made me shiver. I stood on the trunk and stared out the high windows of the solar, watching the eastern wind whip the ocean waves higher. The sea was a hundred hues of inky darkness, the sky filled with dark clouds.

There was a storm coming and it looked to be a fierce one.

It was a bad portent for the day. My sister slept, untroubled, her hair cast across the pillow in blonde waves. She smiled in her slumber, happy at last, and my heart ached at the sight of her.

Merlyn was right. It was time for all old secrets to be revealed, including the one I had clutched so close for so very long. I was resolved.

The earls and the king left Ravensmuir at midday, their pomp and retinue trailing somewhat more raggedly behind them than before. The men had all drunk long into the night in celebration of both Merlyn's survival and the resolution of Ravensmuir's future. Most had been slow to rise, and there had been a great deal of groaning and moaning. At least there were no concerns of having too little food on this day; most of the men had no taste for solid fare.

Merlyn was quiet, wary and watchful. Although I was nigh bursting to share the secret held tightly for so long, it was a tale to be offered in private.

Mavella and Alasdair departed; Ada and Malcolm had already left for Kinfairlie. The squires lingered in the kitchen and there was no sign of Arnulf. I assumed he had gone with his kin, though wished I might have said farewell. I was restless, waiting for I knew not what, and impatient that Merlyn seemed so at ease with his circumstance.

The stone keep brooded all around us, the sea crashed upon the shore in the distance. Ravensmuir felt hollow, yet echoed with secrets and old crimes. I was chillingly aware of how vulnerable we were, that if the keep itself did not defend us, we would be lost.

I stared into the fire of the Yule log. Even though I stood close, the heat did not drive the chill from my bones. I closed my eyes as rain began to fall, cold and forceful. The wind wailed through the high windows, nothing but falling sheets of silver visible beyond it.

"You should hire knights," I said as Merlyn poured himself another cup of wine.

He grimly shook his head. "There will not be time, chère."

I shuddered. He would say no more, but merely stretched his legs out toward the fire, his eyes narrowed as he stared into the flames. Another might have thought his mood grim, but I knew him well enough to know that he reviewed all he had seen and heard. He would wrest every nuance from his observations, and then he would choose his course. There is not so much impulsiveness in my spouse as he would have others believe.

I tapped my toe, never the most patient soul or the most accepting of inactivity. "What do you mean to do?"

Merlyn pursed his lips. "Wait." He did appear inclined to do just that.

"Are you mad?" I asked in frustration. "Do you mean to

simply sit here and wait for some vermin to murder you again?"

He watched me with undisguised amusement. "What do you suggest?"

"Hire knights and men-at-arms. Close the gates and post a watch. Secure alliances." My voice faltered, for I knew little of such matters, knew little beyond the fact that I was not prepared to lose my spouse again. Tears clouded my vision and I looked away, sorely vexed with his scheme.

Merlyn's smile faded and he leaned forward, touching my elbow with his fingertips. "None of that will deter this villain," he said quietly. "It might only delay his assault."

"An indefinite delay would not be all bad."

My husband shook his head. I thought he would say no more, but he spoke with quiet vigor. "I want him to act while he is angered. I want him to think that he is unsuspected. I want him to move quickly, with no clear plan, so that his passion might betray him into making an error." He met my gaze, his own eyes dark. "He must think then, chère, that I consider the matter resolved. He must think me confident in my own safety. He can only think that if I change nothing at all."

"But you might be killed!"

Merlyn's gaze turned steely. "I will not tolerate this threat tainting all the days of our lives, chère. The matter will be resolved, one way or the other, and that with all haste."

"I do not wish to lose you."

He smiled. "I have no intention of dying, chère." He opened his arms and I sat upon his lap, my feet curled up beneath me and my head upon his shoulder. His arms closed around me and we shared the cup of wine, its heat keeping the chill of the day at bay. He leaned back in the chair and we watched the flames together. The hound had found a prize in the rushes and curled at Merlyn's feet, the occasional sound of vigorous gnawing making us smile.

We curled together there and I told Merlyn all that had transpired in his absence.

He was most intrigued by Gawain's claiming of the relic. "What did he say precisely?" he demanded and I recounted his brother's words again.

"The *Titulus*." Merlyn sighed.

"Did you know?"

"No. I knew that whatever the relic was, it had to be a piece of importance. I never guessed that my father had found such a prize. I wonder how it came into his possession."

"Perhaps Gawain knew about it because he had stolen it in the first place."

Merlyn chuckled. "Or my father, not uncharacteristically, told each of us half of the tale."

I touched his arm, sensing his regret. "Did I err in surrendering it?"

He gathered me close. "I cannot fault you for being deceived by Gawain's lies. And I truly cannot be angered that you surrendered such a prize because you feared for my sorry hide." He smiled at me so warmly that I blushed. "But I would have liked to have seen such a marvel. To have touched it, just once."

"Do you seek saintly intercession?" I teased.

But Merlyn did not smile. He rose from the chair and set me on my feet, then strode the chamber beneath the solar. Curiosity demanded that I pursue him. The dog sighed at the inconvenience, picked up its bone, and trailed behind us.

Merlyn stood before one shelf in the chamber below, running his fingers along the volumes there. I felt drawn to his side and, when he continued his survey, I lifted his chemise and pulled the binding away from his wound.

It healed well enough, the scab like a line of rubies across his flesh. One end was less well healed than the other but, as there was no infection, I could scarce complain. I removed the binding and poked the reddish ends of the scar, satisfied that it healed. "You are lucky, Merlyn."

"Doubly so." He winked, then granted me a small smile which heated my blood. "Will you hold this?"

I took the lantern he offered, lifting it so that the light shone over the leather spines of the books. I shivered a little as I stood beside him, for I could smell his skin and feel his heat. I watched his strong tanned fingers move across the leather and could easily imagine his touch upon my flesh.

I was curious at his murmuring to himself. "What do you seek?"

"More detail. I cannot remember all that is known of the *Titulus* and it may be of import."

"Why?"

"It may shed light upon my attacker's identity."

"I thought you had guessed his name?"

"A guess never suffers from more evidence."

I could scarcely argue with that.

"Ah!" Merlyn said finally, then pulled a trio of volumes from the shelf. I put his lamp upon the chest he indicated. He carefully opened the volume there, his finger winding a course over the dense text as he sought some crumb of information.

The vellum was old and turned to a rich golden hue. The ink was blacker than pitch, the script tightly packed as if to save space. The margin was wide, separated from the text by a heavy red line, and graced at intervals with fantastic animals and religious symbols. I spied a lion lying with a lamb, a martyr in torment, a priest driving lively demons from a penitent.

I watched in wonder as Merlyn read, his gaze darting back and forth as he made sense of the small lines that I could not decipher. He seemed to know this text, for he nodded in recollection of a passage here and there.

I confess that I felt an envy to my very bones in that moment. I lusted after the secrets locked in that parchment, secrets so much more tantalizing because they were forever beyond my reach.

I stretched out one finger and caressed the gilded ornamentation that seemed to mark the beginning of the text after every break. "What is this?"

"Hmm? The *Vita Constantini* of Eusebius of Caesarea."

I frowned, feeling that he intended to make me feel ignorant. "I do not understand. You know that I have not had your experiences."

"Nor have you had my opportunities." Merlyn slipped his arm around my shoulder and pulled me against his side. "You have no reason to be ashamed, chère."

I kissed his throat and heard him catch his breath in a most reassuring way. I touched the book again. "What is it, then?"

"*The Life of Constantine*, the Roman emperor . . ."

"Who first became Christian. I know that much of his repute, at least."

There was a twinkle in Merlyn's eye as he opened another book. "And here is the accounting of one Egeria of what she witnessed on her pilgrimage to Jerusalem between *anno domini* three hundred eighty-one and three hundred eighty-four."

I stared at the volume in marvel. "Truly?"

"Truly." Merlyn moved to stand behind me, trapping me between his hips and the high chest. I felt his erection against my buttocks and rubbed myself against him as he folded his hands around my shoulders. His flesh is of a different texture than mine, heavier and smoother, the dark hairs striking against his tanned golden hue. I liked the look of my hand laid atop of his, my foot upon his, his arms around my waist. We were wrought so differently, yet fit together so well.

I had an idea of a good way to pass the time until his trap was sprung. Merlyn bent and nuzzled the side of my neck and I arched back against him. He reached around me, one hand tapping the text, the other folding around my breast.

"It has been copied and recopied perhaps a hundred times, but here, in her accounting of the Easter festivities in Jerusalem, Egeria speaks of the *Titulus*." His finger ran horizontally beneath the lines of text.

"Indeed?"

"She is speaking of the services held on Good Friday," Merlyn said, his wicked fingers coaxing my nipple to a peak, then he began to read. "And specifically mentions the presentation of the *Titulus* along with a piece of the True Cross. She reports an incident of a pilgrim stealing a piece of the holy wood."

"Indeed? How? Surely it was carefully guarded?" I tried desperately to sound intrigued. But I could play his game, as well. I slipped my hand between us and worked the laces free of his chausses. Merlyn inhaled sharply when my fingers slipped under the cloth.

"Indeed, it was, as all treasures should be." Merlyn smiled devilishly at me, then bent and kissed me soundly. His tongue rolled in my mouth, his kiss teased and tempted, his hands made my breasts tingle. When he lifted his head, I was flushed and my blood boiled. His mischievous expression gave me but a moment's warning before he slipped his hand beneath my skirts and touched me boldly.

I moaned at the caress of his fingers between my thighs.

Merlyn cleared his throat and read further. "The faithful were permitted to kiss the relic, and it was in this act that one bit off a piece to steal it."

I laughed despite myself and the subject matter. "People are the same through all of Christendom, are they not?"

"Indeed, they are. And that is why I suspect that even what Egeria saw and kissed was not lost in its entirety."

I fought to keep my thoughts ordered. His fingers made the task an arduous one and I moved against him like a wanton. "Do you think this piece was stolen? A fragment so big could hardly have been bitten from the rest."

"But it could have been claimed earlier." With his free hand, he lifted the volume that he had first grasped.

"Eusebius and the emperor," I remembered.

"Rumor maintains that when Constantine's mother Helena traveled on pilgrimage to Jerusalem, she discovered the True Cross and the *Titulus*." Merlyn frowned at the text. "Though I can find no mention of it here, and Eusebius accompanied the empress upon her journey. But there was considerable construction in the wake of Helena's visit, including a lavish new church upon the site of the crucifixion."

"As might be built to house a marvelous relic."

Merlyn lifted a third volume. "Which brings us to Cyril, who was appointed to be Bishop of Jerusalem in three hundred forty-nine, after Eusebius' and Helena's departure. I enjoy his commentary, for he was unafraid to say what others might not and did not care that he was often banished from his own see."

I smiled. "I can well imagine that you might feel an understanding for such an uncommon churchman."

Merlyn's chuckle made his chest rumble against my back. "And better yet, in the letter I recall, he complains about the proliferation of holy relics, specifically about the number of pieces of the True Cross." He clearly knew this document, for he sought the passage with some familiarity of the rest.

I was fascinated. How many of these tomes had Merlyn read?

"Ah! Here, in his letter to Emperor Constantine II, he talks of the True Cross and *Titulus* gracing Jerusalem." Merlyn was animated, so animated that his caress slowed.

"So it had been found."

"And it was venerated."

"And already there were those who lied about the provenance of the wood they granted or sold to others."

"You miss the point, chère," Merlyn insisted. "The True Cross was found, as was the *Titulus*. Some of those fragments were genuine. In certain circles, there is speculation that the *Titulus* was split after Helena's discovery, the part of the inscription regarding Nazareth taken by Helena to Rome, the rest left in Jerusalem. The Jerusalem fragment has not been seen for centuries. The Roman fragment has not been displayed publicly since the early twelfth century."

"In certain circles?" I echoed. "Is that why you possess these volumes? So that you could concoct a likely explanation for whatever relic you sought to sell?"

"I told you that I have left that trade, chère."

"But still I do not understand why you took it at all."

"There were several reasons." Merlyn stroked the leather binding upon one book, his profile telling me little of his thoughts. Then he spoke low, so low that I had to strain even in this small space to hear him. "Here is one. Because there are true relics, treasures which can be found by one who gathers the hints and searches diligently."

He turned to me then, his face so alight that I understood with sudden clarity something of Merlyn I had not guessed before. He loved the hunt. He savored the prize.

He *believed.*

Merlyn's eyes glowed as he spoke. "There is something about genuine relics, chère. You can almost feel the power of intercession coursing through them, you can sense that which gives succor to so many souls. It is an honor to hold one, even for a moment." He shook his head. "Surely it is only proper that such a prize is within reach of the faithful. I thought that surely in a trade filled with rogues and pirates, there was room for one man to trade honestly."

The discovery of a genuine relic, in all its rarity, was what made his trade worthwhile. My heart leapt, for no villain with a blackened heart would have cared for genuine relics, save that they might fetch a better price.

I had to play the devil's advocate. I had to know the worst

of it even as I hoped for the best. "Even if you also traded in forgeries?"

Merlyn shook his head. "If I could not prove or disprove the provenance of a piece, I told the buyer as much. If the relic was overtly false, I would not trade in it. It was the only way that I could make my peace with this trade."

"You believe what I found to be genuine."

"I know it is, chère. I *know* it, but not by words in any volume or evidence it carries within it. I sense it. I know it with my very innards and my instinct is a finely honed one." Merlyn shoved a hand through his hair. "No matter that if it is genuine, and if people know of it, that would account for the desperation of some nameless soul to possess it."

"How so?"

"The *Titulus* has been seen by few but is known by many. Indeed, it has been vigorously sought over the centuries. It is one of the great relics and its power would be significant."

"It certainly has had a powerful influence on your family's fates."

Merlyn ignored my wry comment. "And here in Scotland, we have buried a king who had difficulties gaining respect, and have crowned one this very year whose ascension was challenged by powerful foes. Fortunes have been made and lost by the favor of these kings, no less their ability or inability to enforce their wills. I would wager that some soul needed the approval of the king and needed it badly enough that he dared not let another lay claim to this gift."

I immediately saw his import. "Someone wished to buy the king's favor, wanted to buy it twice in fact."

"Indeed. The question is who."

I thought immediately of the Earl of March, who had lost so much in the coronation of King Robert. "George Dunbar was only favored by King David near the end of his reign, only after George's sister Agnes caught the king's eye."

Merlyn nodded, his eyes bright. "And now he has had a

taste of what wealth the favor of a king can bring. No doubt the fall from grace this time came more hard."

"Why did you take this trade, Merlyn?" I demanded, hating the position in which we found ourselves. "Why did you abandon your trade in silks?"

Merlyn shook his head ruefully. "That choice was taken from me, chère, by the repute I inherited upon my father's demise. That repute, however, has saved my hide more than once in this trade."

"I do not understand."

"It is useful to be known as a man without scruples in the company of others similarly deficient." His gaze bore into mine.

"Gawain said you killed your own father." I stared up at him but Merlyn steadily held my gaze. "Was that truth or lie?"

"I did kill him," he said with soft conviction.

I found not a shred of guilt within Merlyn's gaze. But once before I had believed Gawain too readily.

Not this time.

I shook my head. "No, Merlyn. There must be more to the tale."

My spouse arched a dark brow. "Even though my brother makes such an accusation?"

"My husband is no lying, thieving rogue, although his brother certainly is. I know there is another half to this tale, a half that will show my husband to benefit." I seized his hand. "I command you to come back to the fire and tell me all of it."

Merlyn laughed with delight. His arms closed around me, and he kissed me so soundly that I nigh forgot my name. I certainly forgot any intent to share a tale, though Merlyn did not. He broke our kiss and swept me into his arms, then returned to the chair in the great hall before the blazing fire.

He studied me, his gaze suddenly serious. He picked up a tendril of my hair, wound it around his finger and smiled crookedly at me. "You are a marvel, chère." His gaze roved over me. "You are always beautiful, but there is a new radiance in your eyes on this day."

"Indeed?"

"Indeed." He smiled playfully. "You might be a woman in love."

"Perhaps I am," I teased, looping my arms around his neck and feeling uncommonly optimistic. It seemed I learned my spouse's affection for some risk. "Are you jealous of the man in question?"

"Should I be?"

I kissed him with such tenderness as to drive any doubts from his thoughts. We parted eventually, the heat between us greater than that cast by the great Yule log.

Merlyn looked rumpled. He offered me the cup, then when I declined, took a hearty gulp of the wine. "Let me tell you of my father, chère. He wanted to feign his death, as I told you, to evade the results of breaking his many promises. And he insisted upon having my aid. You have seen that rocky isle just off the shore of Ravensmuir?"

"It is not that big."

"No. And it is barren. My father said that one of his ships would arrive to meet him at the island in the night, and that all I had to do was to row there with him during the day. It was not uncommon for us to go there when we were younger, to explore the caverns, then row back at the end of the day."

"But he did not intend to return?"

"No. His plan was that I would return alone, distraught, and claim that he had fallen into the sea and drowned. I was skeptical for all knew that he was an uncommonly good swimmer, but he insisted the scheme would work. He said the waves would be unruly and reminded me that even the finest swimmer can be overcome in a rough sea.

"We argued mightily about this lie, but in the end, I thought it a harmless enough endeavor and one that might see him live longer than he would otherwise. There was a desperation about him, and I suspected that he came close to provoking at least one of his potential clients."

"So you agreed."

Merlyn grimaced and sipped the wine. "He bade me row him to the island with first light. I left when you were still asleep."

I remembered awakening to find Merlyn gone, remembered the refusal of all within Ravensmuir to tell me where he had gone. I ached anew that there had been so many secrets between us for so long.

Merlyn's words turned bitter. "And my reward for having done as he bade me, for being the dutiful son he said that he desired, was his betrayal of me."

He fell silent and I nestled closer. I had no doubt that he recounted the truth, for I had seen the betrayal of which Gawain was capable. "What did he do?"

"He attacked me." Merlyn swallowed. "He waited until we were on the far side of the island, where none might witness his deed. Then he punched me, seized me, and he hurled me into the sea."

"No!"

"Oh, yes. He was strong, my father, stouter than me and he had surprise upon his side." Merlyn's words fell in an angry torrent. "I had my wits about me enough to grab at him, and we went over the side of the boat together. In fact, we capsized it. Not that it mattered. We still were wrestling in the water. My father's arms were locked around me like a vise of uncommon strength and I knew that he meant for me to die."

"He was mad!"

"He meant to repay me for not living my life as he had desired. I was an unfit son, to his thinking, for I spurned the legacy he would grant to me."

"You were an ethical son."

"I was traitor in my father's eyes." Merlyn grimly took a draught of wine. "On that day, I fought him, I fought for my life. I slowly whittled his advantage, for I was younger and stronger. He was desperate, though, and furious as I said. He struck me against the side of my head. He kicked me until what little breath I had was lost.

"He was more experienced in the water than me and I know that I drank far more of the sea. And we sank with uncommon speed. I was terrified and fought for my very survival. He stymied my every effort to either escape or save us both."

I gripped his hand in horror, appalled that I had never even guessed at Merlyn's ordeal.

"I turned once, nigh blue for air, and he was smiling at me, his cheeks filled with air and his gaze filled with malice." Merlyn closed his eyes. "Then he lifted his hand and I saw the rock within it just as he swung it at me. Praise be that water slows a strike, for I managed to evade his blow. He snatched at my leg and pulled me down, I clawed for the surface, but my father pulled me to the depths of the sea."

"He meant to kill you."

Merlyn nodded.

"The villain! But you did escape, you must have."

"I did." Merlyn drank grimly. "My boot pulled free. He snatched after me, but I was given new strength by this chance to live. I broke free, desperate for air. He lunged after me, but I kicked, felt the blow connect and did not look back."

Merlyn swallowed.

I covered my mouth with my hands, horrified.

"I broke the surface gasping and shaking, chilled to the bone."

"And?"

"There was no sign of him."

"What did you do?"

Merlyn frowned. "I went back for him. I had to. He was my father, however misguided he might have been. I realized that I must have kicked his head. When I finally spied him, he was sinking fast, faster than any man should. By the time I managed to dive deep enough again, he was limp and drifting with the current. He was so heavy, I could not pull him to the surface. I had to choose whether to die with him or to leave him alone."

"He was probably already dead."

Merlyn bowed his head and his next words were hoarse. "Possibly. His body washed onto the rocks below Ravensmuir later."

"Gawain said his pockets were weighted with stones."

Merlyn nodded. "That was why he sank so quickly. He meant to pull me under, I have no doubt, then empty his pockets and return to the surface. He was a powerful swimmer. He could have held his breath longer than me. Perhaps his ship still did come in the night. I do not know."

I realized my own deeds had done little to make matters better for Merlyn that day. I grimaced as I met his gaze. "Because you returned from this ordeal to find your wife gone."

Merlyn touched the silver ring. "The sole token I had given her lay in the midst of our bed, so that I could not misconstrue the extent of her rejection."

"I am so sorry, Merlyn."

"No. We both erred in this." He pulled me closer. "I should have told you that he had come to Ravensmuir. I should have sought your counsel."

"Why did you not pursue me then?"

His lips tightened. "It was upon my return to Ravensmuir that I realized how clever my father had been. Gawain met me at the shore and called me a murderer."

"I come to intensely dislike your brother," I said with irritation.

"You believed him once."

"Yes, but he is too smitten with his own charm and too concerned with his own advantage."

Merlyn shook his head. "I think he believed this tale, chère. My father had shown his usual skill of accommodating all eventualities. Gawain insisted that our father had told him of my threats against him, threats supposedly rooted in my father's refusal to invest in my growing trade. It seemed that he would not buy me a ship of my own."

"Was that true?"

"I had no ships of my own at the time, that much was true, and it was also true that I could not have afforded one then." Merlyn spoke with heat. "It was not true that I had demanded my father fund one, or that I had threatened him, but he had told so many souls as much that it was as fact."

His words turned bitter. "And this was when I learned that it matters less what a man has done—it matters more what others believe he has done. Whether I died or whether I survived my father's attempt to kill me was immaterial—I was marked as a murderer and my reputation was gone."

He shook his head. "That my father had left every coin in his treasury to my hand provided confirmation to any who might have doubted of my scheme to gain my inheritance early. Perhaps he feared the outcome which did come about. Perhaps he knew that I was stronger than him."

"Perhaps he wished you to believe that you killed him."

"I did kill him. I could not save him from himself nor from the sea." He shook his head. "My father's was an artful scheme."

"And he destroyed your alliances for trade."

Merlyn nodded. "A man can only trade in legitimate goods if his reputation is impeccable, and mine no longer was. The shop in Venice faltered for lack of clients. None in the East wished to make agreements with me. Whatever trust I had cultivated over the years was stolen from me."

"But how did they know? Ravensmuir is not so central as that."

Merlyn smiled, though his expression was without humor. "My father hinted at trouble beforehand, it is clear, perhaps on the journey when he sought me out. And Gawain, in his bitterness, was a very effective messenger. He and my father were close, two of a kind, and he blamed me for cheating him of his own blood."

"You were gone two days," I said softly.

"I came ashore far south of here." He frowned. "And I did not hasten in the walking, for I dreaded having to tell you of what I had done. Then Gawain met me beneath Ravensmuir and I had to consider how best to proceed."

"You should have protested your innocence, Merlyn! You could have told the truth of the tale and cleared your own reputation!"

He regarded me wearily. "Yes, I could have told the truth. I could have sworn to the veracity of my own tale before any magistrate in the land, I could have shouted the truth of what had happened from any hilltop in Christendom. But my family's wicked repute is well known and you have seen yourself how quick men are to mark us all the same." His eyes glittered. "I could shout myself hoarse, denying the testimony of my own brother and the damning facts piled against me. But who would believe me, chère? Who?"

My heart ached for what Merlyn's father had stolen from him—the precious gifts of believing in the good of others, of trusting the pledge of others, or relying upon others for any matter at all. His father had not only betrayed and tried to kill Merlyn, he had stolen his life.

I cupped his face in my hands and held his dark gaze as I whispered the words I most wanted him to believe. "I do, Merlyn. I do."

I barely saw his answering smile before his lips closed

over mine. His arms surrounded me so tightly that the breath was driven from my chest, but I did not care. I surrendered to his embrace and returned his hungry kiss, loving him, trusting him, welcoming all he had to give.

XVI

I pulled my husband back to the solar, determined to have the lovemaking so long overdue. I had never seduced a man but the approval in Merlyn's smile told me that I fared well enough. I recalled suddenly Fitz's jest about all the women his lord had bedded during our separation. It was no matter—I resolved to drive the recollection of each and every one of them from Merlyn's memory forever, and to do so on this day.

I unbuckled my own belt and cast it aside, hooked my fingers beneath my pelisse and discarded it without care for its cost. My robe immediately followed, then I loosed the tie of my chemise beneath Merlyn's avid gaze. I strolled across the chamber, knowing that the light from the candles would glow through the thin linen of my chemise, and locked the portal.

"Now there is no escape," I whispered.

Merlyn grinned and appeared unlikely to protest.

The neckline of my gossamer chemise was gathered onto the tie at the neck. The garment was generously cut and as I walked back across the chamber, I loosed the neck until the chemise could slide over my shoulders. I paused before Merlyn, held his gaze and dropped the chemise to puddle around my ankles.

He caught his breath.

I then lifted my arms over my head and removed the pins from my hair. He watched my breasts, studied my face, as I loosed the length of my hair from the braids. I combed it with my fingers until it cascaded down my back in a coppery mass that fell beyond my buttocks. I shook it, knowing that it would snare the light, and approached him with purpose.

When we stood with barely the width of my hand between us, I let my hands drop to his belt. Merlyn did nothing either to help or to hinder me. His eyes gleamed as I unfastened the belt and dropped it to the floor. I removed his tabard and his chemise, letting my fingers trail across his tanned flesh.

I pushed him back onto the bed and he surrendered with nary a struggle. Indeed, Merlyn smiled. Propped on one elbow, he reached out with his other hand and captured the key that hung around my neck. He gently tugged me closer by the red silken cord around my neck and I could see how his gaze had darkened. I let him steal one kiss, so tender and sweet that it nigh melted my bones, then pulled away.

"Not yet," I murmured. "Not yet." I wanted this to be a coupling we remembered with great fondness, the first of our new covenant, the union of honesty that should have been ours five years past. I wanted to surrender everything to Merlyn and I did not want to make haste about it.

"But soon."

"You cannot retire fully dressed," I chided teasingly. I kissed each palm and set his hands back upon the mattress. "Let me."

Merlyn inhaled sharply. I could feel the tension within him, but he waited.

I straddled his leg and granted him a fine view of my bare buttocks as I pulled off his boot. His hands landed upon me as I repeated the deed with the other boot. He caressed the curve of my rump, then slipped his hands around my hips, drawing me closer to him. I laughed as I tumbled atop him, then rolled across the mattress to seize the laces of his chausses with my teeth.

He halted, eyes glittering, and watched me.

I used both teeth and fingers to unfasten the lace, the heat and the hardness of him urging me to hasten even as my impulse was to linger. On impulse and with uncommon boldness, even for me, I took him into my mouth. Merlyn gasped and whispered my name in a most delicious way.

It was all the encouragement I needed to sweetly torment him, all the urging I required to tease him with lips and teeth and tongue. It was most satisfactory to straighten for a breath and find Merlyn—*Merlyn!*—flushed and agitated. He reached for me but I retreated to the head of the bed.

"I command you to remove my shoes and stockings, sir, before I sate you," I said and lifted one foot in demand.

Merlyn chuckled and I smiled myself. He had never made me ashamed of my own audacity and he had never refused any demand I had made of him abed.

Which opened numerous interesting prospects.

He flung off his chausses, then crawled across the mattress with the fluid grace of a cat. He caught my foot in his hand, eased off the slipper, then caressed my instep with his thumb. His sure touch launched an army of shivers over my flesh and made me ache to feel him inside me again.

Then, without releasing my foot, he stretched to untie my garters with his teeth. His gaze flew to mine and my breath caught, for I knew that he recalled as well as I the night that we had once reconciled abed, when he had removed my garters thus, then driven me wild with desire.

And my flesh heated at the prospect of repeating that again.

His kisses burned behind my knees, trailing behind the stocking as it was urged from my leg, caressing my instep and tickling between my toes. He moved with infuriating leisure, making me shiver and bringing me close to begging. But I would not beg and he would not hasten. It promised to be a most delightful interlude.

Merlyn repeated his labor on the other garter, caressing more slowly and thoroughly. He echoed the pattern of kisses, left a burning imprint upon the inside of my right knee, then halted.

Merlyn lifted his head and regarded me from between my own knees, his eyes burning with ardor. I watched him for a long moment, knowing what he asked of me, knowing how much I wanted it yet wanting to prolong the tension all the same.

When I could bear it no longer, when Merlyn swallowed, I silently parted my thighs. My breath hitched in my throat, and his satisfied smile made my heart stop. Then he eased his broad shoulders between my knees, dipped his head and tasted me.

I fell back against the pillows, closed my eyes and moaned with pleasure. His tongue moved with exquisite languor, his hands gripped me and held me fast, his breath teased. I tangled my fingers in his hair and urged him ever closer, uncertain I could bear his touch any longer, knowing I could not be without it. I hooked my heels beneath his shoulders, drawing him onward, and he laved me with greater vigor. He roused a tempest within me with dangerous ease and I reveled in it. My hips began to buck of their own accord.

My blood boiled and I became dizzy. But still I wanted us to find pleasure together. I seized a fistful of his hair and lifted his head, gasping out my words. "It is not enough!"

"No, chère, it is not." And Merlyn was atop me, lowering his strength into me, claiming me again as his bride. I clutched at his shoulders and held him fast. He caught at the back of my neck and held me fast beneath his demanding kiss. I arched against him, ground my hips, and dug my nails into his back.

I demanded all that he could give and he surrendered it to me, even as he demanded my own surrender. And when the torrent came, it was larger and higher and I tumbled harder and faster than ever I had before. I heard myself cry out, I heard Merlyn roar, then there was nothing but the heat of the man I loved within me.

Afterward I lay still, listening to the storm spend itself against the stone walls, pinned beneath Merlyn's weight as he dozed. Our legs were tangled together, his hand was in my hair, his breath caressed against my cheek. The mattress was soft and the linens fine.

The keep was silent, or as silent as ever it was. The dog snored somewhere near the foot of the bed, the wind whistled as the rain beat against the stone. I let my fingers wind into the dark silk of Merlyn's hair and was—for the moment—content to let matters be simple between us.

I awakened to the tickle of smoke in my nostrils. The solar was falling dark, the wind making more noise than the rain. I jerked but something restrained me.

My hands were bound together, then tied to one of the great columns of the bed. My feet were bound, as well, but not linked to the bed. I writhed, unable to make sense of this nightmare.

But it was no dream.

I pulled hard at my bonds and succeeded only in tearing the flesh from my wrists. I cried out and a woman laughed close at hand.

When I looked for her, I realized that Merlyn's heat was no longer at my back.

He was gone and Ada Gowan stood before me, her eyes wild. She held a lantern, its flame dancing high, and laughed at me as she touched it to one of the tapestries on the wall.

The cloth roared as the fire began to consume it.

"Now comes a reckoning, Ysabella of Kinfairlie," she said lightly. "Now comes the burning due to all witches, without the trouble of a trial before those who might be bent to your will."

"I am no witch and you know it well!" I cried, struggling all the while against my bonds. They were tight, as no doubt she intended.

"A harlot then, burned in her bed of sin." Ada leaned closer to me. "I care not for the details, Ysabella. You are wicked, for you have taken every pleasure that should have been mine. But no more, Ysabella, no more. You will not have Ravensmuir and you will not have Merlyn. I will not suffer to see you sated."

"Merlyn will not wed you." I wanted to keep her talking in the hope that some means of escape would come clear to me.

Ada laughed. "Merlyn is probably already dead, as he should have been days ago. He can no longer help you, Ysabella."

"Where is he?"

"It seems I brought word to him that his ship would soon falter upon the rocky shore. He will never reach the shore, of course, for a predator lies in wait in his own keep. This time Merlyn will not escape."

"Ship?" Fear tightened my throat.

Her eyes glittered. "Oh yes, Ysabella, *that* ship. I shall be rid of Rhys Fitzwilliam, who never liked me, and you shall be rid of your brother, as well."

"No!"

Ada laughed. "I know all the secrets of these Lammergeier. I know how they signal their ships to come to shore with a single lantern burning bright, and I know where that lantern is set so that the ship comes safely through the rocks."

"You cannot be so cruel," I whispered, fearing what she would say.

"Oh yes. On this night, oddly, the beacon has been set in the wrong place. How sad. The weather ensures that none on that ship will see the truth until it is too late, and then no doubt the ship will be lifted by the sea and shattered upon the rocky shore. There will be few survivors, and any fool enough to crawl to shore will die there."

"They will not risk a landing in such weather."

"You underestimate the loyalty of Rhys Fitzwilliam to his lord's bidding. Only the laird sets out the beacon, and the laird's command is not to be disobeyed."

"The laird did not set the beacon on this night."

"The *new* laird has set the flame on this night, and done so to ensure that there are no stray details. It would not do to have a child of Marie Elise of Kinfairlie alive to stake a claim against Ravensmuir. Ravensmuir shall fall to its new lord and lady, with no challenges by blood."

"What of Mavella?"

Ada smiled. "You may rest assured that you will all find your demise in time."

"What have you done to Merlyn?"

She watched the flames, assessing their progress as they leapt to the next tapestry. "As a loyal servant, of course, I could only draw my laird's attention to the ship's mistaken approach."

"You set a trap for him," I said bitterly, fighting fruitlessly against my bonds.

"I set a trap for *you*. The solar door is barred from the other side, if you were so fool as to risk passing through those flames. And we all know of your fear of darkness. Imagine, Ysabella, your sole hope of escape is through the labyrinth, though I will close the portal behind myself so that matters are not too easy. My lover set a trap for Merlyn and my only regret is that I was not able to witness Merlyn's demise."

She sat on the side of the mattress, her manner companionable. "I find it particularly satisfactory that the man who came here to court you turned his eye upon me, instead. I like having stolen a man's regard from you. I like it quite well. I like how it redresses the debts between us."

"Who is this man who would be laird? Is it Gawain?"

Ada laughed. "That scoundrel? Never! He has no care for property and responsibilities."

"Then who?"

"Can you not guess?"

"One of the earls?"

Ada laughed merrily at this prospect. "And how should a wedded man pledge marriage to me?"

"The Earl of March's son?"

Ada shook her head. "Calum of Dunkilber."

"But . . ."

"He is the king's bastard brother, never acknowledged, long denied his rightful legacy. The earls and king say his claim is groundless, they deny him his rightful due, the Earl of March denied him a holding and any status. They would keep him from having any tithes, any wealth to assert his status." Her eyes shone in her defense of his credentials. "They keep him in poverty in the hopes that he will die. They hate him and they fear him, but his day has come. We have an understanding, Calum and I, for we have both faced unwarranted adversity and we shall wreak our vengeance together."

"But if you burn the keep, it cannot be your own."

"Ravensmuir has been rebuilt before. Fear not, I will be Lady of Ravensmuir, though the keep will be larger and finer than this one."

Ada crossed the chamber quickly, then flung open the trunk of clothes Merlyn had bought for me, lifting one gown. "And you will have nothing, Ysabella. Indeed, there will be no sign that ever you were here." She touched the flame to the gown. When I thought the fire would leap to her own clothing, she tossed the gown back into the trunk.

The fire raged there, leaping high, devouring them all.

"I shall have everything you sought to make your own," she said. "I shall have everything that should have been mine and I shall savor every morsel."

"You are mad!"

"I have told you, Ysabella, that advantage must be well secured. Mine will be." She smiled, then flung the lantern at the door that led to the stairs. The vessel shattered, the oil sprayed against the wooden wall, and the flames fed greedily upon it. I could not look upon the wall, so bright was the inferno. The dry wood began to crackle immediately.

Ada strolled toward me, clearly pleased with what she had wrought. "Poor Ysabella, fated to die in such pain." She raised a hand and touched the secret latch with the surety of one who knew precisely where to find it. The portal to the labyrinth slid open, the cool air fanning the flames yet higher.

"You know the labyrinth," I whispered.

"What else had I to do, all those lonely days and nights in this abode?"

"Avery told you of it?"

Ada laughed harshly. "Avery told me nothing. But these Lammergeier are not so clever as I—any fool could see how readily they disappeared and guess the truth." She leaned closer. "I know enough of this family and their wicked ways to see them all rot in hell. No doubt, you shall have all eternity to share each other's secrets."

"What of the plate, Ada?" I demanded wildly, fearful that once she left me here, I would be doomed. "The plate in the chapel that was the thirteenth? Gawain said you brought it to him."

"It is my duty to feed the laird's family," she said, her eyes narrowing. "He lied to me, he made promises to me as well that he had no intent to keep." Her lips tightened. "He took the plate from the labyrinth and I knew not where. You contrived its return to frighten me, I see that now."

She hefted a brass candlestick with a fat tallow candle impaled upon its spike. She crossed the room and touched the wick to the flames, then brought it back to the side of the bed. Her eyes shone with a malice undisguised.

"Now you shall burn, Ysabella, as you always should have done."

And Ada dropped the burning candle on to the bed beside me.

The linens began to burn immediately, the hangings started to smoke. I writhed wildly. Hearing the flames land in my hair, I screamed. Ada laughed as she stepped over the threshold and I knew she would abandon me there to die.

"But how can you destroy the relic, Ada?" I shouted in desperation.

She paused and regarded me with narrowed eyes. "What relic?"

"The *Titulus Croce*, the prize for which Avery was killed. It is there, in that trunk. Ada, it will be lost forever by your deeds!"

Her gaze flicked to the trunk and back to me. "You lie!" she cried, but she was not certain.

"No, Ada. It is truly there." I twisted away from the flames, the bed fairly crackling beneath me. The canopy overhead turned suddenly orange, consumed with flames. "I found it in the chapel."

"But Gawain left with a relic."

"I lied to the liar." I insisted. "He took a forgery."

Ada inhaled sharply. She stared across the solar, gauging the distance to the trunk I indicated.

Then she ran.

The flames danced around the bed curtains with dangerous speed and I tugged at the bond in a frenzy. I glanced up at the heat on my flesh and saw that the fire burned upon the rope that trussed me to the column.

Here was my chance! I pulled upon the rope desperately, willing it to break before Ada returned. It did so with such a vigorous snap that I tumbled. I looked and saw Ada rummaging in the trunk I had indicated, the one whose contents I did not even know.

The solar was filling with smoke, the walls and tapestries too dry to slow the fire. I beat out the fire in my hair and rolled from the bed, landing heavily against the wall.

But I was still bound. I eyed the high threshold and the darkness beyond, guessing that if I leapt, I might tumble down the stairs there.

I had to be free. I shoved my hands into the flames, willing the fire to burn my bonds before my flesh. I bit back a scream at the lick of the flames and pulled against my bonds.

The rope loosed. I pulled one hand free and slapped out the flames clinging to the rope knotted around the other wrist.

Only just in time.

"It is not here!" Ada shouted through the smoke that was beginning to fill the solar. "You lying wretch!"

She raced back toward me, fury contorting her features when she saw that I was upright. She shoved me toward the burning bed. I lost my balance as I fell across the mattress. I twisted and clutched at Ada. She fell on top of me, cursing soundly.

She screamed and her hands closed around my throat. She squeezed and I felt the world around me dim. I choked for breath, flailed across the mattress and found salvation.

My hands closed around the brass candlestick, the metal warm yet not engulfed by flames. I rolled in a last desperate bid for survival and swung it hard behind me.

It hit something.

Ada's grip loosened and fell back. I swung to my feet, gasping, ready to fight anew, but she did not move. There was a gash across her brow and she lay oddly still. I stretched out a hand, but in that moment, the canopy loosed itself and fell.

The entire bed was consumed in crackling flames, the heat pressing against my face and the light blinding me.

There was no time to think of what I had done. I lunged through the door to the labyrinth and felt desperately for the latch that I had once hit inadvertently. The flames danced closer, fed by the cool air, and I feared I would be too late.

I heard the tiny click and my heart fairly stopped. The panel slid back and for once in all my days, I was grateful to have cool darkness enfold me.

It would not last long, though. Orange flames were already outlining the door. I worried at the knot binding my ankles, worked it free, then plunged down the steps into the labyrinth.

Merlyn strode into a trap. I had to find him and warn him, before it was too late.

My fear for Merlyn was greater than my fear of the darkness and it drove me onward. I tended down, wanting to put distance between myself and the flames.

When faced with a choice between passages that both led down, I listened for the wind, heading always toward the taste of the sea. I put my foot in cold water more than once and retreated. I reached dead ends twice, but either retraced my steps or found another way.

I moved with haste. I was cold in my chemise with my feet bare on the stone, and my flesh was raw where the rope had chafed. I did not know how much of my hair was burned and did not care.

I could think only of Merlyn. I could have been in another world, one wrought of nightmares, for there was no hint that another soul drew breath near me.

The wind grew stronger after one turn, its chill making my sweat cold against my flesh. I hastened toward the patch of night far ahead.

The labyrinth fairly spat me into the raging sea. The tunnel ended so abruptly that I almost stepped over its lip into nothing. I looked down and had a dizzying glimpse of waves crashing upon rocks far below. The rain had stopped, but still the sky roiled restlessly overhead.

A path lurked to my right, winding back from the opening, then along the cliff face. I pursued it, falling to all fours when the wind coiled around me and might have flung me to my death. I crawled up the rock face, feeling my way in fearful haste.

I was startled to realize that my path ended on the point beyond the chapel. It was the course Gawain had taken in his flight. Beyond the chapel, a plume of smoke rose from Ravensmuir, black against the churning stormclouds.

I noted no more than that, before someone seized me from behind, one gloved hand closing cruelly over my mouth, the other locking my wrists together behind my back.

"Such a pretty prize," Calum whispered into my ear. "I do prefer to have more with which to wager."

I struggled against him, but he forced me toward the chapel. He pinned me to the wall, trapping me between the cold stone and the hard press of his armor. "What a vantage point you have to watch your lover meet his due."

I gagged on his glove and his words. He whispered in my ear, well pleased with what he wrought. "You shall be witness, Ysabella, to the demise of the old laird and the conquest of the new."

"Ada," I managed to mutter through his grip.

Calum chuckled. "A woman easily deceived. She told me much that I needed to know, and all for the folly of thinking I would marry her. And why? She is too old to bear me the sons I desire and not sufficiently well born for my purposes.

I will have a plump young nobleman's daughter for my bride, even if I have to steal her."

I made a sound of disgust, which seemed to amuse him.

"Have you killed her? I had a wager with my squire that you would best her."

I bit him, but his gloves were thick and he only grunted.

"Watch," he hissed and turned me so that I could see. Far to my right, beyond the stables and the smithy, a single lantern flickered in the wind. "Look, a beacon for the ship snared in the storm, a reference to a familiar harbor."

I could only just discern the distant silhouette of a ship, tossing on the waves. It was as Ada had threatened.

The sea glinted as it flung itself against the rocks to the north of me and I saw that the shoals extended far to sea. The island was there, half hulking below the surface of the rolling waves, a deathtrap for any ship fool enough to be guided or blown that way.

Or one tricked into making that direction.

I recalled that when I had seen Merlyn's ship before, it had been anchored to the south of the chapel. There, the waves broke solely on the shore and I knew then where the Lammergeier's safe haven lay. The overgrowth I had removed would have kept any casual intruders from exploring the point, from finding the access to the caverns below, and from interfering with shipping.

This light beckoned Fitz and Tynan to their downfall.

What could I do?

"Look!" Calum chortled gleefully.

Even as I feared for the ship's fate, a man ran from Ravensmuir's stables, his long-legged stride all too familiar. He raced toward the cliffs, fighting against the wind, then kicked the lantern burning there into the sea. My heart leapt as the flame sputtered and died, plunging the coast into darkness.

Calum laughed beneath his breath. "And they say the Lammergeier are not predictable."

A moment later, I could see Merlyn's silhouette as he stared out to sea. Calum laughed against my back. The ship drew nearer, its hull rising and falling wildly as the sea drove it inland.

"Too late perhaps," Calum whispered, his attention fixed upon Merlyn. "Either way, he will now come to me."

I choked as Merlyn did precisely thus. He ran across the courtyard, ran faster than I might have believed toward the chapel.

I saw the light on the coast flicker to life again, saw that Merlyn was unaware of what happened behind him, then Calum pulled me into the chapel.

It was dark within, but the gleam of his blade was close.

As were the blades of two of his squires.

I caught my breath, even as Calum hauled me toward the altar. "He will come for a lantern to light on the cliff and you will be silent."

He whispered in my ears, his knife blade drawing a line across my throat. My breath hitched when I felt a warm trickle of blood and I nodded, wanting only to make him stop.

The three of them were coiled tense, the boys right by the door. It was clear the boys were meant to distract Merlyn— or at least tire him—so that Calum could take him by surprise.

I closed my eyes and prayed in silence. The chapel doors creaked in the wind, the sea slammed against the shore. I tried to envision Merlyn's progress, tried to see how far he would come and how quickly. I would have only one chance.

I thought he must be close at hand, though the hammering of my heart made it hard to judge the time. I strained my ears and when I thought I heard a purposeful step outside the chapel, I moved.

I bit Calum's hand as hard as I could, not caring if I broke a tooth. At the same moment, I drove my heel up under his tabard, feeling it connect hard with his groin.

He swore, his grip slipped, and I screamed Merlyn's name.

He kicked open the door not a heartbeat later, his blade slashing at the two boys who beset him. The very fact that he had his sword at the ready told me that he might not have had need of my warning. One squire was quickly divested of his blade and fled into the night, while the other fought valiantly against Merlyn's greater might.

I tried to race for the door, but Calum snatched at my hair, dragging me back painfully toward him. He wrapped my hair around his fist, holding me captive in his tight grip and I cried out. Merlyn struck down the second squire, then turned his gaze upon Calum. His chemise was torn, his hair tousled, his eyes dark. He looked unpredictable, unruly and dangerous.

Calum took a step back, pulling me with him. "I will kill her."

Merlyn advanced one relentless step at a time. "I have no doubt of it."

"I will butcher her before your eyes."

"It takes a particular kind of man to kill his own daughter."

Calum caught his breath. "What nonsense is this?"

"Elizabeth recorded the insignia of her assailant in her missive: a gold stag rampant on a black ground."

I gasped, knowing that this was Calum's own insignia. There was not so much difference between his assault upon Dunkilber and that made against Kinfairlie.

"You never read that aloud," Calum scoffed, but there was fear in his voice.

"It seemed tactless to make such an accusation then and

there," Merlyn said smoothly. Calum almost had his back to the wall behind the altar. "I gave it to the king and his justiciar, though. No doubt there will be charges made against you shortly and Dunkilber will be reclaimed."

"They cannot take that from me!'

"They can and they will, Calum, and the charge will bring a heavy price." Merlyn smiled, sparing a quick glance to the chapel. "Unless, of course, you were to repent here and now of your crimes."

"Never!" Calum cried. He flung me aside, drew his sword and lunged after Merlyn. Merlyn parried the blow, then attacked. The clash of steel on steel was deafening, the glint of the moving blades like quicksilver. I backed toward the door, knowing I should flee to safety but unable to not watch.

Calum cried out as Merlyn's blade nicked his throat above his jerkin. He stabbed at Merlyn, but Merlyn swept his blow aside, laughing when Calum dove after him in rage. Merlyn was lithe and fast, younger and more agile than Calum. The older man knew it and deeply resented it. I knew it was because he feared to lose.

When a hand closed around my ankle, I realized it was because he planned further treachery. His squire leered up at me, and made to haul me down to my knees. I knew that gleam in a young boy's eye and this one would have no part of me.

But I dared not distract Merlyn.

This fight was my own.

I struck the boy in the face with my fist, ignoring the echo of swordplay so close at hand. The boy fell back, then came after me with a snarl. I knew then that he would hurt me as well as rape me.

I fought with my fists and my feet, but the boy had mail on the backs of his gloves. His every blow was worth three of mine and he battered me with no care for what damage he wrought. He struck me in the mouth and I tasted blood, before I spat it in his face. He punched me in the belly and when I doubled over in pain, kicked me to the floor.

His companion slipped through the door like the vermin he was. When he seized my wrists and the other opened my legs, my spirit quailed.

The boys laughed as the one between my knees unlaced his chausses. I struggled, earning another blow for my efforts, and moaned.

"Ysabella!" Merlyn shouted. When he cried my name with rage, I knew he had seen.

But the boy chuckled and lowered himself over me, unthreatened. In a moment, I guessed why—I heard Merlyn catch his breath and stumble. Calum laughed and I knew that Merlyn had been wounded.

"No!" I screamed and struggled with new vigor. I fought and bit and was astonished when one boy released my wrists.

The face of the other, leering above me, went slack in the same moment. He fell over me, stunned, and I rolled from beneath his weight. It was Berthe who hefted a stone in her hand, her sweet face contorted with anger.

"Never again!" she cried.

The second squire had released me to reach for his knife, but I leapt up and slammed him into the wall. Berthe struck him as well, and he crumpled to the floor beside his companion.

My heart stopped when I saw that Merlyn lay senseless against the far wall, Calum bent over him. The blood flowed from Merlyn's side and he did not appear to breathe.

I cried his name and took a step toward him.

Calum straightened and turned, outrage filling his eyes.

"Miserable wench!" he shouted and came after us. "I should have seen you dead in Dunkilber," he growled at Berthe.

"Perhaps you should have," she retorted and spat upon his tabard.

Calum roared and lifted his blade.

But he had turned his back upon Merlyn. While the bloodlust burned in Calum's eyes, Merlyn rose to his feet, moving as stealthily as a shadow despite the evident pain in his side. Berthe and I held hands and stood our ground, letting Calum bear down upon us, trusting in Merlyn's speed. He loomed large behind Calum, his blade lifted high.

Then Merlyn whistled.

Calum's eyes widened in shock and confusion. He spun just as Merlyn's sword came slicing through the air. Berthe and I hid our faces in each other's shoulder as the blade slashed across the other man's neck. Blood splattered against us and the chapel walls. We looked up as Calum fell backward at our feet, his blood flowing in a torrent across the floor.

Merlyn stepped over him and caught my chin in his hand. As much as I wished to be strong, my lip trembled and I gripped him tightly. "Chère?" Merlyn tipped my face so that my gaze met his. I began to shiver, realizing how close I had come to losing all I held dear. "Are you injured?"

I shook my head, my tears falling free at the motion. "Frightened," I whispered in a tremulous voice. "And cold. No more than that." I touched his shoulder, looking to the fresh blood, fearing the worst. "And you?"

"A scratch," he said with a wry smile. "No more than that."

"The ship?" I asked, just as a bellow sounded outside the chapel.

Merlyn smiled and tucked me beneath his arm as he escorted Berthe and me out into the wind. Arnulf stood there, grinning with triumph at his own deed. I looked and there was no treacherous beacon on the far point.

And now, a bonfire blazed upon the point beyond the chapel.

Arnulf held the third of Calum's squires by the collar, the boy's hands tied behind his back.

"Well done, Arnulf," Merlyn said warmly and the boy flushed. He nodded and grinned, and Berthe gave him a kiss upon the cheek that made him blush. He ducked into the chapel then, returning only when he had bound the hands of the other squires in turn. He lined them all up, sitting with their backs against the chapel, leaving the chausses of the two undone. They moaned as he trussed their feet together, but once they were helpless we ignored them.

We four watched the ship, its crew visible as they struggled valiantly to change their course. I know that I was not the only one oblivious to my own discomfort in fear for those we could not aid.

Merlyn took my hand in his and squeezed my fingers tightly.

I do not know how long we stood there, our hearts in our mouths, our hands entwined. The wind changed, though, shifting gradually away from the east. With the change, the waves calmed and the ship's crew managed to ease the prow toward the south.

We cheered in relief then, and Merlyn sent Berthe and Arnulf to the keep to fetch some garb. Neither of us could tear ourselves away from the sight of the ship, of our loved ones so close at hand. Berthe found Merlyn's cloak in the hall, though she could not find a gown for me. I did not care, not when Merlyn wrapped me tightly in the fur-lined cloak and held me fast against his side.

It was not long until the first rays of the dawn breached the horizon and the ship drew cautiously into the sheltered bay there. The men sang as they rowed ever closer. They cheered as they finally flung the anchor into the bay and we could see that they thronged the deck.

The surface of the sea turned pearly as they made ready to disembark, the morning bright with promise as it so oft is after a storm. A familiar stocky figure descended the rope ladder and stood in the sea.

He shouted a command and a young boy was lifted high above deck, then passed down the ranks of men to Fitz's waiting arms. Each man teased the boy when he came into their arms and even at this distance, I could see that Tynan reveled in their company.

The men laughed as Tynan was set upon Fitz's shoulders. He waved like a conquering champion as he was carried ashore, the sight of his happiness bringing tears to my eyes.

"Ysabella!" Tynan shouted, waving so madly when he spied me on the shore that he nearly toppled Fitz. The manservant complained loudly, the seamen laughed, but Tynan cavorted once he had his feet upon the shore.

"You see, chère?" Merlyn whispered against my temple. "Your brother was safe with Fitz. Did I not give you my word?"

I looked up at his strong profile, his dark gaze fixed upon the men as they disembarked, his smile at Tynan's antics. His concern was so evident that it might have made me weep.

Merlyn was not only fully the man I had once hoped he was, he was more than that. He was more valiant, more protective, more caring, and more compassionate. He did indeed protect all that was his own. I decided it was time he knew the fullness of what that was.

"Tynan is not my brother, Merlyn," I said.

My husband turned to regard me, no surprise vying with the stars in his eyes. "No?"

I shook my head. "Tynan is my son." I touched his jaw with my fingertips, watching hope blossom in his expression. "Tynan is *our* son."

Merlyn's smile might have challenged the morning sun for brilliance, but I had only a glimpse of it before his lips closed surely over mine.

January 6

Epiphany

XVII

On the feast of kings, we rode to Kinfairlie.

Not the village, but the ruins of the old keep. Merlyn thought it important that I visit the former abode of my mother's family. I was glad it was a clear and sunny day, for I had half a thought that there might be specters there to haunt me.

It was a rather odd destination, in my opinion, though Merlyn seemed surprised when I said as much.

My sister and Alasdair had arranged to be wed by the end of this month and Mavella had not challenged the status of Alasdair's cousin's boy as heir. They were like a small family already, happy together, and I was well pleased.

Tynan adored Ravensmuir. He and Arnulf struck up a friendship based upon the horses, and though Arnulf said nothing, Tynan's chatter more than filled any potential silences. Tynan had been told of my deception and the truth, though I do not know how much he understood of it. For the moment, he was glad to have Merlyn as his father, partly because that meant we would stay at Ravensmuir, where the horses and the ships and Fitz could be found and one's bowl was never empty, and partly because Merlyn fascinated him.

Ravensmuir's solar had been razed in the fire Ada began, though once the roof had burned, the rain had extinguished the flames and they had not spread to the lower halls. The damage would be reparable, though Merlyn's books and the impressive bed were gone forever. Merlyn's box, by some stretch of fate, we found reposing in the ashes, contents un-scathed.

When I jested that his old mentor must have gilded it with some unholy power, Merlyn only smiled.

Dunkilber had reverted to the Earl of March, though he had yet to endow it again. Berthe and her parents—the seneschal of Dunkilber and his wife—had all settled at Ravensmuir instead, a bevy of servants with them. The hall bustled as it had not before, and I had been careful on this morning to store a piece of the Yule log in Ravensmuir's cellars. It would be used to light the Yule log next year, its safe storage providing superstitious insurance against fire.

I still could not think of riding a horse alone, and indeed I much preferred to ride with Merlyn. We rode in companionable silence, the wind in our hair and his heat behind me. He halted the destrier beside the ruins of Kinfairlie. The charred debris was now interspersed with grasses, the black-ened stones adorned with moss. Merlyn dismounted, then reached to grip my waist.

I pulled back slightly. "Why here?"

"Why not?" He had the manner of a man with a secret and I was suspicious.

"Do we have need of more ghosts at Ravensmuir?" I teased.

Merlyn laughed. "Of course not. But I have something to tell you and I thought this to be the place to do so." He took my hand and led me to a tumble of stones. He swept the top one and spread his cloak upon it like a courtier in a bard's tale. Once I was seated, smiling at his antics all the while, he pulled a scroll from his tabard, then presented it to me with a small bow.

"What is this?"

"A reply from the king, in response to my petition made on your behalf."

He watched me keenly, waiting for me to guess what he had done. I thought at first he made a jest, and examined the roll of vellum in my hand. There was a thick red seal affixing the ribbon tied around the missive and it had not been opened. The vellum was so thick, the seal so firmly indented and familiar that it had to be what he said it was.

I looked up at Merlyn. "You know I cannot read it."

"Not yet."

"You will teach me to read?"

"It seems to me that you will have need of such a skill."

I frowned, wondering, then met his steady gaze. I knew then with utter clarity what he had done. He had requested what I would never dare request, even though it was my birthright.

I clutched the missive. "Kinfairlie," I whispered.

Merlyn smiled. "All yours, chère, as it should rightly be."

"Surely you mean it is ours, that it is granted to my husband since I am wedded." I knew well enough how the law worked—I had no quibble with sharing my legacy with Merlyn, for he shared so much with me.

But Merlyn shook his head and indicated that I should break the seal. I did so, and unfurled it, my breath caught at the beauty of the script. Merlyn sat beside me, his arm around my waist, and read it aloud slowly, his finger sliding under the words as he uttered them.

> *"I, King Robert II of Scotland, do solemnly endow the hereditary territories of Kinfairlie upon the eldest daughter of Marie Elise of Kinfairlie, Marie Elise being the sole child of that house to have borne fruit and her daugters being the sole survivors of that lineage. Kinfairlie and its village, its tithes and traditional tolls, the responsibilities of its courts of low justice and the defense of its territories, are hereby granted to the hand of Ysabella, once of Kinfairlie, now Lady of Ravensmuir, in express exchange for the rendering of six knights and their accoutrements to the crown upon demand for the defense of our collective lands."*

I turned to regard my spouse in dismay. "But how shall I render such military service? I know nothing of knights and warfare, and I have not the coin to pay for them."

Amusement made his eyes sparkle. "Perhaps then, my Lady of Kinfairlie, you still have need of me. Perhaps we might make an alliance between Ravensmuir and Kinfairlie."

"I suppose you must have some task to occupy your days now that your former trade is abandoned," I said, considering the document. "Otherwise, you will hover about the hall and take to drinking ale to pass the time."

"I can think of better ways to spend my days," he murmured, then kissed me with gentle vigor. I closed my eyes, knowing I would never be sated when it came to Merlyn's kisses, that I should always yearn for more.

When he lifted his head, sultry promise in his gaze, I smiled. "I love you, Merlyn. I have loved you since the day you matched wits with me in Kinfairlie's market, though I have never had the audacity to tell you so."

"And I love you, chère, as never I imagined any soul could love another." We smiled at each other, besotted fools that we were, then Merlyn's grin turned mischievous. "The fact remains that we have need of another son, chère, to take this legacy in hand," he whispered wickedly.

I looped my arms around his neck. "Perhaps we should celebrate these tidings." I stretched up and kissed his ear languidly. "Perhaps it would be fitting to conceive the child upon his own inheritance."

Merlyn chuckled and tapped my nose with his fingertip. "You would be surprised if I accepted that invitation."

"Would I?" I smiled at him, letting challenge light my eyes. "Indeed, Merlyn, you seem so reluctant that I fear I must dare you to do as much."

His eyes flashed and he swept me into his arms then, leaping from the ruins so quickly that I clung to his shoulders in fear that we would fall. He strode toward a copse of young trees, then paused on the lip of a sheltered hollow. He grinned, holding me fast against his chest, then dipped his head.

"You should know better than to dare me, chère," he whispered against my throat.

"I do, Merlyn, I do." I chuckled until he silenced my laughter most effectively with his kiss.

The steed had long to graze that afternoon, his reins trailing behind him, for it appeared that we had much to celebrate indeed.

The sun was sinking when we finally rode for home, rumpled and flushed and pleased indeed. When we drew near to Ravensmuir, a hoarse cry echoed through the air. Startled, I scanned the darkening sky, my lips parting in surprise when the dark birds became discernible against the sky.

The ravens descended in a spiral, their black wings spread like great shadows. They came, crying each to the other, disappearing behind the high walls of the keep.

"The ravens return!" I shouted, thrilled at the sight.

Merlyn spurred the destrier and we plunged through the tunnel, emerging in the courtyard as the birds began to land. The servants had crowded out of the kitchens and the hall, their eyes wide as they watched the birds.

The hound ran around the birds, barking. Tynan, fearless as ever, ran into their midst, laughing, then mimicking their strut. Fitz watched him indulgently though the birds took little notice of his presence.

"I shall have to teach Tynan their names," Merlyn said and now I did not doubt his assertion. He whistled, lifted his arm, and one bird separated from the flock.

It circled us and the steed snorted, then the bird landed heavily on Merlyn's arm. It bobbed its head and croaked at him, before its beady eyes turned bright upon me. It was almost as if it requested an introduction. I reached up one hand, marveling at the hues of blue and purple and black in its plumage and the bird tilted its head to regard my ring.

"Methuselah remembers," Merlyn said with a quiet smile.

"How delightful to formally make your acquaintance, Methuselah," I said, bowing my head slightly.

The raven studied me for a long moment. It then bobbed its head in turn and screamed, before taking flight with a great rushing of wings. Tynan watched and called to Merlyn, demanding to know how to do what he had done.

We dismounted and I watched Merlyn go to our son, my hand stealing over my belly. I guessed then that my laird's seed took root once more within me and that Tynan soon would have a sibling. And I smiled the smile of a woman well pleased with her secret, a secret I would keep from my spouse only until I was certain of its truth.

For honesty, my friend, is what persuades love not only to stay but to flourish. Merlyn and I have learned that lesson well and it is not one either of us will soon forget.

Dear Reader,

When I was a teenager, I couldn't read enough gothic romances and romantic suspenses. Authors like Daphne DuMaurier, Mary Stewart and Phyllis A. Whitney had me beating a path to the public library. I loved enigmatic and dangerous heroes—especially if they turned out to be honorable in the end. I cheered for intrepid heroines—the ones who got into trouble by doing the right thing, not by taking foolish chances. I loved the dark castles perched on hilltops, the ghosts, the ominous doings. In the end, I always wished there had been a little more romance (I *was* a teenager!) or a little more insight into the relationship that developed.

But I kept reading!

Those books and those authors led me to Ravensmuir and this linked series of my own neo-Gothic romances. What better dark and dangerous hero than Merlyn, living on the edge of legality and possessed of boundless charm? What better heroine than outspoken strong women, like Ysabella? And you can see that I've made things a bit more steamy! Join me for the stories of the other Lammergeier men and the women who capture their reluctant hearts.

Visit my website for up-to-date information on upcoming releases or to join my listserve. Château Delacroix, my virtual home, is at http://www.delacroix.net. Or, you can write to me at:

Claire Delacroix
P.O. Box 699, Station A
Toronto, Ontario
Canada M5W 1G2

Until next time, happy reading!
All the best -
Claire

York—December 1371

Gawain awakened with a wide smile.

His joyous mood was undaunted by his humble surroundings. He grinned at the mire of the bedlinens, he saluted the long and ancient crack in the wall. He chuckled that his pallet was barely fit for a dog and grinned in recollection of the lusty whore who had sated him here just hours past. She was gone, of course, but he expected as much.

He wondered whether he should fatten her purse again before departing from this grim town. He was, after all, in a celebratory spirit.

His mood was not even affected by the steady downpour of grey rain upon the muddy streets of York. The bells of the cathedral rang sonorously, calling sinners such as himself to hasten and repent.

He would never repent of his sins—he enjoyed them too much.

Gawain ran his hands through his hair, splashed icy water on his face, and donned his tabard and belt. He whistled as he pulled on his boots, so well pleased with his circumstance that he could find no fault in the world. He swung his cloak over his shoulder and tied his purse to his belt.

Nothing could be amiss now that the prize which was rightfully his was in his possession again. He had stolen the *Titulus Croce* once at his father's dictate, surrendered it to his father, then lost it through his brother's unwelcome meddling. Gawain had feared his treasure gone forever, but Fortune had not abandoned him.

Merlyn, blessedly, had taken a woman to wife who loved him more than mere coin. What misery people won for themselves with the whimsy of love! Why else would an otherwise sensible woman believe that her murdered spouse might still be alive and in need of her aid? Why else would Ysabella surrender a treasure when Gawain said he would trade it for telling her the location of the fatally wounded Merlyn? That she had made the exchange so willingly proved only that she did not deserve to hold that treasure long.

It was unfortunate that Merlyn was dead, for Gawain would have liked to have witnessed his response to his wife's folly. Gawain chuckled to himself, delighted at his trickery.

Justice was served, sooner or later. Merlyn was dead, Gawain had his due. Perfect.

The only challenge before Gawain was assuring himself of the best price for his treasure. He had to avoid his father's error of offering the relic to too many competing lords, for then only one of a bevy of reliable clients could be sated. Hard feelings did not lead to future sales.

Still, he was consumed with imagining the coin. Oh, he anticipated a merry auction and one that would weight his purse for a long time. Given Gawain's taste for fine living and luxury, that would be quite a feat.

As merry as a man can be, he hefted his saddlebag upon his shoulder, and that deed immediately dispelled his mood.

The bag was too light. Gawain stared at the sack in shock.

He dropped the saddlebag to the floor and unbuckled its flap with uncustomary haste, knowing full well what he would find. His fingers shook as they never had and he riffled through the contents with impatience. His other chemise was there, his wineskin, a dozen other bits of miscellany.

But the relic was gone.

Of the *Titulus Croce*—which would have seen him rich for all the rest of his days, which had been safely nestled in this very bag when he went to sleep—there was no sign.

He noticed that the door was not barred from the inside, but no sooner had he recalled as much than his innards chilled.

The girl.

He saw her laughing eyes again, her merry smile. He felt the soft curve of her breast beneath his hand, felt the imprint of her teeth against his flesh. She had been lusty and demanding, she had approached him with her enticing swagger. He had thought that she had only a whore's instinct for a man in a celebratory mood. He had thought that she targeted him solely for his coin.

His pride had thought she chose him for his good looks and charm. He poured out the contents of his purse and saw that not a single penny was missing.

Oh, she had chosen him, but for a different reason than he had guessed. And he had never suspected a thing. Gawain sat down heavily on the musty pallet. A woman had tricked him! He had been in a mood to celebrate, three cups of ale having diminished any caution he might have shown, and he had thought a common harlot no threat to his prize.

Clearly, he had been wrong. It was no consolation that he was not the first man to have been relieved of his wealth by a whore while he slept.

Gawain swore, he kicked the saddlebag across the floor, he clenched his fists and strode across the small chamber. He thundered down the steps to the main floor, kicked open the door of the common room and roared for the keeper.

That portly man regarded him sleepily from a stool on the far side of the room. "Aye? What ails you this morn?" The keeper yawned, scratched himself and grinned. "Too many bites from the bed for a fine lord like yourself?"

His wife chuckled as she set his ale and bread before her

husband, then turned, wiping her hands, and watched Gawain.

"The girl, the whore, where is she?" Gawain demanded.

"We have no whores in our hall," the wife huffed.

The keeper grinned. "Lightened your purse, did she? You are not the first, sir, to not see past your prick, nor will you be the last."

Gawain gritted his teeth. "Where is the dark-haired vixen who was in this room last evening?"

"Ah, the one you took to your bed," the keeper nodded as he drank deeply of the ale. He indicated the barrel in the corner, in no hurry to part with whatever morsel he knew. "Another draught would sweeten the morn, my lord."

"Drives out the dampness, it does," concurred his wife.

"I want the girl."

The keeper chuckled. "Oh, it is a young man who can think solely of rutting so early in the day." He sighed. "I remember those days well."

"And after a night of it, as well," his wife said archly, then helped herself to a cup of ale. She sat beside her husband and broke off a piece of his bread for herself, then shook it at Gawain. "If you forgive me speaking so bold, sir, you should be on your knees before the priest, begging forgiveness for your fornication, not seeking more of it."

Gawain rubbed his face in impatience, then shouted all the same. "I wish only to *speak* with the girl!"

"But of course," the keeper agreed with a smirk and a wink for his wife.

"If it is necessary that I pay the house for the privilege, then I will do so."

"I have told you that this is no whorehouse," the wife sniffed, but her husband held up a hand to silence her.

"A lesser man than me would take your coin and grant you nothing in exchange, but we have an alehouse of good repute."

"Indeed." Gawain regarded the man sourly.

"Indeed. There are no whores in this alehouse, not any of whom I have knowledge. And I will tell you this. We never saw this girl before last evening—had I known her intent, I would have cast her into the streets. She will not be welcome here again, upon that you may rely."

Gawain blinked. "Surely she is in your employ? Or at least she comes here at intervals?"

The keeper shook his head. "Never has she crossed the threshold. I remember them all." His wife looked suspicious of this but he shrugged. "It is a responsibility, Enid. A man must do what he must do." She snorted and turned away from him.

"But she must be local," Gawain insisted.

"No." The keeper shook his head again, the matter evidently resolved to his satisfaction. "Now, you can take yourself to the sheriff and he may tell his men to seek her, but she is not from these parts. I doubt you will have satisfaction in time enough to sate you, not that I would encourage thievery or any such vice."

"Did she demand a chamber for the night?"

"Curiously, no." The keeper chewed his bread as he regarded Gawain. "Come to think of it, she spied you, she did, and said she had no need of a chamber. I thought at the time that perhaps you journeyed together, that she was a sister of yours or some such." He smiled. "She must have fancied you."

The wife harumphed, her survey of Gawain effectively communicating her opinion of fornicators and whores and their ultimate fate.

"Did she give her name?"

The keeper shook his head, then brightened. "But she left a missive for you. I nigh forgot. I will take your coin for that, fine sir."

A missive? Gawain's heart sank. It was unthinkable that a whore would leave a written message for a patron, particularly one she had robbed. Why leave a clue of her identity?

Gawain's sense that he had been targeted in much the same way that he targeted his own victims increased a hundred-fold.

Had he welcomed a thief to his bed?

The missive, his for a silver penny, confirmed his worst fears.

> *My dearest Gawain,*
>   *So you think yourself a thief beyond compare! Not only have I proven your estimation of your talents undeserved, but I have reclaimed what is rightfully mine own.*
>   *Retrieve it if you dare.*
>   *I thank you, by the way, for the generous gift of your steed in compense for your poor performance abed. (In truth, I had expected a better ride, given your reputation, but we both know that reputations are oft finer than truth.) You need not fear for my welfare while riding such a costly and large destrier, for I am adept in the taming of spirited stallions.*
>
> *Yours in dreams alone,*
> *Evangeline*

It was imprinted with the seal of Inverfyre, the keep from which Gawain had originally stolen the *Titulus*. A more foolish man than he could not have imagined that this was a coincidence.

Gawain balled the missive into his fist and glared at the complacent keeper and his wife. "I need to buy a horse," he said tightly and the wife snorted her ale as she laughed.

"She stole your mount?"

"Evidently. Unless you prevented her from doing so."

The keeper was immediately upon his feet, bowing and apologizing, explaining that theirs was a humble trade and horses so uncommon in their stables that they left guests to tend their mounts themselves. Gawain did not doubt that this Evangeline had slipped a coin across the board to ensure that their attention was diverted, but it mattered little.

She was gone, with his horse and his relic. Not only that, but she taunted him, daring him to pursue her to Inverfyre and retrieve his prize. And she insulted his talents abed. The woman went too far!

He would show her the error of her thinking.

With pleasure.

But even as he schemed his vengeance, Gawain was intrigued. He had never met a woman as clever and crafty as he, much less one as skilled in the same nefarious trade. He recalled the beguiling heat of the lady's kisses, the perfection of her body and her willingness to use it to gain her desire.

He wondered whether Evangeline's passion might be used against her. The prospect restored Gawain's smile. Indeed, he urged his newly acquired steed to race north from the gates of York, so anxious was he to encounter the challenging Evangeline again.